Rhian's Year

Stephen John

Note for Librarians: a cataloguing record for this book that includes Dewey Decimal Classification and US Library of Congress numbers is available from the Library and Archives of Canada. The complete cataloguing record can be obtained from their online database at:
www.collectionscanada.ca/amicus/index-e.html
ISBN 1-4120-2637-7

Printed in Victoria, BC, Canada

Printed on paper with minimum 30% recycled fibre. Trafford's print shop runs on "green energy" from solar, wind and other environmentally-friendly power sources.

TRAFFORD *Offices in Canada, USA, Ireland and UK*

This book was published *on-demand* in cooperation with Trafford Publishing. On-demand publishing is a unique process and service of making a book available for retail sale to the public taking advantage of on-demand manufacturing and Internet marketing. On-demand publishing includes promotions, retail sales, manufacturing, order fulfilment, accounting and collecting royalties on behalf of the author.

Book sales for North America and international:
Trafford Publishing, 6E–2333 Government St.,
Victoria, BC V8T 4P4 CANADA
phone 250 383 6864 (toll-free 1 888 232 4444)
fax 250 383 6804; email to orders@trafford.com

Book sales in Europe:
Trafford Publishing (UK) Ltd., Enterprise House, Wistaston Road Business Centre,
Wistaston Road, Crewe, Cheshire CW2 7RP UNITED KINGDOM
phone 01270 251 396 (local rate 0845 230 9601)
facsimile 01270 254 983; orders.uk@trafford.com
Order online at:
trafford.com/04-0465

10 9 8 7 6 5

For the long term unemployed and minimum wage earners. For the stressed, depressed, and everyone else whoever thought: *'What's The Point?'*

ACKNOWLEDGEMENTS

With special thanks to my partner Lynne for never losing faith in my abilities. Her enthusiastic encouragement, 1000% commitment to the cause, patience, her unflagging ability to put up with my annoying little habits, (Too many to mention on this page.) and much treasured resourcefulness, to know at exactly what hour of the day or night to prepare me a piping hot pot of tea, cafetière of coffee, plus slice after slice of thickly spread marmalade on toast.

CHAPTER LIST

READER WARNING:

If blatant examples of poor punctuation in modern literature send you into an uncontrollable rage, drive you up the wall, bring you out in a cold sweat, spoil your day, or upset your constitution in any way: **PLEASE STOP READING THIS WARNING IMMEDIATELY!** Please return this book to its designated position on the bookshelf, and select something else.

Thank you
Author

Purely for the sake of authenticity, (And author laziness if truth be known.) this modern day tale of apathy is told in Rhian's own words, and slapdash punctuation errors... How many can you spot?

Rhian: I didn't know a semicolon was called a semicolon until Anthony told me. (I had to wait until Anthony came home from school to find that out. My husband Trevor's useless at grammar too. The only time Trevor has use for a pencil is when he's writing out a betting slip.) Anthony did laugh after I'd asked: *'Is a semicolon used when a writer can't decide if he should use a comma, a full stop, or both?'*... I certainly don't know all the laws of punctuation. Its just, I'm not entirely sure how the rules I'm confused about apply?... I wish I could remember what Anthony said an apostrophe is supposed to do again?

Author: In a land where record-breaking exam passes, and recorded numbers of adult illiteracy increase each year. Is it any wonder more and more people rely on the spellchecker to help them create the written word... For the sanity of mankind: *'Why oh why hasn't some bright spark perfected a trustworthy punctuation checker, for us ordinary mortals to believe in*?'

Rhian's Year

Stephen John

Chapter 1: Superstition

I know it's unlucky to hang a new calendar upon the wall before the old year is out, but what about writing an entry in a diary? Should I introduce myself now, wait until after midnight, or refrain from writing my first entry until later tomorrow morning?

God knows my family doesn't need anymore bad luck... If I start... No, I can't do it. I can't risk jeopardising our whole year over this little whim of mine. How would I feel if I began, knowing there could be a chance, (However slim.) I was in the wrong?... No, it's much safer if I wait, or at least try to find out beforehand... Now where did I put my mother's new mobile phone number?

"Please pickup... Hello Mam, can you hear me?"

"Rhian, Happy New Year to you love... Sorry, I'm early... It isn't unlucky for me to wish you a Happy New Year, is it?... It's not unlucky to wish somebody a Happy New Year, before the New Year has began?... Rhian, it's not is it love?"

"No Mam. It's like wishing somebody a Merry Christmas at the beginning of December. Speaking about luck, Mam. Is it unlucky to begin writing in a new diary before the old year is out?"

"A new diary you say?... Oh, I'm not sure love. I know it's unlucky if you hang a new calendar upon the wall before the 1st, but a new diary?... I've never really had much to do with diaries love, new or old. Anyway I thought you and Trevor where coming down to the club tonight?"

"Isn't Trevor there?"

"Oh Trevor's here all right. Trevor and all the gang. We're all here to see in the New Year... A little bird tells me you haven't been feeling very well lately?"

"Oh it's nothing, just an upset tummy. Mam, who's sitting around the table with you?"

"Oh you know, just the girls. Molly Harris, Debbie White, you know the usual crowd... Girls, it's my Rhian on the phone."

"HAPPY NEW YEAR RHIAN."

"Mair, tell your Rhian if she still isn't feeling any better tomorrow morning, I'll pop over with a bowl of my hot winter soup for her."

"Did you hear that love, Molly said she'll bring you over a bowl of her winter soup if you're still feeling a little under the weather in the morning."

"Mam, the lines starting to break-up. Can you ask them about my diary?"

"She's asked me to thank you for your kind gesture Molly, but she thinks she'll be okay... Listen girls, do any of you know anything about bad luck, and diaries?"

"I know it's unlucky if somebody else reads it." sniggered Debbie.

"Especially if it's your husband, and you've been writing about the milkman." Giggled Molly.

"Give over you two, or you'll have me breaking out of my corset." Mam chuckled. "Sorry love. I'm not sitting with a very literary bunch tonight... Listen take my advice, and play it safe. If you're not sure, best to leave well alone until the morning;

but don't you dare go hanging up any new calendars until the bells of Big Ben have stopped chiming... That is unlucky!"

Replacing the receiver Rhian surveyed her living-room with her unopened diary resting upon her lap. Around the room, the Christmas decorations had lost their early December sparkle. Foil packaging debris from a sweet tin (Quality Street) littered the coffee-table, as Rhian quickly flicked through the television channels with the remote control.

"Nothing!"

Turning down the sound, Rhian watched the defining images that were soon to complete the past year, crawl across the TV screen... Rhian sighed.

"Call these edited news clips history!" Rhian moaned aloud. "What have either of those three grinning idiots ever done for the likes of me? Blair, Hague, Gordon Brown and his budget, who gives a toss? I refuse to vote for any of them or their political parties... Posh Spice, and David Beckham, give me strength. How do these people get away with it?... "Rubbish!" Rhian clicked the channel over. "Rubbish!" She clicked the remote control again. "I'm paying the television licence fee and getting nothing in return... Rubbish!... More rubbish... It's New Year's Eve and there's nothing on the box I'd like to watch... I've had enough of this!"

The screen popped, then transmitted a mirrored reflection of herself, as she placed the remote control down upon the arm of the chair.

"I want to write my own history." Rhian mumbled to herself, while thumbing her way through the empty pages of her diary. *'What has this New Year in store I wonder?'* She pondered, as the month of October flashed through her fingertips. "I'm not a very religious person when it comes to the one main God, but I am very superstitious when it comes to the others. (1. The God of: The National Lottery. 2. The God of: 'Life Might Be A Lot Better In The Morning?') Neither Trevor or I are what anyone would call chapel goers. We didn't get married in a church; we also thought it best if we waited until our kids were old enough to decide for themselves, if they wanted to become Christians. (I've three children. None of which were christened... My mother has never forgiven me.) But what my thinking was behind that, I've long forgotten?... Perhaps I thought they might want to turn pagan or something. Either way, I don't think it's had much of an effect on them. Not in this day and age. Not living on this estate... Anyway whatever!"

'What on earth are you going to do with yourself in the New Year?' Employing all her powers of mental agility, Rhian questioned her mirrored reflection staring back at her from the blank screen of the television set. Reclining in a more comfortable position, Rhian waited patiently for a reply. "Just as I thought... You don't know either!" She answered, after the set failed to respond. "And you!" She directed her thoughts towards her diary. "What tales will you tell? What good fortune will becoming my way?" Lifting her diary up, she let the pages quickly flash past her eyes. "You couldn't tell me now, could you? You couldn't give me an inkling of what lies ahead? You couldn't tell me what God has in store for me this year?... Will it be more of the same, or will it be worse?... Was it bad luck, not to get my children christened?... Was it bad luck the day I didn't get married in a church?... Is it bad luck if I christen your pages with ink before the designated date?... I don't know why I'm even bothering to write? I can't spell, and I bet my punctuation's all gone to pot!"

'Diary 2001': Gold lettering sparkled from a navy blue hardback cover, like the north star twinkling on a clear night. Humming a well hummed tune, Rhian allowed her index finger to tap a beat around, along and through the shinny lettering above the well thumbed page.

January 1 - Monday. New Year's Day - Bank & Public Holiday, UK & R of Ireland. Rhian knew the wording of this barren introduction by heart, as she resumed her search for a technicality that would allow her to begin.

"If I were foolish, I could walk in where an angel would fear to tread. But I'm no longer foolish, and do no longer wish to offend... It's the Welshness in me you see. We are a superstitious race, us Welsh. Luck and misfortune walk with us hand in hand... It visits... It turns our lives upside down like a yo-yo on a piece of string. It stays for a bit... Bad luck stays longer mind. Bad luck stays with us one way or another throughout our entire lives... God, I wish somebody would give me a bloody ruling on this diary."

Shaken out of her thoughts by the ringing tone of the telephone, Rhian reached out, lifted the receiver, and answered:

"Hello?"

"Rhian love, it's Mam. Listen I've had a word with a few people in the club, and the feeling is, it's not unlucky to write in your diary providing you don't write on any of the date pages before that date has arrived. Unless of course it's to remind yourself of an appointment, like going to see the doctor, dentist, or to do something else."

"Are you sure Mam?"

"Of course I am love. People write phone numbers, addresses and appointments in them all the time don't they? There are note pages at the back, and people write upon them. It's a bit like the advent calendar at Christmas time. It's very unlucky to open any of the little windows in advance."

"So the same rule applies with my diary, does it?"

"Yes. Nobody opens the little windows on the advent calendar in advance do they, and apart from prearranged appointments, telephone numbers and the like, the consensus in the room is it's very unlucky to write anything down on the date pages of your diary before that date has arrived."

Fuelled with the reassurance she needed, Rhian opened her diary and turned to the section headed *'NOTES'*. Two pages of virgin white paper, ruled with thin black lines met her gaze. On the first line, below the heading she wrote: Diary Eve - The first night of my history, and our new friendship. December 31 - 2000.

Chapter 2: The Introduction

If you and I are to become great friends some sort of formal introduction is needed between us. An introduction of some sort followed by an explanation... After all, you are not one of many. You have no older brothers or sisters to fall back on. Like me you are an only child, and as such I think we should stick together like glue, through thick and thin.

Dear Diary, hello. My name is Rhian Evans. I am married to Trevor, and we have three children Gary (16), Megan (15) and Anthony (13), who everyone apart from me calls Tony. (Before I go on with the depressing part of this introduction, (by the way I intend to make this as brief as possible.) I would like to point out, that throughout our relationship I intend to speak to you like I would a real person, and hopefully think of you as one too.) I am a housewife by trade. More out of fate than by choice, you see Trevor is what the people on this estate call unemployed, again more out of fate than choice. The Evans's are a Welsh family from the Rhondda Valley. Traditionally when the men of our village, (Tragically that would have included my Trevor, but his pit closed down before he left school.) left home to start their shift down the mine, the women (Yours truly.) would be left at home to attend to the children, see to the house, prepare the food, and supposedly worry about the roof of the mine falling down on our poor husbands' heads. (Not that it would worry me all that much, in my Trevor's case... Not during this stage in our relationship, anyway.) So there you have it, an authentic history of traditional family life in the Rhondda Valley, from the year dot.

Some people say, (My Mam included.) always look on the bright side of life... Don't people like that make you sick?... Listen to this classic from my mother: *'Rhian, Trevor may be out of work, but at least your working routine hasn't been affected.'* And that's a good thing, is it Mam? That's something for me to cling to, to pin my hopes upon during the long cold winter nights that lie ahead. *'It could be worse.'* Mam would add. *'At least you still have your housework to keep you occupied...'* Do you know something Diary, if it wasn't for my Prozac I'd probably be crying my eyes out by now. I know I shouldn't say it, but I just can't help it. When my mother opens her big mouth, it really drives me up the wall. (Perhaps I should write a reminder to myself on the 1st of January page: My New Year's Resolution. Allow my mother's words to wash over me, like water running off a duck's back.)

ABOUT ME: What can I say? A woman past her prime, going through life's motions. I'm the wrong side of thirty, but just the right side of forty. (Another one of my mother's little quips.) I've kept a reasonable figure throughout my life, plus I've learnt how to hide the parts of my body that offend... Well offend me, anyway.

Now, I don't want you to get the wrong idea about me Diary. I'm not one of these thirty-nine year old women who think they should still have a body of a eighteen year old. When I say offend, I mean I'm very conscious of the cellulite running down the back of my legs. Cellulite, like all my other little insecurities was caused by the media, or more specifically, the tabloid press. I'd never even heard about cellulite until I read an article about it in the Sun newspaper. Up until that wonderful morning I was blissfully ignorant of the condition. But ten minutes later; after reading and studying a photograph that could only be described as a dimpled piece of meat, I found myself in the bedroom with my jeans around my ankles, wishing I'd studied yoga, as I contorted my body into a strange shape that allowed me to view myself in a little compact mirror I held in my hand. I can honestly say, up until that time in my life the only worry I ever had about my legs, was developing varicose veins like my mother. (To this day when sitting in a chair, I never sit with crossed legs.)

Discovering I had cellulite was a Prozac moment. Realising Trevor would never work down a mine, would definitely have been a Prozac moment, but they didn't have Prozac in those days, so I suppose that would have been a Valium moment, only I could handle what life had to throw at me so much better during that part of my existence... Then, I didn't need medical assistance to help me through the day. How did Dr Reece put it: *'We all can't be happy every day of our lives, can we Mrs* Evans? Have *you ever seen a happy millionaire Mrs Evans? Does the Queen with all she's got look happy to you Mrs Evans? No Mrs Evans, it's all a question of luck in this life. I'm not happy, you are not happy, the majority of my patients are also unhappy, so you see Mrs Evans, you are hardly on your own now are you?'*

I'd now like to introduce you to my children: Gary is my eldest, at sixteen. He left school last summer, and is the only one in the family who has a job. (Slave labour Trevor calls it.) At first I thought my Trevor had it in for Gary because he was jealous of his son finding work, but now I think Trevor's got a point. Gary works five days a week on a Government backed work scheme for The Welsh Development Agency, or the W.D.A in short, for what is the equivalent of double the weekly money he would be entitled to if he was claiming benefit.

Megan, at fifteen leaves school next summer. Like her brother she will also start work on a W.D.A. backed scheme. (Hopefully in an office of some sort.) Trevor wonders, often sarcastically I feel, why Burger King, and McDonald's haven't opened an outlet in our valley. Trevor adds: *'Then all the kids would have a proper job to go to of a morning, instead of prating about on the pretend one the Government supports to keep the youth unemployment figures down.*

Megan on the other hand doesn't seem to care much about her future, just so long as it gets her out of school. Again Trevor, intentionally I feel talks down to the girl at every opportunity he gets: *'Tell me Megan, and what outstanding results can we expect from you after finally completing such a long and distinguished academic career? A scholarship to Oxbridge? Maybe a degree or two perhaps? A couple of 'A' Levels? How about a gold star, and a junior swimmer certificate from the council baths?... You did turn up for your mark each day, didn't you love?*

Trevor can be a sarcastic sod at times, but it all goes in one ear and out the other ear as far as Megan is concerned. She just smiles at her father then goes to play her music in her bedroom.

Everyone but me calls our Anthony, Tony. (Perhaps I should have taken a leaf out of my christening handbook, and called him 'Son' or 'Boy' until he was old enough to choose his own name. Tony - Sorry Anthony being the youngest of my three children, is the only one who's ever taken to schooling. Homework, school dinners, he likes it all. At thirteen, he's top of his class and unbeknown to him carries all my hopes for anyone in this family achieving anything with their life. Trevor, who I've mentioned on a number of times throughout this introduction thinks he's being clever, while I think his comments are just plain nasty; reckons there was a mix-up in the hospital when our Anthony was born, meaning we got the wrong baby. Trevor says: *'There's a family of academics living somewhere in the posh area of Cardiff, wondering what the hell* is *going on.'* Trevor continues with his tale: *'If the unlucky couple are still together, the husband has turned to his wife on many an occasion and said: you can deny having an affair all you want. But there's nothing in the universe that will make me believe that, that thing has come from me!'*

Mam on the other hand is Mam. What more can I say about my mother? She lives in the same street as us, (Further down the road) and is always popping in and out of our house on an errand of some sort. She wears a blue flowery piny at all times, and likes me to give her a home perm, when she goes out on the special old age outings with her pensioner club.

Trevor like me is going through the motions of life, only he has no heart. Don't get me wrong, Trevor's the life and soul of the party outside of the house. He's hale and hearty down at the rugby club with his mates, ale being the operative word. He's an all round good boy to friends and acquaintances. He'll do anything for anyone, often without them paying. But do you think I can get him to do anything for me around the house? His all round attitude when changing a light bulb gives the impression of it being the utmost inconvenience for him, and it's not as if he hasn't got any free time on his hands. There's enough little jobs around this house to keep a fully trained tradesman employed for a couple of years. But can I get him to do anything... Can I hell. Our house should look like a palace, instead of a crumbling derelict building. We have grass growing out of the guttering, that makes the front of the house look like 'The Hanging Gardens of Babylon' in the summer. *'You've always wanted a hanging basket.'* Was Trevor's initial response, after I'd asked him to do something about it. *'You've got an hanging guttering outside, and you're still not bloody happy!'* Well, I don't know if he meant it, or he was trying to be funny, but the grass grew strong and green, then turned brown and withered away, and during all this time Trevor simply ignored it.

Do you know what drives me mad? It's when I pass women in the street, and I overhear them say: *'See her, she doesn't know how lucky she is being married to a man like that.'* I've even heard them say: *'She leads her husband a dog's life.'* My mother has remarked: *'You're too hard on him Rhian you'll lose him if you carry on at him in that manner.'* Then it must be me... It's all my fault. Perhaps I should be the one climbing up and down ladders?... Mowing the lawn?... It's all right Trevor, you sit yourself down love. Have another can of beer darling... Would you like me to turn the television channel over for you dear?... Dinner will be a little late today. I'm sorry sweetheart, but I've got to repair the washing machine you see, but never mind I'll make it up to you. You can have my lamb chop if you like, and I'll stick with the veg... What was that you said my love? Not eating meat will keep me slim!... Oh Trevor you are a one... You do think about me, don't you? Sometimes I forget how lucky I am being married to a man like you. Now don't forget, If you get bored at anytime, and feel like a quick sex session, don't be afraid to give me a shout. I can always repair this washing machine after you've finished screwing me from behind like our neighbour's little dog... For Christ's sake, where did I put my packet of Prozac?

Well Diary, it's nearly time. It's nearly time for the New Year, and your official life to begin - three, two, one - HAPPY NEW YEAR.

Chapter 3: Rhian's Year

January 1: Monday

Umm... Well, yes... I'm determined not to begin this diary with the terrible phrase 'Dear Diary'. (No offence intended, of course.) So here goes... Dear Diary, (Damn!) after reading the introduction, it can come as no surprise that Trevor and I started the New Year off together with a blazing row. Pretending to be asleep at four in the morning, I was crudely stirred from my pretence by a fumbling hand of a drunk, demanding his New Year jump. I asked him how he would feel if I were the one who'd came home the worse for ware, demanding sexual services from him at four in the morning, to which Trevor replied: *'It hasn't bothered me in the past.'*

Ending the argument with the quip: *'You enjoyed New Year's Eve without me. Now I suggest you begin New Year's Day in the same vein.'* (Using hand gestures.) I left the bedroom, and eventually fell asleep on the sofa, downstairs.

I woke-up with a stiff neck, so I popped a Prozac and an aspirin at the same time. (Miles better than a coffee, any day.) Remembered what had happened at four in the morning, and went back to sleep.

Mam called around this afternoon, and said I'd missed a wonderful night out. She said the club was packed, and Trevor had won a bottle of whiskey for his Tom Jones impression on the karaoke. She said he sang: 'What's New Pussycat', and all her friends from the old age club agreed he was very good, they also added: she must feel very proud to have such a talented son-in-law. (Apparently Trevor opened his winning bottle of whiskey in the club, and was congratulated by everyone as he went on a lap of honour pouring a nip of his success into each and every glass.)

Anthony also did very well for himself outside of the club last night: "Look Mam, I made £11.80 wishing the drunks a Happy New Year." He laughed, depositing his hoard of coins upon the kitchen table.

Mam left at tea time, and as the front door closed Trevor entered the room and said: "Thank God for that. I thought the old bag would never leave." Diary, you are the only witness to my dilemma... Only I see Trevor as he really is... He puts this big act on for everyone else. Yet if I try to tell anyone about the way I feel, they look down on me, wondering what right I have to be such a miserable bitch married to a smashing bloke like him!

Stayed in tonight and finished doing the ironing. Trevor watched a video on the telly... Nothing like starting the New Year, as you mean to go on.

January 2: Tuesday

Today is Tuesday. As a rule I go to the Post Office first thing on a Tuesday morning, and cash a money voucher, (Is that the right word?) from my family allowance book... But not today. You see the Post Office is closed today, what with it still being a Christmas/New Year type Bank Holiday, and in any case, I've already withdrew this week's money, last week. Say what you will about my family allowance book, I find it a very kind and comforting friend. No matter what life has got to throw at me, my family allowance book is always there, giving me its reassurance that come what may, every Tuesday there will be

£27.55 with my name on it waiting for me behind the counter... I used to get £37.55, but I lost £10.00 when Gary left school, and the SS ordered Mr Baker the Post Master to confiscate my book, leaving me without any family allowance until the powers that be issued me another book readjusted with the correct amount of benefit. (The weeks I lost were back dated, so I didn't lose any money in the end.)

Trevor says: "The government are trying to stop the rich people claiming child benefit." He also claims: "That's something we'll never have to worry about." Sadly I think he's right.

Megan dropped a bombshell on us when she announced the new trainers we bought her for Christmas were all right for wearing around the house, but she needed a new pair with the correct logo for school. This news prompted Trevor to deliver his speech about trainers being called plimsolls or daps in his day. He added: *'They only* ever *came in two colours, black and white. They had no laces, but slipped easily over my feet.'*

Megan replied: *'Get real Dad, it's not your day anymore.'* Quickly followed by: *'Do you want me to feel deprived wearing these things to school?'*

Trevor informed her, (In between an unnecessary burst of bad language.) she had to make do with what she's got. As the discussion reached its climax, I found myself trying to remember where I'd hidden my home shopping catalogue, as a tearful Megan ran sobbing from the room.

January 3: Wednesday

I awoke this morning feeling great. If there's one thing I've learned, it's when I feel this good, it's best to get as much of my housework done before my mind teeters over the edge again, and I plunge headfirst into my rut. The first job on the agenda was to take the Christmas decorations down... I know Diary. I know what you're thinking. This goes against all you know about me being superstitious. But I have two trains of thought on this subject: One says it's bad luck to carry things from the old year into the new. While the other says it's bad luck to take the decorations down before Twelfth Night. (It's a classic example of sod's law. You're damned if you do, and you're damned if you don't.)

By mid afternoon all of my good feelings had been eroded away to nothing by a combination of constantly nagging children, and an husband who'd just woken up, and wanted to know what I had made him for his breakfast.

Leaving them all to it, I left the house and walked the short distance to my mother's home where I selfishly knew somebody would wait on me for a change. Moments in this oasis are often short,sweet and too far apart. One of the favourite things I like to do is to enter my childhood bedroom, let myself fall into a heap on top of my old bed, silently stare up at the paint crackled mosaic ceiling, and pretend I'm a young girl again at an age when I still had my whole life in front of me, as I listen to the comforting sound of Mam's radio transmitting from a downstairs room. (Feelings like this cost nothing... Why can't we draw on them at our will?) Everything good must come to an end, and the nicer moments in life expire far quicker than most. So reluctantly returning to my fold... The rest of the day was spent refereeing petty disputes and arguments, concerning who owned this, and who's go was it on that, and what were they all going to watch on the television tonight? (When the house is full, I never have a turn of choosing that.) So leaving them to it, I decided to have a early night... Shush Diary, nobody suspects I have began a relationship with you.

January 4: Thursday

Was awakened sometime during the early hours of the morning, by an apologising Trevor,who thought 1.15am was the best time of the day to tell me how sorry he was about his previous behaviour. Needless to say, we celebrated these proceedings with a session or carnal pleasure. Then as Trevor climbed off me, rolled over, and fell immediately to sleep, I was left in the impossible state of being wide awake, with a yearning to discuss our up and coming plans for the New Year.

'Go to sleep - Can't you see I'm tired - I'll talk to you about it in the morning - FOR GOODNESS SAKE RHIAN, GO BACK TO SLEEP AND STOP NAGGING ME MUN!' (I wonder what Trevor would have said if I 'd answered him in that exact same manner, only seven minutes earlier?)

I hadn't the will to live when I finally left the bedroom. All morning I thought how silly I'd been to fall for Trevor's con trick of an apology. After all a leopard never changes his spots... But what made matters worse was the bonk. Where was the romance? Where was the feeling? Last night was a case of: *'Oi, are you awake? - Sorry about, well you know, life and everything. - Well don't just lay there - Bend over - Because ready or not here I come.'*

After that I just let myself drift throughout the day. I did what I had to do, and nothing more. I rallied a little after lunch, and asked

Trevor if he had time to discuss our plans for the New Year? But he brushed me off with: *'We've got plenty of time to discuss that Rhian.'* Adding, *'will you make me another mug of tea love?'*

Well, what do you think Diary? Not a very romantic start to the New Year was it? What's that you say? Why do I stay with him? I suppose it's because I'm Welsh, because I'm loyal, because I believe in the marriage vows I made at the Registry Office, (For richer or for poorer, in sickness and in health.) because I'm on Prozac, because I'm too lazy to do anything about it, or maybe it's a mixture of all the above and more... You're my new friend Diary. I haven't told you all, but from what you do know, I'll let you decide why I live my life this way?

January 5: Friday

Diary, I've some local gossip for you today. The neighbours (Fatty Ham & Piccalilli) have got a new dog. I call him Fatty Ham, and her Piccalilli, because that's what they eat every Friday night after she's finished her part-time shift down at the local off-licence. From the back bedroom window of my house, I can see right into their dining-room. Mind you, I say dining-room, but it's more of a small dinette with a little table and two chairs, pushed-up against a wall, if you ask me.

As I was dusting Tony... Sorry Anthony's room, I heard the unmistakable trill of Piccalilli's voice calling the pup into her home: *'Hear boy, hear boy.'* She twittered. Aye up, I thought to myself Piccalilli's got a new dog, and I was right.

Smiling to myself as I left the bedroom, my happiness quickly evaporated, as I was confronted by a puppy-eyed Megan waiting for me on the landing, holding my home shopping catalogue in her hands, with this question on her lips: *'Mam can you order this pair of trainers for* me *please?'* She inquired, pointing out a pair of 'Reebok Classics' with a manicured nail of her right-hand. *'It says here, if you place an order on express delivery, I'll receive them in time for school next Tuesday.'*

Of course I replied with a carefully rehearsed speech, about having exceeded my credit limit with the catalogue company over Christmas. But after a lot of pleading, I backed down and said I'd have a word with them and see what I could do. This made me the best mother in the world. So later this afternoon I popped around to my mother's house and phoned the order in from there. (I'm sorry, I forgot to say. I woke up to find our phone had been cut off this morning. It was a case of having a Christmas, or paying our outstanding phone bill... Christmas won.) Mam doesn't mind me using her phone if the call is free.

When I returned, I was accused by my two sons of being the worst mother in the world, for buying only for my favourite and nothing for them. I don't know, I was both hero and villain in a matter of hours. But Diary, what's new? In this house there's no difference between me, and the Prime Minister living in Downing Street. We both find it equally impossible to please all of our people, all of the time.

January 6: Saturday

Mam came round this afternoon and asked me if I'd heard the ruckus in the street, during the early hours of the morning? She claimed the Huws's, a young couple living on the opposite side of the road from her, had returned home in a taxi at three in the morning, and had woken the whole street up with their shouting and screaming, bad language and door slamming after they'd entered their home.

"Is this the type of behaviour I'll have to put up with every week?" Mam complained. "I told you they were no good, the day I watched them move in. Common as muck the two of them. Eighteen she is, so Elsie told me. Eighteen, and with three children Hing, Ding, and Bing. Well I don't know what this estates coming too Rhian, I really don't. It's not safe anymore for an old woman like me to sleep soundly in her bed." (At the end of this remark, I was happy Trevor was out of the house.) "Tell me this Rhian. The next time Daddy Huws comes home drunk, what's stopping him from forcing an entry into me?" (At this point I was very happy Trevor was out of the house.)

Mam left around four, with my assurances, and promise that if she bought a new bolt and chain, Trevor would call around sometime during the week to fix them onto her front door.

Trevor spends his Saturdays at the local rugby club. He watches the game, (He used to play for the team, when he was younger.) then spends the rest of the day propping up the bar with the rest of his cronies.

Gary and Megan catch the bus into Cardiff with their separate groups of friends, leaving Anthony at home by himself. (I think Saturday, is Anthony's favourite day of the week.)

After my mother left, the day returned to its normal pattern... Isn't Saturday night telly rubbish?

January 7: Sunday

Trevor woke me again when he came home. But this time I was ready for him, and told him so in no uncertain fashion. He stood tottering in silence, as I told him on this occasion he'd have to go without. Tonight was so bloody typical of my Trevor's behaviour over the past few months. The only time he wants to bonk is when he's pissed. When he's sober he's to bloody lazy to lift his fat backside out of the chair to come anywhere near me!

This morning I found out the name of Fatty Ham's and Piccalilli's little dog. "Billy", can you believe it, they've actually called this one Billy has well.

Oh I'm sorry Diary. You don't understand do you? You see Fatty Ham and Piccalilli have been living at the back of us for nine years, and in all that time they have always owned a dog. Not the same one mind, but they've all been the same breed, and sex. A total of three Yorkshire Terriers to date, making this little fellow, Billy the forth.

My Trevor finds it strange that on average, a Yorkshire Terrier only has a three year life span in their house. Gary reckons three years is all a dog can take living with those miserable gits. (He's never forgiven them for not returning his football when he was younger.) Megan says, she'd try to commit suicide too, if she was cooped up all day inside that house on her own. She also added, she'd seen the previous dogs all staring out of the window, and getting very excited when they saw a bus, van, or large lorry come trundling down the road. *'It's heartbreaking Mam.'* Megan sighed. *'To see their poor little faces pressed up against the windowpane. It can't be right can it, keeping the little things cooped-up 24 hours a day in solitary confinement like that!'*

Returning to the events of the early hours of this morning. Trevor and I are not speaking to each other. (Between you and me, I'm surprised he can remember anything that took place. He was that far gone.) Trevor ate his dinner, and tea in silence. He grunted his annoyance when I asked him to turn the television channel over, before childishly refusing to do so. But he still expected me to make him a mug of tea during the commercial break, when Coronation Street came on... MEN!

January 8: Monday

This morning the White Arrow van pulled up outside our house. I signed for Megan's new trainers by express delivery. Never in my life did I see a girl fall from the realms of happiness so quickly into the pit of despair.

"THESE ARE TOO BIG." Megan screamed, throwing a brand new trainer into the box. "Oh Mam, what am I going to do now?" She cried, running to her bedroom.

"Not bad... These fit me." Anthony said, rubbing salt into his sister's wound. "Can I keep them Mam? It'll be a shame to send them back, what with them being such a perfect fit and all."

At this point Trevor entered the room. "What the Hell's going on?" He demanded, observing the recently arrived invoice from the catalogue company, and forgetting during the heat of the moment that he wasn't speaking to me.

"It's Megan's new trainers Dad." Anthony cheerfully informed his father. "They don't fit her, but they do fit me, and Mam said I could keep them."

"ARE YOU OFF YOUR FUCKING HEAD WOMAN?" Trevor erupted, blowing his top. "No wonder we have no money left in this house, if all you do is blow it all on shit from the catalogue. Anyway, I thought we agreed, no more spending until we've paid off all the Christmas stuff you've bought?"

Still honouring my part of the agreement of not speaking to him. I watched in silence, as Trevor made Anthony remove the trainers from his feet, place them back into the box, tape the ripped packaging together, and stick a return label in its centre.

"Nothing else is to be delivered to this house unless I say so." He said staring at me.

For the rest of the day I heard the sound of Megan scurrying around her room in a vain attempt at finding suitable footwear for her return to school in the morning. The boys on the other hand went out with their friends. Don't ask me where, for the past few years I've found it best not to ask.

Finding myself alone in the room with Trevor, I could feel the tension in the silent atmosphere growing. With no intention of uttering a single syllable in his direction, I watched him squirm in his own juices, until he stormed out of the room. (The 'Silent Treatment'... Grown men can't bear it.)

January 9: Tuesday

At last: the school Christmas holidays are finally over, and it's the first day of term for Megan and Anthony... It's the first day back to work for Gary as well.

Megan said she'd been too hasty in her judgement, and the new trainers were a perfect fit after all. I replied I doubt that very much indeed, even if she wore two pairs of socks over her feet, and pushed another pair down the toe end of each shoe. I watched her face drop, as she saw for the first time her father's neatly wrapped parcel sitting on the coffee-table.

"That's it I can't go." She cried, as Anthony waved his goodbye at me. "You can wear your new ones." I suggested. "But you don't understand." She wailed back. "None of you understand. None of you know what it's like to be me, living in this house." She emphasised her remark by raising her clenched hands to her chest.

I felt like screaming back at the selfish little bitch: *'Never mind you, what about me? At least you still have a chance to do something with your life. You have no idea what it's like to be me, but let me tell you something Megan, it's a lot harder than being you!...'* But my Prozac had already kicked in, so in the end I didn't say a word.

Eventually Megan left the house in an old pair of trainers, with the right label still visible. Apart from Trevor who was still in bed, I had the run of the house to myself. There is no doubt about it, this is the best time of the day for me. A magical time, a two hour respite between the kids leaving for school and work, and the time it takes for Trevor to finally decide to get out of bed.

Heaven for me is watching 'Kilroy' on the telly, with a steaming hot cup of tea in one hand, and a plate of melting buttered toast in the other. Mind you Diary, you could never get me to go on the 'Kilroy' show. Kilroy wouldn't get me to tell my life story to the nation, not for all the tea in China. Not even if the show was titled: 'Life - Where Did It All Go Wrong, And Why?'

At the first stirrings of him upstairs, I left the house and made my way to the Post Office. We are nine days into the New Year, and apart from nipping down the road to my mother's, this is the first time I've had to leave the house on business. Today is 'Family Allowance Tuesday' as I've come to call it. (God it feels good to have some money in my purse again.) After I'd sent Megan's trainers back to whence they came, (Freepost) I had a little potter around the small group of shops in the centre of our estate, and treated myself to a new, or should I say second-hand skirt from the Oxfam charity shop, which cost me 50p. (If only buying my children's clothes were this easy.)

I popped into my mother's on the way home. She said she'd

just been on the phone to the council, and reported 'Big Daddy Huws' to them for being a public menace.

"Him and that tart of his were at it again last night." Mam quipped, greeting me at the door. "Rhian, this end of the street has turned into a ghetto since the council moved him and her in across the road." Then after she'd handed me a cup of tea, she said: "You know Rhian, I really think you should pay the bill and have your telephone reconnected. What happens if they decide to attack my house in the middle of the night. As things stand I'm not able to phone to ask Trevor to come and rescue me!"

Megan came home from school and said: "I've never been so ashamed in all my life. Everyone had new trainers for Christmas except me." Anthony on the other hand said: "It felt great to be back inside the classroom." Adding, "I'd forgotten that there were other intelligent life forms living on the planet." (I'm beginning to think Trevor has a point about him.) Gary came in about 6.00pm, and declared his job was crap, then said nothing more for the rest of the night. (I'm sure there's something on his mind.) Trevor and I are still not speaking, but at least he's not shouting at the children anymore.

January 10: Wednesday

For people living in our circumstances there is no sweeter sound on God's Green Earth, than the rhythm of the postman mailing a double giro envelope through our letter box.

Every Wednesday fortnight is 'Double Giro Day', the day Trevor receives his income support cheque from the government. The so called money the people in power claim, is all my family and I need to survive on for the next fourteen days. We claim £142.90 for Trevor, myself, and two children. We used to receive £173.85, but since Gary started on his government backed work scheme, they've taken £30.95 off us, which Gary now has to make up for in his board and lodging.

"It's hardly worth the boy going to work." Trevor remarked after Gary had handed me his first pay-packet, and I'd deducted the money out for his keep. "Slave labour, that's what I call it. If they want to pay peanuts why don't they employ a gang of chimps?... More fool our Gary and his mates, for putting up with it. But there again. Looking at the state of our boy and that yobbo crowd he works with, the bosses have plumbed for the next best thing. (I repeat: Trevor can be a sarcastic sod on times.)

At first I used to think Trevor expressed himself the way he did, because he was jealous of Gary being able to find work, where he hadn't. But now I'm not so sure. Nobody could survive on what our Gary earns for a living. So I've come to realise that our Gary hasn't really got a job at all. To the powers that be, my son is only a statistic to be removed from the unemployment register, with an excuse for a job that's only function is to get him out of bed, and out of the house of a morning. (Not that I'd tell him mind. Unlike Trevor, I've never been able to kick our son while he's down.)

With the giro cashed, I paid some instalments off our various outstanding accounts, then did a big shop at Tesco's in Cardiff. (I normally go shopping on Friday, but what with Christmas and all; like 'Old Mother Hubbard' my cupboard is suddenly looking very bare.) Mam came with me. It made a nice change for her to tag along... Well, she doesn't get out much these days, not out of Aberheol anyway. She said, the bus ride to Cardiff felt like a charabanc outing to her. She also said a little trip was what was needed to take her mind off the horrible people living across the road. "I don't know what they were doing? But they were up till all hours again last night Rhian."

January 11: Thursday

Well Diary, today is a dead day. By dead day I mean nothing, and I mean nothing remotely interesting happened. So instead of leaving a blank page between your covers, I intend to use these and other dead days which fall throughout the year to inform you of matters concerning the circumstances surrounding my life, and the lives of my family and friends.

On May 6th 1980, the Council Housing Department sent Trevor and I a letter confirming our tenancy of 29, Heol-Y-Haul, on the Lloyd George Council Estate, Aberheol.

My first impressions of the inside of the property with its torn and shabby wallpaper, was wonderful. The size and location of house was perfect for us. There was nothing a lick of paint couldn't put right, and in any case my mother only lived down the road if we needed anything. To be fair to the council they supplied us with ample decorating materials before we moved in, and just in a little over three weeks, Trevor and I had decorated over every square inch of wall, ceiling, door and skirting-board, with either wallpaper or paint.

Looking back, I think those three weeks were the happiest time of my and Trevor's married life. Looking around me now I can find no trace of the freshness that was about me then, and as far as happiness is concerned... For me happiness comes out of a cardboard box in the shape of a little white tab called Prozac.

Trevor and I worked like a pair of beavers to get our home

looking shipshape. I was happy, Trevor was unemployed. (It didn't seem to matter much then.) It meant he could spend all his time working on our home, and even if I do say so myself, we made a smashing job of it together.

Mam on the other hand, God bless her heart. Was torn between two different kinds of emotions. On the one hand she didn't want me to leave home, while on the other she was very determined to help me out in anyway she could.

By the final Monday in May 1980, our new decor was complete and we were ready to move in. (I can't remember the precise date, but I've always maintained whenever you start out on a new adventure, a Monday is the best possible day to begin.) Trevor helped to carry box after box of my personal possessions from my mother's to our new house. Then I helped him carry his stuff (surprisingly little) from his parents' home. The DSS gave us a moving in grant, and we'd made a separate claim for a second-hand cooker and household furniture. Mam said we could borrow my old single bed, until the DSS had processed our claim for our new double divan. Mam's excuse for not letting me keep my old bed: *'Rhian, now that you've left home, I'll never know when surprise guests may decide to drop in on me.'* Surprise was indeed the right word. None had ever dropped in on us, during my entire childhood. *'If Jane suddenly decides to turn-up from Swansea out of the blue, she'll be able to spend the night in your old room.'* The expression on my face asked the question: *'What are you talking about mother?'* Adding: *'You told me yourself your old school friend has been housebound for the past six months, and the likelihood of what you suggest happening was far too remote in the extreme.'* But my mother was being helpful in her own way, so I decided to let the matter drop... Going off on a tangent: Thanks to unlimited housing benefit from the council, my family have been living rate and rent free in this house for twenty years... What is the point of earning a wage to pay for something we can get for free?

January 12: Friday

Mam called in this morning, just after Megan and Anthony had left for school, and immediately stated she'd seen it all now. Apparently old Ivor Smith the newsagent is selling off his surplus Christmas stock of Quality Street, by charging each interested customer 5p per-single sweet. "Have you seen how many individual sweets you get in those big 5lb tins?" Mam protested, taking her frustration out on a teaspoon she rattled around the edge of her tea cup. "He's only got to sell a hundred, to make five quid!"

"What's he going to do with the ones nobody likes?" Trevor asked, butting in on our conversation. (I was surprised to see him up this early in the morning.)

"Well, I don't know, I'm sure." My mother retorted. "I'm not a shopkeeper am I?" She scowled. "I thought you had to sell those sweets by the tin?... Is he breaking the law, Rhian?... Is Ivor allowed to sell tinned Quality Street separately?... It was bad enough when he started selling bread by the slice, and before that it was single fags."

"Well, what's wrong with that?" Trevor interrupted. "Some of the old people around here can't afford a whole loaf, and in any case. I used to buy fags off him for 10p a time when I was a boy."

"Well I think it's wrong, that's all." Mam continued, labouring on in the same vain. "If he carries on like this, he'll be selling individual tea bags next."

I didn't have the heart to tell her, he was.

"Well I for one, always count the number of slices in every loaf I buy from his shop." Mam said, staring at Trevor. "He's not catching me out like that."

"Tell me Mair, how are your new neighbours getting on across the road. Have they settled in yet?" Trevor asked, bringing the conversation to a sudden end.

"That reminds me." Mam replied. "I haven't got time for a another tea or coffee Rhian. I don't like to leave the house unattended for too long." And without another word she was gone.

I listened to Trevor's apology for the rest of the morning: *'I'm so sorry Rhi.'* - *'You know I didn't mean it.'* - *'You know I wouldn't do anything to hurt you.'* - *'I wasn't feeling very well.'* - *'I've missed speaking to you.'* - *'We can talk about our plans for the New Year, if you want?'* - *'Fancy a cup of coffee love?'* - *'I'll tell you what, why don't you let me take you out, tomorrow night?'*

I allowed Trevor to go on and on, forgave him, then settled down to watch 'Neighbours' while Trevor made me a fresh pot of tea, and a plate of hot buttered toast. (No make-up sex took place.)

I felt a funny pain in my side this afternoon... It can mean only one thing!

January 13: Saturday

As predicted the funny pain in my side, turned into my first period of 2001. I hold a secret belief: the day I go on the change, will be the day the Chancellor of the Exchequer announces free sanitary towels for all in his next budget.

Trevor said Smith's newsagents got ram raided again last

night. Trevor claims Ivor Smith blames the BBC News Team, for the damage to his shop: *'You know what the kids around here are like.'* He once told Trevor. *'They only have to see it on the box, and they all want to copy it... No one living on this estate had ever heard of ram raiding until BBC2's 'Newsnight' reported a story about joy riders, ram raiding a shop on an Oxford housing estate. The following night, the police phoned me to ask if I knew I had an abandoned Ford Escort parked in my magazine rack!... The evil little sods!'*

After dinner Trevor went to the club. With the kids all out doing their thing, I spent a pleasant afternoon watching a James Stewart double bill on BBC2. ('The Naked Spur' & 'Vertigo'.) I decided not to go out tonight with Trevor after all. One, I wasn't feeling up to it... Two, I don't know... Just lately, I've changed... I can't be bothered to go upstairs and spend hours putting on make-up and choosing what to wear. Besides; drinking in a smoke filled pub isn't me anymore.

January 14: Sunday

What is it about Welshmen, and their Saturday night jump? Surely life must mean more to them than rugby, drinking, and sex?... Why doesn't my Trevor ever learn?

The events of the early hours of Sunday morning, are as common place to my Trevor, as the events of his average Saturday afternoon. He comes home drunk. He clumsily attempts to gently wake me by licking my ear. Then we fallout when I tell him to leave me alone.

"Don't give me that old period routine." Trevor responded at my refusal. "You were all right when I left the house this morning."

Threatening to show him the evidence... Mercifully Trevor rolled onto his side and passed out.

I woke-up at 8.00am, took a Prozac, then laughed like a drain when Megan told me the name of the Jackson's new baby: 'Sotheby'. Who do the Jackson's think they are?... The poor kid. If ever there is a child destined to be bullied at school, that child is going to be poor little Sotheby Jackson.

The Jackson's: (He's all right, but she drives me up the wall.)

Idris and Mary Jackson have a total of four children, including their latest arrival. Julian,Dominique and Harvey, are all a month or two younger than my children. Idris and Mary attended the same school as me and Trevor... I can't remember a time when Mary and I got on.

"That Mary Peterson (Her maiden name.) has always been envious of you." My mother has always maintained... On hearing Mary was expecting her fourth child my mother remarked: "What's that silly bitch trying to do now?... Go one better?... That's her game is it? Rhian that woman makes me sick. You think she would have something better to do with her time, wouldn't you?... And that husband of hers has never been able to find work with a bad back!"

After I'd finished clearing away the dinner plates, Mam called in and spat out a mouthful of coffee when I told her the new Jackson baby's name... *'No Rhian! Dear, dear me no. Fancy naming a poor little baby after a famous London auction house.'*

January 15: Monday

Anthony came home from school and said, he'd seen Gary hanging around the school playing fields this afternoon.

Megan said, Gary's life was nothing to do with her. He didn't interfere with her life, and she had no intention of interfering with his. (I think something is going on.)

Gary came home at his usual time, looking very tired and withdrawn. He failed to respond to any of my questions concerning his day at work. He offered no response to why he was walking across the school's playing fields. He then announced he was feeling very tired and went to his room. (I must think of another way of finding out.)

January 16: Tuesday

I exited the Post Office with my Family Allowance, just in time to see Gary catching the bus into Cardiff. I worried all day about what he could be up to, but Gary still came home from work at his usual time.

"Leave me alone," and "stop bugging me." Was the only response I could get out of him. I re-questioned Megan, (I'm really worried that she's turning into an unfeeling girl.) and Anthony. (I think he's been threatened to keep quiet by his older brother.) But got nowhere. Trevor said: *'Leave the boy alone.'* And: *'He'll tell us all about it when he's good and ready.'* Am I the only person who cares what happens to my children? I can't believe this was the only reaction I could get out of Trevor... So much for parental concern!

January 17: Wednesday

Baby Sotheby's arrival is the talk of the estate. Mam called around, and once again exclaimed that she'd heard everything now. "Who does that Mary Jackson think she is, giving an ordinary new born baby a stupid name like that?... And where is that weak husband of hers? The poor child's been born less than a week, and Idris Jackson has all ready allowed his wife to turn the dear little mite into a laughing stock. "I tried to calm Mam, but she had already built up a full head of steam. "Their eldest, what's his name again?... You know Rhian, he was in the same class as our Gary at school?"

"Julian, Mam."

"That's right Julian. Poor kid had an hell of a life, what with his mother being the school scrubber and all."

"His mother was the school cleaner, Mam." I reminded her.

"Well, she used to scrub the school floors, didn't she?" Unable to find a suitable reply other than "yes", I decided to let the matter drop.

My mother has never forgiven Mary for marrying Idris in a church. As she remarked at the time: *'If anyone deserved to have been married in church, it should have been my Rhian. How that Mary had the cheek to go through with it, and dressed in white I'll never know. What with her being two months' pregnant and all.'* (I have no proof of course, and to be fair to Mary who wasn't pregnant at the time of her wedding. But in my heart of hearts, I know it was my mother who spread that rumour about the estate.)

Three hours later Mam rose out of her chair and gathering her things together, prepared to make her way back to her own home. (She had a lot to get off her chest today.)

"She's never liked the Jackson's, has she?" Trevor remarked, after Mam had gone. "Sotheby Jackson?... Fancy naming a child that! The tossers!"

January 18: Thursday

Gary said he was too ill to go to work this morning. Trevor

must have been awake because at 7.00am he dashed into his son's bedroom, and reminded him it was pay-day. "Nobody goes sick on pay-day boy." Trevor told his son. "If you want a day off, why don't you pull a sicky tomorrow, and make a long weekend of it."

Gary said he could wait, was in no hurry, and would collect his wages on Monday. But Trevor wasn't having any of it and insisted the family needed his keep today, and something about me needing the money to be in this house tonight, in order for me to do the family shopping first thing tomorrow morning. At this Gary pulled his duvet over his head, and said he'd been sacked. Trevor asked him if he'd been to sign on? While I asked if he was feeling all right?

Answering yes to both questions, Gary revealed he had lost his job on his first day back after the Christmas break for fighting with one of his work-mates. After revealing the name of the other person, Trevor said he didn't think much of him either. In fact; Trevor went on to say he could remember beating the boy's father up at school. "Don't worry about it. He's not worth it. I bet he's just like his father." Trevor commented, after hearing Gary's version of the story.

"Yes." I thought to myself. "Just like their father in both cases!"

Later on, Gary let it all pour out. He'd spent most of his time since his sacking, looking for another job, and at the times his brother and sister had seen him, he was just searching for somewhere to sit quietly and pass the time of day... The other boy, kept his job. "That's only because he's related to the foreman." Trevor said, agreeing with the nodding head of his son.

January 19: Friday

Mam said I should get out more, after she'd agreed with Trevor's opinion of the Lewis family. (The surname of the other person involved in Gary's set to... No assault charges are pending.)

"Rhian, all this staying in is doing you absolutely no good at all." Mam insisted. "Apart form going shopping to Tesco's once a week, where do you go to?"

Deep down I know she's right, but I blame these damn Prozac for making me feel so lethargic. They make my home seem such a wonderful place for me to waste my life in, besides I have nothing to wear,and I can't be bothered to put on any make-up anymore. (I like to think the rest is doing wonders for my facial skin.) God I feel like I'm in a rut, one of those great big ones that curl in on themselves from either side.

January 20: Saturday

My period finished last Thursday, at teatime. Spent most of the day thinking up an excuse for not taking part in Trevor's after-hours Saturday night activities... To hell with it, I'll just tell him I'm not in the fucking mood... Sorry, but I can't write anymore. (Please refer to my previous statement.)

January 21: Sunday

I needn't have spent most of yesterday worrying. (I shouldn't have, if these damn Prozac are working properly?) Trevor never came near me, when he came home. (Why not?) In fact I didn't even hear him come in. (Doesn't he fancy me anymore, or had he all ready had his way with another woman?) I'm thinking about going out with him next weekend after all.

Must remember to see if Trevor's changed any of his personal habits, clothes, hygiene, etc... If he has, he spent the rest of the day doing a marvellous concealing job of hiding them away from me.

January 22: Monday

A proud day for the Evans family. Father and son left the house together this morning, to sign on the dole. (It would be tragic, if I couldn't see the funny side.)

With Trevor out of the house, it gave me plenty of time to search through his pockets for clues of his infidelity. (Am I becoming paranoid?) Two hours later I'd found nothing. It must be all in my mind. My bloody Prozac are turning me into a jealous housewife.

11.00pm. I'm rapidly coming to the conclusion; Trevor didn't disturb me last Saturday night because he wasn't: 1. In the mood. 2. Pissed. 3. Passed out before his head hit the pillow. 4. Combination of all three. 5. Didn't want to disturb me. 6. No longer fancies me!

January 23: Tuesday

My mother's right, I should get out more. "Rhian!" I said to myself. Come on girl you really must make a big effort to do more with your life. So I popped my morning Prozac, and went to collect my Family Allowance money from the Post Office.

I planned to see if they had anything nice for me in the charity shop, but it had been ram raided during the early hours of the morning, so I decided to leave it until tomorrow.

Called in on Mam, and told her the news about the shop. She said: '*It comes to something, when people living around here have to resort to doing something like that, because they haven't got a spare 50p to spend on charity.'*

January 24: Wednesday

Trevor and Gary's unemployment Giros were posted through the letterbox this morning. I cashed Trevor's as usual, but Gary insisted on cashing his own. (It'll be a novelty for him.)

The talk in the charity shop was all about the ram raid. Mrs Howard, an assistant volunteer claimed this raid had come out of the blue. Apparently, all the staff had been expecting a ram raid before the Christmas holiday, but this one had taken them all by surprise. Anyway, there was nothing there I liked, but that didn't stop me from donating 10p worth of copper coins, into the collection box. (Every little helps.) I spoke to Trevor about the raid. Trevor thinks the shop got raided because all their stock is donated by the rich people of Cardiff. Trevor said: *'You bought that nice woollen jumper for me in there last October. I can't recall seeing anyone wearing it around this estate before I had it on my back.'*

January 25: Thursday

This morning I listened to a doctor on 'Richard & Judy', telling the nation that organic vegetables are good for you. The doctor claimed the other sort of veg had all been doused with chemicals. (He didn't mention anything about the vegetables that are put into tins.)

All this talk about fresh veg reminded me of the time Trevor put in a claim with the DSS, for a set of new gardening equipment in the early '80s. Trevor's accompanying letter argued the point, (very well I thought.) that in his opinion, it was very important for a young growing family to have access to a fresh supply of veg throughout the year, and as he couldn't afford to buy any, he'd decided to have a go at growing his own. Trevor inclosed a torn picture from an Argos catalogue depicting the said items he wished to purchase, (Garden spade, fork, rake, pickaxe, wheelbarrow, lawn mower and heavy roller.) and waited for a reply.

A week later a Giro popped through the letterbox for the said amount. (£150) £60 of which helped to pay off part of an outstanding electric bill. £40 reconnected the telephone. (2nd or 3rd time.) The remainder went on a Saturday night out... Those were the days!

January 26: Friday

There was nothing on after 'Coronation Street', so I popped into Anthony's room and spied on Fatty Ham & Piccalilli, eating their supper... I couldn't see the dog there, which was a bit of a surprise because I know Piccalilli likes to eat and feed the dog sitting on her lap at the same time. (I must remember to keep a look out for the poor animal during the week... I hope it isn't dead.) One more thing before I go... Trevor and I had sex last night... It was all right.

January 27: Saturday

1.30pm. I'm writing this now, because I want to spend the rest of the day getting ready for my big night out. (I'll reveal all in tomorrow's instalment.) So far nothing Diary worthy as happened... Still no sign of the neighbour's dog.

8.00pm. Trevor hasn't returned home from the rugby club YET! I feel like a painted tart, without an heart. If he doesn't come for me in the next ten minutes... He'll never come again!

January 28: Sunday

9.00pm, yesterday evening I found myself sitting in the public bar of the Collier's Arms public house. As usual Trevor had put me to sit with the rest of the wives, while he and the other husbands amused themselves by playing darts, pool and exchanging lurid glances at the single young girls drinking at the bar.

Returning at regular intervals with my top-up vodka and orange, I found myself feeling pissed by ten. (I think the alcohol must have reacted with my Prozac?)

Now here's the rub: For some reason Trevor wasn't really all that drunk last night, which is unusual for him on a Saturday. He also turned down a chance of having sex with me, after I'd draped myself across the bed, and provocatively said: *'Come and take me like you've never taken me before.'*

Take it from me, when a member of the opposite sex looks down upon your naked body - laughs - then walks out of the room. It makes you feel like shit, no matter how pissed you are.

Thinking of myself lying there in the nac, makes me want to cringe... THE BASTARD... *'Take me like you've never...'* Why did I have to say that?... The bastard!

WHY WOULD TREVOR REFUSE TO HAVE SEX WITH ME:

1. Revenge? (I've often turned him down in the past.)
2. Screwing somebody else? (Possible?)
3. Wasn't pissed enough? (Hope not!)

Men!... I gave up years ago trying to fathom out how their minds work... I still haven't seen any sign of the neighbour's little dog... Fuck the little dog!

January 29: Monday

Not having Saturday night sex, is still pricking me at the back of my mind... I wonder if Trevor ever feels like this, after I've refused his advances?

It's been... Oh, I can't remember when since we last... I was pissed for Christ's sake. He could have done with me what he wanted... What's the matter with him? Well, I'll tell you this. It's going to be a bloody long time, before I allow Trevor to get me in that condition again!

January 30: Tuesday

On my way to collect my Family Allowance, I noticed a council work gang erecting three concrete bollards around the entrance of the charity shop. "It's bloody typical." I heard a woman remark, as I checked my Family Allowance money at the Post Office counter. "If it's for big business, they're in there like a shot. But you just try and get them to come and see to your plumbing... You've got no chance... You'll have to drop your knickers before you can get one of those idle buggers from the council, to come and repair anything in your home."

Her words were greeted with howls of laughter from the other people in the queue. Walking outside I had to admit. She had a point.

I went out of my way, and walked the long way round to my mother's. This route took me past the front of Piccalilli's house. I'd remembered what Megan had said about seeing their previous dogs looking out of the window as she walked past. But I saw nothing. Not even when a bus with a loud engine roared past... Mam agreed it was about time the council did something to protect the charity shop. She told me when my father was alive, he'd paid taxes in order for the council to do that sort of thing... Mam doesn't like dogs, so I didn't tell her my fears for the little pup.

January 31: Wednesday

Trevor admitted he doesn't find me very attractive when I'm drunk. "Since when?" I protested. He replied, he couldn't put his finger on it exactly, but it's a feeling that's gradually started to come over him during these past few years.

I retaliated by stating he wasn't exactly Mel Gibson when he was pissed either. But he insisted that it was different for men, and some bullshit about only young girls can get away with looking sexy when they were out of it. (What the hell does this mean?... Is there someone else?)

REVIEW OF THE MONTH:

Life hasn't got any better. In fact it's got a little bit worse if you think about Trevor's attitude towards me, and Gary losing his job. But to be perfectly honest with you, January has never been a very lucky month for me, or anyone else in our family.

February 1: Thursday

The studio audience were discussing debt on 'Kilroy' this morning. Trevor and I have been in debt all of our married life. But like Trevor says: *'As long as they don't send you to prison for it, who cares?... What difference does it make if our bank account is in the red? When you're dead, you're dead. You can't take it with you, can you?'*

More disturbingly Gary has started to follow in his father's footsteps, by spending the majority of the morning in bed. He complains there's nothing for him to get up for because all his friends are out working on the scheme. I suggested he began a hobby, model building or something, but he didn't seem interested... Not exactly the start to the month I was hoping for. Years ago a gypsy told my mother if a month started out badly, it would only get worse... Those gypsies are a clever people.

February 2: Friday

The gypsy's curse kicked in big time this morning. Woke-up to find my nerves standing on end. Matters were made far worse, by the dreadful discovery I'd forgotten to collect my repeat Prozac prescription from the chemists.

Aggravated beyond belief I made Trevor get out of bed, and fetch my prescription for me. (I was in no state to leave the house, and Trevor is my DOG!!!)

By the time Trevor returned, I had no nails left on my fingers, toes, and my knuckles were red raw through the constant wringing of my hands. I can honesty say in this condition: if any man, woman,or child had uttered a word to me out of place. I would have flown for their throats.

An hour later, my world was once again at peace... Trevor had returned to his basket... Sorry, I mean bed.

TABLET OF WHITE

by

Rhian Evans

1.

Tablet of white,
You keep my world alight,
And my senses bright.

2.

Without you I'd be lost,
In reality's evil grip,
Tossed from pillar to post,
Like a hulk of a sinking ship.

3.

Demons of the mind,
Often ugly and unkind,
Vanish in an haze,
Taken from my gaze.

4.

When I get out of bed,
Thoughts are swimming in my head,
That I must hide away,
Or I won't make it through the day.

February 3: Saturday

Dear Diary, with everybody out of the house, I've decided to offer you a frank and honest account of my medical history.

Up until the early '90s, I'd been living a relatively healthy, if uneventful lifestyle. During the Spring of 1993 it took a big effort from me to leave the bedroom.... That is to say; I did what I had to do, like sending the children to school, and seeing to their food, but when it came to anything else I'd let it slide, and more often than not find myself returning to the bedroom the moment they'd all walked outside the door.

After two months of this depressing behaviour, Trevor noticed something was amiss, and asked me to tell him what was wrong... How could I make him understand there was nothing wrong with me, apart that is: I felt as if I was carrying the weight of the world around with me everywhere I went. Physically, I was A1... I wasn't going down with a disease... How could I make him understand... Boredom... Tedious, monotonous, boredom... My life wasn't/isn't going anywhere... How could I make Trevor, the world and my mother understand, my tedious nothing life was mentally murdering me a little more each day. Bit by bit, eroding me away, dragging me down?

I didn't want to hear Trevor say: *'Pull yourself together.'* I didn't want to listen to him reminding me: *'You've got children to look after.'* I hated it when my mother said things like: *'She was never like this when she was living with me.'* And the classic: *'Of course, I saw this coming from a long way off. You only have to look at her to see the girl's not feeling well.'*

Eventually I mustered the strength to book an appointment with Dr Reece who reassured me I wasn't going mad, but diagnosed me as suffering a form of depression brought on by the stress and strains of modern life. ("I've heard everything now?" Mam quipped, after I'd told her what the doctor had diagnosed. "My Rhian, - Modern!")

Prescribing Prozac to me for the first time, Dr Reece explained: *'Finish the course Mrs Evans, and with a bit of luck you won't need anymore.'* Obviously I'm an unlucky person, because starting from that spring morning in 1993, I've been taking the prescribed dosage ever since.

Diary, I would also like to state; the people who say Prozac is a non-addictive drug, have obviously never had to take it. You've witnessed what I'm like without mine. The Government worries about drug addicts turning to crime to attain their fix. I firmly believe if Prozac became illegal, the criminal classes would no longer be in the minority in this country... If indeed they ever were?

February 4: Sunday

Trevor came home at midnight, and I let him have his way with me... Why does 'Midnight' hold such a fascination for the Welsh race?... For some reason or other, my mother firmly believes people who are not in bed and sound asleep by midnight, are usually up to no good. "When I was a little girl." Mam kept reminding me: "Only criminals are about at that unearthly hour of the night... You mark my words Rhian, no good ever came to anyone who stayed up so late."

I started to enjoy myself with Trevor, until my brain callously reminded me, he probably only wanted to do it to me because he was pissed. So I played along with him, and went through the motions. (Trevor didn't notice my sudden lack of enthusiasm... If he had, I don't think he cared!)

February 5: Monday

Reread Friday, and Saturday's entries. Enjoyed reading 'Tablet of White' so much so, I've decided to share it with my family. Scribbling the poem down on a note pad, I pretended

I'd just written it off the top of my head. Starting with Trevor and Gary, I read it to them after they'd both returned from signing-on.

Gary stared at the silent television screen throughout my reading, and said nothing. Trevor said, I should ask Dr Reece to increase my dosage, and enquired what he was having for his dinner.

Later on: Megan smiled, then run laughing to her bedroom... Anthony said it was at the cutting edge of surrealist realism, (Whatever that means?) while Mam looked blankly at me and stated, she didn't have a clue to what I was going on about... I think I'll keep my poems to myself in the future.

February 6: Tuesday

Can I ask you a question Diary?... Is ignorance bliss?... Surely what you don't know, can't hurt you... But could knowledge make me a happier person?

Tablet of White has been bouncing around my brain, like a catchy tune I'd listened to for the first time on the radio. With the verse swirling around inside my brain, I entered the charity shop after I'd collected this week's Family Allowance money, and purchased a relatively new copy of William Harmon's 'The Top 500 Poems', for 75p. (Well the book has got over 1,000 pages.)

Turning to page seven, I read the first poem 'Cuckoo Song' written by someone calling himself Anonymous. (Roman or Ancient Greek I expect?) No matter how many times I tried to read Anonymous's poem, I couldn't understand a single word of it.

CUCKOO SONG (C.1250 - C.1350)

by

Anonymous

Sumer is icumen in,
Lhude sing cuccu;
Groweth sed and bloweth med
And springth the wude nu.
Sing cuccu!
Awe bleteth after lomb,
Lhouth after calve cu:
Bulluc sterteth, bucke verteth;
Murie sing cuccu.
Cuccu, cuccu,
Wel singes thu, cuccu,
Ne swik thu naver nu.
Sing cuccu nu! Sing cuccu!
Sing cuccu! Sing cuccu nu!

I refuse to believe this gibberish is any better than my poem!

February 7: Wednesday

Trevor discovered my book, and immediately told Anthony off for not keeping his school books in his bedroom. Then I was accused off wasting our benefit money on rubbish. I could have accused Trevor of wasting our benefit money on booze and fags, but I don't like to argue in front of the children.

'TREVOR'
by
Rhian Evans

1.
Trevor - What do you know?
Trevor - What do you do?
Television, Fags, Booze.
The morning paper, and your all day snooze.

2.
Trevor - I'm drifting away.

February 8: Thursday

I was offered a free calculator today, by a life insurance company. Trevor laughed, ripped the letter up, and threw it in the bin. "We don't need life insurance." Trevor insisted, flopping down on the couch. "If anything happens to us, we don't have to worry about anything. All we have to do is put a claim in with the DSS, and let them sort it out.

Trevor also threw in something about the suicide rate on this estate, and the insurance company not paying out if they get wind of it... This statement slightly worried me. Is Trevor expecting any of us to commit suicide in the near future?

February 9: Friday

'THE MAN I ONCE KNEW'
by
Rhian Evans

1.
He stood out from the crowd,
Lean, hungry, full of life,
Dark hair, dressed in denim,
Be my man, let me be your wife.

2.
You were my man,
A man I once knew.
Where did you go too?
Yet I'm here,
Standing next to you.

Dear Diary, Trevor and I have been together, ever since the day he drew around my fingers with his crayon, at nursery school. Now, I'm not saying we started courting back then, (My mother would have had a fit.) but we have always been together in the sense of us being part of the same group of friends, who grew up on this estate together.

God, it hurts when I think back on how it used to be. From my bedroom window I can see the world as it is, and remember it as it used to be. The streets, and park where we used to play. The bus shelter where he asked me out for the first time. If I look back, through closed eyes, I can hear us laughing. I can see Trevor dart in and out of the tree line, along the edge of the valley walls. With my outstretched arms, I can feel the rough texture of the tree bark against my hands, as my senses fill with the escaping aroma from crushed pine needles trampled under our feet... Then reality kicks in, and around me I see an untidy room. A thing resembling my love asleep upon the bed. A world as far away from the one that I'd like to inhabit, as it could possibly be.

My Trevor, the Trevor of my youth. Fight your way free from your lethargic attitude, become my knight once more, reclaim your throne, return and rescue me.

February 10: Saturday

As I suspected. I became P.M.T active over night. (No wonder I was feeling maudlin, yesterday.) With a slight ache in my tummy, and the house to myself I settled down and discovered 'William Shakespeare'... Page 96, of Harmon's book: titled 'It Was A lover And His Lass'. *'With an hey, and a ho, and a hey nonino.'* (Here is a man who knows what he's talking about.)

On an excursion upstairs, I heard Piccalilli calling to her dog. I looked out of the bedroom just in time to see the little fur ball wag it's tail and jump into her arms. As I was thinking all's well that ends well, Megan storms into the house in floods of tears. I watched her run upstairs, and lock herself in her bedroom.

Refusing to accept food, drink, or even to open her bedroom door, I decided to go back downstairs and leave her to come to herself by the morning.

February 11: Sunday

Last night I thought Trevor took the news about my P.M.T's rather well. Sometime during the early hours of this morning. He woke me... Enquired... Listened to what I had to say... Laughed and asked, why did I always have them on the weekend? I replied by stating, if it was all the same to God, I wish I didn't have to have them at all. On hearing this, Trevor inquired if I was up for anything else? But I only felt it right to inform my dear understanding man, in my present state of mind I felt more inclined to grind my teeth than to suck, so he agreed to let the moment pass.

11.00am. Megan entered the bathroom. On returning she found me sitting on her bed. Bursting into tears she cuddled up to me, resting her head on my lap.

"BOYFRIEND - CHESTY PHILLIPS - SLAG," was all I could understand, between her sobs. But it doesn't take a genius to workout, one of her friends, had run off with her latest beau.

"She pads her bra with 'Kleenex for Men', Mam!" Megan informed me, divulging more information than I needed to know.

"You're better off without him, love." Was all I could think of to say to comfort her... But it did the trick... Dear diary, why do my children only treat me as a human being, when they are ill or in pain. Why won't they occasionally allow me to share in some of the good things that happen in their lives as well?

February 12: Monday

Today was one of those days, where I couldn't get anything done. In full zombie mode I stared blankly at the screen of the television set for most of the day, knowing full well the breakfast dishes were waiting patiently for me in the sink.

Experiencing enough guilt to stir me from my trance, I looked down at the carpet, and wished a cleaning fairy would come along and hoover it for me.

Anthony came home with a note from his teacher, inviting me and his father to a parents' evening then Gary came home and said he and his mates have formed a rock band.

February 13: Tuesday

Neither Trevor or I have ever attended a parents' evening at the school before. (Does that make me a bad parent?) So why has next Thursday's meeting got me so worked up?

Trevor says: *'I send my children to school to get an education. I don't expect to be bombarded with the details. The teacher is there to teach. I don't expect them to come and visit me to see if I'm a good parent. Leave the teachers teach that's what* I *say, and if everyone else thought along the same lines and stopped sticking their two pennyworth in, this country would be a far better place to live in... And further more, the same goes for the people who grass up their neighbours to the DSS inquisition telephone hotline, as well!... I don't need to cross the road to listen to any school teacher telling me my children are thick. I can see that for myself at home!'*... I think I will attend the parents' evening this time. In fact I'm quite looking forward to going.

February 14: Wednesday St Valentine's Day

After all these years of not bothering, Trevor can't understand why I suddenly wanted to attend the school parents' evening. A hush fell over the living-room when I let my family in on my decision.

"You never went to any of ours." Gary, and Megan exclaimed.

"Did you want, or expect me to attend?" I replied.

"Well I'm not going with you." Trevor stated, as the other two shook their heads. "And I can't see why you want to go either..." He paused, "unless this has got something to do with that bloody stupid poem book, you bought the other day?"

Sometimes I think Trevor is blessed with extra sensory perception, because he can read my thoughts like a book... Defending my reasons to the hilt, (What else could I do?) I managed to reassure everyone whatever my motive, I believed I was doing what I was doing for the best even if I couldn't explain what the best was exactly at that precise moment.

Dear Diary I'm standing at the entrance of a tunnel. Far away in the distance I can see a speck of light. A minute chink of light I have called 'Hope'. If I don't reach out for it now, I'm afraid I'll never have another chance to reach for it again... Yes I'm thinking about myself... Am I a bad mother???

No Diary, I haven't forgotten it's Valentine's Day. That is to say I haven't forgotten, but I know a man who has. "It's another rip-off from America isn't it, and I for one want nothing to do with it." So said the man of the house. This year's family card count was also at an all time low:

Trevor: 0 "I've got more important things to spend our money on."

Gary: 0 "Next year, when the bands a success. They'll all be after me."

Megan:	1	"If he thinks I'll take him back after this, he's got another thing coming."
Anthony:	0	"Can I have a computer instead, Mam?"
Mam:	1	"Thank you Rhian. I love you too."
Me:	1	"Thank you Mam, ditto."

For Christ's sake Trevor. I didn't expect a bunch of red roses, or to be whisked away to a fabulous restaurant. But a fifty pence card, is that too much to ask?... Diary, I didn't intend to write my last comment... But I believe we shouldn't keep any secrets between the two of us, and in any case keeping how I feel a secret from you would only make me feel as childish as him.

February 15: Thursday

I felt a complete fool walking through the school gates this evening. Apart from attending the odd car boot or jumble sale, this was the first time I'd entered the school grounds on official school business since the day I left my academic career behind me in 1976.

Straight away I could sense not one of the teaching staff had a clue to who I was. In fact I would go further and say, some showed a great deal of surprise when I told them I was Anthony's mother.

Somebody called Philip, wearing a name badge on his jacket introduced me to each of Anthony's teachers in turn. Everything was going well until I was introduced to Mr Davis, Anthony's English master. (God, why doesn't the ground open and swallow me up?) Thrusting a note containing my poem 'Tablet of White' into his unsuspecting hand, I asked him what he thought about my work?(My work, I ask you?) Immediately the note paper touched his hand, I knew it was a bad idea. Like Sleeping

Beauty waking from a kiss... What was I thinking of?... Instead of finding Prince Charming, I felt ridiculed and embarrassed by my naive actions.

Rushing out of the room, I left the bemused teacher clutching my poem in his hand. (Or maybe it was my glass slipper, I don't know?) And ran all the way home... Where is my happy ending?

February 16: Friday

If suffering from palpitations wasn't bad enough, (My stomach has been turning somersaults all day.) I had to put up with Gary twanging away all morning on an old battered acoustic guitar. (I have no idea where he got it from?)

With Gary learning his cords in the background, my imagination ran riot. I could hear the laughter echoing around the teachers' staffroom: In my mind's eye, I could picture my poem being passed from hand to hand. I could hear Mr Davis telling his colleges about an hysterical mad woman who ran away from the parents' evening: *'You should have seen the state of her.'* I can hear him say. *'I'm no psychiatrist, but I think this poem tells us all* we *need to know about her state of mind... Where that boy gets his brains from is a mystery to me. There must have been a mistake at the hospital when Evans was born.'* (What will Anthony say when he comes home?)

11.00pm. Anthony, and Megan said nothing when they came home from school this afternoon. (I can't believe I've got away with this.)

February 17: Saturday

Gary and the other three members of his band, spent the morning treating my living-room like some sort of recording studio. Placing a portable tape recorder in the centre of the room, they proceeded to produce a demo tape by playing around it... Two thoughts entered my head while I listened to their noise:

1. At this stage of their careers, were The Beatles this bad?
2. Knowing nothing about the music industry. I wonder if it would be a good idea if my eldest son and his three friends learnt how to play the instruments properly, before they began thinking of making a demo tape?

Of course, it goes without saying I will encourage Gary to live out this fantasy until he finds he's had enough and decides to chuck it in. (I give him two weeks maximum!) Mam said, Gary must be following in his father's footsteps, (I hope not) because no one on our side of the family could sing a note. "Rhian, have you forgotten how well Trevor's singing went down in the rugby club on New Year's Eve? Trevor won a bottle of whiskey on the karaoke, and things like that tend to run in the family." Mam then added, more out of helpfulness than anything else. "I'm sure if I had a quiet word with Mr Simon, (the old age concert secretary) he will give Gary and his friends permission to play a live concert for us on a Thursday afternoon, after we've finished playing bingo of course... Rhian,the girls all agree there's been a lack of variety acts on the television lately. They should bring back programmes like 'The Black & White Minstrel Show' and 'Sunday Night At The London Palladium',for us old ones who rarely find the need to venture from our living-room sofas."

February 18: Sunday

Trevor came home at 2.15am this morning. I knew the time was 2.15 am precisely, because I made myself stay awake until I heard him come in. The pubs around here close at 11.00pm on a Saturday night. So allowing him half an hour to drink up, it took my husband the best part of four hours to walk home. *'I went to Mike's for a nightcap and a game of cards,'* was Trevor's only excuse. I don't know if I believe him or not? But I gave him the benefit of the doubt all the same... Strange but true: Trevor didn't seem all that drunk, either?

February 19: Monday

Together, they left to sign on. But separately they returned... Why? Gary came home from signing- on, a good two hours before his father returned from the unemployment centre. Gary said, Trevor had an appointment somewhere or other, and his father had told him there wasn't any need for him to hang around and wait for him. (This is all news to me.) Trevor came home and said the doctor had put him on a course of antibiotics, because he'd been feeling a little run down lately. (Since when?) In the seventeen years I have been married to Trevor, he has never made an appointment to see a doctor in his life.

Trevor's Symptoms:

1. As far as I can tell, unchanged for seventeen years.
2. Seems to be walking funny/with a slight limp?
3. Started biting his fingernails.
4. Moving gingerly when sitting down... Call it feminine intuition, but I think something is wrong!

School half term: Megan and Anthony spent the day moping around the house.

February 20: Tuesday

Overnight Trevor reckons he's developed a water infection. He also reckons Dr Reece told him this might happen. He said it was common for a man of his age, and with his illness to develop it. He also told me not to worry because Dr Reece had prescribed him a course of antibiotic tablets to clear his infection up.

I believe Trevor thinks my Prozac have turned me into some sort of **'THICK-O!'** I agreed it was indeed very common for any man of Trevor's age to develop the symptoms he described. Especially after venturing into the bushes on a Saturday night, with one of the gang of common little teenage scrubbers of the sexy drunken variety, he'd already told me he found so sexy... But after debating the subject long and hard for the best part of five hours. We've both agreed differing opinions was the only thing we could agree on... Dear Diary just in case you don't know where your new home is. You are currently lying on top of a quilt, in the bedroom of my childhood, at my mother's.

Mam said: "Rhian, now you know why I wouldn't allow you to take away your old bed with you when you moved to your new house all those years ago... I had no way of knowing when I would need it again, if someone unexpected paid me a visit!"

February 21: Wednesday

Mam said I could stay for as long as I liked, but it was quickly understood that she was the one who would be in sole charge of the television remote control, and choose what we watched on the box. (When you come to think about it, I suppose the television set to Mam, is the equivalent of what Trevor is to me, but far more intelligent.)

Trevor tried every trick in the book, to make me see him today. First thing this morning Mam turned him away with the quip: “You’ve made your own bed, and now you’ve got to lie in it.” Closing the door behind her, she giggled: “Rhian, I wanted to tell him, if you’ve got an itch, scratch it yourself. But at the last moment, I thought better of it.”

One by one the kids called round, each with a different tale to tell me about their father’s increasingly bizarre behaviour.

“He doesn’t want you back. He says we’re better off without you.” Gary announced, thirty minutes after Mam had turned Trevor way from her door.

“Mam, Dad’s awful upset.” Megan reported, at 3.00pm in the afternoon. “He’s been crying for hours Mam, and he said he doesn’t know what he’d do without you.”

“Dad says you’re a bad mother for walking out on your husband and children.” Anthony informed me at teatime. “He told me to tell you, if you don’t come home now, he’s going to blow his Giro on drink... Mam can I stop around here for my tea tonight?”

The time was a little after 6.00pm. The Post Office had been closed for over half an hour... Trevor was so desperate, he had been reduced to issuing empty threats.

“Are you coming home Mam?” Anthony asked, on his way

through the door. I instructed him to tell Trevor, that I'd speak with him first thing in the morning.

February 22: Thursday

At 10.00am precisely, Trevor open the door to allow me back into my home... Trevor was full of compliments. If I believed everything he said, a night away from him had taken ten years off my appearance. (I think Trevor shot himself in the foot there.) Promising to speak nothing but the truth, Trevor swore on his mother and children's lives, that he hadn't been unfaithful with another woman. He said as unbelievable as the truth he was about to tell me may sound, it was nevertheless still the truth... Trevor claims he caught his infection from one of the toilet seats in either the rugby club, or the pub. *'Rhian, you know the type of people who drink in those places.'* Trevor emphasised. 'Some *of them are really scruffy buggers, who haven't washed their bollocks in ages.*" I was only too willing to agree with what he had to say, and to remind Trevor that he himself was one of them.

SOME OTHER POINTS TREVOR WAS HAPPY TO CLEAR UP:

1. "I couldn't get pissed, because my knob stung when I went to the toilet for a pee."
2. "Sex was out of the question... I was afraid of passing my infection on to you."
3. "I blame that team from Port Talbot for passing this on to me, Rhian. You should have smelt some of them in the clubhouse after the game."
4. "Please come home, I really do miss you, you know... I think the kids miss you as well."

I told Trevor I'll have to think about it, and if I believed his story, I'd let him know in the morning... I made sure I pursed our fortnightly benefit cheque before I left the house.

WHAT KIND OF FOOL AM I
by
Rhian Evans

What kind of fool am I,
To believe all your lies.
What choice do I have,
A part of life's deck of cards.
My life's a game of chance,
Good, bad, indifference.
Better the fool I know,
Than living alone, somehow.
Does he really care?
Am I really wanted there?
Will my foolish heart break?
Or, like a dirty plate,
Am I destined for the sink?

I've made-up my mind to return home tomorrow... Do I believe Trevor's toilet seat story?... I don't know, but anything is possible when a person mixes with the class of people Trevor mixes with... And you can bet Trevor was pissed when he sat down!... If I've told Trevor once I've told him a million times. Trevor you must always remember to wash your hands after using the toilet.

After two days of living with Mam, I now remember why I

was so desperate to leave all those years ago, and find a place of my own.

February 23: Friday

To a man, my tribe greeted me on the doorstep with chants of *'Welcome home Mam,'* and, *'it's great to have you back where you belong.'* Inside the house the table was laid. One of them had found a roughly mauled silver-plated toast rack, and placed six slices of toast within its sections. Somebody else had scooped some marmalade into a little glass dish. A tea cosy had been placed over a piping hot pot of tea, and a fresh unopened tub of margarine had been placed at the side of my plate.

I warned Trevor I was going to give him the benefit of the doubt, but if I ever found any evidence to suggest otherwise, I would be back to my mother's like a shot, and would have nothing to do with him ever again. Giving a man the silent treatment, is one thing. But giving a man the silent treatment when I am not in the same house, and can't keep an eye on him is a totally different matter all together. From now on Trevor will be like putty in my hands. Well until his infection has cleared up, anyway... Dear Diary, do you have any idea where I put that list of jobs that need doing around the house?

February 24: Saturday

Like me; Trevor thought he should give the rugby club a miss this afternoon, so he could concentrate on clearing the debris out of our guttering. Later on in the morning, Trevor agreed our dripping bathroom tap was indeed getting on his nerves, so much so that after he'd made me a fresh pot of tea, he went upstairs to fix it. At 6.00pm, after Trevor had finished his chores for the day and cleaned up after himself, I told him he could go for a drink with his mates, but I expected him home by half past eleven, at the latest... Dear Diary, the time is now 11.45pm. Trevor came home half an hour ago. I've spent a most enjoyable evening creating a new list and thinking up new jobs Trevor can do in the morning... Good night and happy dreaming.

February 25: Sunday

Last night I had one of the best night's sleep since I don't know when. Fantasising about other family members doing my housework, knocked me out before my head had touched the pillow. (Have I accidentally stumbled on the perfect cure for my Prozac addiction?)

Overall, I have to say the day went well. Trevor spent most of his time in the garden, making good the work he should have done, last autumn. Megan and Anthony made the Sunday dinner, and washed up afterwards, while Gary talked to me about his band's first gig at the old people's centre.

Mam called in to check if everything was tickety-boo. I thought Trevor took it rather well when I called him in and instructed him to make my mother a cup of tea... I wonder if I could set myself up as 'Mistress Rhian' the Principalities top dominatrix in Cardiff?

QUEEN FOR A DAY
by
Rhian Evans

I am a Queen for a day,
Waited on by kith an kin.
I am dominant for a day,
Taking advantage, of a weak man's sin?
Am I wrong?
But hasn't he often taken advantage of me?
Are my actions born out of love,
Or burnt from a fit of jealousy?
I am a Queen for a day,
The day belongs to me.

February 26: Monday

Half term is over. (Where did that school holiday go to?) But there's still no school for Megan and Anthony, because the teaching staff are holding a training day... A tactic day Trevor calls it: *'Have you seen the size of some of those children who attend that school Rhian?... Training Day, my arse! 'Teacher Survival Training Day' that's what they should call it!'*

Poor Megan still hasn't got a new pair of trainers to wear. What with all that's been going on between me and Trevor, her trainers have became a casualty of the conflict.

Dear Diary, something extraordinary happened this afternoon. Totally out of the blue I had a surprise visit from Mr Davis, Anthony's English teacher. After attending the training day at the school, Mr Davis called in person to return the poem I'd so eagerly thrust into his hand, before I'd instantly regretted my hasty action; changing into Cinderella, and running away from the parents' evening.

"As I was in the locality I thought I'd return this to you in person Mrs Evans." Mr Davis said,handing me a envelope containing my poem. "I could tell that it meant a lot to you." He said turning towards his car.

Seizing the opportunity with both hands, I heard myself calling him back with the question: "What did you think about it then?"

"Modern - Naive - Spoken from the heart - A topical subject - A mixture of heart felt emotions – I enjoyed reading it, and it rhymed... Have you been writing poetry long Mrs Evans?"

I lied when I said: "Off and on over the years... You know how it is... When I find the time."

"Well Mrs Evans if ever you feel up to discussing your work, and debating other Great Masters of English Literature, you have an open invitation to join me and the other members of the class who attend the adult literary evening, I run over at the school. If you ever feel able to attend, my class is held every Wednesday evening, six till nine... You'll be made very welcome I'm sure... We discuss all forms of the English language, including an open forum where we discuss the merits of each student's work. "

Closing my front door behind me, I felt very much... Clutching my hands to my chest. For the first time in eons I felt very excited to be alive.

February 27: Tuesday Pancake Day

Hurried home from the Post Office, and read fifty poems from my book. (NOTE: Remember to reread poems, because

I can't remember a single word.) All day Mr Davis's offer has been swirling around inside my head.

I can't remember feeling this excited in ages. "If you want to discuss it?" He said. I can't believe it. Somebody wants to discuss something I've written.

I've decided not to attend the evening class this week. I don't want Mr Davis thinking I'm either desperate, or too eager to attend his classes.

DID I WANT TO DISCUSS IT?
by
Rhian Evans

Did I want to discuss it?
He asked in all earnestness.
My answer to him was,
YES! YES! YES!
Discuss it we must.

It's Pancake Day, and in my kitchen pancakes were tossed and eaten with ice cream, Lyon's Golden Syrup, jam, or simply sprinkled with lemon juice and caster sugar. I believe in keeping-up all our country's little traditions, no matter how trivial they may seem to others... There was no pancake race through the centre of the estate for the first time in living memory this year. The organising committee failed to get a Lottery Grant to cover the high cost of an accident insurance policy, the council killjoys demanded the organisers of the pancake race provide before a single pancake had been tossed in anger... Makes me wonder what the people of Wales are playing The National Lottery for?

February 28: Wednesday

Mam called around in a hell of a tizzy, this afternoon. She claimed, first thing this morning, Big Daddy Huws had came out of his house, ranting and raving, gripping a letter from the council in his hand. According to Mam, Big Daddy stood in the middle of the street, screaming: *'I'll get you for this, you bastard. I know who you are, and I know where you live. Nobody grasses me, or my family up to the council and gets away with it.'*

I said: "Mam you didn't?"

"Well Rhian, somebody had to say something. Somebody had to stand up for what's right and decent. Talk about anti-social. He's dragging my end of the street down into the gutter with him and that horrible, skinny, spiked haired, little bitch of his. It's terrible living there on the weekend, what with all the cars, and people coming and going at all hours of the day and night. Do you know what Rhian, I bet they're using that crack drug, and all sorts in there you know."

Mam hesitated, and said: "Rhian I think Big Daddy knows it was me who reported him. Because when he was out in the street, he was looking directly at my house while he was issuing his threats."

Reassuring Mam that she wasn't going to be attacked in the middle of the night, I promised her I'd reconnect my phone as soon as possible. "Rhian I've got no one I can turn to in an emergency. You know what the police around here are like. Look how long it took them to come when I reported Mr Jenkins for driving his car without a tax disc. If I can't get hold of you and Trevor in a hurry, I'll be at the mercy of that scum, and I've been lying awake at night imagining all sorts... It's not safe for a decent law-abiding woman of my age, (72) to live on her own on this estate any longer... I dread to think what Big Daddy and his mates will do to me, when they catch me."

As six o'clock approached, I was having second thoughts about not going to Mr Davis's evening class... I wonder if I'll know anyone there, when I attend next week?

REVIEW OF THE MONTH:

I feel leaving Trevor on his own with the kids for a night or two, was one of the best decisions I've ever made in my life. The consequence of our reunion as resulted in my personal life improving out of all recognition. The possibility of losing me has given Trevor the much needed kick up the backside he needed to get on with the repair jobs that need doing around the house. While an independent critic turned up on my doorstep, with an offer of developing my understanding of the literary world. (Who would have thought all this would have happened, through me spending two nights at my mother's, and running away from a parents' evening?)

March 1: Thursday - St David's Day

I find it comforting to watch the little children going to school on St David's Day, all dressed up in the Welsh national costume. I like to see the little girls dressed in their checked aprons, shawls, and wearing their tall black hats, tied with a big white ribbon under the chin. I've always felt a little pity for little boys on St David's Day. The only thing they have to wear is a Daffodil or leek, pinned to their jumper or coat, but I still like to see them all the same.

Daffodils... That reminds me... After Trevor had cleared up and cut back the overgrown grass from the flower bed, I noticed a nice clump of trumpeting daffodils growing at the far end, of one of our borders... Later, I cut the flowering stems, and along with some unopened buds, brought them into the house... It's very unlucky not to have a bunch of daffodils in the house, on St David's Day.

ST DAVID'S DAY
by
Rhian Evans

I saw the children in their dress.
My mind's eye, did regress.
To a time long ago,
When I just as them,
Wore an apron, a shawl, a tall black hat,
A smile on my face,
Held a song in my heart.
Sang to David our saint, on this special day,
Sang to David our saint, on St David's Day.

It's the first day of spring today. A time for new beginnings... Oh, I do hope so.

March 2: Friday

Trevor had an appointment with the doctor today. I had to laugh at some of the things he's been coming out with lately: *'I've been afraid to touch it for the past couple of weeks, just incase it explodes, or comes off in my hand.'* Trevor explained, looking tentatively down at the effected area. (If I were crude, I'd say something like: *'There's no need to worry about it exploding, Trevor bach. It's been coming off in my hand for years.'* But I'm not, so I didn't.)

Trevor knows he can forget about coming anywhere near me with it, until he's produced a valid certificate stating his penis has passed its medical with flying colours. Later on Trevor came home and told me his John Thomas had passed the test, but I still warned him he'd have to go without for another couple of weeks at least, just to be on the safe side... I added, if he couldn't wait for two weeks. He could always use his hand, to whip it back into shape.

Flicking through the pages of my book of Harmon's top 500 poems. I came across this one on page 679. 'The Owl and the Pussy-Cat' by Edward Lear... I've always thought this was a nursery rhyme?

March 3: Saturday

As unbelievable as it may seem. I never really doubted Trevor's explanation for contracting his unfortunate ailment... And knowing what I do, about the personal hygiene habits of people coming from the Port Talbot area. I find this only adds credence to his story. To be fair to Trevor, he has made a big effort over the past few weeks, and to be totally honest with you, I can't remember our house looking so nice for ages. You should have seen his face light up, when I told him he could go to the rugby club with his friends this afternoon. He acted just like a little boy let lose in the toy shop. But he's still got to be home by 11.30pm, mind.

Mam's favourite film was on BBC2 this afternoon. 'How Green Was My Valley' starring Walter Pidgeon. "I like to see how our valley used to look all those years ago." Mam kept on repeating throughout the film. I've tried to tell her the film was made in America, but she won't have it.

"See that rock, by there, Rhian?" Mam said, pointing at the television screen. "I can remember my father taking me and my mother for a picnic near that spot, when I was a little girl."

March 4: Sunday

Trevor was true to his word. He came home on time last night, slightly the worse for wear. (A very good sign if you ask me. Liquid must be once again flowing freely throughout his system without any stinging pain.) I on the other hand have been feeling so good over the past few days, that I decided to experiment on myself, by giving my Prozac a miss... I don't know if it's psychological or what, but realising I was without my morning dose sent me into an emotional tizzy, resulting in a zombie like trance taking a hold of my body within the first couple of hours of my new found independence. (I wish somebody would substitute my Prozac for a placebo, without my knowing. I'm sure my dependency is all in my mind.)

March 5: Monday

With the kids at school and Trevor and Gary signing on down

at the dole office, I could think about nothing else apart from attending my first evening class on Wednesday. My imagination was racing right the way through 'Kilroy'. In my mind I saw Mr Davis asking me to recite some of my poetry to the class. Then after I'd received a sterling accolade from my new classmates, we would all sit in a large circle to discuss the hidden meanings of my work. (Please God, let it be so.)

Teatime tonight was not the usual affair of everyone sitting around the television set, balancing plates of food on their laps. Tonight I laid the table, and prepared what turned out to be the majorities favourite meal. I say majority, because there will always be at least one who doesn't like what had taken me an hour and a half to prepare. This evening it was the turn of Megan who said: "I don't want mine. Bacon, sausage, egg and fried bread will bring my face out in spots."

Gary insisted, it already had. "One giant pimple, perched on the top of your neck."

Midway through the meal, I made my evening class announcement.

MY FAMILY'S RESPONSE:

Trevor: You what?

Anthony: Good for you Mam.

Trevor: Have you gone off your bloody head woman?

Gary: It's up to her, in it.

Trevor: What does your mother think about this?

Megan: What do you want to go to school for, Mam?

Trevor: It's that bloody poem book again, isn't it? I know something was up the minute you brought that

> bloody thing into the house. Well I don't know what to think... Wednesday evening?... You'll miss 'Coronation Street'. You realise that don't you?

For the rest of the night I had to put up with Trevor making snide remarks at my expense: *'Rhian wandered lonely as a cloud.'* Being a classic example of Trevor's sarcasm... I can see Trevor having to wait another couple of months for sex, if he keeps this up.

March 6: Tuesday

One more day to go, and I can already feel the butterflies fluttering in my stomach. After collecting my Family Allowance, I read the top twenty-five poems in the order of popularity, in William Harmon's book. With a bit of luck at least one of these will turn up at tomorrow's class.

Trevor is teasing me in a playful way. I don't think he minds me attending the class at all. He told me not to worry about a thing. He promised to tape 'Coronation Street' for me while I was out. (I think I will let him bonk me next weekend after all.)

March 7: Wednesday

I bought a new note pad and pen at the Post Office after I'd cashed Trevor's Giro, and scribbled all my poems into it, just in case I'm asked to read some of my work to the class.

I held out as long as I could on the Prozac front. I wanted to portray a natural picture of serenity as I walked into the classroom, but by 3.00pm in the afternoon my nerves were so on edge, that I popped two at once and hoped for the best. To normal people, what I was about to do was no big deal. But to me... I felt like Daniel walking into the lion's den... I was about to re-enter a world that I'd thought I had abandoned forever in 1976.

My clothes are casual yet intellectual. (Jeans, T-shirt, my old trainers, etc... Now I know how Megan felt.) I've decided to go with the fresh faced look, with just a touch of lipstick, foundation, blusher, mascara and eye liner. Even if I do say so myself. For a woman my age, who's been through the wars a bit, I don't look half bad when I put my mind to it... I'm borderline crumpet, that's what Trevor calls me.

I could not believe my eyes when I walked into the classroom. Apart from me, and three other people who didn't live on the estate, sat Big Daddy Huws and his skinny wife, dressed up to the nines in their gothic finery.

"Hello." Daddy said, as I chose a seat in the corner of the room. "Your mother lives on the opposite side of the road from us, doesn't she?"

"Ah yes, I think so."

"Yes she's a lovely old lady, not like some of our other neighbours that we have to put up with. Did you know somebody actually reported me and Anne to the council for holding a '70s fondue party in our home the other Saturday night?"

"Yes it was terrible." Anne said, chipping in. "Just because we dress differently you see... When the furniture removal men were taking our things into the house, you could see the net curtains twitching up and down the street. I turned to Dave and said: there's going to be a lot of jealously directed against us living by here love, and you agreed with me didn't you Dave?"

Dave nodded his agreement at me, I nodded my head back

at Dave... I didn't know what to do or say apart from smile and agree with the both of them.

"I went ballistic the other week, didn't I love."

"Yes." Anne replied, nodding her head reassuringly. "I had to go out, and drag you back into the house, didn't I love?"

"That's right you did. I was in one hell of a state." Dave said with the intensity still burning in his eyes. "After reading the letter from the council, I ran out into the street and started shouting you won't get rid of us that easily you bastard, at the top of my voice. Then Anne here somehow managed to drag me in, off the road and back into the house." Touching me on my hand,Dave said: "If I frightened your mother, you will explain to her what happened, won't you... I'm sure she'll understand after she knows what some people are trying to do to my family"

Well after that, the evening class was a blur. Mr Davis introduced me to the class, and I said hello and nothing more... Wait until Mam hears about this.

March 8: Thursday

I can't believe the thug my mother has labelled Big Daddy Huws and his skinny bitch, have ordinary names like Dave and Anne. In fact I found Dave and Anne to be very kind and considerate... This is oh so typical of my mother, jumping to the wrong conclusions. Talk about judging a book by its cover. I can still remember my mother's words, after she'd discovered me listening to punk music for the first time in 1975... She hated to see me walk out of the house wearing a safety-pin through my ear.

"Rhian, you've always loved the Queen." Mam screeched over my Sex Pistol track. "You've not been acting like one of those delinquents on the telly, have you?... Rhian, please tell me you've been behaving yourself when you leave this house to see your friends... If I find out you've been drawing shame to this house my girl..."

God knows what Man will say if Dave and Anne ever invite me to one of their fondue parties... I'm P.M.T active again. Looks like poor old Trevor won't be getting his leg-over again, this weekend.

March 9: Friday

Trevor took the news about my period well. He said: "Perhaps it's best to be on the safe side, and leave it for another week." Unlike Mam, who warned me not to be taken in by the evil forces that were living on the other side of the street. "Nobody who goes out dressed like them can be all that right in the head if you ask me." She stressed, as I pleaded the Huws's case for them. "Of course, I blame those Prozac of yours, Rhian. They're numbing your brain girl." And I totally gave up the ghost when she came back with: "Last night they were burning candles in their living-room with the curtains open for the whole world to see... Rhian, what do you think of that? Fancy, they haven't been living there for two minutes, and they can't afford to pay their electric bill... I bet they've squandered all of their benefit money on drink and drugs... People who do that deserve to have their children taken into care."

March 10: Saturday

"And another thing," Mam said, carrying on exactly where she left off, yesterday. "Since when has the noise from a fondue party ever kept anyone awake half the night. Especially if that someone is living on the other side of the street, for goodness sake?... Cheese! Even Swiss cheese doesn't cause people to be that noisy, Rhian." A constant pattern continued throughout the day. A distinct lack of evidence didn't stop my mother from accusing the Huws's of everything from drug dealing to dumping their litter in the street. When my mother works herself up, there's nothing anyone can do but clench their teeth and hopefully ride out the storm. Answering her accusations in words of more than one syllable only goes to prolong the agony of the listener. But nodding, and shaking of the head, (As the case may be) goes a long way to speeding up the process, and allowing my mother to get what she's got to say out of her system.

PHRASES TO BE WEARY OF:

1. "I've been up all night thinking about this."
2. "I've been meaning to get this off my chest for a long while now."
3. "Well, I think..."
4. "If you had listened to me in the first place, nothing like this would have happened."
5. "If I were you, I'd..."

Six hours later, Mam said: "Cheery-O." And walked out of the door... Taking my sweeping brush out of the cupboard, I brutally beat Megan's cuddly toy pig to within an inch of tearing its fabric, as it continued to innocently smile up at me from the chair. (If I was pushed, could I become a vicious seal culler? Yes, I think I could!)

March 11: Sunday

I can't believe what I did last night... Trevor entered the bedroom drunk... Forcing him onto the bed, I whipped his trousers off... I gave him what posh people call hand-relief, (violently) then told him to shut-up, and to go to sleep... No one can work me up like my mother.

Trevor's been giving me funny looks all day. I'm sure he can't make his mind up, if last night was a dream or not... I'm not going to say a word to him.

Sunday is Sunday, is Sunday. Just like my mother, is my mother, is my mother.

March 12: Monday

I am no longer P.M.T active, and my didn't Trevor and I celebrate in style this afternoon, while Gary was out, and the other two were at school... Talk about every thrust hitting the spot. You've heard the saying you can't teach an old dog new tricks. Well I say who would want to, if my old dog's routine is as good as Trevor's... I wonder if Mam would have complained to the council about the noise we made, if we were living across the road from her???

March 13: Tuesday

I met Anne Huws in the Post Office today. Both of us were collecting our family allowance, and she inquired if I was going to tomorrow night's evening class? Anne told me she had conceived her triplets at the age of seventeen. Owain, Ifan and Morgan, were born minutes apart, and not the nine months or so my mother had previously suggested. "Talk about feeling like a sausage factory." Anne explained. "No sooner had one been born, than another had popped his head out for a quick look around." I like Anne. Hidden underneath all that doom and gloom make-up and clothing is a very timid girl, who is too frightened to show her face. Nevertheless I find Anne a very warm and charming person all the same.

"We get all our clothes from here." Anne said, as we entered the charity shop. "Apart from the odd scrap or two, did you know that most of it comes from Cardiff?"

"My Trevor suspected some of it might have." I replied.

"My mother's been a volunteer at the charity's main sorting depot in Cardiff for years, and she told me all the donations get distributed equally around all of these little shops in the South Wales valleys." Anne bought three outfits for her children at a pound apiece. "I don't believe all that rubbish about dressing triplets or twins in identical clothing. I don't want to bring up three clones, do I? No, I want my children to develop individual personalities of their own." She laughed then said: "I may look damned in this get-up, but I certainly don't want to bring up the children of the damned if you know what I mean."

I told Anne not to worry, as I had already secured that job.

March 14: Wednesday

Tonight Mr Davis spoke about the effect William Shakespeare had on the English language. I for one was glad, he had chosen Shakespeare. Firstly because I had heard of the man, and secondly because I had read some of his poetry in my book.

During a break in the class, Anne said her husband couldn't attend tonight, because he had been asked if he'd like to do a spot of overtime at work, just as he was about to clock out after his shift. I nearly choked on my coffee when Anne said her husband was employed. "That's why we think some people on the estate have got it in for us." Anne said, whispering her suspicions in my ear. "Jealousy you see. They can't take it, when they see anybody who wants to better themselves, like you and I."

"You and I!" That's what she said. "You and I!" Anne thinks that I want to better myself... I didn't realise it... I couldn't see it... I've been living this kind of existence for far too long... I, I... Of course I want to better myself. I don't want to live on the dole all my life. I've never thought about it before, but I can see it now... I wonder if Anne's Dave can put a word in for Trevor at his factory?... This adult education certainly is a wonderful thing.

March 15: Thursday

Dear Diary, reviewing your pages, I see I've totally failed to mention any news about Gary's band. Fair play to my mother, she kept her word, and booked 'Mandrake' to play their first gig at the old people's centre, this afternoon.

"We are the next kings of rock." Gary proclaimed, as he and the other band members left the house, carrying their equipment the short distance to the centre.

"If you can sing like your father, you won't be going far wrong." Mam had remarked encouragingly, as she told her grandson of his forthcoming engagement. "Gary, all the girls are looking forward to seeing you, and your friends' performance. I told them, it'll be like, being on Top of the Pops."

Trevor also wasn't backward, in coming forward with his advice: "You'd better keep your eyes on those old dears, son. Half of them are veterans of the rugby club's 'Grab a Granny Night' when I was a boy. If you ever come across an old dear by the name of Elsie Sykes, keep your hand on your crown jewels at all times, there's a good lad."

As I watched Mandrake disappear around a corner of our road, I had a gut feeling this would be the first and last gig this band would ever play.

"I've never been so ashamed in all my life." Mam said wiping a tear from her eye. "I'm a laughing stock. All the girls were sniggering at me. They were terrible Rhian. I felt ashamed to be Gary's grandmother, and you know how much I've always doted on the boy. But even I, with the best will in the world couldn't forgive him and his friends for this outrage.

I don't know what kind of home that David Hill comes from, but the f-word was coming out of his mouth every other syllable. I did feel sorry for old Mrs Parfitt. She was using her zimmer-frame to walk past the stage, and he shouted at her to get a f***ing move on.

When Mr Jones went to complain he was told to take Mrs Parfitt outside and give her one up across the top of the hand grips.

Gary phoned later and said he was spending the night around at his friend's house... Wise boy.

March 16: Friday

Mam called around first thing this morning, and asked if Gary had come home yet? "I've been awake all night worrying you know Rhian." She said, occasionally dabbing her handkerchief against her eyes. "I still can't get over it. I don't think I'll ever sleep again until I've asked our Gary what he thought he was playing at?"

While she was waiting, I brought the conversation around to Anne Huws, her triplets, and the unbelievable fact (well around here, anyway.) that her husband had indeed got himself a proper job and had been in full-time employment for a number of years.

"Rhian, you really are the most gullible of girls." Mam replied, countering my statement. "Who in their right mind is going to employ somebody dressed like him?... Triplets, my back passage, excuse my French Rhian, but I've heard that old wives tale being trotted out before you were born... The girl is a common slag pure and simple. They've come to live here, because their name's mud, at their old address... To invent a respectable lifestyle for her husband, and family... Of course, that's if they really are married and not living in sin... Rhian, why can't you understand why your new friend Anne has to make up this story about having all her children at the same time, and by the same father?... But unlike you Rhian, she'll have to get up pretty early in the morning to pull a story like that over my eyes."

My mother has it in for Anne and Dave, its as simple as that.

Gary phoned, and said he was stopping out for another night at his friend's house.

March 17: Saturday

Over breakfast, Trevor said that Mandrake were the talk of the rugby club. "Old Bill Motson told me, if he ever sees our boy and his mates walking past the old age centre again, he'll get the law onto them." Grinning Trevor added. "Your mother's friend, Debbie White, told me that she hadn't laughed so much in years. She said, I should have seen the look on your mother's face." Trevor began to chuckle. "She said, she must stop thinking about it or she'll be wetting her knickers again."

Gary sneaked back into the house, when he knew I would be the only one at home. He claimed things had gone from bad to worse the moment some old boy on the door had asked him if he had anyone to sign him in.

"You should have seen it Mam." Gary said, sitting ready to confess. "It was a total nightmare from start to finish. While we were setting up right. These old people were milling around, and asking if we could guess what they did during the war. Some old boy claimed his son had his own skiffle band in the late fifties." Rubbing his eyes, Gary admitted: "Hill's was the first to lose his patience. He told one old boy to f-off, and another old boy of about eighty to get a life. For Gran's sake I just smiled and nodded at everyone, but inside I wanted to scream: *'LEAVE ME ALONE. I CAN'T BREATHE. YOU ALL SMELL OF PISS AND I WANT TO* GET OUT.'

Hill's at this stage, along with the rest of the band had totally lost it. They were effing and blinding at them all, and then the hall's bouncer, together with some other men who could walk unaided came over and asked us to leave.

"So you didn't actually play then?" I enquired.

"Play! They didn't even have enough plug sockets, for us to plug our guitar amps into." Gary responded.

"Why didn't you come home last night?"

"I saw Gran's face as they kicked us out... I couldn't deal with the hassle... I didn't need to hear her going on and on. You know what she's like. So I stopped with a friend."

On the bright side, the free publicity generated from the gig (Non-event) had made the band famous on our estate, and the surrounding area. Gary reckons, 'Mandrake's' notoriety, and shock value should be enough to help them secure a string of gigs in the future.

March 18: Sunday

Dear Diary, apart from resuming my role as a committed participant in my husband's Saturday night sex frolics. Sunday did what Sunday usually does, and I fell asleep in a chair. Tonight I've decided to tell you about the dole, and why we've been claiming unemployment benefit for so long... In other words: 'How I Got Lumbered With An Existence I Don't Foresee In My Childhood Bedroom.' After all, I was the little girl who was destined to marry the king of Romania!

As children, school meant very little to me and others of my generation. Trevor, myself our friends. We laughed, we joked, we played, we turned up at school for our mark to be placed inside the register, and that was about it as far as we were concerned. *'I don't need to worry, I'll be going down the mine with my old man.'* Trevor used to boast. *'What good will geography be to me down there?'*

All through his childhood, and into his early teens Trevor had been promised a place. And then,just as he was about to claim his inheritance, they snatched it away from him... So he claimed the dole instead... Fair enough. That's Trevor sorted out but what about my career I hear you ask? Life was so simple back then. While Trevor was down the pit, I was the one who would see to our children, wash, bake, and clean. To scrub his dirty back for him in an old tin bath in front of an open coal fire. In our whitewashed, picturesque thatched miner's cottage, with roses forming an archway over the door... How the young dream, and what rubbish they believe. What would the people of London do, if all the business's shut-up shop and moved to pastures new? Because that's exactly what happened here. One man didn't lose his job, the whole community did. Trevor left school at the age of sixteen in 1976. From that day until this, he's never had a full-time job in his life. Yes, he's worked on government schemes, and schemes for this and that, but never in what you would call a full-time situation... Trevor's approaching forty-one. I think he retired before he began... The one good thing about living on the dole is you are free to choose how to spend your day. On the BBC's 'Kilroy' programme, I've listened many a time to the so called spokespeople who speak for,and on behalf of the mass ranks of the unemployed. (Mainly well to do types from London or there about.) Complaining bitterly of the underclass's plight; with concern for young and old alike who are not receiving an adequate amount of state benefit from the Government... Permit me to strike a line through all this guff to announce: the benefit system in this country is a godsend to people in my and Trevor's situation. With little or no education, (Neither Trevor nor myself attained any exam qualifications while we were at school.) and without the safety net provided by social security, both Trevor and I would be forced to slave away day after day in dreadful working conditions for the minimum wage or less in our 24 hour, never-ending struggle to earn our daily bread... Today the uneducated equivalent of Trevor who found himself in a similar situation, (With a wife and three pre-school children to support.) would find it near impossible to independently earn the sum of money required to live from hand to mouth, within a mountain of debt he would surely accumulate along the way.

Our Government tempts its underclass with differing rates of employment allowances such as 'Family Credit'. A top-up benefit, a bribe in any other name. Tax payers' money the politicians hand to low income families. The scheme government hopes will induce the underclass to loosen its grip of the benefit system. An alternative the powers that be hope the minimum wage earners will accept instead of claiming all they are otherwise entitled to from the state... It's not about the dole money a person has in his pocket each week. It's about the little extras that come with it. It's about the free housing. It's about the free council charges, rates, poll tax, housing category band A, B, or C or whatever it is they are calling it this year, while the unemployed never have to pay... I know families who are claiming the annual income equivalent of £25,000 a year on a range of unemployment and sickness benefits. If Trevor was offered work tomorrow, his basic salary would have to surpass £15,000 to break even... Where is the incentive to get out of bed? Who in their right mind is going to pay an unskilled Trevor £15,000 to work for them? How can someone find themselves financially worse off if they find themselves a job? Why can it be financial suicide for an unskilled married man with three children to support, to sign-off the dole?... My God, when I look about me on this estate. Trevor and I may not have as much as some, but I am certain we have a lot more than most.

March 19: Monday

How quickly the fortnights pass. It seems like only two weeks ago, that Trevor and Gary went to sign-on... That reminds me. I must remember to ask Anne Huws if her Dave knows of any vacancies at his factory for my Trevor?... After he'd returned from signing-on, I walked with Gary down the road to his grandmother's house to apologise. What a bunch of softies we Evans's are.

Mam said: "Gary I've always thought the world of you." Immediately bursting into tears, after completing her sentence.

Gary replied: "Sorry Gran." Then he joined her, in sobbing his heart out.

"Let's all be friends again." I said, then broke down sobbing in a chair.

We are all as weak as dish water in this family... The lot of us!

March 20: Tuesday

There was an uproar in the Post Office this morning. The relief post master, had been caught trying to diddle an old age pensioner out of his pension money.

"YOU SHORT-CHANGING LITTLE CUNT!" The lady in front of me screamed, the spittle from her mouth splattering against the bullet proofed, Post Office window. "You just wait until Mr Baker hears about this, you 'Gog' piece of shit... I watched him count out this old gentleman's pension money." She said, turning to face me, and the others who were standing behind me in the queue. "I watched him count it out, then I saw him palm a fiver of this gentleman's pension money into his pocket."

Locking himself in his cubicle for his own safety, the relief manager ordered the Post Office to be closed, then telephoned for the police and waited for them to escort him safely from the premises. Which they did forty-five minutes later, past an hate filled mob who lined the short distance between the entrance to the Post Office and the police car. One irate man threw a punch, (Missed) another stuck out a foot and tried to trip the relief manager up, (Caused a stumble) many issued threats of violence against his person. (With the Post Office closed I'll have to collect this week's family allowance, when I cash Trevor's

Giro tomorrow... Damn it all!) Which just goes to show what would happen throughout the country, if the government tried to hold back the social security benefits from the people.

March 21: Wednesday

I'm in the money today... Family Allowance, Trevor's double giro, Gary's board and lodge. My purse was awash with cash right up until I paid some instalments off my debts, and bought the weekly groceries in Tesco's, and now I'm right back where I started... Broke! Never mind, it felt good while it lasted.

At evening class Dave promised, he'll keep his ear to the ground, and let me know if anything suitable turns up for my Trevor and Gary. (I felt a little like Joan Collins in 'Dynasty' this evening... Networking my business contacts.) Dave told me a bus takes him to and from work, but if he works any overtime, he has to make his own way home. (This can be a problem in obtaining a lift, because Dave is the only person working at the factory who lives on our estate.) The bus picks him up on the main road, that runs past the main turning into the estate.

"Rhian, I have the whole bus to myself for the first six miles of the journey." Dave laughed. "Mind you, I'm lucky to have a job. My boss would have thrown my application form in the bin, if I'd applied from my new address."... What hope is there for Gary, Megan and Anthony finding work, when they have to fight this form of 'Post Code' prejudice?

March 22: Thursday

I was very disappointed with Trevor's attitude towards my business connections:

Trevor: Where did you say this factory is?

Me:	Out Merthyr way.
Trevor:	How am I supposed to get there then?... It'll cost me an arm and a leg in bus fares.
Me:	No it won't. A work's bus will pick you up, and bring you home.
Trevor:	How much does the job pay?
Me:	I don't know... I didn't like to ask.
Trevor:	Bloody hell woman, are you thick or what? Arranging an interview for me without bothering to find out if it will be worth my while or not?... I don't know Rhian. All this going to night school is turning your head love... Now don't be silly!... You need to find out what the job pays, before you start making any arrangements for me."

Of course Trevor was right in this respect, the benefits we receive far exceed the going rate for unskilled labour in this part of the world. But he was in full agreement with one aspect of my plan. Finding our Gary full-time employment, would be a real eye opener for the people living around here.

Dear Diary: no matter how Trevor feels, I'm far from giving up on the idea of finding him a job. I just need to do a little bit more research, that's all.

March 23: Friday

Gary walked into the house with a brand new electric guitar this afternoon. He said, he'd ordered it from David Miller's mother's catalogue. He said he'd agreed to pay £2.50 a week, for the next 150 weeks. Or in his own words: *'If 'Mandrake' make the big time Mam, I promise to pay off the outstanding balance with one payment.'*

March 24: Saturday

Dear Diary, there are some people who shop for pleasure. I on the other hand gave up that little past time on the 6th May 1980. Yes I know what you're thinking. You've heard that date somewhere before, and you'd be right. The day I moved into this house, was also the day I found it I impossible to shop solely for myself.

Apart from my wedding day, and the dates of my children's births, the 6th of May 1980 is probably the most important day of my life. On this date new thoughts entered my head, like: *'Can I afford this?'* And, *'what will Trevor say, when he finds out I've spent my housekeeping on that?'*

Oh yes, it was easy at first. But a month or so later, the bills started pouring in, and I had *to* organise payment books for this and that, and the other... Well, to cut a long story short, my personal shopping... The shopping I did for pleasure... (Sorry I can feel the tears welling up as I write.) Went for a burton, as I set my mind to the pleasures of window shopping for the rest of my life. (Or as I put it: *'Touch it, feel it, pick it up, examine it, try it* on, *twirl it around your head if you like, but never put your hand in your purse to purchase it.')*

I was so happy the day they added non food, and household lines at Tesco's. (Clothes, toys, etc.) For starters, I didn't feel any guilt in touching the products without purchasing. In other shops, I'd always been very conscious of the staff watching me, as I'd enter, walk around, examine this and that and exit without buying anything.

'Why pay 35p on a branded product, when you can buy this tin of beans for 15p?' Trevor would insist, until I stopped him coming shopping with me all together. (Not a very dif-

ficult thing to do.) Quality and taste were the two words that only come out of Trevor's mouth, after he'd looked down and complained about the food on his plate. He somehow failed, or refused to make the connection: that as far as he was concerned, the food chain began and ended with what came out of that 15p tin.

British summertime begins tomorrow, meaning the clocks go forward an hour tonight... Trevor's happy. We've reached the time of year when we begin to save some money on the electric bill.

March 25: Sunday - Mother's Day

The gentle rays of the sun softly coaxed me out of my sleep. Outside on the window ledge a sparrow and a blue tit sweetly serenaded me with an exclusive rendition of the dawn chorus.

"Here you are my darling." Trevor said, handing me a beautiful bouquet of roses of the deepest red. "You deserve this and a whole lot more besides."

"Can we come in Mam?" I heard Megan call, from behind the bedroom door. "Happy Mother's Day." She announced, entering the room, carrying a silver platter of hot buttered toast, a piping hot pot of tea dressed in a wooly tea cosy, orange juice, and a metallic wrapped foil present, which glistened in a myriad of different colours in the early morning sunlight.

Behind her the smiling faces of Gary and Anthony expressed their kind regards, as Megan rested the platter upon the bed. "Happy Mother's Day Mam." They all said in unison, simultaneously kissing me on each side of my cheek.

"Now Rhian, don't you dare move out of this bed." Trevor said playfully, wagging his finger at me. "Gary, Anthony, bring the television up for your mother to watch, and don't forget to bring the Radio Times, and the Sunday newspapers up with you for your mother to read. Megan, you can see to the cooking and the cleaning of the house today. While you're all doing your chores, I'll be spending my time in the garden. I've got to get the potatoes in, and as a special treat for your mother,I'm going to plant those climbing rose bushes, she's always wanted trailing over the door, and up the side of the house..."

DING-ALING-ALING-ALING... Thrusting my arm forward I turned the alarm clock off. The hands were pointing at eight o'clock. I heard the harsh call of the crow welcoming the grey dismal morning of low hanging clouds, that threatened a heavy down pour of rain. "Happy Mother's Day." I said to myself, as Trevor farted his kind regards, before rolling onto my vacated side in the bed.

"Here you are Mam." Anthony said, handing me a card, as I stared zombie like at the crumbs resting on top of the kitchen table.

"Here's mine." Megan quickly responded, handing me a large red envelope.

"It's not your birthday is it." Gary said, wondering what on earth was going on. "Only I thought it was in April?"

"It's Mother's Day today stupid." Megan said, as Trevor passed through the room. Looking up, he said: "Fine." Then carried on reading his newspaper.

After that, Sunday carried on in its familiar pattern, the only change being I popped round to my mother's with a card, and a box of Milk Tray for her. "Milk Tray! Rhian, you know I prefer Roses... Oh well, I'll have to keep these for when my

Grandchildren call round." Mam sighed, placing my gift into a draw of her sideboard.

A MOTHER'S LOVE
by
Rhian Evans

1.
Never wrong, but always right.
A calming presence, in times of strife.
To nurse you better, if you feel bad.
To cleanse your bruises with an healing kiss.
I need my mother at times like this.

2.
With nowhere to go I turn to her.
Abandoned by life, there's a welcoming home.
A friendly face, that's never cross.
Confidence returned, I regain my strength.
Healed in spirit, I depart the nest.

3.
A mother's love, builds my strength.
A mother's love, my confidence boosts.
A mother's love, a comforting friend.
Against a world both cruel and hard,
A mother's love will carry me through.

March 26: Monday

Mam inquired if putting the clocks forward, had caught me out over the weekend. She continued: "If you wasn't, I bet that scum across the road were. You should have seen him, that Big Daddy thing this morning, Rhian. Running out of his house and down the road as if his backside was on fire."

He must have been late for work." I replied.

"Don't be soft girl. Late for a drug deal, or a Crown Court appearance more like. The pair of them should be ashamed of themselves, doing that sort of carry on with three little children in the house. You think the welfare people would at least make a visit to see if everything was all right, wouldn't you?"

Refusing to leave my mother's until she'd promised me that she wouldn't ring the social services, to report Dave and Anne Huws to the child welfare people, I spent the rest of the day worrying that she had.

March 27: Tuesday

Mr Baker, (The Post Master) had returned from his week's holiday, and was letting everyone know that last week's little misunderstanding had been sorted out, to everyone's satisfaction.

"Sounds more like a cover-up to me." One lady remarked, as she waited in line at the miscellaneous counter, with a birthday card in her hand.

I began my Christmas shopping today. In the charity shop I discovered a pen set in mint condition, and still in it's original box for 99p, and an unopened collection of 'Body Shop' bath oils, and bubble bath for 75p. (A present each for Megan & Anthony's stockings.) Don't get me wrong, not all of my children's Christmas presents will come from the charity shop. They each pick a main present from my catalogue, but I like to purchase little surprises, good quality but inexpensive stocking fillers throughout the year, when and if I'm lucky enough to came across them.

March 28: Wednesday

Dave and Anne Huws didn't attend class this evening. (He probably had to work late again, and she couldn't find a sitter.) So I more or less spent the entire evening on my own listening to Mr Davis announce to the class: "As you all know, Easter will soon be upon us, so I thought it would be a good idea if we organised a recital evening to take place on the final evening before the Easter break."

'At last', I thought, my ears pricking up at this exciting announcement. *'Here's a chance for my work to be judged by my peers.'* (By my peers... Judged by my peers. Isn't life strange, Diary? Here's a phrase I never thought I'd use, unless I found myself in court.)

"As we're only a small gathering." Mr Davis continued. "I thought each of you could recite three of your own creations, we could follow this with a light discussion on the merits of each piece. With the added incentive of the winner winning a bottle of cheap plonk from the local off-licence."

Leaving the classroom I knew that bottle of wine was as good as mine.

March 29: Thursday

What a night we had of it last night. What with joy riders chasing each other around the estate, police sirens going off at all hours of the night, helicopter searchlights, cars on fire, the Fire Brigade coming to put them out. It was a wonder any of us got any sleep.

"Did you hear that carry on last night." Mam asked, as she

popped her head around the door. "It must have been two-thirty to three o'clock in the morning before I finally drifted off to the Land Of Nod, and on a school night and all."

"Trevor reckons all the joy riders on this estate catch a bus into Cardiff, then pinch other people's cars to drive themselves home in." I remarked, offering a simple explanation to my mother's query.

"Well I don't think they, or anyone else should even think about going all the way to Cardiff, if they haven't got enough money for the bus fare home." Mam replied, without fully understanding what I'd been trying to say.

Not really wanting to go into why anyone would want to do this sort of thing for fun. I immediately changed the subject. "Anne Huws and her husband didn't attend class last night." I began.

"What did I tell you Rhian. You don't have to tell me anything, because I've seen it all before. Those sort of people like the Huws's are good starters, but poor finishers. They can never stick anything through to the end." Mam rejoiced, happy that her diagnosis had turned out to be correct. "I knew all along, that this sort of thing would happen. They'll soon get fed up of it I said to myself they wont be attending evening classes for long I said... You see Rhian love, you don't get to my age of life without realising what those type of people are really like. If they wanted an education, they should have learned something while they were at school like everyone else."

I wanted to scream at her: *'WELL WHAT ABOUT ME, THEN? I NEVER LEARNT ANYTHING AT SCHOOL EITHER!'* But I let it drop.

I'm a day late!

March 30: Friday

Dear Diary, it's 2.30am. Since my mother went home, her words have been constantly on my mind. I can't sleep... For two pins I feel like running around to her house and having it out with her... Trevor has ordered me to stop fidgeting in the bed, and to lay still, so that's why I find myself wrapped in my nightgown, locked in the bathroom, sitting on the toilet seat, writing this short communication to you, while using an old Ali Baba basket as a desk. (I hope this will help to drive my mother's words from out of my head.)

At about four this morning I finally give up all hope of falling to sleep. The instant my brain accepted this fact, I instantly fell asleep on the sofa in the living-room.

In my dream my mother won the bottle of wine with a poem entitled 'Nobody Knows Rhian Better Than Me'. All I can remember about her poem is, she received a standing ovation after she'd recited it, and this one line: *'I've often tried to talk to my daughter, but she's never wanted to listened to a word I say.'* (I do hope this is not one of those dreams that come true.)

I spent the rest of the day worrying about bad omens, and the fact that I'm two days late, period wise.

March 31: Saturday

Remembered another line from Mam's winning poem: *'She's been behaving like this, for the best part of forty years.'* (Whatever happens in the future... I must erase this dream from my memory.)

'Gone With The Wind', was this afternoon's Saturday matinee on BBC2. (I thought they would have kept this film for Easter time.) "I don't give a damn." Rhett Butler said to Scarlet O'Hara, the exact same phrase I intend using on my mother, the next time she offers me a opinion on the Huws family.

THE REVIEW OF THE MONTH:

Another so, so month. Apart from Gary's embarrassing gig at the old people's centre, the Evans family continued living an unnoticed existence in the background of life, as if we wasn't really living at all. Meanwhile, out in the real world, March proved to be the month the Government got its knickers in a twist, because of the **'FOOT & MOUTH** epidemic sweeping through the countryside ... I've never mentioned any of this in my diary before... Why should I?... What the hell has it got to do with me?... I'm three days late with my period, and the poor farmers think they've got problems.

April 1: Sunday

Dear Diary looking back through your pages, I find I took part in a very frantic sex session with my husband on the 12th of last month. Quoting myself: *'His thrust hit every spot.'* (Please God, I pray he missed one.)

I'm four days late. This is all I need... I really couldn't cope with another... I don't want a baby, I want to be a poet.

LATE
by
Rhian Evans

Late - I sit around and wait.
Late - I build into a state.
Late - A ten pound test and then.
Late - Three minutes pass in hell!.
Late - The square window, lets me know.
Late - Am I reprieved, or is it woe?

Well that's it then. First thing tomorrow morning, I'm going to buy myself a home pregnancy testing kit... Happy April Fool's nightmare... The cruelest joke of all.

April 2: Monday

While Trevor and Gary were signing on, I hurried to the chemists and bought an home pregnancy testing kit... Talk about sod's law... Why, oh why didn't I take my time, and eat that remaining slice of toast this morning?

I'm sitting on the toilet seat... I've got my knickers around my ankles... I've broken the seal of the pregnancy testing kit's packaging... I'm reading the instructions in my hand... Bastard, bastard, bastard... My period started, and I've just blown ten quid for nothing. (Trevor will go mad if he finds out about this.)

Now what am I supposed to do? The chemist will never take it back, not with the seal broken.

I'm very happy that I'm not pregnant. But bloody hell, ten quid!!!

RELIEVED
by
Rhian Evans

I thought I was, but I wasn't.
For me the pressures off.
Free from a state of unhappiness.
Free from the frightening costs.
Free to carry on living.
Free to remain who I am.
Relieved not to be burdened.
Wretched, wretched, of man.

April 3: Tuesday

I woke-up this morning feeling fine. I brushed my teeth, then descending the stairs I noticed an unwelcoming reception committee, waiting to threaten me, stacked high upon the doormat, underneath the letter box.

Standing on the third step from the top of the stairs, I saw an assortment of official brown envelopes of the ugliest kind. This quarter's statement sent directly from the mailing room of the South Wales Electricity Board waited patiently for me on the top of the pile... £123.84, January to March. Thank God I've an ongoing arrangement to clear my outstanding balance in £10 weekly instalments, at the Post Office.

We pay all of our bills, (Electric, gas, water, etc.) on weekly budget plans. £10 a week each for electric and gas, £8 for water, the monthly catalogue payments go up and down, but I never pay more than £25 a month no matter what threatening letters they send me... We don't pay any rent or poll tax/rates, or whatever they call it these days. (These are paid for by our housing benefit.) We don't own a car, so after I've paid for our food, all that's left over, (Which isn't a lot.) can be spent on luxuries for my family... Dear Diary, now that I've written it down, I promise I will never write about this boring subject again... Unless it's linked to another story.

P.S: Although I have a weekly budget plan. I settle my account payments every Wednesday fortnight, because that's when the DSS send Trevor his unemployment Giro.

April 4: Wednesday

Anne and Dave didn't show up at evening class again this week. Although I enjoy listening to Mr Davis and the other class members' points of view. I miss Dave and Anne not being there. I know it might sound strange, but because they live in the same street, I feel under all that gothic make-up, they are in the same boat as me.

'Empathy'! - Dear Diary, I've just looked this word up in Anthony's dictionary, and I feel very strongly that myself, and the Huws's have identified mentally with each other, during our contemplation of our literary interests.

April 5: Thursday

With my curiosity getting the better of me, I decided to call on Anne Huws today, making sure my mother had already left for the old people's centre first. (Dear Diary, I'm nearly forty years of age, yet I still feel very conscience of the fact that I'm sneaking to a house of a friend my mother doesn't want me to be seen with.) First, making sure my mother had indeed gone out, and wasn't spying at me through her net curtains, I knocked on Anne's front door.

Inside the house there were visible signs of Dave's unfinished DIY projects, but overall the house looked very much as how I imagined it would be, with throws draped over the furniture, and candles in ornate metal crafted holders dotted around the room. In a chair facing the window Anne sat with her three children playing at her feet. A waste paper bin, brim full of crumpled paper tissues give the game away, and as I stared into the darkness of her panda stained eyes, she said: "Take no notice of mammy kids, mammy's being silly again, isn't she!"

"What on earth is the matter Anne?" I asked, as her three children gave their mother a worrying glance.

"Oh, don't mind me." Anne said, snatching a tissue from the box. "God knows, I try not to swear in front of my children, but there are some evil bastards living on this estate."

Anne carried on in more detail: "I had a visit from child welfare the other day. They said they'd received an anonymous complaint, that my children were in danger, because Dave and I are drug addicts who aren't caring for them properly."

I fought wonderfully hard to suppress the word 'MOTHER' from seething from my lips. Only by employing my utmost will power did I manage to keep my feelings under control...

It helped that Anne's eyes was constantly looking at the floor... I don't think I would have got away with it if Anne had been staring at my face.

"It's because we're different you see." Anne began, her voice growing angrier as she spoke. "The jealous bastards." She reached down and ran her hand over the top of her three children's heads. "They see me and Dave dressed to the nines in our gothic finery, and they don't understand, or know what to make of us. They see Dave going to work, and they say: Why hasn't my husband got a job to go to, too?... They see me, pushing my pram to the shops, and they say: What has she got to be so happy about?... It's all about jealousy Rhian. You know what the final straw was, don't you? When Dave started to put decking down in the back garden. I bet they said we're not having this, why should they have a nice garden, while ours is overgrown and full of weeds?"

Not knowing how to reply, I waited for Anne to finish her cigarette: "After giving up for three months, I'm back on these fucking things, because my nerves are in shreds." I observed the look of anguish on her face, and witnessed herself chastisement for using the f-word in front of her children.

"Do the people around here think we are animals, or what?... Do they really think we practice black magic, or Devil Worship?... Do they really believe that I sacrifice my children to the Devil every night, on our alter come kitchen table?... Am I a witch?... Is Dave a warlock?... Are my children's toys really voodoo dolls?... Is my Dave really a vampire?... Let me tell you something about my Dave, right, Rhian. He's so squeamish that he won't even go to the dentist on his own." At this point Anne broke down, and I wanted to grab my mother by the throat.

"They even picked on my candles." Anne sobbed. "They

said we shouldn't have naked flames lit around small children. Rhian, my, my, my children don't even know how to strike a match!... Do our neighbours really think we are the Adams Family?"

Realising that this was not the best time to discuss poetry, I waited for Anne to regain her composure, then making my excuses I left on the pretext of crossing the road to visit my mother.

April 6: Friday

In last night's dream, my mother took the role of 'The Witchfinder General'. In horror I watched as she callously danced around a giant bonfire, as the Huws family were burnt at the stake. (The time has come for me to put a stop to this.)

Two hours it took me. Two hours of soul searching for the correct questions, answers, responses and arguments, to arm myself for the battle that surely lay ahead.

After 'Richard & Judy' had ended, I put on my coat and made my way to face the lioness in her den. Halfway down the street I turned around and walked back to my house. I suddenly remembered. Mam had gone to Tenby for the day, on an old age outing.

April 7: Saturday

With a plan of battle firmly ensconced in my mind, I advanced upon, entered my mother's home, and secured a strong defensive position, in a high backed Queen Anne chair near the coal fire.

"Why did you do it Mam?"

"Do what exactly love?"

"Report Anne and Dave to the child welfare people?"

"Anne and Dave is it?... You're getting very friendly with the people across the road all of a sudden, Rhian."

"They're nice people Mam, if you give them a chance. OK, they might look different, and..."

"Are your nice friends accusing me of anything love?"

"No, they think that you are a nice old lady who lives across the road."

"So why are you then?"

"Because I know you Mam. I know what an..."

"That's nice coming from my own daughter. But that's you all over isn't it. Always siding with others, against me... I don't know why I should expect anything different at my time of life... That's a nasty trait of yours Rhian, and you've been doing it to me all your life."

"But you did report them didn't you, Mam?"

"I'm so happy that your father isn't alive to hear this... This daughter of mine turning on her own mother. It's no wonder Gary's turned out the way he has."

"What is that supposed mean?"

"Rhian, that boy was a perfect little angel. And now look at him. Thanks to you, he's turned into a foul mouth yob."

"There's nothing wrong with my Gary, he's just going through a difficult phase that's all."

"Look at Megan. She's only fifteen, yet you allow her to leave the house dressed like a painted tart."

"All the young girls dress like that these days."

"Well don't come crying to me, when she gets herself pregnant. I only hope that Anthony gets away from you before it's too late."

"What is that supposed to mean?"

"Don't you dare play the innocent with me Rhian. You know

what I mean. If he stays around that idle sod of an husband of yours, he'll turn out the same way as our Gary."

"You've never liked Trevor, have you Mam?"

"I like your Trevor, about as much as your Trevor likes work. But unlike you, I say nothing, and hold my tongue for the good of the family. I try to get on with people you see Rhian. God above knows, (Mam looked up and pointed to the heavens.) I could go round calling Trevor to all in sundry, but I don't. At least I know the importance of family values, and of family loyalty Rhian. Even if you don't!

You've really hurt me Rhian. (A sudden attack of the sniffles, causes my mother to reach for the handkerchief she'd hidden up her sleeve.) How can you say I don't care, when yesterday I bought you all a stick of rock back from my old age outing to Tenby?"

My mother is a past master of the family argument. Finding herself on weak ground, (She couldn't defend her actions, against Anne and Dave.) she immediately switched the direction of battle, and did what she's always done throughout my life, turn the spotlight of the discussion onto me. (The battle was lost.)

I could go on with page after page of script, but I'd rather forget about it... In any case it would make for some very ugly reading, but suffice to say, at the end of it all, Mam had the final word: "Rhian I'm glad we've taken this opportunity to clear the air. If only more families could sit down and do this sort of thing. The world would be a happier place, and maybe the people living across the road wouldn't have the people from the child welfare banging on their door at all hours of the day and night."

April 8: Palm Sunday

In the comfort of my own home... I've come to the conclusion, Prozac has stopped me from throttling my mother by the throat, on more than one occasion.

How does she do it, let alone get away with it?... My mother must have a will of iron. How does she get through life without the aid of the happy drug? If my mother was working for the DSS, I honestly believe a record number of benefit fraud claimants would be prosecuted overnight.

At the top of the page, I see it's Palm Sunday. I used to know what that meant, when I attended Sunday school... Is it the day Jesus rode into Jerusalem on a donkey?... I'd like to see somebody try to nail my mother to the cross.

IN THE WRONG
by
Rhian Evans

You are right, and I am wrong,
Our worlds will never change.
What's good for me, is bad for you,
The points I've made, are lost on you,
The thoughts I have, are frowned by you,
My dreams, you toss aside.
Yet you are right, in what you do,
In what you say, your beliefs run true,
Your respected thoughts, and dreams anew,
An iron will, and point of view,
A drug free world, and clear head,
With you, I walk behind.

April 9: Monday

"Hello, is anyone at home?" Mam shouted, on entering my home uninvited by the backdoor. (This woman knows no shame.) "Rhian, I think your friends had another visit over the weekend. I saw a man with a clipboard walk down their garden path. Mind you, without knowing the full details of his visit, I suppose he could have been a double glazing salesman, or something. But whoever he was, he didn't take any children away with him when he left." (This woman also knows no tact.) "I was only saying to the girls on our outing to Tenby the other day. It's a shame when a nice little family like the Huws's, have to have their children taken into care. (Nice family???... This woman does not know the meaning of the word 'hypocrite'.) Of course I blame Dave and Anne's parents for all this. If they had brought them up properly, and taught them right from wrong, and how to respect their elderly neighbours who live across the road from them. Well, I don't think they would have got themselves into such a mess in the first place... What do you think Rhian?"

Dear Diary, I think this little speech was my mother's way of telling me, that she will leave the Huws family alone in the future.

April 10: Tuesday

I called around to see how Anne was feeling this morning, after Megan and Anthony had left for school. I also called to see if she wanted to walk to the Post Office with me to collect our family allowance money together?

Anne looked, and said she'd felt a lot better, since my last visit. She said: "A man called from child welfare last Saturday afternoon. He said all of the accusations against them were groundless, and he hoped we could appreciate the difficult complexities his job entailed.

He said, he and the department were very sorry for any distress which may have ensued, but by law it was the department's duty to investigate all leads that came from the general public, no matter how groundless those leads were proved to be."

"Well, at least it's all over with now." I replied, hopefully.

"Like Hell it is." Anne retorted. "There's somebody out there who's got it in for me, Dave and the kids, and Dave and I won't rest until we find out who it is."

On a happier note, Anne agreed to return to evening class tomorrow night. She seemed very interested in the poetry competition, and agreed with me it would be a great way of taking her mind off the past week's unhappiness. (Please God, I'd die of shame... Please never let Anne find out it was my mother who was to blame.)

April 11: Wednesday

Like the F.A. Cup, and all the other great sporting trophies of the world, the glass bottle of Liberfraumilch twinkled under the fluorescent schoolroom lighting, as a slight draft emanating from a crack in the classroom door caused the bow tail of a red ribbon to flutter gently against the prized bottle‘s slender neck.

Reading a poem titled 'Oblivion', (A joint effort from Dave and Anne Huws.) Anne announced: "This is the reason Dave and I have missed the last few classes."

OBLIVION
by
Dave & Anne Huws

Darkness, darkness, everywhere,
No solace could we muster.
Our babies have been spirited away,
From the bedroom where they clustered.
Some say they were taken by gypsy cart,
Their pitiful cries, we keep hearing them still.
Some say they were taken by fairy folk,
For their kingdom lays under the hill.
Woe is me, and my husband true,
For no children can we find.
Woe is us, and others wronged,
By happenings of this kind.
Oh where, oh where, are our little ones kept?
For we hear them calling us still.
Return our brood, to our loving nest
For God is merciful still.
For oblivion called, while we were away,
And fear is crippling our minds.
But all are returned, to our loving nest,
Happiest, happiest, of times.

Of course there wasn't a shadow of doubt in Mr Davis's mind... After listening to the passion of Anne's trembling heartfelt delivery... There was only one winner of the bottle of wine after that.

Others wrote poems about the countryside, and wildlife. We

heard about fish swimming in the sea,and foot and mouth grazing in the meadows. Somebody wrote a poem about Britain's first openly gay Prime Minister, with a demand for free Vaseline for all. While I stuck to three of my favourites which after all said and done went down well, but on the day were no match for the tremor in Anne's voice and the tears in Dave's eyes as he stood upright, like a magnificent marble column at his wife's side.

I've learnt a lot tonight. The power or tenderness you put into your performance, is as important as the poem itself... Tonight Dave and Anne portrayed their emotions just right.

P.S: Dear Diary, because of the forthcoming Easter holidays, the DSS have advanced Trevor his fortnightly Giro. (Not always as good as it sounds.)

April 12: Thursday

Only Anthony attended school today, the final day of term before the school broke up for the Easter break. As it was an half-day Megan said she couldn't be bothered to attend, adding: "It isn't worth the effort of washing my hair, not for half a day... Nobody will be doing anything, anyway... My friends will be spending all their time looking out of the classroom window, while our teacher spends his time looking at his wristwatch... Put it this way Mam; I'll spend more time putting my make-up on, than I'll actually spend sitting in the classroom."

Anthony said she didn't want to go because all of Megan's friends had told her they weren't going, and as she was one of the sheep, she had to follow the flock 'Baa, Baa, Baa'.

As far as I was concerned, I couldn't see half a day making any difference to Megan's education, so I let her stay in bed...

Anyway what with last night's competition and all, I had too much on my mind to worry about it, and in this situation saying 'Yes' was far, far, easier, than living through an argument that would be the result in me saying 'No'.

After cashing Trevor's Giro I bought a 'Kit-Kat' Easter Egg for each of the kids, (They were selling them off, three for a fiver in the newsagents.) and two little cream eggs. (One each for me and Trevor.) I don't buy an Easter Egg for my mother. I got her a small carton of 'Roses' chocolates instead.

April 13: Good Friday

It's 'Good Friday' & 'Friday the 13th' all rolled into one. (Perhaps one will cancel the other out?)

At Christmas we eat turkey, and on Good Friday we have fish for dinner... At teatime I make sure everyone eats at least one hot cross bun too! (I like to keep this country's little traditions going whenever possible, as I've mentioned before.)

Dear Diary, There used to be a fish and chip shop on this estate called 'Sgod & Sglods'. (The Welsh for fish & chips.) But Mr Best the chippy had to close down because the price of fresh fish had risen to such an extent, that not many on the estate could afford to buy it anymore. While the shop was open I used to buy two large portions of fish and chips, for us all to share, (A bit like the story of Jesus, and the loafs and fishes.) because it worked out cheaper than paying for five regular size portions for us all... Six if you count my mother.

Being a very superstitious person I hope it's not unlucky to serve my family fish fingers instead of fresh fillets of fish, on Good Friday. But in this matter I really do not have any choice. The price of fresh fish has priced us out of the market, meaning my family are reduced to eating the scraps Bird's Eye put into fish cakes, and fish fingers. (Economy packs, of course.)

On any ordinary Friday the 13th, I'd wrap myself in a blanket and resist all attempts from my family to prise me out of my chair... I refuse to go anywhere near the kitchen, and if I'm forced to go out, I find it very difficult to cross a road... To cut a long story short, on Friday the 13th my list of worries and phobias are somewhat exaggerated and intensified.

I worry about everything, including stepping on cracks in the pavement, a black cat crossing my path, walking under ladders, cutting myself with a knife, or on a tin in the kitchen. Falling down the stairs, tripping over and banging my head on the coffee-table, Trevor and the children being hurt in an accident, Mam being rushed into hospital, a faulty electric plug burning the house down... I could go on and on, but I think I'll take another Prozac and try not to worry about it.

Trevor on the other hand claims Friday the 13th means absolutely nothing to him. Like he always says: "They closed the mine and my future down on a Friday the 13th, sentencing me to a lifetime on the dole. What on earth can it possibly do to me after that?" (I'm sure Friday the 13th will think of something, if Trevor waits long enough. But I'll say nothing, there's really no need to worry him... Not just yet anyway.)

April 14: Saturday

GROCERY SHOPPING:

I hate it with every inch of my being - It's the most boring thing I have to do - I feel like a pack animal, lugging all of those plastic carrier bags home - I can never afford what I really like to get -After this entry you will never find me writing about this subject again - How can I put this as delicately as possible?... "I Fucking Hate Shopping For Food." Supermarkets are definitely a double Prozac type situation.

Dear Diary, every Friday fortnight... Why Friday fortnight I hear you ask?... Well every Friday Tesco's send a free bus to this estate... But I only board it, once every two weeks.

As you know Trevor receives his double Giro every fortnight, and with eighty pound of his hard earned claim in my purse, (£40 per week.) I board the free bus that transports me to the supermarket to purchase my family's food rations for the coming two weeks.

As you've probably worked out, forty pounds a week isn't a lot to feed a family of five, especially a family that eats as much as mine... Before I carry on, I'd like to point out that, my food money also has to pay for all the toilet, and household cleaning products I have to buy.

Everything I purchase comes from the Tesco range of blue line products. If you don't know what that means?... It means I buy 'THE CHEAPEST' of everything on sale.

Bread, tin beans, tin fruit, washing powder, toilet rolls, biscuits, furniture polish, toilet cleaner, toothpaste, packets of cooked ham, bacon... I really believe one day I'll be held to account for damaging my family's health, by feeding them all this rubbish... I bet I'm not doing the Ozone layer any favours either?

The list goes on: Shampoo, potatoes, pop, squash, (both lemon and orange) chickens... If my children all develop cancer in later life, I'll never be able to forgive myself. But like the fresh fish I wrote about on Good Friday, I really can't afford to feed them on anything else... I read in the newspaper that illegal immigrants feel like second class citizens because they have to use vouchers to pay for their weekly shopping... How do they think I feel pushing a trolly full of Blue Line packaging around Tesco's?

One thing I will say in Tesco's favour. They do accept all newspaper and magazine money off coupons even if I don't purchase the product advertised on the face of the voucher... So there you have it, a truthful and honest account of my mundane fortnightly shopping expeditions to the supermarket, in a quest to find a range of bland, uninteresting products with myself in the guise of Sherpa Tensing, lugging the weight of eight to ten plastic carrier shopping bags home alone with me on the free Tesco bus...

Footnote To Expedition: If we run out of anything between shopping trips, I top-up supplies by spending my family allowance money at Ivor Smiths's over priced local corner shop.

Summary note: I've never enjoyed shopping for food... I don't want to go shopping for food, and I'm determined never to write another word on the subject again... Unless, something extraordinary happens while I'm standing in line at the checkout, with my eighty quid and money off coupons in my hand.

April 15: Easter Sunday

I read in the paper that sixty-four percent of school children living in London, didn't know the true meaning of Easter. The article went on to say Jesus was crucified on Good Friday, (What's good about that?) and became resurrected on Easter Sunday, and some other gibberish about the ever altering date of Easter having something to do with the stars. Testing my family's religious knowledge against the paper's questionnaire entitled 'Christian or Heathen, Which One Are You?', I quickly found out that apart from Anthony the children from London were not the only ones who didn't know the true meaning of this Christian Festival:

Trevor: Pontious Pilate, crucified Jesus on Easter Sunday, but Jesus came back to life on Bank Holiday Monday.

Gary: I'll go along with what Dad says.

Megan: When I was in the infants, I can remember my teacher telling us that we have hot cross buns on Good Friday because that was the day Jesus died, but I can't remember why?

Mam: Rhian, I haven't got the time for any of this.

Me: I have to admit, I believed Jesus died on Easter Sunday as well... Does this mean we are more heathen than the people of London?

The Bank Holiday weather kept up its tradition of letting everyone down over the weekend. It started to rain at 5.00pm Friday evening, and it hasn't stopped yet. "Imagine how disappointed we'd be, if we owned a car." Trevor remarked, as he watched the huge droplets of rain running down our windowpane.

"Yes." My mother agreed. "Hardly picnicking weather is it."

After dinner, (Mam insisted on making the gravy... Her very special gravy... The recipe for which she's threatened to take with her to the grave.) we all sat around eating our Easter Eggs while watching the Easter movie. ('The Greatest Story Ever Told' on Channel 4.) "Don't mind me." Mam said, watching us all tuck into our eggs. "I'll go and get myself some bread and dripping... I don't want to disturb your enjoyment of the film Rhian, and what with my bad leg playing up and all. This could very well be my last supper."

April 16: Bank Holiday Monday

"Mandrake are playing their second gig in Cardiff this afternoon." Gary announced, as a crackle of thunder detonated above the house. "They are holding a 'Battle of the Bands' competition in the beer garden at the back of The Hope & Anchor, and we've been booked to go on at 4.00pm."

"What, in this weather?" Trevor asked, questioning his son's judgement as another flash of lightning interfered with the reception of our television set.

"No worries." Gary responded. "The storm will have blown over by four, and in any case. If we don't turn up the landlord has threatened to blacklist us, so we will never be able to get a gig in the area again."

Dear Diary, doesn't a Bank Holiday drag when you have nothing to do. If this was a normal Monday morning, Megan and Anthony would be at school, while Trevor and Gary would be on their way to sign on at the dole office, leaving me alone to watch 'Richard & Judy' on the television in peace... But this isn't a normal day, and instead of enjoying my own company, I find myself cooped-up in a box with four outdoor loving people, who through no fault of their own find themselves trapped indoors by the weather.

Anthony: Mam, what can I do, I'm bored?
Me: I don't know?
Trevor: Rhian, is there anything good on the television today?
Me: I don't know?
Anthony: Mam, I'm bored.
Gary: Mam, what's on the other channel?
Me: I don't know?

Megan:	Mam, have we got any of those biscuits left?
Me:	I don't know?
Anthony:	Mam, I'm bored.
Trevor:	Rhian, where's the remote control?
Me:	I don't know?
Gary:	I can't stand watching this crap anymore.
Megan:	Mam, are you sure we haven't got any more of those biscuits left?
Trevor:	Right, will everybody stand up and see if the remote control has fallen down the side of your chairs.
Me:	(Hoping for the best, after swallowing a couple of Prozac.) Sun please come out... Please come out from behind the clouds, and allow my family to get out of my hair.

THE FEELING OF THE DAY
by
Rhian Evans

Together, when we need to be apart.
Bonded, when we need to be free.
A family of five, shackled by the storm.
Five souls turned in, instead of blazing alone.
A dismal cell, for a family home.
Forcing us to be where we don't want to be.
Together, sharing purgatory.

April 17: Tuesday

Would you believe it? It stopped raining. At 7.00am this morning, the sun discovered a gap in the clouds to shine through... It stopped raining... Blue sky appeared, in time to greet Dave Huws who was on his way to work. Dear Diary, I read somewhere that we are the playthings of the Gods... When things like this happen... Well, you know what I mean.

After I'd collected my family allowance from the Post Office, Gary told me yesterday's gig had been a complete wash out. "The beer garden resembled a swamp Mam." Gary said, describing the venue. "They had to put sandbags down to stop the rain water from flooding the pub floor."

"Perhaps it was for the best." I remarked. "After all, you're only sixteen, and you shouldn't have been in the pub in the first place."

"But Mam, we were playing for a hundred quid." Gary protested. "That's ten quid each for the five of us in the band, and fifty quid for Hill's mate who let us borrow his van."

Two Questions I Wish I'd Asked Gary:

1. Who was driving the van? (No one in the band has passed their driving test.)
2. How were they going to pay the fifty quid van rental if they didn't win the competition?

On second thoughts, perhaps he'd be better off sorting this out on his own.

April 18: Wednesday

I've come to the conclusion Mandrake are the most unluckiest rock group in the world. Two gigs, both abandoned... I think the band should change their name to 'Jinxed'!

Today has been a day of 'No's'... No evening class, and because Trevor had received his early, no Giro. Dear Diary, now do you understand, why I wrote: *'receiving a Giro in advance is not always a good thing.'* Without proper planning and organisational skills, my family could easily have found themselves without any money for food for the next fourteen days.

April 19: Thursday

No one would think it... Anyone who watches television, or reads the newspaper, would never come to the conclusion that Wales is in fact a third world country... Or should I say Principality?... But we are.

Today is the day I collect my food parcel from the EEC. In much the same way as prisoner of war detainees collected their food parcels from the Red Cross during the Second World War... On certain days throughout the year the EEC, (European Economic Commission.) distributes quantities of food to the benefit claiming populus of Wales, direct from the European Food Mountain which is situated somewhere near Brussels.

Going on past parcels. They normally consist of two pounds of butter, two pounds of cheese, and eight tins of stewing steak, which arrives in packaging depicting the flag of the European Union. (A circle of gold stars, on a dark blue background.)

To claim this gift, all you have to do is prove your eligibility by showing a benefit book, or letter from the DSS at a local pickup point. (Usually a local Community Centre, etc.) Once your eligibility has been established, volunteers will be on hand to distribute your ration.

Why I Think Wales Should Join The EEC:

1. The Celtic people of Wales are used to foreigners (mainly English) telling us what we can and cannot do.

2. We would get more out of the EEC, than we would ever have to put in.
3. Without any real leaders of our own... I can't believe the EEC would treat us any worse than the English have over the years. (I can't remember receiving any food parcels from them.)
4. A change is as good as a rest.

Why I think The English Shouldn't Join The EEC:

1. Nobody likes them.
2. They'll demand a finger in every pie, and wont be happy until they have interfered, and meddled with everything.
3. They have a: It's my ball, and I'm not letting you play with it unless you do what I say, mentality.
4. Nobody likes them... It's well worth mentioning again!

April 20: Friday (My Birthday)

Trevor made me laugh first thing this morning. He said: "Happy Birthday Love." Before throwing back the duvet cover to reveal his 'John Thomas' trussed up in a red ribbon... Unwrapping my present, I spent the most enjoyable stamina sapping six minutes of the day... Who says 40 year olds don't know how to have fun!

At the breakfast table I was showered with cards, and little gifts: "Nice card isn't it Mam?" Megan grinned, as I opened the envelope to find a cartoon drawing of a teenage girl opening a box of sparkling white training shoes. Inside the inscription read: 'Happy Birthday To You' and in brackets: (Especially to your Feet.) "You have remembered it's my birthday on Monday, haven't you Mam?" Megan inquired, handing me a box containing a little ornament of a mouse nibbling food, perched on a giant triangle of Swiss cheese."

"Me next." Anthony insisted, handing me what felt like a card inside a brown paper bag. "I used a computer at school, to design it." He blushed, as I found myself staring at a picture of my face superimposed onto the neck of Miss World. Inside Anthony had printed: *'Dreams can come true, they can happen for you, if you're young at heart.'*

"I'm sorry I couldn't buy you much Mam, but I found this book in a charity shop. It only cost me 20p but I thought you'd like it." Inside another brown paper bag, I found a well thumbed copy of 'Shirley Valentine by Willy Russell', and they say that children don't understand what their parents are thinking!

She's 40 today, she's 40 today.
She's got the key of the door,
Never been 40 before...

Before Gary could hand me his card, Mam uninvited, burst into song on entering the room.

"How's my birthday girl then?" She asked, thrusting a Tesco carrier bag into my hand. "Just think forty years ago today, I was in Merthyr General Hospital giving birth to your mother." She said addressing my children. "Forty years ago today it was, and I can remember it as if it happened yesterday."

"Come on Mam." I said, responding to her dabbing her eyes. "There's no need for all this now, is there?"

"It's your birthday Rhian, and I'll cry if I want to... Now go and try that top on. It's the one I saw you looking at in Tesco's a couple of Friday's ago."

"Here you go Mam, Happy Birthday." Gary said, handing

me a card and a packet of 'Fox's Glacier Mints'. "Well I didn't know what to get you, and what with it just being Easter and all, I thought you would have had enough of chocolate... Anyway these mints won't melt, and I thought you could easily pop them into your bag when you go to your evening class or if you just pop out for a walk... I think it's nice to have something to suck on, if you go for a walk. Don't you Mam?"

I've been dreading reaching the big **FOUR-O**, but now that it's here??? Why on earth do I suddenly expect my life to get worse???

"Has everyone gone out?" Trevor asked, popping his head around the living-room door. "Only I know how much you enjoy opening presents, and as we're on our own... I thought you might like to open this one again." Entering the room with only a red ribbon wrapped around his genitals, Trevor winked, then with a swish of his arms carried me off to the bedroom. (I didn't say anything at the time, but I wish Trevor had bought me a real present... Just this once.)

April 21: Saturday

Dear Diary in the past I have been known to get my birth control pills, and my Prozac tablets into a muddle... This has caused me more than one sleepless night in the past... The mix-up occurs because I pop both tablets at the same time of the day. IE, first thing in the morning. Which as you know isn't the best time of the day for me.

If I take two Prozac by mistake, then the world is a happier place, and to hell with the pill... Only life isn't that simple. I could fall pregnant, and have to put myself through all that rigmarole, which happened at the beginning of the month.

On the other hand, if I pop two of my birth control pills

by mistake, I have literally been known to go through hell, (Mentally) until I've worked out what has happened, and correct it.

Taking everything into consideration, I've decided that Trevor must have a vasectomy.

April 22: Sunday

Last night

Midnight: Trevor took the news of his forthcoming operation well.

This morning

10.00am: "Rhian, last night... Who did you say was going into the hospital for an operation?"

This morning

10.05am: "You're going off your bloody head woman. Why should I be the one who has to go into hospital?... There's nothing wrong with me!"

I tried to explain my point of view.

This morning

10.30am: "So what you're saying is, I have to go under the knife because you can't be trusted to swallow two bloody tabs before you brew the tea!"

By 11.00am this morning. Trevor and I were no longer on speaking terms with each other.

April 23: Monday Megan's Birthday

Megan is sixteen today... First thing she came bounding down the stairs, eagerly anticipating her birthday present... She opened her birthday cards:

"Where's my present than Mam?"

"I've been meaning to have a little talk to you about that love." I said watching the smile slowly fade from her face. (This is another example of an early giro throwing the family's finances into chaos.) "Well you know your Father didn't receive his giro last week, and because of Easter and everything, we're a bit strapped for cash at the moment. (I was walking on egg shells.) So if it's all right with you, I thought you could take a day off from school when Dad's next giro arrives, and we the two of us could go into town on a girlie day out, and buy a pair of those trainers together?"

"I suppose it'll have to be all right, won't it." Megan snapped storming back to her bedroom.

God, If only I'd remembered to put a fiver in her card to soften the blow.

Thing's didn't get any better at tea time: "Where's the birthday girl?" Mam called out, entering the living-room holding a red Po Tellytubby shape birthday cake in her hand. "I know this cake is really for little children, but I couldn't resist buying it Rhian... Don't you think his little face looks a bit like Megan's when she was born."

Poor Megan... All in all, not a very memorable birthday to remember. No new trainers, and for the rest of the evening she had to put up with her brother's calling her 'Poo Face'.

"Happy birthday Megan." Mam said, pinching both of her Granddaughter's cheeks. "Sweet sixteen and never been kissed."

"Don't you believe it." Said Gary, until the look on my face told him to shut his mouth.

Trevor and I are still not speaking... Anthony's teachers held another training day at the school.

April 24: Tuesday

The kids go back to school today... I woke-up feeling very guilty this morning. I couldn't get Megan's disappointed features from out of my mind... There's nothing for it, I'll have to let her order the trainers out of my catalogue again. (But this time they won't be delivered by express delivery.)

> TRAINERS
> by
> Rhian Evans
>
> When I was young, we called you Daps.
> Black or white, you came in a choice of two.
> Comfortable slip-on, slipped gently over my feet
> Ideal for the gym, but never to be worn around the town.
> Have all your ideals, and your dreams come true?
> For now you are a classic shoe.

Collected the family allowance. Trevor and I are still not speaking.

April 25: Wednesday

It felt good to get away from the tension of the house this evening. That's right Diary, you've guessed it. Trevor hasn't thawed to my vasectomy proposal yet.

Discussing Trevor's reluctance to participate, with Dave and Anne Huws. I found to my surprise that Dave had, had his operation shortly after the triplets were born: "Well it stands to reason, doesn't it." Dave explained, placing a comforting arm around his wife. "If we are capable of knocking them out, three at a time. I realised something had to be done." (Why doesn't my Trevor feel like this?)

"The operation itself only lasts a couple of minutes." Dave continued. "Don't get me wrong, I was shitting bricks as they wheeled me into the theatre."

"They didn't knock you out, did they Dave?" Anne interrupted. "You think they would have wouldn't you?" She said, turning to me. "Because my Dave may look big and bad, but underneath it all, he's just a big old softy... Aren't you, you big old soppy thing."

"They injected me downstairs." Dave said with a wince. "And when it went numb, they did the business. I could have seen everything on the monitor if I'd wanted to, but I just closed my eyes and told them to get on with it."

"And there were no complications, afterwards?" I enquired.

"No, I was a little bit sore for a day or so... You said I was walking like John Wayne, didn't you Anne. But a day or two later I was soon in the saddle again, wasn't I love?"

"Dave!" Anne blushed, nudging her husband in his side. "Not in front of the evening class, please David."

April 26: Thursday

At midday the silence was deafening. Trevor had been up an hour, and was reading his newspaper in the chair, while I sat on the sofa staring at the television set with the sound turned down:

"Dave Huws had his operation done, soon after his triplets were born." I said beginning the argument.

"So you've been discussing our private business with your weirdo friends in your evening class... God it was bad enough when you discussed everything with your mother. But now I've got your evening class on my back as well."

"Dave said he didn't feel a thing. He said the whole operation only took a couple of minutes. He said he'll come over and talk to you about it if you like."

"Are you fucking insane woman? No fucker is coming over here to tell me what happened to his cock!"

"There's no need for that Trevor. Why can't we sit-down and discuss our problems like adults?"

"Because I'm the silly fucker who has to have his fruit and veg cut off. And another thing, why can't you take one pill in the morning and one pill in the afternoon?"

"Because mistakes can still happen."

"Listen Rhian, if you were thirty, instead of forty I could understand your point of view. But how many child bearing years have you got left in you? One, two maybe. For all we know you could be past child bearing age already."

"So you're still refusing to have it done then?"

"Look, Dave Huws is one of those new men. He's a lot younger than me. His wife is a lot younger than you."

"Trevor... Just Fuck Off!"

"Now where are you going?... I thought you wanted us to behave like adults?... Rhian, don't run away, we can sort this out... Rhian!"

"FUCK OFF!"

"The truth hurts, doesn't it love?... Anyway, why don't you get yourself sterilised, if it's worrying you that much?"

Dear Diary, forget the snip. Nothing short of castration will do for me now.

TREVOR, YOU BASTARD
by
Rhian Evans

She's younger than you, he said with a grin.
Knowing he'd hurt me, knowing he'd win.
To save himself he turned on me.
Twisting the knife with his cutting phrase.
I fled to my bed, feeling battered and dazed.
Below I heard laughter, then a turn of a page.
I cried on my pillow, then wrote on this line.
Trevor, you bastard - You treacherous swine.
Trevor, you bastard - Your life will be mine.

April 27: Friday

I tossed and turned all night. I haven't been this worked-up for ages. When I finally drifted off to sleep, I dreamt about my mother: *'I told you so, Rhian. I warned you, he was not the man for you.'* Over, and over again she reminded me what she'd said, just two hours before my wedding.

Trevor spent most of the day in the garden. I don't know if he's finally got into horticulture, or if he's only using it as an excuse to get away from me?

I can't make my mind up at what hurt me the most. Trevor's statement about my breeding capability, or the reference to the age difference between me and Anne Huws?

The more I think about it, the more it makes sense. Trevor is jealous of Dave Huws. He refuses to apply for a job at Dave's factory, and as soon as he heard about Dave's vasectomy, he went completely off his head.

April 28: Saturday

Saturday afternoon, (Alone at last.) a time of reflection on my part. I'm P.M.T active once again... Yes Trevor, I can still reproduce!

At this moment in time, I feel wonderfully sleepy sprawled across my couch. I expect it's a combination of my Prozac, and my menstrual cycle mixing together... What a wonderful sensation this is. On one hand, my Prozac is telling my brain to relax, and not to worry about a thing. While on the other hand, my P.M.T's are urging me to kill, kill, kill.

PROZAC
by
Rhian Evans

A calming friend, a mystic haze,
The seconds tick by life and fade.
Without your help, I'd hate the day,
No light, all dark, my mind in pain.
Relaxation lost, for thoughts within.
My one true friend, to see me through,
For days of light, and hopes anew.
Without your aid then all is lost,
No time is spent to count the cost.
I need you friend, to live this life.
A stronger bond than man and wife.
For with you I achieve a peaceful soul.
I exist in a world, not in a hole.
My teenage years were full of light.
Darkness stressed my adult life.
But you, you blew the clouds away.

Medically kept my mind at bay.
Little friend, my white knight 'tis true,
I still wield control, because of you.

Isn't it funny what your mind thinks about in its semi-conscious state... Now I begin to understand how people experimenting with hard drugs become such good poets.

April 29: Sunday

Smelt a funny smell, as I passed by Gary's bedroom this morning. Stubbed out in an ashtray, I found the remains of an hand rolled fag. (I have an horrible feeling that 'Golden Virginia' was not the only substance contained within the papers.)

"Gary I don't want you to smoke in your bedroom any more." I said, confronting him with my discovery. "You could fall asleep, and set the whole house on fire."

"All right Mam."

"How long have you been rolling your own?" I enquired. "You know how I feel about that disgusting habit?" (OK, I admit it. I used to smoke in the past, but I gave it up for my children's sake... I gave up drinking and smoking at the same time... Did I really give them up for my kids?... It was all such a long time ago.)

"Only a couple of days or so." He responded. "I thought I'd give it a go, before I die."

"Well I don't know how you are going to afford it, if you decide to take it up properly." I warned him. "Where are you going to find the money from to feed your habit, when you've got your board and lodge, and weekly guitar payments to take into consideration?

"Relax man. Every things gonna be just fine." Gary answered as if he didn't have a care in the world.

"Listen Gary. You're not being clever you know. I know what's going on. You'll have to get up pretty early in the morning, to pull the wool over my eyes, good boy." I said attacking his lacklustre,devil may care attitude.

"So you know then?"

"Do I know, of course I bloody know. (I try not to swear at my children.) What do you think you are playing at."

"It's the rock and roll lifestyle, in it." He smirked. "All the rock groups are doing it..." And then he spoke about how it helped him to relax. How it helped him with his music, in both the playing and the writing of his songs. (I wouldn't say so much, but he only started smoking this weekend.)

"It's just the same as your Prozac Mam." Gary said in defence of his recent actions. "You take what you need to get by, and now, so do I."

This conversation isn't over by a long shot.

1. I get my tab's prescribed to me for free.
2. The doctor says I need to take them.
3. My drugs don't stink the house out.

I'll wait until he comes down off his cloud, before bringing this issue up with him again. I hope Trevor doesn't find out... We're still not speaking.

April 30: Monday

Gary looked a little dejected this morning, as he left the house to sign on with his father. (I'll have another word with him, when he comes back.)

White Arrow delivered Megan's trainers. (Please God, let them be the right size.)

10.00pm: I told Gary what was out of sight, was out of mind, but if he ever brought that shit into the house again, he'd have to find himself somewhere else to live.

He once again threw my Prozac up to me, but I reminded him that I had the law on my side and he didn't. I also pointed out, that if he wanted to live the alternative lifestyle, he could find himself some alternative accommodation live it in.

Threatening to put his name down on the council housing list, he immediately stormed upstairs,and locked himself in his room.

I think 'Mandrake' have corrupted my son's mind... Is this the defining moment where my family finally falls apart?

Megan was very happy with her new trainers.

REVIEW OF THE MONTH:

I found out my eldest son smokes pot. I discovered this while his father and I were no longer communicating with each other. I don't feel like writing anymore after rereading this statement. Is my writing this diary causing my family to have bad luck?... Is writing my life down on paper unlucky?... At least Mam isn't picking on the Huws family anymore. Why is that silly sod of a son of mine smoking pot?... Am I a bad mother?... Do I set him and my other children a bad example?... Why is Gary picking on me for taking Prozac?... It never seemed to bother him in the past. I want to go to sleep... Why has this been sent to try me?

May 1: Tuesday

Dear Diary; sorry about insinuating you were bad luck in the previous entry. Only, I felt under a lot of pressure last night... Anyway when I eventually finish writing my entries upon your pages. I'd like to believe our relationship together is blessed with a happy ending.

Well another month has started, and I entered into it on the back of another sleepless night of worry. (What's got into our Gary, and what's making him rebel like this?)

Some good news for a change... Trevor and I are back on speaking terms again. (The good old silent treatment worked its magic once more.)

"Look, I'm sorry if I offended you by suggesting Anne Huws is younger than you." Trevor began, trying to select the correct words in making his apology.

"I'm not disputing the fact Anne is younger than me." I replied. "It was the nasty way you implied it, I didn't like."

"Rhian, about the vasectomy. I can't do it for you love. You know I would if I could, but I can't. Call me a coward if you like. Call me selfish, too. But I just can't do it for you love. I'm sorry, and all that, but there it is... Please don't let this come between us."

As he spoke, Trevor cupped his hands around mine. He added phrases like: "We'll have to be more careful in the future." And the evergreen classic: "We can work through this thing together."

I could tell he was determined not to go under the knife, so offering a little resistance to his protests, and a few disappointed glances in his general direction, Trevor agreed to a compromise... Trevor is going to decorate our bedroom. After he'd made this decision, Trevor was very disappointed to discover that I am still P.M.T active... Come to think about it, so was I.

May 2: Wednesday

After I'd cashed Trevor's Giro, I did some Christmas shopping in the charity shop. I purchased two 'East 17' CD's for 98p. (49p each) Megan used to like listening to this group when she was younger. I hope these CD's will become as nostalgic to her, as my old 'David Cassidy' and 'T-Rex' LP's are to me.

My big chance is here at last: "After the success of our end of term poetry evening, I feel it would make a very interesting experiment if you each submitted a poem of your own choosing, to a ladies' magazine of your choice." Mr Davis, announced to the class. "Of course there are a few basic rules we all have to follow, but there's nothing to worry about, as we'll all be doing this together."

With my pen in hand, I scribbled down this advice:
Market Research

1. Know your market. Find out which magazine publishes reader's poems.

   Question from the class: "We can't afford to buy all these magazines on our dole money."
   Answer from Mr Davis: "You don't need to buy anything. Thumb through the magazines on sale at the newsagents, W.H.Smith's or somewhere else that has a large selection.

2. If you can't find any poems. Write a poem about an article written in the magazine. Then write accompanying letter

to the editor, explaining why the article had moved you to pen your verse.

Question from the class: "Isn't this lying?"
Answer from Mr Davis: "Let's call it poetic licence."

3. You've got to be in it to win it. - Who dares, wins.
Question from the class: "Is there any money involved?"
Answer from Mr Davis: "If you are successful on the reader's letters page, you could receive anything from fifteen to twenty-five pounds. If you win a poetry competition in a magazine, you could win more. But more importantly if you are successful, you will become a published poet."

I'm so excited. *'You will become a published poet'*, Mr Davis said. If I do become a published poet. The world will be able to read my work... I can feel the tears welling-up in my eyes.

I am no longer P.M.T active. (That was a short one. Perhaps Trevor is right after all... Am I about to go on the change?)

May 3: Thursday

Midnight: I told Trevor about Gary's rock and roll lifestyle... Trevor did not take the news well:

"I'm not having this." Trevor said marching to his eldest son's bedroom. "If he's got money to burn on that rubbish; better he pay us a bit more for his board and lodge than damage his already stupid brain cells."

"Listen to me Dad." Gary pleaded, as he held onto his duvet cover for dear life. "We all need our little something to see us through the day. Mam's got her Prozac, you've got your fags and drink, and I've got my blow... Where's the harm in it, mun?"

"Nobodies ever smoked that stuff in our family." Trevor

shouted, ignoring his son's protests. "Not even your Uncle Wyn, and he used to go to all the open air rock concerts when he was younger."

"What's going on?" Anthony screamed, frightened out of his sleep during the commotion. "Has Dad gone mad?"

"If you want to be a junkie, you can be a junkie somewhere else." Trevor panting, finally let go of the duvet cover. "I'm not having it boy, do you hear me?... I'm not having it, in this house."

As Trevor left the room, I stared at Gary who rolled over onto his side. "I'm not allowed to do anything in this house." He muttered as I switched off the light.

"Some of us have got school to go to in the morning." Megan yelled from inside her bedroom.

"My brother the junkie." Anthony laughed, as he prepared to go back to sleep. "I've got a junkie for a brother... What a tosser!"

Trevor got up early this morning, and admitted that worrying about Gary's altered state of mind had kept him awake for most of the night.

"I don't know what's got into the boy Rhian." He said, at the breakfast table. "He used to love to watch the television, but lately he's never in."

"He's growing up you see Trev. It's a different world to the one we used to live in." (I can't remember the last time I called my Trevor, Trev. But I was really touched by how much concern he was showing for our son.)

The remainder of the day was spent discussing the best way, to save our son from a life of drugs... After ten hours of anguished debate, we came up with nothing. (I hope my mother doesn't find out about any of this... The news could kill her!)

PARENTHOOD
by
Rhian Evans

We wished for a future, that's now arrived.
We've nurtured their growth, at our parental side.
Once babes in arms, our dream's alive.
Enter the world, both naive and true.
A judgement on us, and the spirit in you.
To walk a straight line, or a crooked path.
Our peers sit, and observe their tread.
All actions of ours are taken to task.
Our young, one by one, step out of the nest,
Influences abound, both good and bad.
Temptations enough to undo our work.
Pitfalls a plenty, unseen at the time,
Creep-up on your mind in later life.
And as quickly as that, you run out of time.

I can be deep at times... This poem has really surprised me.

May 4: Friday

My figure is one of the few things I've got to be proud of. Cross my heart and hope to die. I have never been on a diet in my life, and give or take a pound or two at different times throughout the year, (IE Christmas.) I have remained at the same weight for the past twenty something years... I've never been on a diet, because I've always had worry on my side... Stop laughing Diary... I know you don't believe me... Okay, okay. When I say I've never been on a diet, what I mean to say is; I've never seen a diet through... I've never had to. Worry is a tremendous ally, in the battle of the bulge. Some people smoke, some drink, do drugs, eat... I rock back an fore on my sofa, biting my nails, my stomach in knots... On a purely weight watching basis, I find this the best method.

In a way, I suppose it would be fair to say worry has been with me all through my adult life. But since I've been married, it has been my daily companion: I started to worry about our unpaid household bills. When I fell pregnant I worried that there was something wrong with my womb. I worried my babies would be born deformed... Every kick was the babies way of telling me something was wrong.... Cot death syndrome was a big worry at the time, and became a big part of my life. Night after night I'd wake, and run into my children's bedroom to find out if they were still breathing, with my heart pounding loudly in my chest. Then I went through a phase where I worried that they were going to fall down the stairs, or find and drink a bottle of bleach in my cupboard.

'The Home Is A Dangerous Place. Most Accidents Happen In The Home.' Those newspaper headline screamed out at me, scaring me half to death. I don't think I was ever born to be a natural mother, the responsibility of it all was slowly killing me.

Even today, nothing has changed. I'm still worrying. I try to employ the pretence: 'What Mother Doesn't Know Won't Hurt Her.' But it's all an elaborate illusion on my part, which doesn't really help. I worry what everyone are doing, when they are out of the house. I worry about the kind of people they mix with, and the kind of people they call their friends. Who are they? Are they living on this estate? Or are they outsiders?

Boys will be boys but Megan is my biggest worry. The magazines she reads, (I'd feel embarrassed if I saw my mother reading them. Some of them have a position of the month, with diagrams.) and the company she keeps... You can't tell me her friends are still virgins. And if that wasn't bad enough, now I've got Gary... My Gary... A boy that was no worry to me at all, until he joined a rock group.

One good thing to come out of this; Trevor's shown he does care what happens to his family... Sometimes, it's hard to tell. On the bad side: Hell has once again re-entered our living-room.

Like I said at the beginning of this piece. I've never had to worry about my weight... I pray to God every night. I thank him for not letting me fall into the trap of the comfort eater... If I had, I'd be over twenty-five stone, and too fat to lift myself off the couch by now.

Trevor is still very worried, (He hasn't said anything but I can see it in his face.) Gary hasn't seen the light... Telling Trevor wasn't a wise move on my part. In fact I think I've made matters worse... Men are no good in these kind of situations. (If they cant rip it open, or beat it into shape) Not only am I worried about Gary, but I'm starting to worry about Trevor now... He's not used to handling a large amount of stress like me... Is life a vicious circle or what?

May 5: Saturday

Staying with the dietary theme. I watched Shirley Valentine explain her F-Plan diet during the Saturday matinee on BBC2 this afternoon. I wanted to shout at the screen: *'YOU SHOULD*

TRY MY W-PLAN DIET, LOVE.' But then I thought, what's the point, and let the matter drop. (It's not like she could hear me, is it?) But apart from that I enjoyed the film. I've seen it a couple of times before. Anthony presented me with a copy of the book on my birthday, that reminds me I must make a start on reading it... God, if anyone needed to be Shirley Valentine at this present moment in time that someone should be me.

This afternoon was one of the few occasions during our married life that I've insisted, Trevor go to the rugby club. Fair play to him mind, he was quite prepared to spend the day discussing our Gary's problem with me, but I insisted he went all the same.

Reasons For Trevor To Go To The Rugby Club:

1. I work better on my own.
2. A drink with his mates, will take his mind off things for a while. The last thing I want is for Trevor to have a nervous breakdown... Oh God, I'm worrying about that now!

Gary phoned and said he was staying with friends tonight. Well, that's that then. My son is spending the night in a crack house, or an opium den hidden in the Welsh valleys... There's no need for Trevor to know about this until tomorrow. I wish he could spend the night in the pub.

May 6: Sunday

Gary came home before Trevor got up, looking as white as a sheet... Come to think about it: Trevor looked as white as a sheet when he got up as well.

"Never again Mam. I've had a terrible night. I've seen all

sorts of things I wish I hadn't." Gary mumbled, as he went to his room.

11.00pm: What a brilliant day. Gary spent most of it in his bedroom, repenting. While Trevor silently impersonated a statue, in between fighting off sudden and very violent attacks of nausea and diarrhoea: "I must have drank a bad pint love." He complained.

4.00pm: Gary leaves the confines of his bedroom to announce to the family: "The band and I departed company last night. I am no longer a part of 'Mandrake' anymore. Owen Hunt now owns my guitar, and has agreed to carry on making the outstanding payments on it."

I feel so proud, I could sense the tears filling my eyes

"Why's that then?" Trevor asked, until I kicked him on the shin.

"I'm sure Gary will tell us when he's good and ready, won't you Gary?" I said, glaring at Trevor not to push the boy. "You go back to your room and have another lay down love. You look worn out to me." I instructed my prodigal, as both Trevor and I watched him leave the room.

May 7: May Day Bank Holiday Monday

"I was never cut out for the rock and roll lifestyle, Mam." Gary admitted, as I carried a mug of tea into his room. "I was missing the television too much, for that." He continued. "It was just one of those things I suppose. Something I had to try that's all. I had to get it out of my system, didn't I... It was just one of those... You know, we all go through them while we are growing up."

Sitting on the edge of his bed, I listened and nodded my head: "And what about that stuff you smoked?"

"I didn't really like it... I couldn't inhale... I didn't know how to... I don't smoke... But I couldn't let the others know that could I?... It was just something I tried with the boys... I only wanted to rebel a little bit... Do you know, I felt sick while I was doing it?... Hill's says it was because I couldn't get the smoke down into my lungs properly... I never liked smoking you see Mam... Mam, I didn't want to become a junkie."

What a great Bank holiday this is turning out to be. Trevor was absolutely delighted when I told him the news, and best of all my mother hasn't found out... Just one disappointment to the day: The council in it's wisdom has failed to erect a Maypole for the estate virgins to dance around this year... Just what is the Lottery Charity Commission spending our money on?... Perhaps the Maypole organising committee couldn't find any virgins over the age of twelve living on the estate???

May 8: Tuesday

I knew my luck would be too good to last: "Rhian, please tell me it isn't true. Please tell me what everyone is saying about our Gary is a pack of lies."

"What are you talking about Mam?"

"Our Gary was seen entering the Hunt house last Saturday night... Rhian, you know as well as I do, to what goes on in there... It's a den on iniquity... That woman Mrs Hunt, who has the brassneck to call herself a mother... It's disgusting, running after young boys at her age... There should be a law against it... She allowed that out of control son to rule the roost ever since her no good husband runaway... It's not right Rhian. It's not safe for a sensitive boy like our Gary to be seen going in and out a places like that. For the good of the boy I think you should put a stop to it. Nip it in the bud Rhian, I really do."

"Gary sold his guitar there, that's all." I said, hoping to bring the conversation to an end.

"And that little bit of business took all night, did it?" Mam replied, then persisted in her usual fashion. "Only Debbie White saw him leave the Hunt house first thing last Sunday morning. Debbie said he looked terrible. As white as a sheet, she said. Well I wondered what he'd been doing all night, so..."

"Well, it's all over with now, isn't it." I said, interrupting my mother's flow.

"I should think so too. Rhian, I should have a word with the boy if I were you. He's going to end up in trouble if you don't. You mark my words. I know you've let him stay out all night in the past, but he is only sixteen after all."

"Well, it's all over now Mam." I repeated, wishing that she would think of something else to talk to me about.

"Yes, for you no doubt. But I'm too old you see Rhian. I'm too old to move house at my age, and if the family name gets dragged through the mud... Well, you know what I mean. Nothing any good ever came from mixing with the Hunt's. Even Mr Hunt realised that, just before he runaway. I'll tell you this my girl..." And she carried on, and on with her predictions of doom and gloom for the family, if Gary, Megan and Anthony were all allowed to continue to go through life unchecked.

"Of course I'll have to resign from my old age club... I'll be a pariah in my own community... I'll be nothing more than a prisoner in my own home. Rhian, can you imagine it? Trapped, a recluse residing within the same four walls, day after day, with nothing to look at but the wallpaper... I'll turn into a cat woman, or some other type of horrible outcast. I'll be too ashamed to let my face be seen in the street. I'll have to wear a head scarf everywhere I go..."

Please God, don't let my Mother find out about Gary's seven day drug habit.

May 9: Wednesday

I love my evening class. For me, it is the highlight of the week... So why do I continue to feel upset when events around me begin to crumble, as they always have done throughout my married life?

"Hi Rhian, I've brought an old school friend of yours to the class with me tonight." Anne excitedly announced, as I entered the classroom. "Mary and I are both volunteers at the local nursery group. We were having a conversation about tonight's class, and what with one thing and another I decided to ask Mary if she'd like to tag along with me tonight."

My heart sank, as the grinning face of my old adversary made herself known to me.

"Hello Rhian." She said with that toffee nosed voice of hers. "I was totally gobsmacked when Anne told me about the evening class... You never struck me as the literary sort... You never showed any interest in the subject while we were at school."

Dear Diary: this is one woman that I'd happily do time for. Mary has been a constant thorn in my side for the whole of my life, and the funny thing is... I don't know why? We sat inside the same classroom at school from beginning to end. Whatever I did, she made it her business to go one better:

Music:	I'd buy the single, she'd buy the album.
Dress:	She'd wait until the last moment to buy her school uniform, so she could say that hers was newer than mine.
Make-up:	When she was thirteen, she'd cry if her mother ever bought a cheap brand.
Boyfriends:	It nearly killed her when Trevor and I started courting. She tried every trick in the book to get Trevor to dump me.
Wedding:	My registry office v Her church service.
Children:	Rhian 3 - Mary 4 (She scored in the last minute of extra time with baby Sotheby.)
Husbands:	My Trevor beats her Idris hands down in the masculine look department... Any fool can see that, even her...I'll never forget that time she made her Idris wear a wig.

"I hear your Gary isn't working on the Government Scheme anymore?" She hissed. "Only my Julian is doing ever so well on his. Mr Hurst the florist, is very impressed with him. He can't praise him high enough. My Julian has always been very artistic with his hands you see." She said turning to Anne. "It comes from my side of the family."

Your Julian is has gay as a bunch of daffodils. I wanted to scream at her, but I didn't want to start a slanging match with Mary... Not then. Not in the classroom... It wouldn't be right.

May 10: Thursday

"I wondered how long it would be before she was back on the scene." Mam remarked, after I'd told her my news. "What does she know about poetry? And that Julian of hers, he's as limp as a wet lettuce... Florist, did you say he's training to be?... Well Rhian, that's just about his mark, isn't it!"

And of course once Mam started on the subject, I had to sit and listen to the full gamut of her opinion of Mary Jackson, from school right through to her marriage and children.

"...And if you ask me Rhian, I think that husband of hers is as bad as she is. Now I came to think about it I do believe Idris Jackson, is jealous of your Trevor."

"Don't be silly Mam."

"No, no, you didn't see his face when Trevor won the karaoke on New Year's Eve... If looks could kill... Mind you we did have a laugh when his Mary forced him onto the stage, and made him sing that Charles Aznavour song... Rhian, you know it. What's it called?"

"Dance In The Old Fashioned Way?"

"Can you imagine it Rhian. A little toad of a man like Idris singing a song like that, while making all those sexy hand movements behind his back... It was nearly enough to put me off my drink."

Looking on the bright side. At least this bit of gossip, has taken my mother's attention away from Gary spending the night at the Hunt's.

May 11: Friday

Today Anne called round pushing the triplets in their buggy: "Which magazine are you going to send your poems to?" She asked, after settling her three children down on the floor to play with a box of building bricks she'd brought with her.

"Magazine? What magazine?" I stared blankly at her for a moment, then I realised: "Of course our homework."

Dear Diary: OK I admit it! Encountering Mary Jackson in

the classroom had once again completely knocked me off my stroke.... Last Wednesday's class passed me by in a haze. I heard and saw nothing, apart from asking myself this one question over and over again: "What the hell is she doing here, now?"

"Mary seems like a nice person?" Anne said, removing a green plastic brick from one of her children's mouth. "Mind you it was funny how we met. Out of the blue she knocked on my front door and asked me if I wanted to become a volunteer and help out with the local nursery group, down at the community centre. She said she'd seen me speaking with you on a number of occasions, and as you were an old friend of hers, she thought it would be okay to ask me if I was interested."

Listening intently, I allowed Anne to continue.

"Mind you I was getting bored in the mornings at home, so it worked out all right for me, and my three enjoy playing with their new friends, don't you boys?" Anne hesitated. "Rhian I hope you don't mind me saying this, what with her being an old friend of yours and all... But that Mary Jackson does go on a bit, doesn't she? She's always going on about what her family has got, and how well her children are doing at school. I think Julian must be her favourite, because she's forever going on about him and praising his fabulous bouquet designs, which are apparently in great demand by Mr Hurst's rich clients in Cardiff. Mary also told me her husband was the first man to become a house husband on this estate."

At this revelation both Anne and I stared into each other's faces before bursting out in a spontaneous roar of laughter.

"Her husband has been on the dole longer than my Trevor." I said, trying to respond in between shrieks of giggles.

"No, she won't have that." Anne replied, her three children looking up at us in amazement. "She insists that it was her husband's choice to stay at home and to care for their children, and she decided to stay at home with him because she didn't think it fair that he should have to stay at home all day on his own.

May 12: Saturday

What a bitch that Mary Jackson is. Fancy embellishing innocent Anne into her evil little schemes. Before her visit ended Anne admitted Mary had more or less invited herself to last Wednesday's class... This time I hope curiosity really does kill the cat.

With the family out of the house I gathered-up as many of Megan's old magazines as I could find,and settled down with a pot of tea to see if anything caught my eye.

MAGAZINES:

CHAT: I read a letter from a woman who was having sex with her husband's two brothers... I bet these people live on a farm.

MORE: The position of the month looked extremely difficult... You have to be young and supple to do something like that.

JUST 17: Teenage rubbish. The crossword: 8 down dildo, 12 across love eggs... Megan had filled in each clue correctly... Should a young girl of Megan's age be reading something like this, let alone know the correct answers?

WOMAN - WOMAN'S OWN - BEST:

If you ask me the teenage magazines are more juicy than the adult ones.

After two hours of skimming through the pages I couldn't find a poetry competition in any of them,(Mind you some of the magazines I read were nearly a year old.) but I did find a story that caught my eye in a recent edition, so I decided to compose a poem on that.

THE PENSIONER
by
Rhian Evans
(Poem inspired by an article in
'Woman' magazine 10/4/2001)

1.
Alone, on my own, my television, my telephone.
Excluded from the postman's thoughts,
My ever dormant letterbox.
While I sit here alone.- Hankering to hear a ringing tone.

2.
There's no need to be alone,
So say the people who inhabit my screen.
So say people on the street,
To the people who they meet.
I watch my neighbours greet.
Hello - How are you - Nice day.
Someday I hope they come to visit me,
Home Help - Samaritans - Meals on Wheels,
Any one from three, please come and talk to me.

3.
Thoughts are painful on my own.
The memories they creep, from mind to heart.
Often exaggerated and unkind,
Kept at bay, by substance length,
Take one three times a day after meals.
The mind is a fragile thing,
Take care of it, and it will take care of you.
I've read the pamphlets, and I've watched the news.
But I have no friends you see,
No friends to came to visit me.

4.
So I am alone.
I witness the dawn - Noon - Sun set.
A prison home, for an ancient being.
Outlived my youth and purpose.
Survived while others fell.
The last of my kind in history and kin.
My world holds only one within.
And soon the curtains are drawn.

Put that in your pipe and smoke it, Mary Jackson.

Tonight is one of the great television nights of the year. Saturday the 12th of May: the night of the Eurovision Song Contest, and this year it didn't disappoint. We had it all. We had a good selection of Boom-Bang-A-Bang songs, outlandish outfits, and an abundance of schizophrenic and political voting. Terry Wogan was on sparkling form once again. (What are these European's on?... They are clearly living on a different planet from us.) It came as a great shock to everyone when Estonia won. (Terry Wogan, and I couldn't believe it.) I liked the Dutch song best, (Nobody judging seemed too.) but I can't remember the name of the singer, or the song now that I think about it. (I don't feel this is important, because it's the Eurovision experience that counts and not just the music.)

EUROPE AND US:

1. If you don't understand anything about the workings in Brussels, simply spend four hours watching the European Song Contest, and everything will become abundantly clear to you.
2. The voting system... A mirror image of the European Parliament.
3. Blatant political voting. (See point 2.)
4. Terry Wogan should be made president of Europe.
5. Why do the people of Europe hate us, when we helped them to remain free during both World Wars?
6. Are Israel and Turkey strictly speaking apart of Europe?

May 13: Sunday

Sex was wonderful last night... I felt so happy, I was so full of myself... I was so excited, the humiliation of an enemy was staring me in the face, and I'd never felt more alive.

I honestly believe I can write poetry, and the thought of listening to Mary Jackson's tongue tied offerings drove me to distraction.

Poor Trevor must have been wondering what was happening, because I was all over him like a rash. (Of course it goes without saying: if Mary Jackson turns out to be a brilliant poet, I'll have no option but to take an overdose of sleeping tablets, Prozac and aspirin to end my life!)

May 14: Monday

This morning, as Trevor and Gary left to sign-on, I imagined how wonderful it would be if Dave Huws could get Gary an interview, and I announced my son's newly found position to everyone in the middle of my evening class... Florist indeed!... I'd rather Gary stay on the dole.

May 15: Tuesday

Mam walked with me to the Post Office today. While I collected my family allowance, Mr Baker the Post Master answered her queries concerning her pension book. (I think it had something to do with an increase in payment. Mam says nothing about her financial status to me. (She's very secretive about things like that.)

"So she made a point of approaching Anne, (Yes Diary, I couldn't believe it myself. Mam's calling Anne, Anne now, and not that skinny little bitch from across the road.) in her own home did she?... The cheeky madam!"

Nodding my head at everything my mother said, I allowed her say her piece. "It's about time you put her in her place Rhian. Her and that house husband of hers."

May 16: Wednesday

Disaster, disaster, disaster! Standing to address the class I said: "I couldn't find any poetry competitions in any of the magazines I read, but I did find an interesting story about an old age pensioner living on her own... Mrs Bates is eighty-nine years old, she lives on her own, and she's outlived all of her family and friends. My poem: "The Pensioner" (Oh God, I don't believe it. I've just made rabbit ear signals to the class.) was inspired by her story, and is my interpretation of how I would feel, if I ended up in a similar situation.

I recited my poem to the class.

Mr Davis: Any comments from anyone?

Anne: I thought It was very good... I thought it caught the mood of the article perfectly.

Mr Davis: Yesss!... Any others?

Mary: I also liked it. But I felt, it was patchy in places.

Mr Davis: Well, I also liked it. But I don't think it suitable for publication in a woman's magazine. Can anyone tell me why?

Mary: Wrong subject?

Mr Davis: No not really.

Mary: Too depressing?

Mr Davis: Well... It could be, but I was thinking more along the lines of the length of the piece... You can sit down Rhian, if you wish.

Like a fool I'd remained standing all the while, while I'd listened to Mr Davis unravel my confidence like an old sock.

Mr Davis: Let me explain Rhian. The only realistic hope you have of getting a poem published in a magazine, is on the publication's reader's letter page. And the best chance you and the rest of the class have of achieving this, is if you keep your poem short, quirky, and to the point... Remember everyone, to a successful magazine editor; space is everything.

Totally deflated I took the criticism on the chin. Sporting a silly grin, and outwardly acting as if I didn't give a damn... But inside I'd been cut to the quick, and to make matters worse Mary Jackson had been present to witness my humiliation.

May 17: Thursday

I had a nightmare last night. After reciting her poem to the class, Mr Davis presented Mary Jackson with a fabulous bouquet of red roses for her rendition of: 'Why I'm Better Than Rhian'.

1.

I have four children, that's one more than you.
I have an house husband, not a benefit scrounger like you.

12.

...Rhian a poet, it will never come true.
A loser at birth, sentenced to a lifetime of gloom.

After the fifth encore, and order had once again been restored to the classroom, Mr Davis announced: "My brother is the editor in chief of 'The South Wales Echo', and I have no hesitation in offering Mary Jackson a lifelong contract with the paper, which allows them to publish a selection of her work for as long as she cares to write poetic verse."

Dear Diary how is it, I can remember the full twelve verses of this abuse by heart, but have great difficulty in remembering a single line of my own work?

May 18: Friday

From one nightmare to another. I discovered this morning that Anthony is being bullied at school: "Stop fussing Mam, I can handle myself." Anthony protested, after I'd confronted him with the torn blazer pocket of his school uniform. (Frantic fifteen minutes followed stitching the pocket back into the correct position... No black cotton. White will have to do, until I borrow some black thread from my mother.) "They're all brain dead you see." Anthony explained. "Every kid in the computer club gets stick at one time or another, just because we can walk straight into the canteen at dinnertime, and not have to queue for our dinner with the other pond life who drag their knuckles along the floor."

"All nerds deserve a kicking." Megan proclaimed in very unladylike tones, as I questioned her on her brother's predicament. "I wouldn't worry too much about it, if I were you." She insisted. "Brainiac brings a lot of it on himself... Why does our Tony always want to be different. Why can't he just fit in like everyone else?"

"Well look at him. He's asking for it, isn't he." Gary remarked, during the commercial break of 'Emmerdale Farm'. "If he stopped reading books, and hung around the estate with the other kids more often, none of this would have happened."

"Boy, if anyone hits you, you hit them back, do you hear me?" Trevor said, offering his son the benefit of his experience. "Remember there's no shame in getting beaten up, as long as you get one good one in first... If you find yourself knocked to the ground roll yourself up into a tight ball."

So much for my caring family. I was appalled by their overwhelming reaction to my suggestion of having a quiet word with Mr Davis during my evening class:

Anthony: Please Mam, please don't say anything.
Trevor: This isn't about poetry woman. This is about real life.

Anthony: Dad, tell her not to say anything.

Megan: (BABY VOICE) Mammy's going to have a 'ickle word with the teacher, about the nasty bullies for you then.

Trevor: Rhian, leave it drop. The boy is big enough to fight his own battles.

Gary: It's his own fault for not playing with the other kids in the street.

Trevor: Do you want him turning into Julian Jackson?... For Christ's sake woman, he'll want to train as a florist next.

May 19: Saturday

Dear Diary, I won ten pound on the National Lottery tonight. My number's were: 3-13-23-29-33-43. Numbers 3-29-33 were drawn, so that means, I've won a tenner. I've never won more than a tenner on the lottery in my life. I've had three numbers and a bonus ball before now but the bonus ball doesn't count unless you've got five numbers. (I play the same numbers each week... You never know. They may come up?)

"I've always been lucky at gambling. I used to win the ten pence jackpot regularly, on the penny slot machines when the Autumn fair came to town. My favourite machine used to be called 'The Log Jam'. (I say used to be, because the fair disappeared from this area in the early 1980's.) On 'The Log Jam', I'd feed two pence coins into a slot. They would fall down a shot onto a flat surface where a buffer would push them into a stack of two penny pieces, where hopefully they would cause an avalanche of overhanging coins to fall into the pay out tray below.

Trevor on the other hand gambles the odd pound each week

on the horses, on something called an accumulator. He's never won, but he often remarks, that only one horse had let him down.

Dear Diary, when I first started going out with Trevor, there was a television programme on ITV every Saturday afternoon called 'The World Of Sport'. On that programme, they used to have something called 'The ITV Seven'. A horse racing bet, that involved picking the winners of the seven televised races.

"Why does 'BAR' run in every race?" I asked a room full of astonished, future, male-in-laws. "The horse is always being mentioned in the betting, but he's never mentioned during the commentary, and to my certain knowledge I've never seen him win a race."

To my eternal shame I can still hear their laughter ringing in my head to this present day. Leading me out of the room by my arm, Trevor said: "You've done it now... I've never been so ashamed in my... I'll be reminded about this for the rest of my life."

"Unlike you Trevor." I embarrassingly responded. "I was never brought up to understand the goings-on inside a den of iniquity before."

May 20: Sunday

Dear Diary, isn't it funny how one embarrassing memory, triggers off another one: Way back in my youth the 'Heinz'... Or was it 'Campbell's?... Anyway one of the soup companies brought out a range of square shaped soups, that were contained inside a square carton, instead of the usual tin. To publicise this product on television, a gardener was shown growing and picking a selection of square shaped tomatoes off the vine.

"Can we grow that square shaped variety of tomato?" I

asked Trevor years later, when he was thinking about getting a greenhouse.

"I'll tell you what." Trevor replied in that cocky tone of his. "If I built a cold frame, I could grow some of those oblong cucumbers, while on my bamboo canes, I could grow some triangular runner beans as well." The cheeky sod. You won't believe this Diary, but Trevor still gets a buzz out of inspecting the tomatoes on sale in Tesco's, and announcing to the world that the square ones still haven't come in yet... God, I must have been so naive.

May 21: Monday

Anthony left for school carrying a lot of useless advice from his family, with the pocket of his blazer stitched back into position, the best way I know how. (Mam had also run out of black cotton... Navy blue had to do.)

Trevor:	Don't forget son, get one in first. It only takes one good one, and you'll feel much better and they won't be bothering with you again.
Megan:	Computer Club, or no Computer Club, you should queue up for your dinner, like the rest of us.
Gary:	Instead of doing your homework tonight. Go out, and hang around the streets with the other kids.

But there was no need to worry. When Anthony came home he said the bullies had found somebody else to pick on. *'Somebody with pocket money.'* He added.

I finished reading William Harmon's book of the best 500 poems today. On reflection there was a lot that I liked, and a lot that I didn't, and many that I couldn't understand, but I enjoyed reading each and everyone of them all the same.

Top Poem: The Rime of the Ancient Mariner. by Samuel Taylor Coleridge... God knows, I'm been living that life, what with my mother and Trevor taking it in turns to play the Albatross around my neck.

May 22: Tuesday

Dear Wall, after collecting my family allowance, I read the first fifty pages of Shirley Valentine. I really do know how Shirley feels when she confides her innermost thoughts to you... You see, I've been banging my head against others of your kind for years... I'm with Shirley. A woman can only take so much.

Trevor collected my repeat Prozac prescription from the chemists, this afternoon.

May 23: Wednesday

From out of the blue, Dave Huws handed me a letter, containing the most incredible information anyone in my family had ever received in living memory.

LEWIS & HUDSON LTD
Unit 5, The Old Mine Ind Est
Merthyr Tydfil

Dear Mr G Evans.
On behalf of Lewis & Hudson LTD, I would like to offer you an interview at the company head office, on Friday May 25, at 10.30am for the position of trainee warehouse person.

Yours sincerely
Mr George Parker (Personnel Officer)

PS: Please be punctual. Our address is on the heading at the top of the page.

I can't believe it... A real offer of a job... Not a scheme, but a real job... I'm so excited I didn't know what to think, or what to do:

"Are you all right Rhian?" Dave asked me, after I'd read the letter.

"Y-y-yes f-f-ine." I stammered, fumbling the letter back inside it's envelope.

After that, my class passed me by in a whirl. My mind was so full of excitement, that whatever was said about 'Dr Johnson', was lost on me. Sitting at the back, I was grinning like a Cheshire cat. My ears heard additional names mentioned like Milton and Browning, but nothing to link them in between.

A cocktail fuelled by adrenaline, Prozac, my emotions, and the sound of Mr Davis's voice wishing us a good night, was enough to send me rushing out of the school gates, and in through my front door:

Me: (Screaming at top of my voice.) GARY, GARY, COME QUICK... TREVOR, TREVOR. GARY, GARY, TREVOR, TREVOR, YOU'LL NEVER BELIEVE WHAT'S HAPPENED TONIGHT.

Sitting around the television set, my family looked up in terror, as a screaming banshee burst into the room.

Trevor: (Jumping out of his chair.) What's the matter with you woman? You haven't been mugged or anything have you.

ME:	LOOK, LOOK. (I said, thrusting the letter, the greatest letter ever into my husband's hands.)
Trevor:	Bloody hell, I don't believe it. You can forget about applying for a job in McDonald's boy. Your mother's got you an interview for a job in a bloody cardboard factory.

Tossing the now crumpled communication into his son's lap, Gary finally got to read his extraordinary communication.

Me:	(Calmed down.) Isn't it wonderful news Gary?
Trevor:	Well, what have you got to say for yourself boy?
Gary:	Yeah... Great... Thanks Mam.

And that was that... We've got hope.

May 24: Thursday

"NEVER!... RHIAN, OUR GARY'S GOT AN INTERVIEW TOMORROW. WELL, WELL,WELL." Wiping her hands on the apron of her piny, Mam carried two freshly drained cups and saucers from the sink, and placed them on a tray on the kitchen table.

"Dave Huws, that man from over the road, got him an interview you say?... Well who would have thought it with his hair?... Then again who would have thought Dave Huws would have had a job in the first place?"

"Now Mam, let's not start all that again."

"Well, this is a turn-up for the books, Rhian." Mam said, but I could sense a big 'BUT' coming along at any moment. "But let's not get too carried away with your good news at this stage of the proceedings. After all Dave's only got our Gary an interview, and I think it's far too early for us to get carried away with it all at the moment... Never count your chickens before they are hatched."

No, No, No, I was not having this. For once, I was a bearer of wonderful news to my mother. How many times had I heard her complain: *'Rhian, why do you always bring your problems to me? Why can't you bring me some good news for a change?'* And here I was doing exactly that, and it still wasn't good enough... I spent the next two hours trying to prevent Mam from putting a damper on my family's future.

Me: But Mam, why would Dave Huws go to all that trouble of getting our Gary an interview, if he didn't think Gary would have a good chance of getting a job?

Mam: Rhian, is Dave Huws going to interview our Gary? Does Dave Huws have the final say, if our Gary gets the job or not?

Me: No, but he must have put a good word in for him.

Mam: Good word or not, I don't intend building my hopes up... I've learnt my lesson in the past with you!

Please God, if there's any justice left in the world, let the man from Lewis & Hudson say yes.

May 25: Friday

7.00am: Mam called round with my father's old suit tucked neatly over her arm. "Our Gary's about the same height and build as your Dad Rhian, so I've brought Sam's old suit for him to wear at his interview... You never know, it might bring him some luck."

Handing me the neatly folded, mothball infused, suit of clothing, Mam poured herself a cup of tea, and said: "I've been up all night washing and ironing Sam's best Sunday suit, ready for this morning. I knew it was too good to throw away that time, The Salvation Army left me a bag for all my unwanted clothing. Rhian, you can still feel the quality of the thread." She said, gesturing at me to feel one leg of the freshly pressed black pinstriped trousers.

"Please!" I begged, handing Gary his Grandfather's suit. "Please do this one thing for me... Please put it on, just to show your Gran how you look. Please Gary. For me. Please!"

Leaving the bedroom before Gary had a chance to change his mind, I waited nervously on the sofa for Gary to make his entrance: "Rhian, I thought your father had just walked into the room." Mam trilled, then burst into tears. "I can see him now, on that outing to Tenby. I was sitting on a bench looking out to sea, and he was crossing the road carrying an ice cream cone in each of his hands."

"Mam, I haven't got to wear this, have I." Gary pleaded, also looking as if he was about to burst into tears.

"If only I had saved some film in my camera." Mam sobbed, as Gary trudged back to his room.

9.00am: "It's a lovely suit Mam, but it doesn't suit our Gary I'm afraid." I'd tried my best, but Gary refused to attend his interview looking like a down and out who had just been handed a suit of new clothing at a refuge.

"Well, I don't know why I expected any different." Mam snapped, gently folding her husband's suit over her arm. "Whatever I try to do for this family, it always seems to get thrown back into my face... So what if it wasn't a perfect fit. All it needed was a belt to keep the trousers up, and Gary didn't have to button the jacket together if he didn't want to."

9.15am: Gary left for his interview wearing his new jeans, (Well they were new last Christmas.) white cotton T-shirt, trainers, and denim jacket. (I had also been up most of the night, making sure his clothes were clean.)

Trevor: (Before Gary had left the house.) Do your best boy. Nobody can expect anymore of you than that... I don't care who they are.

Anthony: (Before he left for school) You've got no chance, you loser.

Megan: (Before she went to school.) Mam, have you seen my bag anywhere?

Mam: (Before storming back to her own house in a huff.) Tell Gary I'll be thinking about him, and I'm sure his Granddad will still be at his side, if he wore his suit or not.

Me: Don't be late... Make sure you get there in plenty of time... It's better to be a little bit early, than a little bit late... Have you got the right money for the bus?... Remember, be polite, and don't forget that it's manners that make the man... Are you sure you don't want to go to the toilet before you go?...

Trevor: For God's sake woman, let the boy get on his way.

Me: Good luck son... Running to the front bedroom window, I watched Gary until he'd disappeared around the corner, on his way to the bus stop.

1.00pm: Trevor & Me: Well?

Gary: I got the job, and start next Tuesday, after the bank holiday.

12.00am: Dear Hiary I'm pissed... I'll well you all about it tomorrow... OUR GARY'S GOT A LOB!!!

May 26: Saturday

Dear Diary, I feel like death warmed up this morning. I've got a terrible hangover, my tongue and my throat feel like two very dry abrasives rubbing against each other, and if that wasn't bad enough two seconds after opening my eyes, I discovered I had become PMT active during the night.

Dear Diary, what a nightmare I found myself in this morning. Can you imagine trying to remove a soiled bed sheet from underneath your sleeping husband, while he's unconsciously hanging onto the sheet for dear life, like some demented paperclip? Anyway, to cut a long story short I removed it from underneath him, and got it into the washing machine before anyone had a chance of discovering the mess.

1.30pm: What a relief. Now that I'm totally alone, I can begin to make some sense of the past twenty-four hours.

THE SHORT VERSION:

1. My son has got a job.
2. We partied like it was 1999.

THE LONG VERSION: P:1 "TELL US WHAT HAPPENED?"

Trevor: Well, did you get it, or what?

Gary: They've given me a chance, and I start on Tuesday.

Me: (SCREAMING HYSTERICALLY.) YOU GOT IT?... YOU REALLY GOT IT?... I CAN'T BELIEVE IT... I DON'T KNOW WHAT TO SAY. YOU'VE GOT IT, YOU'VE REALLY GOT A JOB.

Gary: Yes.

Me: (STILL HYSTERICAL) AND IT IS A PROPER JOB ISN'T IT? IT'S NOT ONE OF THOSE GOVERNMENT SCHEMES?"

Gary: No, it's a proper job, all right.

Trevor: So what's the matter with you then soft lad? You're the first person from our branch of the family, who's not being employed or subsidised by the government... My God boy, you'll be buying your own house next.

At this point of the proceedings Gary informed us that he wasn't very happy with the working conditions he'd been asked to work under.

Gary: I'm on a month's trial. I'm not entitled to any paid holidays, or sick leave until I've been working there for three years. I'm starting on two pound an hour, which will be raised to two pound-fifty an hour if they decide to keep me on. I have to supply my own overall, and steel toe-cap boots... I can buy these from the work's stores, and the cost will be deducted from my wages each week. I start at eight each morning, and finish at five-thirty each evening. I get a fifteen minute tea-break in the morning, and a forty-five minute dinner break in the afternoon. I have to take my own flask of tea and sandwiches to work with me, but there is a canteen for us to eat them in, plus there's a man on the industrial estate who sells burgers, hot dogs, and things. Oh yes, and there's a free mini bus that picks me up in the morning, and drops me off at night.

Me: (Calmed down) We all have to start somewhere you see Gary. From little acorns.

Trevor: Say thank you to your mother boy... Go on, thank her for giving you this chance.

THE LONG STORY: P.2 THE PARTY

"I knew your Granddad wouldn't let you down." Mam said, kissing her eldest Grandson on his cheek. "I bet he was by your side all the way through that interview."

"I thought Granddad was dead." Anthony said, turning to me after catching the end of his Grandmother's sentence.

"He is love. I think your Gran was talking about his spirit being present at your brother's interview."

"Drink up working boy." Trevor said topping up his son's glass. "Come on, get this down your neck."

"Well Rhian." Mam said, siding up to me. "Perhaps it was a good thing our Gary didn't wear his Granddad's suit after all."... Apology number one.

"And maybe I was wrong, when I said attending evening class would be a waste of time."... Apology number two.

"And while I'm overjoyed with my Grandson's good fortune. I don't mind admitting that I was slightly wrong in my judgement of the Huws family."... Apology number three. But wait for it...

"But Rhian, even you've got to admit, it's a mistake anyone from my generation could have made."

"Can I have your attention." Trevor announced, clinking the side of his beer glass with a teaspoon. "Have everyone got a glass of the poison of their choice?... As you all know this is a very special day for our little tribe. After being on the dole for the best part of five months, my son and heir has become the first person to find himself a proper job, a job that is, that's got nothing to do with the government... Granted, he won't be able to be ill or to go on holiday for the next three years, but like his mother has already pointed out, he's got to start somewhere. And this sweat shop, come slave labour camp in Merthyr is as good a place as any to start... So I give you our Gary."

"SPEECH - SPEECH."

"I'd just like to thank my Mam, for giving me this opportunity. Gran for offering to lend me Granddad's old suit, and Dad for having total faith in me to succeed in the end... Thank you."

At this point, my mother and I were in floods of tears, and we started repeating things like: "I can remember when we used to push him around the estate in a pram", and "I don't know where all the years have flown too... It only seems like yesterday when..."

"I don't know." I heard Trevor say, nudging his son in the arm. "From druggy to a respectable working man, in a couple of weeks. I don't know the youth of today. Your mother and I didn't get up to any of that sort of malarkey when we were your age."

May 27: Sunday

A FAMILY'S DREAM
by
Rhian Evans

Out of darkness and into light.
A family dream bursts into life.
Was just a dream for sixteen years,
Now all at once begins to stir.
Escapes the cobwebs trapping light,
Fills dismal places, with hopeful sights.
I held this dream, on his day of birth,
My son may walk upon the earth.
That he would lead us all away,
To another zone, and a better life,
To better days, and to peaceful nights,
To heal the heartbreak, of our decay,
To chase our night time demons out,
A job, his career, will do the trick,
First step on the ladder, scale the tower of fame,
Our life for the better, will not be the same.

What a Bank Holiday weekend this is turning out to be, and it's not even raining.

May 28: Bank Holiday Monday

Me and my big mouth. A flash of lightning, brighter than a beam from a lighthouse, quickly followed by a crack of thunder, bullwhipped over our house at 2.30am this morning, and stubbornly remained for a further three hours, lighting up the estate and the surrounding hillside.

Normally I've been known to sleep through such storms, but this time... "This is so bloody typical of the weather that we have to put up with, blowing in from England." Trevor barked, as a shaft of light from another bolt of lightning dived through the gap in our curtains: "I bet those bloody English had their storm, at a bloody reasonable hour of the night... But not us, oh no." Fidgeting heavily onto his side, Trevor reached out for the bedside alarm clock, as another flash of lighting lit up, and illuminated the clock's hands, and dial. "Oh no, we get ours in the middle of the fucking night... The English bastards!"

Breakfast didn't start until 11.00am this morning, yet we still managed to resemble a family of zombies around the table. 'Uprooted trees, flash flooding when The River Severn broke its banks... Two inches of rain fell in three hours, a mini hurricane has spent the night zipping around the country ripping up roofs and fences... How did the weathermen get it wrong?... As Britain starts to clean up after a night of misery, we ask the question is this the first sign of global warming?... Also on the news: The Queen, is she value for money?... While in the Middle East..."

"Turn that bloody rubbish off." Trevor growled out his command at no one in particular, but demanded that somebody immediately switch the radio off. "Million pound computers my arse, I'll tell you the best way of finding out what the weather is going to do... Stick your head out of the bloody window, you lazy bugger." He screamed at the recently turned-off broadcaster.

After that the day went from bad to worse. I don't know how

I did it, but I managed to get Gary's clothes, and sandwiches ready for him in the morning... But we were all hit for six after our poor night's sleep, and one by one we all drifted to our beds for an early night.

May 29: Tuesday

7.00am: I peeped out of my bedroom window, in time to see Gary carrying his snap-tin and flask, make his way to call on Dave Huws who had kindly offered to walk with him to the bus stop... Please God, let Gary get on. Please God, let Gary like going to work to earn a living.

11.00am: Collected my family allowance, and started a seven hour vigil of looking at the clock while simultaneously worrying about Gary's first day on the job... I have no nails remaining on my fingers and toes.

5.45pm: Gary came home looking very embarrassed, and whispered something to Trevor about white spirit?

Me: Well, how did it go then?
Gary: All right.
Me: They didn't work you too hard on your first day did they?
Gary: It was all right.
Me: Did you like it?... Do you get on with the people you were working with?
Gary: They were all right.
Me: Come on Gary... Tell me what you did then.
Gary: You know. This and that... Things.
Me: Is it better than being on the dole?

Gary: A bit.
Me: Is it...
Trevor: For God's sake Rhian, leave the boy alone.

6.15pm: Trevor entered the kitchen laughing his head off. "Rhian, you should see the state of him out there." He said pointing at the shed. "Our Gary's been black balled."

"You, you, you, mean Gary's work-mates have sent him to Coventry, and want nothing more to do with him?" I stuttered.

"No, I mean they've painted our son's balls black." Trevor grinned.

"No, the poor dab... Does he want me to go out and help him to get it off?" (What am I saying?)

"Leave him. I've given him a bottle of turps and enough rags to do the job himself... It might sting a bit at first, but he'll be all right in the end... It's best if we leave him to it. He'll come in when he's ready."

"Well I think nobody should mention anything about it when he does." I begged, but my family were already in a high state of hysterics. "Come on now, you wouldn't like it if it happened to any of you." I protested. "Trevor promise me you won't say a word."

6.45pm: "How's it going black balls?" Trevor laughed, as his eldest son entered the room. "Did you get it all off, or would you like your mother to run you a bowl of warm water, so you can dunk your tackle into the bowl some more?"

11.00pm: "Trevor." I whispered, as I felt him still quivering with laughter in the bed. "That black paint they daubed on our Gary's privates. It won't stop him having children in later life, will it?... Trevor, will you please stop laughing. I'm trying to sleep"

May 30: Wednesday

Trevor said, while he and Gary were out in the shed. Gary had told him what his first day at work had been like: "Well, they put him on the brush, didn't they." Trevor remarked, as I watched him spread marmalade across his toast. "Of course they do that to all the young boys in those factories. On the brush, and making tea, that's all our Gary will be doing for the next six months. Then another new boy will start, and our Gary will be moved onto something else."

"And what about painting him down there." I enquired. "I suppose they do that to all the young boys as well."

"That, or shaving off his pubic hair." (An image I found disgusting at the breakfast table.) But saying that; with all the rubbing our Gary was doing in the shed, I bet he's already erased most of his pubic hair himself!"

Poor Gary, what was I thinking of sending him to work in a place like that. Gripping a tea-towel in my hand, I began to subconsciously wring the tightly twisted towelling material around my fist.

"I've heard some stories about the goings on in some of those factories." Trevor, laughed into his cereal bowl. "One bloke I know was made to walk home in the nac on his first day... I also know of a midget who'd been stapled to a side of a door with a nail gun... It's no different to when we were at school, and dunking the new boy's head down the toilet."

I looked at Trevor blankly: the tea-towel cutting off the circulation to my fingers.

"Of course you remember what happened at school Rhian... By the way, did Gary tell you they nicknamed him 'Sweep'?"

"Sweep?... Why?"

"Because he's on the brush silly... A brush in one hand, and a teapot in the other, and all for two pound an hour... It makes you feel so proud seeing your son getting on in the world, doesn't it love?"

WHAT HAVE I DONE TO MY ELDEST SON?... AM I A BAD MOTHER???

May 31: Thursday

Mam said: "They should all grow up, and act their age." After she'd found out what had happened to poor Gary on his first day. "I've got a good mind to have a word with the managing director." She said, handing me a bottle of calamine lotion; and without saying another word she mimed I was to give it to Gary to dab on his nether regions.

"It will help to make him feel a little more comfortable." She inferred, after a shared moment of embarrassed silence. "You know, down there, on his private parts... Calamine is very cooling for that sort of thing."

I can't get the image of Gary sweeping the factory, and making all those mugs of tea from out of my mind.

1. Gary doesn't drink tea, and has never brewed a pot in his life.
2. I have never known Gary to pick up a sweeping brush in his life either... What will happen if his boss finds any dust under the machines?... I wish I'd taught Gary more

about housework, while he was growing up. I'm fantasying about asking my mother to help me break into the factory at midnight, to do a bit of spring cleaning before the workers return to work in the morning.

Why do I feel so guilty when all Trevor ever does is grin quite contentedly in his chair???

"Of course Gary knows how to use a sweeping-brush." Trevor laughed, rocking himself back and fore on the sofa. "He's watched you use one often enough hasn't he, to figure out what he has to do for himself?"

REVIEW OF THE MONTH:

GOOD 1. GARY HAS GOT A JOB.

BAD
1. Mary Jackson has joined my evening class.
2. Mr Davis didn't like my poem.
3. My eldest son works in a sweatshop armed with a teapot and brush.
4. Gary started to smoke pot... But he give it up after a few puffs, which is good.
5. Anthony was bullied at school... But isn't now, which is also good.
6. Nobody likes us in Europe, i.e. Eurovision Song Contest.

All in all I would say this has been an indifferent month.

June 1: Friday

Well Diary, we've reached the midway point of the year. (Does this mean you are middle aged?) This morning, after 'Kilroy' and his audience had finished discussing 'Why Does My Husband Need To Have Sex With Other Women', I turned the volume of the television set down, and browsed through your pages.

My first thoughts were: a lot seems to have happened during the first five months, yet why do I feel as if I've spent most of it sitting in this house?

My second thought was: am I writing you correctly?... Are there any diary rules I don't know about, but should be following?... Do other diarists describe their lives in this manner?... Must remember to look out for secondhand editions of 'Adrian Mole', 'Bridget Jones', 'Samuel Pyps' and 'Hitler' in the charity shop.

Naively I hoped that we would be the forgotten people. Buried away in this valley, I thought the mountains on either side would protect us from the invasion that was about engulf us... Sadly it hasn't!

8.00am: The first General Election junk mail was forced through my letterbox... Tony Blair's face was grinning up at me, from my doormat. Ten seconds later he was staring up at me from the bottom of my kitchen pedal-bin.

4.30pm: At first I thought it was another joy-rider driving around the estate, with his music blaring at full volume. But as it drew nearer I began to make out the distinctive crackle of a hand held megaphone, controlled by a party fanatic urging me to vote for the Liberal party.

"NOISY BASTARDS!" Trevor complained, as the din from the megaphone drowned out an interesting piece of dialogue from the 'Tellytubbies' as it drove past. "That's bloody typical that is. You don't hear a peep out of the buggers for four years, and then they're all over you like a rash."

"Who are you going to vote for Dad?" Anthony asked, wondering if his father had any strong political leanings, or indeed any political opinions at all.

"Me and your mother don't vote son." Trevor answered, without turning his head away from the television screen. "We learnt our lesson a long time ago boy... You see, for people like us it doesn't really matter who gets in, because they are all the same. And as long as I get my Giro every fortnight, I couldn't give a damn which of the three main political parties sends it to me?"

"So you and Mam are both members of the Apathy party, then?" Anthony responded.

"Boy, your mother and I were life members before you or that what-you-ma-call-it party were invented." Trevor roared, clearly happy with his response. "Your mother and I have always been trend setters son."

"Well, I'm going to vote for Plaid Cymru when I'm old enough." Megan suddenly announced.

"Since when have you been interested in politics?" Trevor questioned, shaking his head at his daughter in disbelief. "I thought we brought you up better than that."

“Oh, don’t worry Dad. She only saying it because her friends said they were going to vote for them when they are old enough.” Anthony retorted, dumping his sister’s political aspirations in the bin.

“You listen to your old man.” Trevor said, turning to face his daughter. “The less you have to do with liars like Blair and that crowd, the happier your life will be... Go on, ask your mother if you don’t believe me.”

Thank you Trevor I thought, as the eyes in the room fell upon me. “Well, your father’s right.” (For once) I agreed, as Trevor smiling and nodding his head, turned away to continue concentrating on the television screen. “For people like us it really doesn’t matter who gets in. Because after the election is over, we’ll be still living here, they’ll be still living there, and never the twain shall meet.”... So ended the political lesson for the day.

June 2: Saturday

Woke up this morning and found William Hague and Charles Kennedy grinning up at me from my doormat. I quickly introduced them both to Mr Blair in the pedal-bin.

Across the road the Lloyd’s have a collection Labour, Liberal and Plaid Cymru Party posters neatly arranged in their front windows. (Not even the Lloyd’s would dare to display a Conservative Party poster, for fear of half an house brick visiting during the night, via the front window.) “That’s what comes of allowing free speech in the house.” Trevor observed, before sitting down to compile his ITV Seven, horse racing accumulator, *or* whatever the bet is called today upon the coffee-table.

3.00pm: The BBC2 Saturday matinee starred Burt Lancaster

> and his little mute, deaf and dumb friend, Nick Cravat in 'The Crimson Pirate'. The film was marred when the Labour and Conservative motor cavalcade, complete with identical crackling megaphones, drowned out the sound of the film in turn, as they slowly drove passed my house.

"crackle... KEEP THE TORIES... crackle... OUT... crackle... Tony, TONY... crackle... IS OUR MAN... crackle-screech... IF HE CAN'T... screech-crackle-screech... NO ONE CAN."

"FUCK OFF YOU NOISY BASTARDS!!!... I'M TRYING TO WATCH A FUCKING FILM."

"William Hague... screech-crackle-screech-screech-crackle... Sorry about that, I've got the sound turned down too low... TESTING - ONE TWO, TESTING... crackle... crackle... crack, SORRY ABOUT THAT... squeak... AS I WAS SAYING. WILLIAM HAGUE IS THE MAN TO HELP YOU... screech-screech-screech..."

Where is the natural justice in the world? How would Blair and Hague like it if I made a noise outside of their homes on a peaceful Saturday afternoon?... All I want to do is to watch a film!

SUGGESTIONS FOR PUBLIC MEETING OF COUNCIL TENNENTS:

1. Barricade all entrances leading into estate.
2. Entrance into estate only allowed to occupants. (Including family and friends who don't live here.)
3. Also buses, taxi's, white van men delivering things, (IE, from the catalogue.) Postmen, (Delivering benefit etc.)

4. Make it legal for children to throw stones at any form of transport with a megaphone secured to a roof-rack.
5. Also at people wearing political rosettes, and dressed in designer suits. (Just to be on the safe side.)
6. People carrying clipboards... People who stop fellow estate dwellers, to ask who they are voting for. Any stranger who knocks on more than one door in the street per visit.

June 3: Sunday

Trevor came home in an highly sexed state of arousal last night. He claimed to have spent most of the day debating the sex lives of this country's politicians, with a knowledgeable posse of drunken friends, down at the rugby club.

TOPICS DEBATED BY TREVOR AND FELLOW DRUNKS:

1. Would any attractive, intelligent, self-respecting Welsh woman agree to marry William Hague, if he lived on this estate and was not leader of the Conservative Party?
2. Charles Kennedy, is he: 1. Gay? 2. Married? 3. Both? 4. Living in sin? 5. Has he got a girl/boyfriend? 6. Does anybody care? 7. When he was younger, did he used to be Jeremy Thorpe's favourite rent boy?
3. The Blair's: 1. Who wears the trousers in that family? 2. Do they both take it in turns? Trevor believes it's option two, because he can see Cherie dragging Tony through the Court Of Human Rights, if he doesn't give into at least 75% of her sexual demands... Trevor also mentioned something about him and his mates believing Cherie uses a strap-on during her more intimate moments with the Prime Minister, but I've no desire to say any more about that!

Sunday the Sabbath, a day of rest. Not even the politicians would be so ignorant as to call round and spoil our piece and quite on a Sabbath afternoon... But then again why should they, when they've got my mother to do their dirty work for them: "Rhian, you won't forget to vote on Thursday, will you love?"

"Mam's not voting this year Gran." Megan announced... Her work done, quickly retreated to the sanctuary of her bedroom.

"Not voting! It's because of people like you, we all had to put up with Thatcher for all those years." Taking off her coat, Mam settled herself down in the chair. (I took this to be a bad omen.)

"Mam, you know Trevor and I never vote." I said, stating my position as firmly as I could.

"And look where its got you."

"What does that mean, 'Look Where Its Got You?' (God, you must help me break this annoying bunny rabbit habit, my twitching fingers have developed recently.) "Do you really expect me to believe that scratching an X in a box on a little scrap of paper, and posting it into a ballet box, would have helped my family to move away from this estate?"

"Well maybe not away from, but it might have helped you to feel more a part of the community... Gave you more of an interest, and a chance to take more of a part in things and all."

"Community!" (God, I'm doing it again.) "Why should I want to feel more of a part of this rat hole, when all I ever dream about, is getting away from here as soon as possible."

"Well perhaps you want to get away from me as well?" Mam said, rising to get her coat.

"Now you know I didn't mean that."

"Well I'm sorry Rhian,I really am. I'm really sorry your

father wasn't a multimillionaire." Mam had already fastened her first button of her coat. "Perhaps we should have waited until we could have afforded to have you." The second button fastened shut. "I'm truly sorry you had to put up with me and not a nanny , to bring you up." Through gritted teeth I watched her fat fingers feed the third button, through its eyelet. "But most of all I'm sorry your father and I forced you to live in this squalor." Checking herself to see she was all buttoned up, Mam picked up her handbag. "Remember Rhian, people died to give you the vote. But if that's not good enough for you... After all, nothing I did seems to be." My back door slammed shut. (I have to be so careful what I say in this family... It's like walking on egg shells 24 hours a day.)

Thinking about the sex lives of our politicians has got me in the mood... Tonight Matthew I'm going to be Ffion Hague.

June 4: Monday

It was the turn of Plaid Cymru's Ieuan Wyn Jones to wish me a good morning, this morning. (Or 'Bore Da' as we say in Welsh.) Like his political cohorts before him, Ieuan soon found himself joining the political debate in the pedal-bin... My bin is now the proud owner of a full set of political party literature. Armed with the knowledge gained from the various party manifestos, and containing my and Trevor's torn in half polling cards. I have great confidence the bin will come to the correct conclusion, and remain standing next to the cupboard under my sink.

June 5: Tuesday

Two days before the General Election: After collecting my family allowance, I gave up the will to live... Knocking upon my door, and accosting me in the street, outside of the Post Office and charity shop... God, why wont this deluded, mutant race of clipboard carrying disciples, leave me alone to get on with my own life in peace?

June 6: Wednesday

General Election Eve: Please refer to previous statement.

A zombie like trance took over my central nervous system, prohibiting me from attending tonight's evening class... Fucking Election!!!

June 7: General Election Thursday

8.00am: Well it's started already... I turned the television on.

BBC: "Voting has got off to a slow start, but all parties have issued a statement stating, they expect to see the volume pickup throughout the day." Click.

ITV: "Sir, can I ask you why you voted?" (Man in grey mac: "Because I heard there was a £1,000 pound fine if you didn't.") I think you may have got that mixed up with the census." Click.

C4: "On the Big Breakfast this morning we'd like you to vote on which one of these politicians has got the biggest tits? Is it A. Ann Widdecombe. B. John Pres...". Click.

C5: (Picture out of focus) "Here is the Channel Five news. Britain is in the grip of election fever." Click... Television Off.

Radio: "Voting is reported to be slow throughout Wales, but the..." AAHH!

9.00am: Two at school, one at work, one in bed, my mother in her own house, I popped a Prozac and hoped for the best.

9.05am: "CRACKLE... THE POLLS ARE... screech-crackle... NOW OPEN... screech... COME AND HAVE YOUR SAY... crackle-screech-crackle... AT THE OLD PEOPLE'S CENTRE..."

"SHUT-UP YOU NOISY BASTARD." I heard Trevor scream out of the bedroom window. "SOME OF US ARE TRYING TO GET SOME SHUT-EYE UP HERE."

3.00pm: The cease-fire was over. At half hourly intervals, for the next two hours:

Lab: (Knock on Door) On behalf of the Labour party, I would like to remind you the polls are open, and will remain open until 10.00pm.

Trevor: (Re-enters living-room after answering the door.) If that woman had been a man I would have told him to fuck off!

Con: (Knock on Door) Oh, hello little girl. Is your mother or Father in?

Megan: No!

Lib: (Knock on Door) Hi, I wonder, if it's possible to speak to either Mr or, (He looked down at his clip-board.) Mrs Evans, please?

Anthony: I'm sorry to say both my parents refuse to vote on principle. I know it's a waste of a vote and all that, but there it is. I on the other hand fully intend to use my vote when I come of age but that's not for a few years yet.

When I vote I intend to make my vote count, by voting for a party that can actually do something to change the world. Tell me, what do you think about the May Day Riots?

Lib: Well, well, I...

Anthony: Exactly. You Liberal Democrats don't know much about anything do you? Goodbye. (Slams door shut.)

Trevor: That's my boy.

P/Cymru: (Knock on door) Mrs Evans I presume?... Mrs Rhian Evans?

Me: Yes.

P/Cymru: Come and make your mark Mrs Evans... Wales needs women like you to stand up for her, in her hour of need.

Trevor: (Barging past me.) When are you going to declare war on England then?

P/Cymru: Well, that's not in our manifesto as yet, Mr Evans. (Then in a sarcastic tone.) We leave that sort of thing up to Cardiff City supporters, when their team plays away.

Trevor: Well when you do declare war on England, maybe then we'll come and vote for you. (Door slammed shut again.) The cheeky git.

8.00pm: Things must be starting to get desperate down at the polling station. Party vehicles, customised with megaphones, are perpetually cruising around the estate, hoping to tempt the infirm and the naive out of their homes.

Trevor: Apart from the old people who always vote. I think the apathy vote amongst the young will be about 100% on this estate.

Popping out for a pint of milk. Trevor came back with tales of people's homes being ransacked on the eastern side of the estate. "Gangs of youths are following behind the party vehicles as they arrive to give the elderly a lift to the polling station. I've heard some of the electorate are complaining about being too frightened to go out and vote, just in case their homes are broken into before they return... "It's a crying shame isn't it Rhian." Trevor said, placing the carton of milk into the fridge. "We don't vote because we don't want to. But I feel very strongly that everyone should still have the choice to vote, if they want to or not."

10.00pm: The polls have closed, thank God for that... Now it's all over, perhaps everyone will leave us to live our lives in peace for another four years... So why am I feeling guilty???

HOPES FOR THE NEXT FOUR YEARS:

1. To be left alone.
2. To be a poet.
3. To be happy.
4. No longer need to take Prozac.

June 8: Friday

Experienced a very strange dream last night. Tony Blair, in the guise of a tomato kept insisting that he really cared. William Hague, togged up to the nines as a packet of pork scratching insisted; he was a bloody good laugh. While poor old Charles Kennedy said nothing, but wandered lonely as a cloud through a field of golden daffodils. Then out of the darkness I heard this voice: *'Wales needs women like you, you, YOU!'*... I think I'll vote for Plaid Cymru in the next election.

"You'll never guess what?" Anne gushed, during our free bus ride to Tesco's. "Dave and I have been invited to a barbecue."

"Have you?" I innocently remarked.

"Mary's invited the whole evening class around tomorrow night."

"When did this happen?"

"During last Wednesday's discussion. She said she was going to ask you and Trevor, but as you weren't feeling up to attending class, she felt you wouldn't feel up to attending her barbecue either... She said, it was probably something to do with your nerves."

Bloody cheek! If I had been feeling well enough to attend class last Wednesday night, there would have been no barbecue invitations issued to anybody... I'm the last person Mary wants rummaging through her private property.

"So how is Rhian feeling?" Anne said changing the subject. "Were you feeling well enough to go out and vote yesterday?" I shock my head. "Never mind, it's not as if our votes counted in any case. Labour always get in, in this area. Dave says, they could stick a Labour rosette on a dead donkey's bum, and the people around here would still vote it in.

Dave and I voted Plaid Cymru... Mr Davis during last Wednesday's class called for a snap poll, and we all voted for Plaid Cymru, except for Mary who voted for the Conservatives."

I don't care what Trevor says, I am definitely going to vote for Plaid Cymru at the next election...

Oh yes, before I forget. Tony Blair's Labour Party won the 2001 General Election by an overall majority of... Well, it was a lot anyway?... I can't believe John Prescott hasn't resigned after punching that mullet haired farmer, who threw an egg in his face... Mam calls him a lout and a big fat toad... She told me she can picture Prescott in her mind's eye, sitting on a lilly pad catching flies in his mouth... Trevor thinks Prescott's a classic example of why we shouldn't vote... "Rhian, would you buy a second-hand car off that fat git?... Neither would I."

June 9: Saturday

"Oh it's you Rhian, is it? I suppose you'd better come in then."

"Look Mam, you know I didn't mean any of those things you accused me of thinking the other day." I apologised, handing my mother a box of 'After Eight' mints.

"Oh it's not you Rhian, it's your father you see. He was a big one for the vote was your father. He was a big believer in a show of hands, and I know he would have been disappointed by your attitude in refusing to vote, if he had been alive today."

"Look Mam, will it make you feel any better if I promise to

vote next time." I said, as she reached for an hanky. "I suppose you voted for Labour again, did you?"

"Of course I did."

"Why?"

"Because of your father silly. Sam was a big Labour man, and a lifelong member of the union and everything. When I go to vote, I cast my vote for him more than anything else, and that's why I keep going on at you. Who's going to vote for your father when I'm not here to do it for him?"

So there you have it diary. It's got nothing to do with polices, manifestos, objectives, schools, policing, pensions, Hague, Blair, Kennedy, Ieuan Wyn Jones, or Uncle Tom Cobleigh and all. As far as my mother is concerned, my father was a member of the Labour Party during the fifties and early sixties, and what was good enough for him then, is good enough for her today... I haven't got the heart to tell her that Daddy will be voting Plaid Cymru at the next election. This is one secret that shall remain between me and the ballet box.

June 10: Sunday

I worked myself into a frenzy today. I must build up my strength, I must start to believe in myself. *'Wales needs women like you!'* That's what the Plaid Cymru canvasser said. I must have confidence in my work. I'm going to take the bull be the horns, and send my poem to the magazine:

Dear Editor.

After reading about the plight of Mrs Nelly Bates, in an article entitled 'Home Alone'- It's not only children who are left to fend for themselves.' I was moved to pen you this verse.

In my poem 'The Pensioner' I tried to imagine how I would feel if I found myself under similar circumstances to that of Mrs Bates.

Yours sincerely,
Rhian Evans

PS: Please could you send my poem back to me if you don't like it... Thank you.

If 'The Pensioner' gets published it will be one the in the eye for all at evening class... Mr Davis can't be right all the time.

June 11: Monday

I got up early to call Gary for work:

Gary:	I'm not going in today Mam.
Me:	Why not... You're not feeling ill are you?
Gary:	No. I'm going to sign-on with Dad today. I told them at work, that I've got to go to the dentist.
Me:	But you've got a job now Gary, you can't sign-on.
Gary:	I know that, but they're only paying me two pound an hour. And anyway, I've got to pay you and Dad rent... Mam, if I don't sign-on, it won't be worth me going to work.
Trevor:	What's going on?

Me: Your son says he's still going to sign-on with you this morning.

Trevor: Is that all?

Me: What do you mean, is that all?... Don't you think that, that is enough?

Trevor: Everybody's doing it Rhian. I'd be doing it too, if I had a job... Listen, Lewis & Hudson are ripping our Gary off by paying him slave wages. Our Gary is ripping the Government off because he can't afford to live on what he's being paid. Rhian, our son through no fault of his own is not earning a living wage. It's catch 22. It's a vicious circle love, that's all.

And with that they both went back to sleep, issuing a request for me to give them a wake-up call later in the day... What does Gary mean he can't live on his wages? I pondered at the breakfast table. Until Lewis & Hudson had offered him full-time employment. Gary had been living on ten pounds a week pocket money, for the past six months!"

Making sure no one was looking. I kissed the envelope containing my poem, before posting it in the pillar box. (Please God, let me receive a result.)

June 12: Tuesday

5.30am: I sat bolt upright in my bed and shouted, "MINIMUM WAGE!"

"You what, what's wrong with you?" A startled Trevor

inquired, then realising the house wasn't on fire, slumped back down on his pillow.

"What about the minimum wage. Isn't it illegal or something if Gary isn't earning over three pound an hour?"

"It's five-thirty in the bloody morning mun. Can't this wait until the morning?" Trevor sleepily stated, picking-up and adjusting the distance he held the clock from his out of focus eyes.

"Well, is it or isn't it?" I insisted, elbowing my semi-conscious husband in his back.

"Yes... No... Maybe, I don't know Rhian mun. Not now, not like this, not at this time of the day."

10.00am: Trevor had just entered the living-room. "Well, am I right?... Are Gary's bosses ripping him off, or what?"

"Of course they bloody are." Trevor replied in his bear like growl. "And there's nothing he can do about it." Two mugs of tea, and a bowl of cereal later, Trevor was in better spirits. "Our Gary had two options when he was offered the job... Take it or leave it. One, take the job and graft away for a lousy two pounds an hour. Or two, leave it and walk away. No ifs no buts, that's it, and that's all there is to it."

"But what about the minimum wage Trevor?"

"What about it?... Haven't you got to be eighteen, twenty-one, or something before you can qualify?... And in any case, what's the minimum wage got to do with it? Don't get me wrong Rhian, it may work in places like London with 100% employment, but here. Come on love, you and I both know people on this estate who would work for a lot less than what our Gary is getting."... And the sad point is, I knew Trevor was right.

June 13: Wednesday

Thank God I had my wits about me this morning.

"I thought your Gary had found himself a job?" Mr Baker in the Post Office inquired, as I handed him Gary's unemployment benefit Giro.

"Yes he has." I admitted. "But he has to work a month in hand, so the DSS have agreed to pay him his benefit until he receives his first week's wages." That's the trouble with living in a small community, everyone knows your business... I think I got away with it?

I told Trevor what had happened when I came home, and he said Gary would have to change the Post Office where he cashed his giro in the future. "Our boy is going to have to tell the DSS he wants to cash his Giro in Cardiff." Trevor said, after he'd thought the problem through. "Then you can cash it for him, when you do the shopping." Trevor also said something about not shitting on your own doorstep, but I didn't question him about it any further.

Needless to say Gary accepted his father's helpful advice when he came home. "Good thinking,Batman." He said, understanding his father's plan. "Well done Mam." I was also congratulated for my quick thinking... Am I the only one who thinks we're treading a dangerous path?... What will happen if the DSS or my mother find out we are defrauding the system?

June 14: Thursday

Today was one of those days, where you take stock of your life, and if you are me, you burst into tears.

It's June - Six months into the year - I've only had ONE NIGHT out, (Not including evening classes.) and I feel like Mrs

Bates the lady in my poem, and if that wasn't bad enough my eldest son is about to enter into the world of benefit fraud... If Gary gets caught, what effect will it have on Trevor's claim?... Will we be charged with aiding and abetting?... Will our Anthony be taken into care by the social services?

After taking stock, I've decided to take control of my life beginning on Monday the 18th, because I think Monday is the best day to start anything new, including changing my life.

June 15: Friday Gary's Birthday

After handing Gary his birthday card, I said: "Your father and I have agreed to cover the cost for all the protective clothing you need for work, as a birthday present." (Total cost £50... Deducted at £5 p/w from Gary's wages.)

Trevor and I both thought Gary was delighted with his present, but I didn't think Trevor was entirely correct when he said it was traditional for all factory workers to take a day off on their birthdays to buy their father a pint... Not when this worker had just started a new job, and was on a month's trial.

"Seventeen Rhian." Mam said, handing her eldest Grandson his card and present. "Well, I don't know where all the years have gone to, I really don't... Seventeen, an handsome young man with a job to go to each morning. Upon my soul there's plenty living on this estate who wish they could step into Gary's shoes, Rhian. Before you know it he'll be getting married, and raising a family of his own."

'Or in court accused of benefit fraud.' I thought to myself, not daring to breathe a word.

11.00pm: Trevor has just informed me Gary has made a new arrangement with the DSS, and will be cashing his Giro at the main post office in Cardiff from now on.

June 16: Saturday

Dear Diary, in order to take control of my life, I feel the need to come clean, and get one or two little things off my chest.

DRINKING: The truth about my drinking is I love it... Or should that be, I used to love it?... Or maybe, I still love it but I don't dabble with it anymore... Okay, I got pissed when Gary got his job, and on the night I went out with Trevor... Well anyway, I was never what you call a Chablis, or a Champagne drinker. Tall stem wine glasses or flutes were not for me... I was... I saw myself has more of a can drinker actually. For me a good vintage was measured purely on the high alcohol content number, printed in a corner of the label.

Was I a social drinker?... I suppose it started out that way, having a drink with friends, but that soon stopped when I developed a taste. Dear Diary, all this happened in the days before, and just after I'd discovered Prozac. A time before my children were born... Or if I'm being totally honest, when my children were very young... Gary was about five... I pray he and Megan remember nothing of that time... Thunderbird wine numbs the brain, and mixed with Prozac... At least I did know what I'd been doing, (Sometimes) where I'd been going to, and with whom.

'Rhian was a very naughty girl in those days, weren't you love?... Well at least until I had my little scare.' You see how I talk down to myself Diary... You've never heard me chastise myself have you?... When I turn on myself... Enough! Allow me to return to the point... Dear Diary, the person you see before you today, is most certainly not the person I was then... Okay! Here it is. My story in all it's grisly detail.

Pissed out of my head, I agreed to go for a ride in this bloke's car... Are you getting the picture?... I know what you're thinking... Only there wasn't just one bloke... Is the picture I'm painting becoming any clearer for you?... It could have turned nasty but it didn't. Trevor, (My white knight) dragged me from the back-seat... But the point is, this sort of thing happened on more than one occasion, and although I can understand how stupidly I acted then, it doesn't stop the shame and embarrassment of my past actions from returning to haunt me today.

Take my only night out this year for example. I still ended up getting pissed, (After promising myself I wouldn't.) and begging Trevor to bonk me... For heaven's sake have I learned nothing?... I stay at home for my own safety, because I'm weak, and this is one of the reasons way I need my poems to come through for me... If I'm a published poet, my self-esteem will grow strong, and I will be able to bask in self-confidence and pride.

So how did I move from Thunderbird to Prozac?... Well Diary, I feel I know you well enough to let you in on a little secret... I give the drink up just like that, and my nervous system fell flat on its face like a pancake. Yes, I saw and understood everything Trevor and my mother were trying to tell me, and just like that... Before I made the decision to quit alcohol my mother begged me to stop drinking. "The shame... The shame you are bringing down on me, the children, all of us, yourself, the family name... The darling little things, having to witness their mother letting herself fall into an alcoholic stupor." If I close my eyes very tight... To this day I can still hear my mother's words rattling about inside my head.

With a snap of my fingers, I gave up the booze (and fags) for my family... Mam would also say: "If you won't do it for yourself, do it for your children, Rhian." As I tried to sober myself up in the morning. "You're lucky you've got Trevor my girl. You're lucky he still cares about you after all the trouble you put him through... I know plenty of men who would have walked away for far less."

So I did... I give it up just like that... I made up my mind and I stuck to my guns, and my mind took over... Demons filled my head, and I could no longer get out of bed... I felt sad, I thought I was going mad, my mind was acting strange, I was feeling hellish strange. The world looked different somehow?... Unbalanced? My universe, and everything in it seemed out of kilter. I no longer recognise the person I'd become... And at this point, or close to it, I was introduced to Prozac, and we have been getting on like a house on fire ever since.

MY LIFE TO DATE:

1. Childhood = Happy.
2. Teenager = Happy Mostly.
3. Young Mother = Drunk.
4. Middle age = Confused / Tolerable With Prozac - Unbearable Without.
5. Am I Happy? = How The Hell Should I Know?

June 17: Sunday Father's Day

Dear Diary, seeing that this is a weekend of confessions, let's talk about my cellulite. Picture this: There I was sitting on the sofa, with a mind full of personal demons battling with the calming effects of my Prozac. When low and behold on the health pages of 'The Sun' newspaper what do I see: *'Cellulite - A new form of disfigurement.'* The article went on to say bathing beauties all around the country, were too embarrassed to be seen in bikini's, because of these mysterious blotchy, come pimple like embellishments that have mysteriously appeared on their thighs.

Now on the face of it, I agree with you. It's oh so trivial, but that doesn't take into account the mixed-up state of my mind at the time. Running to the bedroom, I laid the paper's diagram on the bed, and with the aid of an hand mirror I examined myself for the corresponding marks. *'I've got it!'* I cried, *'I've got Cellulite!'* I screamed devouring every piece of information over and over again, in my eagerness to discover if it was life threatening.

'I've got it, I've got it.' I kept repeating over and over again. Thank goodness everyone was out at the time, because I dread to think what they'd have thought, if they'd discovered me rolling around on the bed with my jeans around my ankles. But as they say, time is the great healer and things did get better... Well that is to say, I became calmer, the Prozac helped me to relax; it diminished my stress, and the tension my stress levels caused to my family inside the house... Believe it or not I became so relaxed, that I actually began to laugh when the final reminders popped through the letterbox. For the first time in my married life I began to understand what Trevor had been trying to explain to me for all those years: *'What can the*

bastards do to us if we don't pay Rhian?... Oh yes they can cut our gas and electricity off, but apart from that what can they actually do? Take us to court?... So what!... So take us to court then... We're unemployed mate... Okay, you'll get your money in the end, but you'll have to wait for it. We can only afford to pay fifty pence per week... Fuck you!'

I'm going to make a pot of tea... I'll be back in a bit.

Sorry about that Diary. Sorry about my little rant. Now getting back to my cellulite: I've learned to live with it, but I can't bring myself to look at it. I even feel uncomfortable touching it when I'm in the bath. (We've no shower.) On bad days, I bathe with the bathroom light off. Maybe it's because I discovered cellulite during a time when I was feeling at my lowest... I don't know. Maybe my mind wasn't functioning as it should have been at the time. But whatever the reason... To this day I can never bring myself to go out of the house unless I'm wearing leggings, a pair of jeans, or trousers of some kind.

Father's Day: Trevor roused himself from his bed, then came down and opened his single card that I had bought, and made the children sign. After reading the sentiment, Trevor placed the card on top of the mantelpiece, thanked everyone, then threw the crumpled-up envelope into the wastepaper bin... So ended Father's Day for another year... Happy Father's Day Trevor.

June 18: Monday

8.00am: Today is the day I take control of my life. Today is the first day of the rest of my life, and to mark it as such, I have decided to do something out of the blue. Something that I wouldn't have dreamt of doing last week, last month, or last year... I have decided to get fit. I have decided to get fit in the open air. I have decided to go for a walk right away around the Lloyd George council estate on my own.

12.00pm: I've been very lucky with the weather this morning. The sun was shining, and a light cooling breeze blew down the valley as I began my walk. It is true what they say, the simple things in life are free, and I couldn't believe how good my little walk made me feel, as I strolled around the estate in the summer sunshine.

Dear Diary, I've lived on this estate all my life. As I passed each house on a route that took me down streets I hadn't walked along in years, the memories came flooding back. I began to remember who lived here and there. (Some still do.) There are parts of this estate that I haven't set foot in since I was at school. Trees I used to climb. The children's play area my children used to visit, (Maybe they still do?) with rusting roundabout and slide.

The eastern side of the estate looks dead common if you ask me. Talk about rough. I counted two burned-out cars waiting to be towed away, while I watched a scrap metal dealer operate a lifting mechanism that raised the fourth of a job lot of seven abandoned vehicles off the ground. I also saw a further three burned-out wrecks abandoned on a patch of waste scrubland bordering the rugby ground, (Thank God I live on the west side.) and if that wasn't bad enough, it seemed to me that every property I passed had an old car in bits parked outside, half on and half off of the pavement.

QUESTIONS THAT I NEED ANSWERING:

1. Do joy-riders steal cars for their parts?
2. What are the chances of any of these cars passing the MOT?
3. Can anyone living in this part of the estate afford to pay for a MOT certificate?
4. If so can they afford road tax?
5. Apart from sentimental value, why would anyone want to repair an Hillman Imp?
6. What are the chances of a joy-rider stealing an Hillman Imp?
7. Will parts from a Golf GTI fit into a Hillman Imp?

Returning home I soon discovered my walk had done me some good. The backs of my legs began to ache gently, (There's no gain without pain.) and I discovered a healthy rosy glow to my complexion when I looked at myself in the mirror.

TAKING CONTROL
by
Rhian Evans

1.
Free from the confines of the wall.
Outside the boundary of the gate.
Standing alone with no place left to hide.
Taking control of my life and loves.
What's done is past.
Hesitancy, has got a grip.
Then quickly brushed aside.
I am the ruler, I rule my mind.
Please don't criticise.
Right or wrong, I face my fate.

2.
Who can say they tread the righteous path?
Who can say they escaped the sentence passed?
Who can say they have stepped out of the light?
Not scraped, not scratched, no mark of any kind.
To the body or to the mind.
Like a phoenix, born of a broken dream,
I rise to retake my family seat,
Make the tempest show it's face again.
Let our dance complete.

Next time I decide to go for a walk, I'll think I'll give the eastern side of the estate a miss.

June 19: Tuesday

THE GOOD: I feel as if a spark has been ignited inside me. I'm full of pent-up emotion, and feel as if I want to burst out of myself from my inside... I feel great... I am at one with the world. I want to be a poet... My God, do I want to be a poet... Lord, please let me be a poet.

THE BAD: Megan ended her academic career at the local Comprehensive School on June the fifth and I've failed to mention/write anything about it in my diary... Does this prove once and for all, that I care more for my two boys than I do for my only girl?

Dear Diary, I woke up this morning in a wonderful mood, full of the joys of Spring, (Or early summer.) and then it hit me... 'Bloody Hell' I thought I haven't written so much as a dicky bird about our Megan's decision to leave school.
The school broke up for a week, last bank holiday... I'm still not sure if this was 'Whit Monday' or not... Okay, I can hear what you're saying. Why didn't I write about any of this either?... But you have to remember there was a lot going on, and I couldn't fit it all in... Okay, okay, I know it's a lame excuse... Okay, I admit it... I'm a bad mother. I'm a selfish person. I thought about myself, before I considered the feelings of my daughter... Of course it fucking was... Of course it was fucking important. Megan left school without any qualifications, for Christ sake. But that wasn't all my fault... Honest to fucking God, it wasn't... I did try to warn her, but would she listen to my advice... NO!... I tried, Trevor tried, so did my mother, who said: *'You sit your exams my girl. Do you want to end up like your mother?'* But she still wouldn't have it.

Subconsciously... Yes, subconsciously I must have decided to ignore the situation... File it away to the back of my mind... Keep Megan out of my diary, and thoughts.

Let me state here and now: I'm sorry Megan. I'm sorry if I've let you down in anyway shape or form. I'm sorry if you think I don't care about you love... I'm sorry, but I do.

11.55pm: I can't sleep I'm not feeling very happy at all. I don't understand why I keep doing this?... I've blanked out an important part of my daughter's life for the best part of fourteen days... Why?

Yes, I've spoken with her... Yes, we've had our little face to face confrontations... Yes, we've yelled and screamed at each other... Yes we've slammed doors, and sulked into rooms... So why haven't I mentioned any of this to you Diary; my one true friend?Subconsciously... It's the only reason I have. Subconsciously I must have wanted to hide it away... God, I feel terrible!

June 20: Wednesday

As you can imagine I didn't have a very good sleep last night. I don't intend to go into minute detail; the for, against, where, why, and everything else. But I will say this for Megan, she stuck to her guns, and got herself a job on a Government financed, work related scheme, which she begins next Monday... Good for her.

Megan won't tell anyone the name of the company that's taken her on. Gary thinks it's because Lewis & Hudson have taken her on as a trainee secretary... Trevor says if that's the case, then we'll soon have one child making tea for the workers, and another making tea for the bosses. (God, I wish I'd encouraged my children to do more in the kitchen when they were growing up.)

Tonight at evening class, I tackled Dave Huws about the working conditions, at Lewis & Hudson and I found myself very surprised, by what he had to say... During the break Dave said, apart from earning the minimum wage he was entitled to claim other benefits for his family called 'Working Credits'.

This came as a great shock to me, because apart from retaining your family allowance, I thought all other benefits would be stopped or at least means tested when anyone entered full-time employment. The longer I listened to Dave, the more I found what he was saying very hard to believe. What Gary was claiming illegally, Dave was perfectly within his rights to claim legally. For the remainder of the evening I couldn't help thinking: *'Does Trevor know anything about this?'*

"Trevor, did you know that you can still claim benefit if you are working?" I enquired, as soon as I walked through our front door. "Only, Dave Huws said he is, and we've got the same number of children as they have to support."

"Yes and no." Trevor replied, in a flippant manner. "Yes, I knew all about it, and no because there was no such benefit for me to claim when our kids were the Huws's children's age."

"But you could still claim if you had a job, couldn't you?" I asked in a pleading manor.

"What's the point of that?" Trevor countered

"Well, if you found a job, you could still claim some benefit, so we wouldn't be any worse off."

"I agree we wouldn't be any worse off, because we'd be exactly the same. Rhian, if you can give me one good reason for going to work to earn exactly what I'm claiming in benefit for free, then I'll happily go down to the dole tomorrow and find myself a job."

Ten minutes of silence passed between us.

"Why is Dave Huws doing it then." I rounded on Trevor, feeling a second wind surge through my body. "Why is he doing it, if there isn't any point?"

"Bloody Hell Rhian." Trevor said, resisting my surge. "I hate it when you come home with your head full of these half-cocked ideas. What the fuck do you think I've been doing all these years? Do you think I've been sitting on my arse, in this fucking chair out of choice?... Do you really think I've given up?... Don't you think there's not a minute that goes by in the day or night, that I'm not thinking: what the hell can I do to get us out of this mess?"

For the first time in I don't know when, I felt the passion in Trevor's eyes, and the strength of feeling as his words left his mouth. "Dave Huws works for his benefits, that's the only difference between him and me... Yes, Dave has a job. Yes, Dave is not classed as being unemployed. But that's only because the Government top up his wage packet each week... Look at it like this Rhian. Dave's job should pay him a living wage for him and his family to live on... Am I right?"

I nodded.

"Come what may, everyone who is in full-time employment should be paid enough money for them to support his or her family... No ifs, no buts, everyone should be entitled to a living wage, and be independent of the state."

Again I nodded my head in agreement.

"But life's not like that is it?... I'm fucked if I'm going out to work for the same money more or less that I'm claiming on the dole ... Oi Blair!... You want me to work, you pay me a decent fucking wage, that's all I've got I say.... Fuck um all to Hell Rhian, fuck um!"

June 21: Thursday

This morning, sixty hours after taking control of my life I had a panic attack. After mulling over Trevor's words, I came to the conclusion that life is an illusion. Dave and Anne were deluding themselves with dreams of full-time employment... Maybe Trevor and I have got our lifestyle right after all, without really realising it... Or maybe life is all a game for the amusement for the Gods, or the Blair Government!... I don't know?... But what I do know is this: I could only walk as far as the shops today, before I gave up the ghost, and felt an urgent need to return home.

It's nearly six months to Christmas, and I've hardly got anything in.

June 22: Friday

Still feel very weak... I can feel my nerve endings standing out on stalks... In regimented lines... Like army battalions standing to attention all over my body. This afternoon I read about Shirley Valentine practising her F-Plan diet with some Greek God who she'd met on holiday. That reminds me, neither Trevor, the kids or I have ever been on a proper holiday... Day trips, yes... Holiday never.

Megan still hasn't said anything about her new job. She also hasn't shown any sign of being nervous at starting her first day. She just scoffed at Gary when he warned her, the men would shave her head on her first day, if she started work with him...

I made Gary admit that this was just a joke when the others had left the room... I don't think my nerves will be able to take much more of this."

June 23: Saturday

Don't ask me way, but my mind as decided that my body is going through the change. At quarter to five this morning I woke-up, and it suddenly dawned on me what was happening. God, I feel horrible... God, if you're going to take something away from me, do you have to make me feel as bad as this?

Abandoned on the sofa with only the television, and the Radio Times for company. I let out a little groan when I heard my mother enter the kitchen via the unlocked back door.

"Trevor popped around on his way to the club." Mam said, as I heard her filling the kettle. "He said you weren't feeling up to the mark this morning."

Thank you for that Trevor I thought, then whispered a: "Yes." Followed by a, "do you think I'm old enough to be going through the menopause Mam?"

After my mother had completed carrying out the medical checks she'd practised on me throughout my childhood. (She's since added a meningitis checking glass tumbler to her routine.) I said: "Only I thought I was approaching that age when that sort of thing happens, and..."

"Listen Rhian you know I don't like talking about such things." Mam interrupted, as wave after wave of embarrassment spread across her face. "I don't mind advising you about diarrhoea, chicken pox, or any other childhood diseases, but you know I feel really uncomfortable about talking about things like that... You know, things downstairs... In any case, that's what doctors are for."

I wanted to ask my mother what her experiences had been like?... What effect the change had been on her life?... Did she suffer with the same symptoms as me?... But no such luck. Deciding I wasn't feeling physically up to an argument, I listened to her unrelated advice: "Well Rhian, why don't you go and have another word with the doctor about your worries." Then we settled down to watch the Saturday matinee 'The Great Race' starring 'Tony Curtis' on BBC2.

June 24: Sunday

MEGAN'S NEW JOB:

Me:	Why won't you tell me where you are working?
Megan:	Because it's private... It's my business, and it's got nothing to do with you.
Me:	Well, are you going to work with Gary at Lewis & Hudson or not?... You'll have to let me know Megan. Do you want me to make some sandwiches for you, yes or no? Because I won't be getting up first thing in the morning to make them for you, you know.
Megan:	I don't want you to make me anything... Stop fussing Mam, I'll be all right.
Me:	Why won't you tell me then?... You're not ashamed of your job are you?
Megan:	What are you talking about?
Me:	(In a low whisper.) You haven't agreed to do anything stupid have you?... You haven't got a job as a stripper, lap dancer, or something sordid like that?
Megan:	Mam, what kind of person do you think I am?

Me:	Then why won't you tell me?
Megan:	That's for me to know and for you to find out. (She gets her attitude from her father's side of the family.)
Me:	You won't be going to work tomorrow, unless you tell me where you are going to.
Megan:	We'll see.
Me:	Yes indeed, we will see my girl!

Dear Diary can you see how stubborn she is? I can't do a thing with her. She won't listen to a word I say. She wouldn't listen when I tried to talk to her about staying on at school... She looks like a tart when she leaves the house. Okay, I know that's a lousy thing to say about my own daughter, but it's the truth. Her make-up, her clothes, she doesn't listen when I ask her to tone them down. I don't know what to do with her... Mam said she felt the same way about me, when I was Megan's age... She also added: "Rhian, now you know what it was like to be me, in the seventies."

Trevor thinks it's just a phase Megan is going through. I said if it is, it's been going on for the best part of sixteen years. But Trevor just laughed and replied: (I hope he wasn't being serious?) "She'll soon grow out of it Rhian. It won't be long before Megan finds herself a steady boyfriend, gets herself up the duff, and settles down to a life of drudgery, standing next to the chip pan, with three assorted kids biting at her ankles!"

June 25: Monday... Wimbledon Monday

Trevor, Gary and Megan left the house to catch the bus at the same time this morning. Trevor and Gary have gone to sign-on, (As far as Lewis & Hudson are concerned, Gary has got a dental appointment every Monday fortnight for the foreseeable future.) and I still have no clue to where Megan is going too. (After signing on, Trevor has promised he'll look around the shops, just in case Megan has found herself a job in one of them.)

11.00am: Trevor and Gary return home... Report on Megan's whereabouts - Negative.

6.00pm: Megan returns home carrying a large bouquet of flowers for me.

Gary: What church did you rob those from?
Megan: (Ignoring him) These are for you Mam. Julian Jackson made them for you.

What a nice thoughtful girl my daughter is... Perhaps Trevor is right after all, and it's just a phase she's going through.

Gary: You've got a job working with Julian Jackson?
Megan: (Ignoring him again) Mam, I know I've been horrible lately, and these are just to say sorry.

Kissing me on the cheek Megan handed me the bouquet, then while we were all sitting around the table having our tea. Megan (After changing out of her work clothes.) gave us a blow by blow account of her first day in her new job.

"Julian's a nice enough boy." She stated, twirling her teaspoon around the rim of her cup. "He's a little bit gay of course, but that doesn't stop him cutting a crisp stem, and Mr Hurst thinks he's a natural born florist. It was Julian who arranged Mam's bouquet from the left over flowers in the shop."

We all turned to admire the flowers, now arranged in a glass vase on top of the sideboard. "Julian can do wonders with carnations, and if I ever get married, he's promised to do the flowers for me at cost."

Dear Diary, isn't it funny how things turn out. I've been worrying to death over nothing, yet if I dare to drop my guard for an instant, life has a nasty habit of turning around and kicking me in the teeth.

Wimbledon

I am not a big lover of sport. Football does nothing for me. Rugby is a man's game, (Trevor calls me a traitor because I never get excited when Wales play.) but I do love my tennis. I started watching with mother, and I haven't missed a Wimbledon since the early seventies. Every day for the next two weeks I intend writing a little piece on the day's play at the Lawn Tennis Championships:

Wimbledon: Day 1

The sun shone, I relaxed in my chair. There were wins for Henman, Sampress, Capriati and Rusedski. At Wimbledon all is well with the world. Trevor says: *'It's the dream of every ice-cream seller to park his van inside the main gates.*

Women's number 1 seed Martina Hingis was eliminated by an unknown French girl (Pascual) in the first round 6/4 6/2.

June 26: Tuesday

Our telephone bill was paid today:

Mam: I've been thinking Rhian. You really should have the phone put back on, you know.

Me: I'd like to Mam, but I can't afford to reconnect it at the moment.

Mam: You can't afford to have the telephone reconnected, but Trevor can still afford to waste money on his fags and drink... I don't know Rhian, you've got two at work who can't get in touch with you if something happens out of the blue. I would think a telephone is a necessity for you at the moment... How much do you owe British Telecom did you say?

Me: We did owe £256, but now I've got it down to about £200... I've been paying them back ten pound a month... These things take time I'm afraid.

More out of worry for her Grandchildren than anything else, Mam walked with me to the Post Office and paid the outstanding balance of my bill. She also lent me her mobile phone until our phone had been reconnected... I have to pay for my own phone cards, of course.

Mam: Now Rhian, when you ask them to reconnect you. Tell them you only want incoming calls only, then you shouldn't get into trouble with BT again.

Trevor remarked, after hearing my mother had paid our outstanding bill: "Nobody knows, how much money that woman is worth?"

Wimbledon: Day 2

The temperature rose to a scorching ninety degrees on centre court this afternoon. There were wins for Venus Williams,

Agassi, Rafter and a couple of Brit's no one has ever heard of before.

On one of the hottest days of the year there was no sign of sun block anywhere in the crowd, and the woman's rule was introduced... I don't know what the rule means exactly, and I don't think anyone playing knew how to take advantage of the rule either?

June 27: Wednesday

"Rhian, a little dicky bird tells me, your Megan, is working with my Julian." Mary said, slithering up to me in the classroom. "Julian says she's very slow at the moment, but I'm sure she'll pick-up speed if she sticks it out."

Smiling as she spoke, I was determined none of her little pin pricks would find my tender spot. "Of course not everyone can be a natural with flowers like my Julian. I do believe he made you a charming little bouquet the other day. Made out of rubbish, left lying on the floor, wasn't it? He often comes home with some of his little creations for me, orchids and the like. But as it was Megan's first day he thought it would make a nice welcoming gesture if he made something for her to take home for you, as she couldn't afford to purchase you one from the displays in the shop."

"Thank Julian for me, won't you." I replied through gritted teeth, secretly wishing I had the bouquet with me at this moment, so I could ram it down her throat.

"Isn't life funny how life works out?" Mary trilled, leaving me with no option but to listen to another one of her observations. "I was at school with you. My Julian was at school with your Gary. My Dominique was at school with your Megan. My Harvey is in the same class as your Anthony,and now my

Julian and your Megan are working together." Agreeing with her that it was indeed a small world, I literary cringed with embarrassment, as Mary emitted a ear piercing false laugh, and gushed: "Oh I nearly forgot. We attend the same evening class together, don't we?"

MY SHADOW
by
Rhian Evans

1.
Why are you forever in my face?
Why won't you give up the chase?
One step forward, two steps back,
The inconvenience of an over laden sack.
Wherever I look,
Be it east, or be it west.
Your hound dog determination,
Stands the test.

2.
Why me, and not someone else?
Did I fail some ancient rite?
Am I cursed until my dying day?
Please leave me alone, please go away.
What is it about me that you like?
Or is it, you want to live my life?
If you could, you'd soon stray.
But since you can't, you've pledged to stay.

I don't know what it is, this woman thinks I've got. But whatever it is, she'd desperately like some of it.

Wimbledon: Day 3

On a day when the sun popped in and out, defending champion 'Pistol' Pete Sampress was taken to a five set thriller by unknown Brit Barry Cowan in the second round. There were also easy wins for Rusedski, Henman and Capriati.

June 28: Thursday

Once again my brain, accompanied by my overactive imagination, were proved to be wrong... Last Saturday's revelation about being on the change came to nothing; once again I became PMT active... This was a shame because I was looking forward to saving some money on my sanitary towels.

Dear Diary, I don't think it matters if I was on the change or not, for all the notice Trevor has been showing me recently. Do you realise, he hasn't come near me this month. And it's not as if I've had to turn him away... Well Trevor, it looks like you're going to be out of luck, if you try it on with me this weekend... And it will serve you right.

Wimbledon: Day 4

Rain showers interrupted play throughout the day. Rafter, Venus Williams and Agassi all booked their places in the third round... Fifteen Brit's started, four days gone and only 2 remain.

June 29: Friday

What a day... A day of firsts... A day that money poured into the house. Today was also the final day of Gary's trial period with Lewis & Hudson. They've decided to keep him on. Trevor said: *'They must be mad!'*

Firstly, I cashed Gary's Giro on the way to Tesco's. Now I know I've promised never to write anything about shopping again, but it was so funny. Trevor came with me, and turned what would have been an ordinary shopping trip into an hilarious scene from a Carry-On film, by turning innocent phrases I said into sexual innuendo.

"Push it in, Trevor," and "give it a pull." Had us rolling up the aisles, but in reality they were only remarks made about depositing a £1 coin, to release the security chain on a shopping trolley.

I turned away in embarrassment when Trevor asked the lady shelf stacker where the store kept its Dick? (Ready meal 'Spotted Dick' dessert.) But the best laugh was kept for last. Trevor nearly choked on his pic-n-mix sweet, when I told him: "I'd been dying for it all afternoon." After taking a sip from my Coke can to quench my thirst.

6.00pm: Gary came home with his first wage slip... His pay had been paid automatically into his bank account. (Another first for Gary. Having a bank account I mean.)

Megan came home shortly after, with more flowers. (I'm running out of vases.) She had also achieved a first. She had completed her first week at work, but looked slightly jealous of her older brother, especially when he started taunting her with his wage slip.

I'm happy, Trevor's happy, the kids are happy... Oh God, how long can this last?

Wimbledon: Day 5

There was an annoying kid standing in the crowd on centre court. (Well annoying for me anyway.) He was standing... Leaning against a wall at the back of the court, during the Capriati v Panova match. Dressed in jeans, Nike sweatshirt, white baseball cap and sporting a face I'd like to slap. Capritati won the match 6/4 6/4... But bloody hell, that kid got on my nerves.

There were wins once again for Hen, Rud and Samp.

June 30: Saturday

Anthony's school held a car boot sale on its playing field this afternoon in order to raise some much needed money for school funds. About forty car boots turned up, mostly outsiders, but I did recognise a few people from the estate selling their odds and sods, as I walked round.

Now here's a funny thing. As you know, normally on a Saturday afternoon I'm to be found at home, lolling on my sofa watching the afternoon film. But not this week. For the first Saturday since I don't know when I have some money in my pocket... Lets shop!

Christmas Shopping List:

Name:	Item:	Condition:	Cost:
Anthony	6 x Books Sci-fi	Nice - Not Torn	£1 the lot
Mam	BHS Potpourri gift box, bowl, & scented candle	Mint	£1.50
Trevor	Lee Cooper Jeans	Worn	£2.00
	Ralph Lauren Green, Red, & White Polo shirts.	V. Good	£1 each
	2 x white shorts (For next summer)	V. Good	50p each
	Cable knit cream sweater	V. Good	75p
	Denim After shave boxed gift set	Box tatty	50p (After haggle)
Megan	Black Shoulder bag (very roomy)	Good enough for work	£1.00
Gary	Real Leather Belt (Nice Buckle)	Respectable	20p
		(I haggled down from 35p.)	

With Christmas only six months away. I feel a lot happier with this lot in the house.

REVIEW OF THE MONTH:

After all said and done, June has proved to be a very good month for us. I've got two children at work, another who is doing well at school. I've sent a poem to a magazine, Mam has paid our outstanding phone bill. I'm happy, (I'm not on the change, yet.) Trevor's happy, the kids are happy. I've started my Christmas shopping. My house is full of flowers. A quote from June 29th: *'Oh God how long can this happiness last*?'

Wimbledon: Day 6

Showers once again interrupted play, but not the car boot sale at the school. All my favourites made it into the second week - The Fourth Round.

Rafter, Venus and Agassi, all won in straight sets.

July 1: Sunday

Another day of firsts... Yesterday, Gary spent some of his first month's wages on a mobile phone. (A first for this house... Actual mobile phone owner, I mean.) While Megan opened her first back account.

First Gary: "Well, I need it mun, don't I?" Gary insisted, as Trevor scoffed at his reasoning. "It's like Gran said. If I'm working late, I'll need it to let you know what's happening."

"How much did that thing cost you soft lad?" Trevor inquired, while his son fiddled with the buttons of his new toy. "Fifty notes bar a penny."

"FIFTY QUID!" Trevor exploded. "I don't suppose it crossed your mind, it may workout a little bit cheaper if you just popped 20p in the call box at work, now and again!"

And now Megan: "The Nationwide Building Society. What made you open an account with them then love?... Trying to save up for your own house, are you?" Sometimes, Trevor speaks to his children in such a condescending manner.

"Well, I was thinking about opening an account at the Halifax, but they didn't offer me anything. So I choose the Nationwide instead... They give me a free CD voucher for joining."

"That's my girl... Oi, Earth to telephone boy, did you get anything free when you bought that thing?"

"As a matter of fact I did." Gary replied, lifting his head up in triumph. "They give me a free ten pound phone card, with the phone."

"And who are you going to have your first one to one with, then boy?... Gary, you do know your Gran's mobile telephone number don't you son?"

Dear Diary, something very strange happened this evening... I had a very interesting conversation with my daughter. It wasn't planned, there was no pressure, in fact I didn't even begin the conversation.

After dinner I was pottering about in the bedroom, I think I was trying to find a better hiding places for the things I bought in the car boot sale, when Megan knocked on my bedroom door, and asked if she could come in for a chat.

"Can I come in Mam?"(This was very strange behaviour to start with.) "Mam, I've been thinking about you and those Prozac you take."

"Yes?"

"How do you know, you still should be taking them, if you don't see the doctor?"

"Take my word for it Megan, I know."

"But how do you know Mam? Dad picks up your repeat prescription for you every month... Well I don't think the doctor should be giving them to you anymore, unless he sees you at his surgery."

Taken aback by my daughter's sudden interest I asked: "What's brought this on then love?"

"Are you a Prozac addict Mam?"

"Don't be so silly. You can't get addicted to Prozac, (I lied.) it's just that I suffer from my nerves that's all. There's nothing for you to worry about. I'll be all right.

For one insane moment I thought about discussing the dark side of my life with her, or should that read the dark side of my mind?... But I turned it around by asking what made her decide to leave school without sitting any exams?

"Tell me Megan, now that we're having this woman to woman chat, why did you do it?... You know it won't be easy starting out in life without any qualifications, don't you?"

Her answer astounded me: “Is it better to be me, or the person somebody else wants me to be?” As she spoke my eyes began to open, and I saw her skirt wasn’t short anymore. “It’s my life and I will walk the path I choose to go down, not another’s.” Her face looked scrubbed clean, lovely and fresh, I couldn’t believe it. For the first time since she became thirteen, she wasn’t wearing any make-up. “I’ll live or die by my own decisions. I will not allow pieces of paper to gain control over my destiny.” I couldn’t believe this was the same girl, who yesterday afternoon had chosen which building society to join, simply by accepting a bribe of a CD voucher. “It hurts me to say this Mam, but I intend to control my life, and not have it controlled by any foreign substances.” Megan’s growing her hair, her clothes are loose and free... My God, she’s not wearing her birthday trainers, she’s got on some sort of open toe sandals on her fee... “Megan, are you turning Hippy?”

Wimbledon: Day 7

Rest day.

July 2: Monday

“Those bastards, those dirty fucking bastards.” Trevor moaned, after reading his latest communiqué from the social security. “They’ve called me in for an interview on Wednesday the eleventh... There’s no need for that now, is there Rhi... Why can’t they just leave me alone?”

Later on in the day the telephone was reconnected. Mam phoned shortly after to check it was working... She also said she wanted her mobile back. “I’ve been trying to phone you every half hour since eight o'clock this morning." She twitted. "Rhian, apart from the human voice, did you know some people use the telephone lines to invite that internet porn into their home?"

Just one more thing to add before I close for the day. The white arrow man delivered my winter home shopping catalogue this afternoon.

Wimbledon: Day 8

The king is dead. God save the king. Ex-champion Pete Sampress lost his crown in a five set strength sapper to Roger Federer on centre court.

And then there was one... One Brit anyway. Greg Rusedski lost in straight sets to Goran Ivanisevic. Meanwhile Tim Henman is down two sets to one against Todd Martin, before play was suspended for bad light.

On a very hot and humid day there were also wins for Rafter, Agassi, Capriati and Venus Williams who all progress into the quarter finals.

July 3: Wednesday

I felt very guilty collecting my family allowance today. Megan's employed on a Government Scheme, but I'm still claiming my family allowance for her... Is this wrong?... Is it really up to me to tell the DSS my business?... If the DSS can't be bothered to ask the school if my daughter has left, than I can't be bothered to tell the DSS that my daughter's got a job.

The more I thought about it, the more I came to realise I wasn't the one who was in the wrong... They were!

WHY IT'S NOT MY FAULT:

1. The DSS sent Megan her National Insurance Number.
2. Her job was given to her by an official government body.
3. The school is also an official government body.
4. Megan told the school she was leaving... The school's career officer encouraged her to accept a place on the scheme.
5. Megan accepted the job off a government official.
6. If all these official departments refuse to speak to each other. Why should I do their job for them?

After I'd worked this out, I felt a lot better within myself... God it's hard work being a parent.

Wimbledon: Day 9

I am the Jennifer Capriati of this estate. We both share the same fighting qualities needed to conquer our respective insecurities... Jennifer Capriati is a true tennis goddess, if only I could handle a pen as well as she can handle a tennis racket. I was on the edge of my seat watching the way she fought back from the dead to defeat Serena Williams 6/7 7/5 6/3. What a match. Serena tried every dirty trick in the book from slow play, to halting play all together and running to the toilet. But to no avail. Well done Jennifer... Henman beat Todd Martin... Venus also won.

July 4: Wednesday

Dear Diary, isn't it strange how one day changes from another?... One day I had three children in school, and the next I have two at work... One day I am married to a eunuch, the next to an over sexed, sexual acrobat... My period concluded for a month, Trevor and I were at one with each other... To quote something Trevor whispered in my ear: *'It feels great to be back in the saddle.'*

At evening class Mary Jackson was bragging about how many exams her Dominique was sitting or sat... I only caught part of her speech... Then she droned on about how many A's or B's Dominique needed before she'd be accepted into this college or that.

"Isn't it exciting Rhian?" She gushed. "Oh to be young again, with all of your life in front of you. I do wish I'd gone to college when I'd had the chance."

'So do I.' I thought. *'But you were too busy copying me weren't you?'*... But I just smiled, and said nothing.

"Of course, if my Dominique is offered a college place, she will be the first person from my family to step-up and bridge the gap between the state school and the echelon of higher education."

At this point, somebody behind me said: "You must be proud"

"Yes, I am... I feel very proud, as a matter of fact." For one dreadful moment I thought Mary was going to wipe a tear away from her eye, but she continued. "My Julian was always very bright at school. But his talents lay in his eye and hand co-ordination, as Rhian will tell you." At this, the eyes were upon me, but not for long as Mary pressed on: "Rhian's daughter Megan, is working under my Julian. There's little over a year in age difference between them, but what that boy doesn't know about cutting roses, you could write on top of a safety pin.

As the group broke up, and made their way to their seats. Mary sided up to me and said: "I hear your Anthony is very bright, and not at all like your other two. They must be such a disappointment to you. I was only saying to my Idris the other day, children can be such a dis..."

"Fuck you!" I hissed, in a form of a vicious whisper, that was only heard by the two of us.

"Excuse me?"

"You heard." I growled. "One more disparaging remark about my kids, and I'll give you a slap." Thinking about it now I can't believe I said it to her... Just as I can't believe the menacing tone of voice emitting from my mouth... Have I got a demon living inside me?

"Very lady like, I must say." Mary retorted turning her face away from my now bulging eyes, and trembling lip... Last Sunday Megan asked me if I still needed to take Prozac?... Megan my love, those little white pills were at that moment the only thing preventing me from slaying your work colleague's mother, with a single blow that would have broken an elephant's neck!

Wimbledon: Day 10

Ivanisevic, claims his superstitions have helped him into the semi-finals... I knew there was something in it all along!... He now meets Tim Henman who defeated the conquer of Pete Sampress, Roger Federer in a fourth set, tie-break thriller. Rafter and Agassi also make it into the semi's.

July 5: Thursday

Anne called around after she'd finished her stint at the preschool nursery, and immediately burst out laughing when I opened the door: "Rhian... Rhian, I nearly pissed my knickers, when I heard what you said to Mary last night... And your voice... That tone you used... Where did that come from?"

"Do you think anyone else heard me? I asked blushing profusely. "Only, I thought Mary was the only one who could hear what I said."

"Rhian, you turned into the exorcist last night. I heard your every growl, and I expect so did everyone in the class." Then Anne had another fit of the giggles, and said: "Didn't you notice Mr Simpson who was sitting in front of you?" I shock my head. "I swear to God, he sat bolt upright in his seat because he was too frightened to move, with all the little hairs on the back of his head standing to attention... I know for a fact there were other people in the class who were too afraid to look round at you."

"Well that's it then." I said throwing my arms up in the air. "I can't go back there now."

"Don't be silly... Dave was talking to the others later on, and they all agreed that Mary had deserved it... She'd had it coming... She's always talking down to you... Some of the class had wondered why it had taken you so long to put her in her place."

"So they are all on my side then?" The relief of this news was clearly etched upon my face.

"To a man... But Rhian, I haven't told you the latest yet. Mary didn't show up at the nursery today. She phoned in sick. She said she'd been suffering with one of her migraines." Then in a tone of voice not too dissimilar from the one I'd employed last night, Anne growled: "The lying bitch!"

Throughout the day I was continually pestered by the fallout of my actions... Had I gone too far?

Anthony:	(Home from school) Harvey Jackson told me you and his mother were fighting in the classroom last night Mam.
Megan:	(Home from work) What have you been doing? Poor Julian Jackson came into work in a hell of a state this morning... Do you realise he's been sobbing into his floral bouquets all day?
Mam:	(On the phone) Rhian love, it's all over the old age club... Good for you love. It's about time somebody give that Mary Jackson a taste of her own medicine.
Gary:	Entered the living-room after work whistling the 'Rocky' theme.
Trevor:	(In bed, after sex) I didn't know you had it in you love.

Wimbledon: Day 11 - Ladies Semi-final

I am gutted. Jennifer lost 6/2,4/6,2/6 in a rain affected game against Belgium's Justine Henin. (Not that the rain made much difference.) Jennifer lost after coasting through the first set and a half. Henin will now meet Venus Williams in the final.

July 6: Friday

YES! YES! YES! My God it's happened, I received a reply from 'Woman' magazine.

Woman Magazine.
London.
4-6-2001.
Dear Mrs Evans.

Thank you for a very interesting letter and poem. On behalf of everyone connected with the story of Mrs Bates, (Home Alone) I would like to thank you for the concern you have shown, and for the time it took you to compose your verse.
Unfortunately, I am unable to find a space in the forthcoming editions of the magazine to publish your poem, but I have taken the liberty of passing your poem on to Mrs Bates. I am sure your composition will gladden the old ladies heart, and help to reassure her that there are still some kind and considerate people in the world, who are thinking of her.

Yours sincerely,
Carole Russell (Editor)

PS: For future reference. Please enclose a.s.a.e with all your future correspondence. I know a lot of editors who get just a little teensy-weensy ticked off when subscribers fail to do so.

What a brilliant letter. Armed with this, I feel justified in making a triumphant return to the classroom.

AMAZON
by
Rhian Evans

Over the years they put me down.
Whatever I said,
Whether right or wrong.
I knew my place,
Never rocked the boat.
Feelings trod under,
No second look.
But I rose again,
By the mighty pen.
Words that are written,
Live longer than,
The speech on the tongue,
Or a bandied phrase.
I've used this method for forty odd years.
With a pen my friend, I cut through my tears.
And reborn am I, to an Amazon Queen.
Known for my words,
My life slips by - Unseen.

Wimbledon: Day 12 - Men's Semi-final Day

When I first started to watch Wimbledon in the early seventies, the last Friday of the tournament used to be Ladies Final Day... Nothing lasts forever.

Pat Rafter made it into the final for the second year on the trot by beating Andre Agassi 2/6 6/3 3/6 6/2 8/6. Henman's game with Ivanisevic was suspended by rain in the fourth set. Henman's trying to be the first Brit to win the championships since Fred Perry in 1936. Bunny Austin was the last Brit to reach the final in 1938.

July 7: Saturday

Dear Diary, I've come to the conclusion that standing up for myself has bought its own reward.

1. I received a excellent reply from an editor of Woman magazine, who liked my poem so much, she sent it on to the old lady who I'd written about, while at the same time hoping I wouldn't think it a liberty she did so. She also sent me some very good advice for the future... I think I've made a contact there.
2. To a man, the evening class is on my side, in the dispute between me and Mary Jackson... I stood up, she went down.
3. All this standing up for myself is good for my sex life. Trevor and I have been at it like rabbits since last Wednesday night.
4. For the first time in years, my mother is proud of me. Mam said: "I'm proud of you Rhian."
5. And so am I.

Megan went to town this morning to withdraw her first wages from the hole in the wall. I've started a new family tradition. (Well, new for this family anyway.) Anyone starting work, can keep their first week's wages... With this in mind, Megan blew every penny on a new mobile phone. (I can see the estate phone box outside of the Post Office losing a lot of money, if this craze catches on.) Within a space of five minutes, Gary, Megan and I were holding down a total of three separate telephone conversations in the living-room, with poor Anthony putting in an added complaint that he couldn't hear what the people were saying to each other on the telly... Who would have thought any of this would have happened to my little band, a month ago?

3.00am: It's three o'clock on Sunday morning, and I've just nipped out of bed to get myself a drink of water. There's no doubt about it. When he's pissed, Trevor turns into a fabulous lover.

Wimbledon: Day 13 – Ladies Final Day... Oh No It Wasn't!

Rain delayed play until 5.30pm. What play there was concerned Tim Henman and his semi-final match against Goran Ivanisevic... Hopefully the game will be completed tomorrow. The score is two sets all, and it's with serve in the fifth.

Ladies Final Day will be rescheduled to Men's finals day, (Tomorrow) which in turn will be held on Monday, a day after the tournament has officially ended... Confused?... So am I.

July 8: Sunday

Dear Diary, firstly I'd just like to apologise for my hasty entry during the early hours of the morning. I also sincerely hope my somewhat eager action won't condemn me to a spell of bad luck bridging the gap between today and the end of the year... After writing my 3.00am comment, I instantly realised I'd written it on the wrong page. (IE: yesterday instead of today.)

Back to business:

Trevor must have been awake before me this morning, because he woke me up in an unusual manner, and I don't mean by poking me with his hand... Six minutes later I was standing in the kitchen making breakfast, while Trevor sat reading the newspaper on the sofa: "Oh shit!" Trevor groaned pointing at the headline: 'Labour Promise To Crack Down On Benefit Cheats.' "Rhian, I think the DSS are on to me!"

"Don't be silly." I said, trying to put his mind at ease. "Not after all these years surely."

Dear Diary, I hope Trevor's interview on Wednesday with the DSS will only be a formality... Call me suspicious but somethings got my Trevor spooked. I can't put my finger on it at the moment, but for most of the day Trevor's annoying habits have been getting on my nerves. Constantly rising himself up and down in his chair: "Trevor have you got ants in your pants?... Trevor you're like a 'Jack in the Box'... For Pete's sake, sit still, will you!"

Paranoid of any stranger passing the house... Spying out of the window at every opportunity... Searching for a snooper lurking in the bushes: "I'm on the lookout for any DSS grassers watching this house." Trevor explained, before focusing his enquiries onto my mother. "Your mother hasn't been blabbing her big mouth off down at the old age club again, has she Rhian?"

"Of course not."

"You know what she's like after she's had a drink."

"My mother knows nothing about what's going on in this house, thank you very much. And if she does know, she certainly didn't hear it from me."

"Who's told her then?"

“Told her what?... I don’t think she knows anything... What’s going on Trevor?”

“David Rees gave me twenty quid for helping him to move his daughter’s furniture into her new flat... You don’t think your mother found out about it do you?”

“Forget my mother, what did you do with the twenty quid Trevor?... I bet you’ve pissed it all up against the Rugby Club wall, haven’t you?”

And from there it got ugly... Yes, I’m happy to be the first to admit, in the past my mother has indeed been known to report benefit cheats to the DSS... But she’s never tried to hide money from the fam... Well, of course she is very secretive about her old age pension, but if she finds any money in the street, she always comes and tells me about it before putting it in her purse... But unlike Trevor my mother has never tried to hide any money from her late husband or only child. (ME!) Trevor and I are no longer on speaking terms... Trevor owes the family twenty quid, and I pray to God my mother never gets to find out about this, or her Grandson’s little wheeze.

Wimbledon: Day 14 - Men’s Final Day

On Men’s Final Day the rain couldn’t stop Venus Williams from retaining her Wimbledon crown for the second year in succession. She beat Belgium Justine Henin 6/1 3/6 6/0.

Tim Henman lost his three day semi-final, to complete a black weekend for British sport. (Australia beat England at cricket, and the ‘Lions’ at rugby.) Henman said he’ll be back... What a heartbreaker.

July 9: Monday

It's signing on day, or as I now call it: 'Benefit Fraud Monday'.

Trevor had a very restless night in bed, and it serves him right... What do people say?... There's no rest for the wicked, and in Trevor's case they're absolutely right.

Just in case you are wondering, Trevor and I are still not on speaking terms with each other. Defrauding the Government is one thing, but ripping off your own family is something else... Okay,the case for the defence is: he didn't actually spend any of the family's benefit money on fags and drink, but that's not the point. All monies received should be made known, and accounted for in the family pot. If this type of behaviour isn't immediately nipped in the bud. Where will it all end?

Remaining cold and aloof, I listened to Trevor's fears on his return home from signing-on: "They were all giving me funny looks, when I walked in." He whinged, "and you're no different, sitting like Cleopatra on her throne... So, I should have told you about that twenty quid, but I didn't. Now I suppose you are going to crucify me for the rest of my life."... Trevor was never any good under pressure.

"The dirty rotten bastards," he complained. "Why couldn't they get it over and done with... Why couldn't they have interviewed me this morning?... They're sadists, that's what they are... They're dirty fucking sadists. Trying to make me sweat, that's what they're trying to do to me Rhian... The dirty bastards."... I hope Gary shows more backbone if he gets caught!

Wimbledon: Day 15 - People's Monday... I honestly believe it was.

Call it what you will, God, Fate or Destiny but something helped Goran Ivanisevic win the Wimbledon title at his fourth attempt.... Classic, Classic, Classic. The atmosphere inside centre court was electric, (This is the kind of unique occasion that only happens when the people in charge allow ordinary people to fill the stands, and not the indifferent corporate box rabble.) but I do feel sorry for poor old Pat Rafter. (Loser for two years running.) If he'd been playing anyone else, God and I would have definitely been on his side.

If I was a man, I'd be the Goran Ivanisevic of this estate... I too will never give up on my dream, until I succeed.

July 10: Tuesday

Mrs P Bates
28,The Old Road,
Manchester.
7-7-2001

Dear Mrs Evans.
I'm just penning you these few lines to say thank you for a lovely poem. I've been overwhelmed by the response I've received from the general public to my story. I have received over a hundred letters written by well wishers from around the country; some containing cheques, which I have passed onto charities with the sender's kind regards. I never realised there were so many kind people like yourself left in the world, and reading what you said in your letter gladdened my heart.

I have placed your poem, in my scrapbook, along with all my other letters at the side of my bed. (I like to read them before I go to sleep at night.)
Once again I would like to thank you, and wish you and your family all the best for the future.

Yours sincerely,
Mrs P Bates.

THE GOOD:

Well, well, well... I've been published after all, in an old lady's scrapbook.

THE BAD:

1. Mrs Bates has made Trevor's actions seem all the worse. I can't see Trevor donating any of his windfall to charity.
2. It grieves me to say it, but Trevor and I deserve each other... I didn't write my poem because I was personally moved by the plight of Mrs Bates. I wrote the poem because I wanted to see it published in a magazine... Trevor took the twenty quid, and I've preyed on an old lady's feelings... God, Trevor and I are both council house scum.

July 11: Wednesday

It was my turn to have a restless night's sleep. At one point I wanted to get up in the middle of the night, and write Mrs Bates a letter, confessing all... My conscience demanded I apologise to Mrs Bates, and explain to her that I wasn't the good kind person, who she thought I was... But I didn't know where to begin... Guilt is a great burden to carry around with you, especially if like me you are already carrying so much of it around with you each day, inside your head.

TREVOR'S INTERVIEW DAY:

There was no guilt on Trevor's mind, as he left the house this morning... No guilt but plenty of fear. Fear that he would lose his benefits, and be forced to find himself a job paying the minimum wage.

At 11.30am this morning Trevor's swollen head entered the house like the king of the world: "I've done it Rhian." He screamed, triumphantly raising his arms in the air. "This time I've fucking done it love... Rhian, I'm on the fucking book."

Dear Diary, My Trevor's on the book.... On the book at long last... Dear Diary, do you have any idea what wonderful news this is?... No, of course you don't... Being on the book is the 'Holy Grail' of the benefit world... On the book... My Trevor's on the book... I can't believe it. It's like a dream come true... I'm so happy for Trevor, I feel as if I'm about to cry... On the book, and he's still in his early forties... Trevor you make me feel so proud.

WHAT ALL THIS MEANS TO US AS A FAMILY:

1. Trevor doesn't have to sign on at the unemployment centre anymore.
2. He will be able to draw his benefit money from a weekly benefit book, instead of a fortnightly giro.
3. He will be no longer classed as unemployed, and his name will be crossed off the unemployment register... Trevor claims this is called adjusting the unemployment figures...

Trevor also claims, the government will tell everyone concerned that he is no longer on the dole.

4. All in all, you could say the government have given up on my Trevor ever finding a job.
5. Trevor has more or less taken an early form of retirement, on full benefits... I will write more about this on another day.

MY EVENING CLASS:

If Trevor entered the house like the King of the World, then I entered the classroom like an 'Avenging Angel'. I couldn't believe the reception I received from my classmates... The moment I entered the classroom fell silent. I felt like John Wayne bursting through the swing-doors of the Cattle Baron's Saloon in Rio Bravo. "Rhian!" Anne's yell greeted from the back of the class, as everyone smiled as I sauntered by.

"Mary isn't here Rhian, she hasn't shown up." Anne nervously giggled, as I greeted her in my customary fashion. "She's been off on the sick all week from the toddlers' nursery, so I don't think we'll be seeing her tonight." Then a smiling Dave joined in and said: "I still can't get over what you said to her last week. You had me on tenterhooks... I was up and down off my chair all night. At one point I thought I'd have to step in and pull you off her at one stage... But Rhian, that scary voice of yours, bordering on the demonic or the possessed... No wonder Mary's been on the sick all week. I think I would have been too, if you spoke to me like that.

"If you could all settle down please, and if Mrs Evans could refrain from frightening the other members of the class. I would like to press on with tonight's poet and poem." Making a joke of my past action, Mr Davis gave me a wink, then said:

"This evening I would like us to discuss Edgar Allan Poe's, 'The Raven'."

An hour later and I was fit to burst. After the midpoint break in the class, I heard myself say: "I received a reply from 'Woman' magazine last Friday, and another letter from an old lady called Mrs Bates last Tuesday morning."

After reading both letters to the class, Mr Davis agreed, that the letter from Carole Russell come out of the top draw of rejection replies... Normally, you only get two lines saying thanks, but no thanks, or a standard photocopy missive signed at the bottom. But as Mr Davis said, the editor must have enjoyed reading my poem, because she took the time to write me a personal reply.

I was walking on air as I left the classroom. Both my letters had been circulating, and read by everyone in the room. Anne said my failure was an inspiration to them all. Others said, I had inspired them to send off letters of their own. I was treated like a celebrity, for the final forty-five minutes of the class, and it felt great... My only regret being, Mary wasn't there to see it.

Dear Diary before I sign off, I'd like to thank God for giving me a brief taste of what life could be like, and for making me feel special. I would also like to thank him for Trevor's benefit book, and to beg him not to destroy this illusion as quickly as he's destroyed all the others... Thank you God, love Rhian Evans, amen.

July 12: Thursday

All this success has gone to my and Trevor's heads. It's also gone to other parts of our bodies as well, because we were at it like rabbits again last night.

At the breakfast table Megan and Anthony were giving me some funny looks, and at one point Megan started to giggle. (Thank God, Gary had left for work.) Embarrassed beyond belief, I made my excuses and left the room... There and then, I vowed never to have sex again with my children in the house... That sounds bad doesn't it!

REASONS TO BE SEXUALLY DISCRETE:

1. The walls are like paper.
2. I tend to become very loud when excited... A gag's no good. I find it difficult to breathe.
3. I'll never have to feel this shamed again.
4. I've tried to understand how my children feel, by imagining my mother having sex... God, I need a Prozac.
5. Our bed is nearly twenty years old, and it sounds it's age.

The postman came late this morning... By the way, only Gary's Giro came yesterday. Trevor personally collected his final Giro in person, after he'd attended his interview... You'll never guess what Diary. The Census people are threatening to take Trevor to court, for not returning our completed census form on time. (Looking back through your pages, I see I've never mentioned the census to you before.) Trevor's excuse was: *'I didn't think we counted?'*

It took me the best part of four hours, to hunt out our missing census form. During my search, I discovered at least half a pound of salted peanuts hiding under each of the cushions of our three-piece suite. And if that wasn't disgusting enough, Trevor decided to gather them all in a bowl: "Rhian, these aren't half bad you know. They're not too soft, and they've still got plenty of salt left on them."... Trevor ti mochyn brwnt! (You dirty pig Trevor!... I only know the odd phrase in Welsh, and how to call someone a dirty pig is one of them.)

To cut a long story short I eventually found the Census form at the bottom draw of my kitchen unit. I filled it in, and made a special journey to the post box to post it. The nosy bastards! Don't the authorities know enough about my family as it is?... And another thing; what's it got to do with them, who was visiting my home on the twenty-ninth of last April?

July 13: Friday... Friday 13th - Explains everything really!

Well Diary, there's no such thing as good luck in this house... Not today, and not... But to be fair, the day had been very quiet up until the time Megan came home from work, and then it bit back at me with a vengeance:

Megan:	I'm going out clubbing tonight Mam.
Me:	You're not old enough. You're only sixteen.
Megan:	But I look eighteen, and I'm working.
Me:	I don't care if you look thirty-two, you're not going discoing to Cardiff.
Megan:	I'm working now. (She repeated.) I can do what I like.
Trevor:	Not in this house you can't... Now listen to your mother, and do what you're told.

The bad language... The foul, disgusting language Megan replied in response... Well, I've never heard anything like it in my life... Not directed at me from the mouth of one of my own children anyway. Even our Gary was shocked, as he tried to calm his sister down. Trevor wanted to throttle her, and poor Anthony ran and hid in his bedroom... But Megan, nothing anyone could say would calm Megan. She continued to swear at Trevor and me like a demented banshee. I couldn't get over the difference in her from the kind, considerate girl who had so tenderly spoke to me in my bedroom.

"Independence has gone to your head girl." Trevor yelled, as Gary finally managed to force her up the stairs, and into her room.

MEGAN'S ACCUSATIONS:... Deleting the F-Word, and most of the other expletives.

1. Trevor and I were accused of being bone idol council house scum.
2. We were also accused of being a disgrace to Wales.
3. We were accused of needing to find a life.
4. I am a drugged zombie. Trevor is a drunk.
5. Trevor is a big headed know all, on nothing.
6. Gary follows in his father's footsteps, and is as thick as sh*t.
7. The house is a rat, come sh**hole.
8. My mother is an interfering old bag... She said nothing derogatory about Anthony... She must like him?

Before I went to bed, I heard Megan crying to someone on the other end of her mobile phone. I don't know if this was out of anger, frustration, or regret... There's more to this than meets the eye.

July 14: Saturday

Dear Diary, when is a child not a child?... When its left school, when its turned sixteen?... Is a girl a woman, on the date of her first period?... What are the right and wrongs of it all?... By law Megan can go to work, have sex, have a baby, get married and do what she likes, apart from vote, watch an over eighteen film, and have a drink in a pub... So is she a woman or not?... Will people point me out in the street and say: there goes the mother of that out of control girl. When in fact that girl is a woman in disguise?... What's that you say Diary? You don't know either?... Well that makes the two of us, because I'm sure I haven't got a clue too?

12.00pm: Megan waited for the others to leave the house, then came down to apologise.

Megan: It's not right you know Mam, keeping me a prisoner in my room.

I said nothing.

Megan: If I'm old enough to go out to work, then I'm old enough to go out for a drink with my friends.

I employed the remote control to switch the channel over on the television set.

Megan: Julian Jackson's invited me to his sister's end of examination party tonight.

I read about this afternoon's film in the Radio Times.

Megan: His parents are spending a night at a Barry Hotel.

I looked into Megan's eyes, and I felt like slapping her across her face.

Me: Who the hell do you think you where talking to last night?... Don't you dare try it on with me in my own house, good girl... And for your further information, both your father and I have tried our best to give you the best of everything.

Now, it was Megan's turn to sit in silence.

Me: And for another thing, just because you are in work, it doesn't give you the right to look down upon me or your father.

Megan, head bent, sat sobbing in the chair. "I know what I said was terrible." She mumbled, amongst her tears. "But I couldn't help it... I had a terrible day at work yesterday... I messed up the till... Mr Hurst told me off, and told me to take an early lunch... I nearly ran home when he told me to go... All I wanted to do was to go out, and have a laugh with some of the girls I used to hang around with at school... Can I go out tonight Mam?... Can I?... Please?"

At the end of every sentence, Megan went through a delicate little routine of wiping her nose, and dabbing the tears from her eyes... I then observed her complete outlook brighten, and her tears immediately dry, after I'd given her my permission to attend the Jackson's party... Dear Diary, you can call me an old cynic if you wish, but there's no way Megan's little outburst had anything to do with Mr Hurst telling her off... The job doesn't mean that much to her.

July 15: Sunday

1.00am: I watched Julian Jackson walk my inebriated daughter home… Call it woman's intuition, instinct, or whatever you like, but I think there's something going on here.

MY CONSPIRACY THEORY:

1. I've got a house full of cut flowers.
2. Recently, the quality of cut flower has been getting more expensive.
3. Recently, Megan's been talking about Julian and work non-stop.
4. Has it definitely been proved that Julian is gay?
5. Megan hates Dominique. (The story about her party could have been a lie.)
6. Why would Mary and Idris Jackson want to spend a night in an hotel in Barry?

Until I discover some firm evidence that collaborates jointly with all the facts, I have decided to remain silent on the subject for the moment.

NEW WORRIES:

1. I hope Megan isn't one of those women, who think they can turn a bent man straight.
2. Trevor's going to go off his head if he finds out.
3. So is Mam!

Dear Diary before all this blew up, I intended telling you the story of Trevor's DSS interview, but that can keep until another day... I have too many thoughts buzzing around inside my mind.

July 16: Monday

The DSS are asking for proof of my illness, so I have to make an appointment to see the doctor... I'm sorry Diary, you don't know what I'm talking about, do you?... So here it is then. The full story of Trevor's DSS interview:... Before I start, just let me say before the interview started, Trevor did have a little bit of luck on his side. Instead of a man, he had a lady interrogator, and although she'll never admit to it in a court of law. The ladies do fall for Trevor's child like charm.

THE INTERVIEW COMPLETE AND UNABRIDGED:

DSS Lady: Please take a seat Mr Evans... Slight pause as she glimpses at Trevor's folder... I see you were last employed in 1993 Mr Evans. By the Welsh Development Agency I believe.

Trevor: Yes, that's correct bach.

DSS Lady: And you've been out of work ever since?

Trevor: Yes. (I would like to point out at this point, Trevor was employing the tactic of pretending to be both stupid, and pig ignorant at the same time... An intelligent strategy when dealing with the authorities.)

DSS Lady: Have you applied for any work, or attended any work related interviews since 1993 Mr Evans?

Trevor: Um... No, I can't remember any off hand, like.

DSS Lady: (By the way, she's writing all this down.) Is there any reason that you can think of why you can't go to work, if you were offered a job of work this morning?

Trevor: What do you mean?... Reason?

DSS Lady: Is there anything preventing you from going to work Mr Evans?... Are you currently suffering from an illness of some sort?... Are you an invalid in any way?... Are you caring for someone at home, who constantly needs you at home to care for them 24 hours a day?

Trevor: What was that last one again bach?

DSS Lady: Are you currently caring for somebody who needs medical attention at home, Mr Evans?

Trevor: What, like the wife you mean bach?

DSS Lady: Well yes, or dependent children, ageing relations, anyone who personally needs you to be with them in order to administer around the clock medical supervision.

Trevor: Well in that case, yes there is bach.... My wife, Mrs Rhian Evans.

DSS Lady: (Taking another look through Trevor's file.) I can't find anything about your wife's illness in your file Mr Evans.

Trevor: (In all innocence.) What's it got to do with you, if my wife is feeling a little under the weather?

DSS Lady: Quite a lot Mr Evans, if Mrs Evans illness has kept you from finding full-time employment all these years... I think that it's got quite a lot to do with us indeed.

Trevor: Why's that then bach? (Trevor employs a very strong Welsh accent to his advantage. When speaking to educated people in authority, a strong

Welsh accent can actually make you sound thicker than you actually are.) You're not going to stop giving me my benefit money because my wife is ill are you bach?

DSS Lady: On the contrary Mr Evans. If as you say your wife is truly suffering from any form of prolonged mental or physical illness. You will be classed as her carer, and taken off the unemployment registrar altogether.

Trevor: (In all innocence.) Will I bach? And what does that exactly mean then, like?

DSS Lady: Yes... You will no longer need to sign on, and you will be issued with a benefit payment book, which you can use to draw your weekly benefit at your local Post Office.

Trevor: And I'll still be entitled to what I'm getting now, will I bach?

DSS Lady: Let me see. You might be entitled to a little bit more Mr Evans... Excuse me for a second while I find out... I hope you don't mind waiting. I'll be back in a moment.

Trevor told me at this point in the proceedings, it took all of his powers of concentration to stop himself from bouncing up and down on his chair. "Rhian, I couldn't believe it." He said to me afterwards. "I saw my chance opening up before my very eyes, and I went for the jugular love." Trevor also said he had to remain very calm, just in case they were using a two-way mirror to secretly film his reactions in another room.

DSS Lady: (Returns with a handful of forms.) Well now Mr

Evans. I've had a word with a colleague specialising in these matters, and depending on how ill or, should I say what type of illness Mrs Evans is suffering from. You may be entitled to back date a claim for the money you were entitled to, at the start of Mrs Evans's illness.

Trevor: A backdated claim... A... Some sort of rebate, you might say, like?

DSS Lady: That's correct Mr Evans. What you need to do is fill in these forms. This one needs to by filled in by your family doctor. (She handed Trevor the forms.) Fill them in, then post them back to us as soon as possible Mr Evans, and we'll take it on from there.

Outside of the unemployment office, and on the bus home, Trevor said he'd wanted to scream his head off in triumph. "I felt like a winner on one of those television game shows, Rhian." Trevor spluttered into my face. "The only thing missing was a bikini clad DSS girl handing me a Golden Giro as I left the building."

I have an appointment at doctor Reece's surgery for Friday the twentieth.

July 17: Tuesday

Trevor said he can't wait to get his benefit book, because catching the bus into town to sign-on every two weeks was wearing him out... Then with the house to ourselves he began to seduce me with a 'Toffee Crisp'.

I love 'Toffee Crisp'. When I was a little girl, it was a toss-up between a 'Toffee Crisp', and an 'Aztec Bar', but they don't make Aztec bars anymore, so I've stuck with a 'Toffee Crisp' ever since. Sometimes I think I'm going mad, but I love the way the toffee and the chocolate hug around the little 'Rice Krispie' things, and the chewy texture on rough... Rice grains, I think?... And the smooth chocolate melting in my mouth.

While I was imagining the first taste on my tongue, Trevor was gently manoeuvring the opened chocolate bar along my inner thigh... Sorry Diary, not even for you... This is as far as this story goes. I'll leave it to your imagination to guess what happened next?

July 18: Wednesday

On the evening of the final evening class before the school break-up for the summer holidays. The room was awash with excited aspiring writers, who had recently mailed a cross section of assorted submissions to a wide range of unsuspecting magazine editors of Great Britain.

Of course Mr Davis was there, offering both equal amounts of helpful advice, and criticism, in that unbiased manner of his, which to us students didn't offend... The class was swinging. Everyone expected everyone else to have become a published writer or poet by the new school term. Then, just as Mr Davis was about to make his end of term speech. Mary Jackson: suspended between a pair of crutches, her right-ankle covered in plaster, entered the classroom.

"Rhian, you didn't?" Anne silently mouthed at me, as Mr Davis helped Mary to a chair. "Of course not." I mouthed back, before settling myself down, in preparation to listen to what she had too say.

"As you all know." Mary began, agonisingly shifting her raised foot to a more comfortable position on a moulded plastic seat. "I have missed the final two classes of the term through ill health. Nevertheless, I'd hate for my little illness to upset anyone else, so I've arranged a surprise party, come barbecue for you all at my house next Saturday evening." (Apparently Mary's previous barbecue had been a success... Can't think why I've never mentioned anything about it before?)

In stunned silence the entire class stared at the smiling hostess, then at each other, as each mind individually struggled to come to grips with the ramifications of this invitation.

"Are you sure you'll be feeling up to this, Mrs Jackson?" Mr Davis enquired, in a fruitless attempt of finding an excuse. "Only it's very short notice, and I don't know if we'll all be free on Saturday even..."

"No need to worry." Mary interrupted. "I checked what everyone was doing before I made the arrangements." As Mary spoke, everyone bar me remembered the little conversations they'd held with her on the few occasions they'd met.

"And I don't want to see anyone of you worrying about me." She insisted, pointing at each of her perspective guests with the bony index finger of her right-hand. "My husband Idris will be in full control of the food and drink. Leaving me free to socialise, with my Julian pushing me around the garden in my wheelchair."

Realising all further resistance was futile; to a man the class with heads bowed reluctantly accepted their personal hand written, embossed, barbecue invitations from her hand.

"Perhaps we could take it in turns to hold recital evenings throughout the summer." Mary gushed, as she chattered to Mr Davis. "Perhaps we could all pop round to Rhian's, the week after next?"

"Me and my big mouth." Anne said, as we stepped outside into the night air. "I told her all about your reply from 'Woman' magazine, and now look what she's making us do."

"Am I fuck!" Came Trevor's reply, after he discovered he'd be spending next Saturday evening around at the Jackson's.

July 19: Thursday

Trevor's worked it out, and according to him, my mental illness started in 1993. He's pretty sure about the date, because he can remember collecting my first Prozac prescription, a month or two after he'd finished working on his final Government Scheme.

"FUCKING HELL RHIAN, THE SS OWE US NEARLY NINE YEARS WORTH OF BACK DATED INVALID BENEFIT." Trevor screamed, punching the air in triumph.

"Now you've got your story straight, haven't you?" He asked, five hours later, after we'd spent the afternoon together concocting our stories... Mind you, I for one will be glad when this is all over. All this talk of mental illness, is making me think that I may be a little mad after all.

Megan came home from work with an extra large bouquet of flowers for me. "I had to pay for these myself." She said, resting them on my lap. "These are just to say sorry for the upset I caused last weekend." (And the interesting bit.) "Julian's invited me to come with you and Dad to the Jackson's barbecue next Saturday night."... Dear Diary, you can't tell me that there's not something going on between these two?

July 20: Friday

What a good, kind, and very considerate gentleman Dr Reece is. He knew exactly what was expected of him, from the moment he saw the top of my DSS forms poking out of my bag.... I began to ramble, as I handed him the forms: "My nerves are in shreds, doctor... I can't bear it any longer... To be left at home on my own I mean... My Trevor, my mother, or one of my children has to be with me every minute of the day and night... My nerves have got worse over the years Doctor... You don't know how much of an effort, it's taken for me to come and see you today... I'm at my wit's end Doc..."

"It's all right Mrs Evans." Interrupted, Dr Reece. "You just leave them here with me, and I'll see what I can do for you." Then he gave me a little smile, and a knowing wink, which came across, as meaning: *'Why on earth haven't you asked me to help you before, you silly woman?'*

My consultation lasted less than five minutes, and before I knew it, I was on my way home to Trevor with the good news, and a fresh prescription for another course of Prozac.

Trevor and I celebrated in the usual fashion... Dear Diary, there have been times this month, when my legs have never been closed... Well, it's certainly felt like that on times... Trevor said we should make this a special one, because what with it being the final day before the start of the school summer holidays and all, we might never find another chance to be alone together until next September.

WORLD NEWS:

Fellow writer Lord Archer got sentenced to four years for perjury today... I hope this is not a bad omen, and they don't put me away for four years for aiding and abetting benefit fraud.

July 21: Saturday

Today is the day of the Jackson's barbecue, and wouldn't you know it, the weather's perfect for an alfresco occasion... The weather was ideal when I got up this morning, and the weatherman predicted it would remain so for the rest of the day.

Trevor is unhappy. "Where's the bloody rain when you need it." He remarked, looking up at a blue cloudless sky... In common with the rest of my evening class, Trevor doesn't relish spending an evening, let alone a Saturday evening around at the Jackson's, and was relying on the weather to give him his excuse not to attend.

I on the other hand am looking forward to it, very much. I wasn't last Wednesday, but I am now. Megan is also looking forward to it... Trevor hasn't added two and two together yet.

A mixture of sex, the prospect of obtaining a benefit book, and my agreeing to see Dr Reece finally tipped the scales in my favour. With the battle won, Trevor had no option but to agree to escort me to the party without complaint... Well, I have done a lot for him lately.

Mam called around this afternoon to help me with my hair... Megan helped me to adjust it later after she came home from work.

"This will be like going to a Buckingham Palace garden party." Mam remarked, securing a curler to the back of my head. "Now don't forget to keep your eyes open Rhian. I'll expect a detailed report when you come back."

4.30pm: Trevor kept his promise and came home after the game... The rugby club, becomes a cricket club during the summer months.

6.00pm: Megan had come home from work, and the two of

us are upstairs getting ready... I feel like a teenager again; getting ready for the big night out.

7.45pm: We are ready for the off. Megan looks lovely. Trevor says she looks the mirror image of me, when I was her age. He also said, we look like sisters... Flatterer... Trevor looks presentable, (He scrubs-up well.) and he's promised to be on his best behaviour... May God, have mercy on us all.

July 22: Sunday

It all began pleasant enough. Julian invited us in, then led us through to the back garden. (Apart from the modern furniture and decor, the Jackson house looks very much like our own.) Idris sporting a chef's hat, and a blue striped apron, was taking advice from Dave Huws, on something or other, while poor Anne had been press-ganged into pushing Mary around her patio in her wheelchair, and was being bored to death with talk of plants in patio containers.

"Rhian, Trevor and Megan. Nice of the three of you to make it." Mary gestured, as Anne pushed her chair towards us. "Now there's no need for anyone to be shy. There's plenty of drink for the men, and my Julian has volunteered to make a selection of his wonderful cocktails for us ladies." As she spoke I noticed Julian offering Megan something I believed was called a 'Harvey Wallbanger', during my drinking days.

"All the gang are here apart from Mr Davis, and Mr Simpson. Both have made their apologies, but you know how it is, unforeseen commitments, and all that."

"Well, all the more for us then." Trevor responded, before offering an apology of his own. As spray released from the ring-pull of his lager can splashed down the front of Mary's cream blouse.

Insisting that Trevor join the men huddling around a fire topped with chard meat, I felt obliged to help Anne, manoeuvre Mary back into her house in order for her to change her top. "I've been collecting Capodimonte for years." Mary said, while we waited for Anne to return from her bedroom, with a clean blouse. "Of course, I purchase most of my pieces from Q.V.C the shopping channel on Sky. Have you got digital television, Rhian?" Then before I could answer. "Of course, Idris and I wouldn't know what to do without it. So many channels to choose from, and so few hours in the day to watch them all."

"Is this the one?" Anne asked, holding-up a navy blue creation, draped on a floral padded hanger.

"Lovely... You've got Sky, haven't you Anne?"

"Yes."

"I was just telling Rhian, she doesn't know what she's missing... Mind you, I'm surprised that you haven't got satellite Rhian, because you do spend a lot of time at home on your own, don't you?" At this unexpected revelation, I could do nothing but laugh, while poor Anne nervously tried to back herself out of the room without the two of us noticing. "Well, this won't do, now will it. Can't have my other guests thinking I am allowing you two to monopolise me all evening." Then with all the ease in the world Mary manoeuvred her wheelchair out of the room and onto the outside patio, with all the pomp and ceremony of a reluctant actress taking her fifth curtain call from the wings.

Two hours later the white ash of the barbecue, was left to cool on the evening's breeze. Occasionally a droplet of fat spitted on hot coals, as the gnarled bone of a pork chop, joined the paper plates and napkins in the waste bin.

"I would just like to thank you all for coming." Mary announced, to her hushed audience. "It's been an absolute pleasure, for my husband and I to entertain you all tonight..."

"Mam, can I say something?" Julian interrupted. "Ummm, I, I'd just like you all to know that I've met the girl of my dreams..."

"What's he talking about?" Trevor whispered in my ear.

"Megan." Julian held out his hand, and my giggling daughter joined him and his stunned parents on the edge of the patio.

"Mam, Dad, Mr and Mrs Evans, I have fallen head over heels in love with Megan, since the first moment she walked into the shop... Mr and Mrs Evans tonight I have asked your Megan if she'd do me the great honour and consent to get engaged, and she's said yes."

"Is he off his fucking head?" Trevor asked, as the lover's kissed.

"Julian, Julian, you're, you, you... Little fool." His mother stammered.

"Hang about... I thought the little cock-sucker was fucking gay." Was, the future father-in-law's initial reaction, to the happy news.... This was quickly followed by another sarcastic comment "I'm not having my daughter not knowing which way to turn in the middle of the night."

"Julian, Julian, you're breaking your mother's heart."

Anne looked at me and shrugged her shoulders... Dave cheered the happy couple... Idris shook his son by the hand, and admitted he'd had sleepless nights worrying about his son's leanings in the past... Trevor threatened to kill the dirty little pervert if he ever came anywhere near his daughter again... I stood in silence and took it all in, while the audience around us didn't know whether to laugh or cry... The barbecue broke-up shortly after with Trevor dragging a sobbing Juliet away from her Romeo's clutches.

Closing the Jackson garden gate behind me I heard Idris yell: "Julian, phone for a doctor quick. Your mother is having one of her funny turns," with Julian responding: "That drunken thug (Meaning Trevor) will never keep us apart."... Dear Diary, it's been hell in this house today, and I haven't the heart to write anymore.

July 23: Monday

Megan went to work on an earlier bus this morning... Personally I think she just wanted to get out of the house as soon as she could... An hour later Trevor and Gary left to sign-on. (Trevor still has to sign-on, until they send him his new benefit book.) Anthony is delighted that everyone has gone out,and so am I.

Dear Diary, yesterday was a living nightmare... A test of wills between Megan and her father, with me in the unhappy role of piggy in the middle, trying to keep the peace.

"I'm not having any queers in this fucking house... Can you hear me in there?" Trevor yelled, his abuse spraying the outside of his daughter's barricaded bedroom door. Then with a thump of his fist upon the woodwork. "The marriage will take place over my dead body, do you hear me?"

"Our Megan... Marrying that thing... Who would have..." If looks could kill, Gary would have fallen dead on the spot, after being on the receiving end of one of Trevor's menacing stares. While poor old Anthony... I honestly believe I saved his life after he'd made the remark. *'As long as he* makes her happy, what difference does it make who she marries?'

"Is it me Rhian?" Trevor asked, during a cooling off period. "Why him Rhian, why?"

I didn't know the answer.

"Well I never thought it would come to this." Trevor continued. "He's a fucking queer, for fuck's sake."

"But is he though?" I questioned. "Has he ever been out with, or has anyone ever seen him out with a boyfriend before?"

For a moment Trevor stared at me in silence, then swept my notions aside. "If it walks like a duck, quacks like a duck, and swims like a duck, then it's a fucking duck... Rhian, you can't tell me that, that mincing, feminine sounding, long streak of piss is normal." Then turning to his eldest son. "Did you ever hear about Julian bumming any of the younger boys at school Gary?"

"Well he never played games, if that's what you mean?" Gary replied. "He always carried a sick note form his mother to excuse him from gym. We all called him gay, but I've never seen him with anybody."

Deflated by lack of evidence, Trevor sat silently and pondered the real reason behind his hostile reaction, only to be reawakened by his daughter's bad timing. "If I'm old enough to go to work, then I'm old enough to go out with who I like." Standing at the midway point of the stairs... Megan had twisted her body in readiness to make a quick escape back to the sanctuary of her bedroom.

"Not in this bloody house you can't." And as her bedroom door slammed shut. "You are not going to work at that poof's palace anymore."... This is probably another reason why Megan left for work earlier than usual this morning.

I was feeling drained, and worn-out by six o'clock yesterday afternoon. Sunday dinner had consisted of a jam sandwich, and a cup of tea. The others got what they could catch, but in truth none of us were very hungry, which was just as well... Lord, sometimes I wonder why I bother to leave this house at times, because I always seem to hear bad news on my return.

During a break in 'Coronation Street' Mam sarcastically thanked me for letting her know about her Granddaughter's engagement, before slamming the phone down on me. (There are no secrets on this estate.) Gary and Megan have no credit left in their mobile phones, so I couldn't phone my mother back, and explain. "I bet Megan blew all of her credits telephoning that tosser." Trevor said, breaking the ceasefire that had lasted for the past three hours.

On their return from signing-on, Trevor and Gary reported they had witnessed Megan and Julian giggling at one another in the florists... Before he left to sign-on this morning, I'd made Trevor promise me he wouldn't say or do anything to Megan until I'd had a chance to speak to her on my own.

I tried to explain all to my mother this afternoon, but she refused to answer the door to me. Snapping at me through her letterbox, she told me to go away.

Megan came home from work two hours later than usual this evening... To keep the piece I made Trevor promise not to say a word.

July 24: Tuesday

I've been stabbed in the back... After collecting my family allowance, I tried once again to make it up with my mother. This time not only did my mother let me into the house, but before any trace of an apology could pass my lips, she proceeded to give me a lecture on family unity, which ended with the question: Did either I or Trevor realise we were breaking our only daughter's heart?

Megan came home late last night, because she had taken Julian to meet her Grandmother, who of course was now on their side.

"What lovely manners Megan's Julian has got. It was please may I have this, and thank you very much for that, all evening Rhian. I know you've had your falling out with Mary Jackson in the past, (*'Mam, you know you've always hated her too.'*) but you can't fault her on the way she's brought that boy up."

"Mam, don't you think he's a little bit gay?"

"We're all happy at that age Rhian."

"No! You know, do you think he's one of them?" I asked this question impersonating a teapot.

"Noooo. Julian! Of course he's not. Our Megan wouldn't go out with one of them... Oh I can see where all this nonsense is all coming from. Trevor thinks Julian's one of them just because he says please and thank you, and works in a flower shop, doesn't he. Rhian?... I sometimes think your Trevor is simple in the head."

Mam wouldn't have a word said against Julian after that. She brushed my and Trevor's fears under the carpet with her observations. "Well, I think they make a lovely couple." She said, showering them both with her approval. "A credit to both families, if only the pair of you weren't too dim to see it."

Back home Trevor claimed my mother had lost the plot. (No change there then.) I on the other hand have yet to catch Megan on her own. I think Julian is a nice enough boy, no matter what his sexual preferences may or may not be. (If they do get married, I only hope he doesn't come out of the closet during the honeymoon.)

July 25: Wednesday

I've done it again Diary. This time Anthony is the person who's achievements have been overlooked by your pages... What with one thing and another, and my mind being what it is. I've failed to mention anything about Anthony's exam results. But take them he did, and his school report reported he'd achieved great results. Mam said he's a credit to us all. Trevor agreed, and promised to ask the DSS for a claim form to pay for Anthony's fees while he's at university. (Apparently the government are trying to encourage young people from poorer backgrounds into universities.) Megan and Gary only scoffed at Anthony, and told him his exams he sat were meaningless and were nothing more than little boys' tests. I put an end to the conversation when I reminded Gary and Megan that they were a fine pair to talk, as both of them had never passed a single educational examination in their lives.

On a more personal front, this morning I discovered I'd became PMT active once again. (So ends one of the more active periods of my sex life... But then again; looking on the bright side, I could do with the rest.)

I was feeling a bit run down this evening... I miss my evening class, (This is the first Wednesday since the school broke up for the summer holiday.) I also miss the sex.

July 26: Thursday

Trevor has grounded Megan. (When she's not at work.) Megan has spent her entire wages on mobile phone cards, in an attempt to thwart her father's plan. Trevor doesn't know this, and thinks Megan is upstairs crying in her room. I am still piggy in the middle, and just when I thought things couldn't get any worse, Mam decided to pay us a visit.

"What's all this nonsense I hear about you grounding Megan." Mam, directed her question at the front page of the 'Sun' newspaper, Trevor held-up in front of his face. "I received a rather upsetting phone call from my Granddaughter late last night, begging me to call round and help to sort her problems out."

Trevor folded his paper across his lap. "She may be your Granddaughter Mair, but she's still very much my daughter, and I'll say what goes on in my own house."

"It's a bit late for that, isn't it?" Mam countered, then before Trevor had a chance to reply, "for you to suddenly take an interest in the welfare of your family... I mean. Who are you to pretend you care about the fate of your children at this late date?... Where has your interest been in the past?... With little or no help from you, your family has muddled through all these years on their own. You've got a wife, my daughter who's a nervous wreck. (But, I am getting stronger I thought.) Against all the odds you've got one son who's doing very well at school, one son who's got a proper job, and a daughter who's in employment. (I'd never heard my mother talking like this in my life.) So what if Megan is going out with Julian Jackson. He's not going to slap her around like some on this estate would, is he? He's not going to give her crack, or whatever it is they take these days. OK, I don't like his mother either. But Julian is a nice boy, and living on this estate Megan could have done a lot worse for herself than going out with him?"

"But he's gay!" Trevor said in despair. "There's no man in him. His walk, his talk, I can't bear to be in the same room as him."

"Who says you have to?" Mam continued in the same tone. "I mean, Megan's the one who's got to live with him. How many years have you been married to my daughter, Trevor? And in all that time, how many times have you called at my house to visit me on your own?"

Dear Diary this was another first. In all the years my mother has interfered in my life, this was the first time her interfering had done any good, let alone made any sense. Anyway to cut a long story short; Trevor reluctantly agreed that the gossip concerning Julian's sexuality was all hearsay, even if his personality suggested otherwise. He also agreed, that there was a lot of heterosexual idiots living on this estate, and Megan could find herself in a lot more trouble if she'd been going out with one of them. So a compromise was reached. Megan's grounding was lifted, and Julian would be given the benefit of the doubt... Until it was proved otherwise!

July 27: Friday

Dear Diary, thank God all this pressure has been lifted from my brain. Mam phoned this morning and said Megan had phoned her from work, and was very pleased with the outcome. She also said Megan and Julian had called around on their way home from work, and presented her with a beautiful bouquet of flowers for sorting things out. Trevor thinks that Mr Hurst must be rolling in it, if he can allow his staff to take home all the unsold flowers in his shop for free. I said it was known as perks of the trade, and no different from working in a cake shop.

I didn't receive any flowers on this occasion, but Megan warned me to expect some exciting blooms in the near future.

July 28: Saturday

One of my little pleasures in life is the Saturday matinee on BBC2. Now I know this doesn't mean a lot to most people, but to me, and at times, it has meant the world.

During the period I spent trying to wean myself off the drink. The beginning of my Prozac years... The quiet moments caught during my babies afternoon naps... I honestly believe the images of Stewart Granger, Cary Grant, Rock Hudson and others have gone a long way to the preservation of my mind. Their existence on my television screen, has helped me to escape from mine. So it will come as no surprise when I tell you, anything that interferes with my Saturday afternoon ritual, is looked upon by me; with how shall I put it... With a less than sympathetic eye.

Five minutes before the start of 'Kim' starring Errol Flynn... For some reason Megan had stayed at home this afternoon. Paying no attention to this, I settled down to watch the film.

Megan: Mam, can I ask you a favour?

Me: Can't it wait until after the film love?

Megan: Can Julian listen to some music in my bedroom with me?

Me: It's too early yet love. Give your father some more time to come around to the idea of the two of you courting, before you invite him over.

Megan: You are just like Julian's mother. She doesn't think I'm good enough to go out with her son.

Me: And she's told you that, has she?... She said it to your face?

Megan: No, Julian told me.

Me: Well then, don't just stand there, get on your mobile and tell Julian he can call around for his tea... Megan, after the film has finished, okay!

Mary Jackson's got a bloody cheek saying my daughter is not good enough for her son. She'll be gutted when she hears that he's coming for his tea.

11.00pm: Yes Julian was very polite. Yes, he said all his please and thank U's in the correct places... I personally found him very easy going. He made me laugh with some of the things that he said, especially when he mimicked his mother dusting her precious ornaments, or her 'Crap-poo-da-ponty' as he called them.

Yes, over all I have to admit to liking Julian. He didn't annoy me as much as I thought he would. In fact, watching him mincing across the room, made me smile more than anything else. Even Trevor is coming around to the idea. Before he went to the club this afternoon, he remarked: "What hope did the boy have, after his mother cut off his father's balls on their wedding night?"

During tea, (Megan hurriedly made some 'Spam' sandwiches, and arranged a number of 'Rich Tea' biscuits on a plate, (Plain and jammed) while I finished watching the film. Julian admitted that his mother was dead against him going out with Megan, and more than a little bit surprised that Trevor and I didn't feel the same way. He also let slip that Mary and Idris are not in agreement on this issue,and are no longer communicating with each other. Then shaking his head, he said: "She tried to bar me from leaving the house, after I'd told her where I was going this afternoon... I'm seventeen next birthday, and I had to run out of the backdoor before she had time to bolt it."

July 29: Sunday

The day began the same as the majority of others in this house. Worry, boredom, confusion, but by midday the place was in uproar, with the entire family dancing around the living-room, screaming and cheering their heads off, like demented fools.

10.45am: Trevor got out of bed and descended the stairs like the missing link. I handed him his mug of tea, then watched him tackle the Sunday newspaper.

11.15am: Trevor was on his second mug, while he hunted through his pockets for his pools coupon, and betting slip.

11.18am: "Bloody Australian rubbish." Trevor said, throwing his football coupon in the bin.

11.25am: "YES! FOUR NIL, FOUR FUCKING NIL! RHIAN I'VE FUCKING DONE IT, LOVE!" Then he started to sing: We're in the money, we're in the money. Na-na-na-na-na-na-na-da-da-da-da.

11.45am: At last I'd managed to get some sense out of him. "My horses came up Rhian. My fucking four horse accumulator came up darling... I said it fucking would, and it fucking has. It's taken me the best part of twenty-five years, but I knew it would happen in the end. I've stuck by my system through thick and thin, and now it's finally paid off."

Dear Diary, like me I bet you don't understand what the hell Trevor's talking about. Apparently for twenty-five years Trevor has been placing a pound wager on something called a long odds accumulator, and yesterday his bet came up. Or in other words, his four horse selection won.

"How much?" I yelled, after I'd finally realised what was happening. "How much?" Gary, Megan and Anthony asked, when they were told the news. "How much?" Mam asked, over the phone, and ten minutes later after bursting into the living-room via the back door.

"I, I, I'm not sure... But it's a lot." Trevor replied, as he scribbled his calculations around the edge of the newspaper.

12.15am: In the bedroom. "Trevor, this win?... It will be definitely more than fifty quid, won't it love?" I asked, before rolling on to my side, and falling to sleep.

July 30: Monday

Trevor's pink face turned bright red, then along with his body, began to shake excitedly in the chair. At first I thought the bastard had done it to me again... He'd built my hopes up, only to send them crashing down.

"Rhian, Rhian, Rhi... I ran all the way home from the betting shop." His shaking hand dipped into his pocket, his large staring eye's bulged out of their sockets, as he lifted a bundle of fifty pound notes from his pocket, and placed it directly on top of the coffee-table. "Four thousand, five hundred, and sixty-five pounds, and thirty-nine new pence." He whispered, tossing the lose change into the ashtray on the table.

“Dad, did you know your pound a week gamble has cost you £1,300 in stake money over twenty five years? Anthony asked, showing his father the total displayed on his pocket calculator. “According to these figures, your win means you can continue to be a pound a week loser for the rest of your life, and still end up being an overall winner in the end.”

Trevor, Anthony, and I stared at the money on the table. Mam stared at it when she called around. As did Gary and Megan when they came home from work. Now you may find this strange, but it was odd having all that money in the house. For one, most of it was in fifty pound notes. A type of currency, we as a family have had very little to do with in the past. (I’ve never been given a fifty pound note when I’ve cashed my family allowance or unemployment benefit at the Post Office.) Trevor was worried we’d get robbed. He said, now that we’ve got something worth stealing in the house, we’ll have to be extra careful to lock all the doors and windows before going to bed tonight. Before she returned to her house, Mam had been sworn to secrecy, along with the rest of the family, until Trevor and I have decided what to do with the money for the best.

Dear Diary, it’s been a strange old day, with all that money in the house. In many ways it truly is a big responsibility, and a heavy burden not knowing what to do with our windfall. (God help us, if we ever win the lottery.)

July 31: Tuesday

Dear Diary, last night Trevor and I had a very restless night worrying about the money. (I’ve never noticed before, but this house makes a lot of noise during the night.) After a lot of tossing and turning, we decided to blow the lot before the DSS finds out about it. Our plan is to clear all our outstanding debt for the first time in our married lives, buy everyone in the family something special, and hopefully have enough money left over for us all to go on a family holiday together.

With notepad and pencil in hand, I made a list of all the people we owe money to. (This made for some very depressing reading.) Until I saw it in black and white, I never realised how deep into the shit, our family is. (Financially I mean.) Including the household bills, catalogues, (I'm only allowed credit from one at the moment, but I owe money on four.) and Trevor's outstanding court fines. (More about them at a later date.) I discovered the Evans family are in the red to the tune of £5,794.81... Trevor and I both agree we should forget about settling our outstanding debt, and concentrate on enjoying ourselves for once in our lives.

Trevor said we should buy a new television and video, and I agree. Trevor, who keeps abreast of new technology said: "The government are changing the television signals, so if we don't buy one of those new digital televisions now, our old set won't be able to receive a picture in a couple of years time."

THE WHAT I WANT LIST:

Trevor: Television and video. "It's my choice, but I don't mind if you all watch it with me."

Gary: I don't know really? (Shrugged shoulders) I don't mind, whatever... I'll be happy with the new box too.

Megan: I want you to pay for Julian to come on holiday with us when we go. (Trevor whispering in my ear: "I don't think we'll be able to afford to go on holiday after all love.")

Anthony: A new computer... Then I can be like everyone else in my computer club."

Mam: Rhian, I'll be happy with anything you give me, love. (I still think she looked disappointed, when Trevor repaid the money, she'd spent on settling our outstanding telephone bill.)

Me: I want what money can't buy, unless you count bribery. I want to be a successful poet, or writer of some sort... Now that I can afford what I like, I find that I want, or need nothing. It's all comparative when you come to think about it... Okay, I could do with some new clothes, and some decent make-up, but it's not life threatening is it. When it comes down to it, I'd also like a new television, and video... And a new three-piece suit, a new cooker, and fridge-freezer wouldn't go a miss as well.

REVIEW OF MONTH:

What an helter-skelter ride this month has been. Megan and Julian. The Jackson barbecue, and the fallout there in. My sex life, and of course the icing on the cake, Trevor's win. It took Trevor nearly twenty-five years to achieve his dream. How long will it take me to realise mine???

Four and a half grand... Fucking Hell!!!

August 1: Wednesday

My period ended on the 30th of July, but alas. Trevor and I, have been feeling too stunned to do anything about it. Trevor has hidden the money beneath a loose floorboard under our bed: *'Safer than the bank of England, this is.'* He declared, before gently rapping the board down, and rolling the carpet back into place.

I on the other hand feel worn-out by it all. My wrist's ache from continually writing lists for the things we want, then crossing them out when we think of something else we need to buy. If only they'd ache from writing poetry, then I wouldn't complain... But that's life I suppose.

August 2: Thursday

Trevor nearly give the poor bus driver an heart attack, when he asked him if he could change a fifty pound note. Laughing all the way to his seat, Trevor left me to pay the flustered driver our 45p fare.

Inside Curry's Cardiff branch, I turned my head away in embarrassment, as I watched Trevor trying out his haggling technique on the sales assistant.

Assistant: This digital television is a 28" Widescreen. It's Nicam stereo of course, Teletex, remote control, plus a lot of built in features like a built in menu, child lock, and the like.

Trevor: And it comes complete with a video, does it boy?

Assistant: With or without, it's up to you sir.

Trevor: Well, we'd like a video as well you know.

Assistant: Well, you've come to the right place, and on the right day. For instance, if you decide to take this

	television video combo sir. We can deliver it for free, and one of our staff will set it up for you at your home.
Trevor:	How much is this little lot, going to set me back then son?
Assistant:	Eight hundred and ninety-nine pounds sir.
Trevor:	How much for cash?
Assistant:	Eight hundred and ninety-nine pounds, but I can do you a special deal with a Sky satellite receiver if you'd like one?

An hour later Trevor had spent over two and a half thousand pound:

Television/Video combo	=	£899
Electric Cooker	=	£499
Computer	=	£599
Fridge/Freezer	=	£399
Kettle	=	£35
Toaster	=	£49
Ice Cream Maker	=	£29

Satellite Box, Dish, & Installation = Free, but we have to pay Sky £34 a month for the full programme package. (I can't believe Trevor signed-up for Sky. Don't get me wrong. I'm delighted we're getting it, but I'm married to a man who complains when I spend two quid a week on television licence stamps.) Needless to say the kids were all ecstatic when they heard the news too.

Trevor insists he's going to get some of our money back, by selling off our old stuff in the free-ad's via the local paper, and by placing a card in the Post Office window. As for Sky TV:

'*Don't worry about it.*' Trevor explained after kissing me on my cheek. '*The rise I'm expecting in my benefit money, will more than cover our Sky commitment each month.*'

August 3: Friday

Glorious, glorious day. How the other half lives. Food shopping around Tesco's today was like a dream come true. Trevor and I pushed a shopping trolley each, no shopping list, no pen and paper to tally up what everthing cost... pure bliss. Everything we fancied went into the trolley, and not a blue line label in sight.

TWO HUNDRED AND FIFTEEN QUID, FOR A WEEK'S SHOPPING!... I nearly pissed my knickers laughing, watching Trevor pay the checkout girl... On our way home Trevor asked the taxi driver to stop at the discount furniture warehouse. Forty-five minutes later and one thousand pounds lighter, we climbed back in the the taxi cab and drove home.

12.00am: "Bloody marvellous place that discount warehouse is." Trevor remarked, cuddling up to me in bed. "One new double bed, three singles, a flat-pack wardrobe unit and a new three-piece suite; all for a little under a grand!"

"Yes, I know." I reminded Trevor. "I can't believe it myself."

August 4: Saturday

Yesterday I forgot to mention that I had to ask my mother to store some of our food in her fridge freezer, because ours isn't large enough. At first Mam wasn't too happy about the arrangement, but she soon changed her tune when I invited her around for Sunday dinner.

TREVOR'S FINES:

In the past, around about the same time that I was getting pissed. Trevor had his own share of trouble... All right, at this point I would like to point out that some of the scrapes he was getting into were my fault... Like the numerous times Trevor beat-up those blokes for calling me a slag, even when I was acting like one... And the time he got himself arrested for being drunk and disorderly when I was the real culprit who was behaving aggressively about the town... But the shoplifting at Christmas time, and the football hooliganism he was involved in were scrapes entirely of his own making.

Every time Trevor got caught and pleaded guilty, the Magistrate would fine him whatever, and because Trevor was nearly always unemployed at the time, the Magistrate would allow Trevor to pay off his fines in ridiculously low amounts like fifty pence a week in most cases... In his time Trevor has been arrested twice for shoplifting, once for threatening behaviour, (That's when he took the blame for me... He told the policeman to leave me alone, or he'd ram the policeman's truncheon up the policeman's bum.) and three times for violence inside and outside of a football ground.

All this took place during the late seventies and early eighties, but Trevor's continued to pay off his fines ever since. (£10 still outstanding for threatening a police officer.) To this day, Trevor scoffs at the idea of football hooliganism being wrong. *'At certain times in your life, it's good to fight.'* Trevor tried to explain to me one night. *'These soccer pundits on the telly who call it a disgrace, don't know what they're talking about. They've never experienced the excitement, or danger of coming face to face with the enemy coming at then from the opposite side... Inside a football stadium I felt like a gladiator, it was great. Singing, chanting, charging, battling, fighting, surges of adrenaline, fucking great mun.'*

Well, I couldn't understand Trevor then, and I don't understand him now. Men! Who knows what's going on inside their heads?... I'm all for a quiet life myself, and luckily for me Trevor now feels the same way... Age you see... We all grow older and wiser... After all Trevor wasn't all that bad in his youth. He stuck by me through thick and thin, didn't he.

August 5: Sunday

Our old cooker must have had the shock of it's life when I placed a £10 leg of lamb inside it's oven,and turned up the setting to full power. Telepathically I heard it say: *'Where's the tray of lamb chops you usually allow me to turn into charcoal for you on a Sunday afternoon?'*

After dinner Mam said: "You can't beat a nice bit of Welsh lamb, can you?" For dessert I bought one of those ready made fresh cream family size trifles. (£4.99 that cost.) After we'd consumed it,Anthony remarked: "That was better than Christmas dinner Mam."

Megan said: "I wish I could have invited Julian to dinner. This was so much better than giving him Spam sandwiches the last time he came."

"Yes love." Mam agreed. "As you go through life, you'll find everything is better when you've got a bit of money behind you."

"And now for my surprise." Trevor smiled. Taking a selection of photographs from his blazer pocket, he spread them across the cleared table. "Dai West... You remember me telling you about him Rhian. He's on the committee down at the club... You must remember him, he owns a carpet shop in Cardiff."

Offering nothing but a blank expression on my face, Mam chipped in: "I think I went to school with him. Wasn't his father killed in the war?"

"I don't know." Trevor replied, in a desperate attempt to end this avenue of conversation.

"West, West, or was his name Best? Rhian, do you know anyone named Best, who had his father killed in the war?"

"Forget all that." Trevor said pointing at the photo's. "My mate Dai West's got one of those static mobile home, type caravan things sited down in Cornwall, and he said I can rent it off him over the bank holiday weekend for one hundred and fifty quid."

Dear Diary, isn't it funny how when you've got no chance of going, you think wouldn't it be nice to get away from it all. Yet when a holiday is offered to you on a plate, a thousand and one reasons crop up, that make you wonder is it really worth going after all?

Mam:	I suppose I'll be all right staying on my own over the bank holiday. You needn't worry about me Rhian. You'll only be away for a few days won't you?
Me:	I can't go if my mother's not going.
Megan:	Can Julian come if he chips in a few pounds?
Me:	Anyway, I've got nothing to wear.
Mam:	Don't let me spoil your holiday for you Rhian.
Megan:	You can borrow some of my clothes Mam.
Me:	No, it wouldn't be right. If my mother can't go, then there's no point in me going... I'll only worry about her while I was there.
Mam:	Don't let me spoil your chance of a holiday Rhian.

Megan: Julian can come, can't he Mam?

Me: Trevor, is this caravan big enough for us all to sleep in, or what?

Mam: Don't let the idea of me being all alone in my house, put you all off from going Rhian.

Three hours later the caravan sleeping arrangements had been worked out to everyone's satisfaction. Mam (reluctantly) agreed to join us: 'As long as it's not putting anyone out.' And Trevor (reluctantly) agreed to allow Julian to tag along, providing his mother was willing to let him out of her sight ... Personally, I didn't think there was any need for Trevor to make this remark after Megan had excitedly ran to her bedroom, to phone her boyfriend: 'If I have to sleep in the same caravan compartment as Julian. I bags sleeping with my back against the wall.'

August 6: Monday

Trevor and Gary signed on today. The DSS still haven't sorted Trevor's benefit book out yet. "It was sickening on the bus into town Rhian. "Trevor remarked on returning home. "The two of them were all over each other like a rash. Laughing, giggling, tickling, whispering in ears. I bet if Gary and I weren't sitting directly behind them, Megan's tongue would have ended up down Julian's throat."

Julian called round with Megan after work, and thanked us for inviting him to come to Cornwall with us. He assured Trevor his mother would be delighted when he told her about the trip. Thankfully Trevor remained silent, but tipped me a knowing wink.

8.30pm: Megan came down the stairs clutching her mobile phone, and said there were riots going on around at the Jackson house. According to her, poor Julian had to lock himself in the bathroom in order to make his telephone call. Poor Megan, I suppose we all should have been more understanding, but the mental picture of Julian cowering on the pan, making his SOS call, while his rampant mother was outside beating down the door with her crutch, was more than any of us could stand... Our howls of laughter sent Megan scurrying back to her bedroom in tears.

August 7: Tuesday

Dear Diary, Trevor and I have blown all his winnings on a wild spending spree. The evidence of which will be arriving at this house throughout the day in various delivery vans. In a way I'm sad all the money's gone, but on the other hand, I'm happy that we spent it on new things for the house,instead of pissing it up against the rugby club wall.

10.00am: A Curry's delivery van pulled up outside and lowered it's tailgate, as a crowd gathered to watch the men deliver a new range of household gadgets to our door.

"I don't think many people living around here have one of these." The service engineer said, as he installed our new Widescreen digital television and video combo. "Come-up on the lottery, have you?" He remarked, while his colleagues struggled to manoeuvre our new cooker into the kitchen.

"Horses!" Trevor replied. "Horses, and twenty-five years worth of faith."

11.30am: A van from the discount furniture warehouse pulled-up outside, just as the service engineer was giving Trevor a basic lesson on how to turn on our new computer.

"We bought it for our youngest boy." Trevor said, feeling overwhelmed by the sight of the new technology. "Don't worry about trying to explain it to me." Trevor reassured the service engineer who realised he had bitten off more than he could chew. "The boy will know what to do with it when he comes home from school."

1.00pm: Everything had been delivered apart from our new three piece suite, and our satellite dish. "Very nice." Mam remarked, after she'd had a good look round. "Mind you this room needs redecorating, Rhian... The walls are making your new television look scruffy."

4.00pm: Trevor had been upstairs for the best part of five hours trying to erect our new flat-pack wardrobe. During that time the bad language seeping out of our bedroom window was terrible. On more than one occasion, I caught sight of a passer by looking up at our window in disgust."

8.00pm: "I don't know." Trevor yawned from his chair. "You spend eight hundred and ninety-nine quid on and new digital widescreen telly and video combo, and there still isn't anything worth watching but repeats!"

August 8: Wednesday

Trevor went to bed later than me last night. When I entered the living-room this morning I found this note waiting for me on the kitchen table:

Rhian.
I've written out this card for you to stick in the Post Office window when you go to cash my Giro this morning? I don't know what time I'll be getting up in the morning/ afternoon. Erecting that flat pack wardrobe wore me out last night.

See you when I see you,
Trev.

Under the note (Dear Diary, hasn't Trevor got lovely hand writing?... I've Sellotaped the top of this note to your page.) I found, and read the card:

FOR SALE
TELEVISION = £50 ono
VIDEO = £50 ono
FRIDGE-FREEZER = £50 ono
ELECTRIC COOKER = £50 ono
ALL IN GOOD WORKING ORDER
BROWN DRAYLON THREE PIECE SUITE
- WELL LOVED & LOOKED AFTER = £50 ono
TELE: DAY - 0007 888111 NIGHT - 0007 888111

Another good thing about Trevor's win; over the past two weeks I haven't needed to spend any of our benefit money on food or bills. (I've managed to stash most of the savings away, in a safe hiding place... We'll need it when we go on our holiday.)

It's costs 20p a week to place a card in the Post Office window. I spent 40p, and put it in for two weeks.

August 9: Thursday

Received a letter from Sky TV this morning. They say they are calling next Monday to connect us. Megan's been very unhappy since last Monday night. She claims Mary Jackson's health has taken a sudden turn for the worse, and Julian feels so guilty that after work he spends his evenings reading aloud to his mother from the side of her bed.

"No, no, no, Rhian. This time you are asking too much." Trevor protested, after I'd finished telling him my plan to get the two lovers back together again. "Please not another barbecue... Please tell me you're not serious... A bloody barbecue Rhian! You want us to invite the Jackson clan to a barbecue next Saturday night?... You haven't forgotten what happened at the last one, have you?"

Then Trevor said: "We haven't got a barbecue." To which I responded: "You've still got about a hundred quid left of your winnings. Why don't you buy a cheap one, for thirty quid in Argos?"

A little more coaxing, and Trevor agreed to my plan: "That girl of ours is more trouble than she's worth!... We should have only had boys Rhian, and kept it at that."

With my plan swinging into motion, Anthony printed me out two exclusively designed invitations on his computer. (One each for the Jackson's and my mother.) Anthony came up with a comical design of a mad cow barbecuing some burgers. I posted Mary's off, with a first class stamp. (I'd love to be a fly on the wall, when my invitation lands on her doormat.) But I hand posted my mother's myself, when I knew she'd be out... Well, it'll be a nice surprise for her when she gets in.

August 10: Friday

Mam phoned first thing this morning, then went into raptures when I told her Anthony had exclusively designed the invitation for her. "It's very good isn't it Rhian. He's very clever is our Anthony, and you say he made it on the computer, did he? Well Rhian, you can tell him from me that I think his card is wonderful. I've never received a designer invitation before. Wait until I show the girls down at the old age club. They'll be wanting him to design their birthday cards, and everything from now on, I bet."

At midday I received a phone call from a Mr Jones: "Hello. I saw your card in the Post Office window. Have you still got your three piece suite for sale?"

"Yes." He asked for, and I gave him my address.

"Right, I'll be there sometime in the next half an hour."

"Okay." I put the phone down.

"Trevor, there's a man coming to see the furniture." I yelled up the stairs. Then I heard a mad scramble, a loud curse and the sight of my half dressed husband rushing down the stairs.

"Well don't just stand there woman, bring me the hoover." Flinging the cushions to the floor, Trevor proceeded to hoover the slightly soiled lining of the sofa. Instructing me to clean the two chairs; Trevor ran his hand down the back and along the sides of the sofa, finding one pound twenty-two pence worth of loose change in the process. "We want them to look nice Rhian." Trevor said, as I found another fifty-six pence down the back of the chair. "But we don't want to be giving money away, do we."

There was a knock on the door: "Hi, I phoned about the three piece suite." Trevor answered the door and let him in, while I went and hid in the kitchen.

Mr Jones: Do you mind if I look under the cushions?
Trevor: Feel free. You can sit on it as well, if you like.

While all this was going on, I was listening with my ear pressed up against the kitchen door. I don't know why I was hiding in the kitchen. Trevor certainly didn't tell me to go in there. Subconsciously I didn't want to be in the room when our furniture was rejected. Or more to the point, I didn't want to see the disappointed look on the man's face when he rejected it.

Mr Jones: Fifty pound or nearest offer, the card said in the window. What's the lowest you'll take?
Trevor: About forty-nine pounds, and ninety-nine pence?

Trevor, this is not the time to piss take, I thought to myself behind the door.

Mr Jones: Well I'll take it, but you'll have to come up with a better deal than that.

Forty pounds and Trevor's promise to help him carry the furniture to the eastern side of the estate; the deal was done. First the two chairs were carried out of the house. Balancing them upside down with the seat on top of their heads, and gripping tightly to the arms I watched Trevor and the man disappear up the road. I actually cried when they came back for the sofa. Standing in the space created by the absent furniture, a terrible thought suddenly occurred to me. 'WHAT ON EARTH

ARE WE ALL GOING TO BE SITTING ON NOW?' And if that thought wasn't bad enough, my next thought sent me into a state of panic: 'WHAT WILL THE JACKSON'S SIT ON, WHEN THEY ARRIVE ON SATURDAY NIGHT?'

August 11: Saturday

This is so typical of Trevor. He goes charging ahead with his schemes, without a care of the consequences his actions may cause to others... Tonight we have invited guests to this house, and apart from the four chairs around the kitchen table, and a battered old pouffe in the living-room, there isn't a stick of alternative seating to be found anywhere in the house.

"If you think this is bad, you should have seen the state of the house that poor sod has got to live in." Trevor remarked, after I'd called him a idiot for selling our old furniture, before our new three-piece suite had arrived. "No word of a lie Rhi, the place stunk to high heaven of cat's piss, but they were really landed with our old suite. You should have seen how happy his kids looked bouncing up and down all over it."

A shudder went down my spine on hearing this... My old friend... My poor sofa... My comforting sofa was being abused!

Mam also called Trevor an idiot when she found out what had happened. Stating the obvious she said: "Of course Rhian. You do realise, the Jackson's will never believe your story about the furniture, don't you? Trevor's really landed you in it this time my girl. Good and proper."

"I know Mam, but what can I do?"

"She'll be landed to come in here and find your house in a state like this. And it's too late to cancel, because if you do, she'll accuse you of not being able to organise a barbecue."... I think the rain and my tears began to fall at the same time.

"Look the long range weather forecast says it's going to rain non-stop for the rest of the day." Trevor said, finding the information on Teletext. "Why don't we forget about having a barbecue, and have a 'Kentucky Fried Chicken' bargain bucket evening instead?"

'Great!' I thought to myself. 'No chairs, no barbecue, but we do have a bargain bucket... If Mary can't convince her Julian to stay away from our family after this, nothing will."

6.00pm: For once the weather forecasters got it spot on. It's been teeming down all day. Like the trooper she is, Mam came through at the last moment and allowed us to borrow four of her dining chairs. (Trevor says, if Mary comes in her wheelchair, that will make the grand total of nine, plus one pouffe.)

I'm ready. At this moment Trevor should be on the bus with at least three bargain buckets. Mam has arrived, (She's wearing her best summer flower cardigan from M&S.) Megan is nervously staring out of the window, and twiddling with her hair. Both the boys are watching the television, in T-shirts and jeans. By the way, I'm trying to create the gypsy look dressed in my flowing skirt, and off the shoulder top. (Rather appropriate in this house at the moment.)

"MAM, I CAN SEE THEM ALL COMING AT THE TOP OF THE HILL." Megan screamed at the top of her voice. "JULIAN'S PUSHING MRS JACKSON IN HER CHAIR."... Please God, let this party go with a swing.

August 12: Sunday

I don't care if the bitch is in a wheelchair, I'll fucking kill her!... Mam was right, she didn't believe the story about our furniture, but she did ask me if our sofa used to reside against the wall, because she could make out its ghostly outline on the wallpaper. The time is now 8.00am, I'm writing this while the memory is still fresh in my mind... Oh my God, I've just remembered Julian is sleeping in Gary's old sleeping bag, on the living-room carpet... I think I'll leave off writing anymore, until I come to myself, a little later in the day.

9.00pm: First of all Trevor missed the bus from town, which meant he had to wait an hour for another one. That in turn meant, I only had twiglets, and some other nibbles for them to munch on for an hour and a half while they waited.

"Lovely telly, you've got there." Idris complemented, hoping to jolly everyone around.

"Yes, lovely." Mary agreed. "I'm sure it will go with your new furniture, when they deliver it."

"What do you think about Rhian and Trevor inviting your Julian to go away with our family to Cornwall over the bank holiday weekend?" Mam, Mam, Mam, Mam, Mam!... So World War three began.

"So now we know why we've all been invited, don't we." Came Mary's reply to my mother's innocent question. "I had a feeling I'd be walking into a trap. Idris! What did I say before we left the house this evening?" Before her husband could reply, Mary answered the question for him. "I said there was an ulterior motive, and more to this than meets the eye, didn't I. My God, you must be desperate for your daughter to get her hands on my son, Rhian... You invite us to a barbecue in the middle of a tropical monsoon. Only for us to find out, that the menu's been changed at the last minute. You've sold every stick of furniture in your house. The proceeds of which are at this precise moment being spent by your husband at some greasy spoon, for quite frankly food my family don't like or wouldn't want to pop into their mouth. And all because you hope I'll give you my blessing. You want me to give you my blessing for my precious son to walk hand in hand with your darling daughter into the setting sun of Cornwall. Well, let me tell you that will never happen..."

Stunned into silence by our guest's unwarranted outburst, Mam and I could only stare open mouthed at each other, as Gary picked up the gauntlet on our behalf. "You are one horrible bitch, do you know that?" My softly spoken son, informed the gnarled face of the dragon.

"Steady on now son." Idris tried to intervene.

Undeterred Gary pressed on. "Horrible, nasty and jealous. I warned my sister about your son, and about you if it comes to that. But for some reason unknown to any of us here, she loves him, and if we can put up with him, then I think that you should give her a chance."

"Here, here." Said Mam, patting her Grandson on his back. "Don't think you can fool us Mary Jackson. Coming here in a chair. I've seen you standing-up to hang your washing on the line."

"Julian, Idris, you two." Mary said pointing her bony finger at Dominique, and Harvey. (Baby Sotheby had slept through the whole thing on her lap.) I'm not staying here to listen to this anymore. I'm..."

"I'm not going." The room fell silent. "I'm not going home

with you Mam." With his hand entwined tightly around my daughter's waist, Julian made his stand. "Mam, Mrs and Nana Evans don't deserve what you've said tonight. (Thank God, Trevor missed the bus.) Along with Mr Evans,the whole family have been very kind to me. Kinder than you have been with their Megan."

"You stupid fool!" She spat back in his face. "Don't you know when you've been taken in boy?" Mary said, pointing at me. "Rhian only wants you to go out with her daughter because she knows it will get up my nose."

"Please play fair, Mam." Julian pleaded, kneeling at her right wheel. "Please give me one good reason why we all can't be friends?"

"Because she's not good enough for you Julian. Do you want me to spell it out for you son... She'll pull you down to her level. You'll never save enough money for a little flower shop of your own, with a girl like that hanging around your neck. Look around you. Look at the way these people live." Then like the wicked witch I always knew she was, Mary rolled her chair to the front door, stood-up, opened the front door, sat back down again, before manoeuvring herself through the exit.

In the garden, under the umbrella her husband was holding above her head, Mary gave her son her final ultimatum. "It's us or them, Julian. If you are not home within the next hour. I will take it for granted that you would rather break your mother's heart and stay with them... Oh Julian, whatever did I do to make you turn your back on me?"

A confused looking Trevor greeted the departing Jackson's at the garden gate. "What, going already?" He quipped as Mary led her families retreat up the street.

"What's the matter now?" Trevor enquired on entering the

house balancing three bargain buckets in his arms, as two plastic carrier bags dangled from his wrists.

Sitting in a semicircle in front of our widescreen television set, my family sat silently eating fried chicken: "I'm sorry to have to say this Julian, but I think your mother's mad." Mam said, in between sucking on a bone.

"I know that, Nana Evans." Julian nodded, sitting astride the pouffe.

"My Rhian offered your mother the hand of friendship, but Mary only took it up to throw back in my daughter's face."

"I understand that Nana Evans."

"Mam." Anthony interrupted. "Why does Julian call Gran, Nana? When we all call her Gran?

"Shut-up boy." Trevor said coming to the rescue. "Shut-up, and have another portion of chicken... Would you like another piece Julian?... No, well how about another glass of pop then?... There's some Arctic-Roll in the freezer if you like? "

Crumbling slowly down the side of the pouffe, Julian buried his head and sobbed upon Megan's knee. "I-I-I-am so-oo so-oorry Miss-rs Evvv-ans." Between each syllable a large tear dripped from the end of his nose.

"This is so sad." Mam whimpered, dabbing her eyes on a free napkin, advertising the chicken.

Trevor, Gary and Anthony looked at me and shrugged their shoulders. Megan comforted her boyfriend, and told him everything was going to be all right. "He can sleep here tonight, can't he Mam?" She asked, pleading with her eyes.

Sitting on a kitchen chair balancing a bargain bucket full of discarded chicken bones on my lap I began to laugh. Nervously at first, but nevertheless it was a definite laugh all the same. Trevor raised an inquisitive eyebrow in my direction then quickly followed suit. Soon we where joined by Gary and Anthony. Sitting on her chair Mam didn't know whether to laugh, cry or run to the toilet. With a look of horror on her face, Megan stared at us, looked down at Julian, patted him on top of his head, then rolled off her chair with an hysterical fit of the giggles. Even poor Julian saw the funny side in the end. "No offence lad." Trevor said, using a Kentucky wet wipe to cool his face. "But there's only one thing to do when you meet people like your mother... FUCK-UM!" He yelled, sticking two fingers in the air.

Julian had a terrible night by all accounts. Megan said: "I felt so sorry for him Mam. I could hear him crying from my room."

I must admit the thought of Julian, weeping all alone in a strange room, tugged at my heart strings too... Now what am I supposed to do?

At 2.15pm, Idris turned up with Julian's clothing in two black bin bag liners. He also handed Julian a note from his mother. It simply said:

DEAR JULIAN.
MY HEART IS BROKEN. I NEVER WANT TO SEE, OR HEAR FROM YOU AGAIN.

LOVE MAM.

Escorting Idris to the door, Trevor offered him this advice: "It's about time you grew another set of balls, and stood up to that wife of yours before it's too late."

August 13: Monday

Julian ironed his and Megan's work clothes, but refused to have anything more than a cup of tea for breakfast: "I wish I could say I was looking after my figure." He said patting his stomach. "But you know how it is. Living on my nerves has always given me a jippy tummy." (I thought what a funny thing for a young boy to say.)

With the two lovers and Gary at work, Anthony upstairs on the computer, and Trevor speaking to one of the men who were installing our Sky satellite dish. I decided to take the bull by the horns, and go and make peace with the Jackson's.

Approaching the house I noticed a number of heads pop-up on the inner-side of the net curtain. Nearer the garden gate, I heard the back door slamming shut. Walking up the path I saw a blur in the frosted glass, and heard the thump, thump, thumping of feet running up the stairs. I knocked on the front door... No answer. I rang the front door bell... Greensleeves... Followed by no answer. Stepping back from the door, I saw the net curtain of a upstairs bedroom window twitch. I pressed the front door bell again... Edelweiss... Followed by no answer. I walked through a side gate, and entered the back garden... Deserted... I knocked on the back door... No answer. I tried the back door... Locked... I walked back to the front of the house. On my little journey I heard a host of overhead feet following me first to the back, then to the front of the house. I pressed the door bell for the final time... I'm Forever Blowing Bubbles... No answer. In a fit of temper I rapped heavily upon the brass door knocker... No answer. I screamed through the letter box: "Open the door. I know you're in there you shits."... No answer.

Back home Trevor sat cross-legged on the carpet in front of the newly installed Sky satellite box channel hopping his way through the channels to his heart's content: "Crap!" Click. "Crap!" Click. "Crap!" Click. "Rhian, Pink Floyd were right after all. *'Over sixty channels of shit on the TV to choose from.'* He said quoting a lyric from 'The Wall'.

With the two lovebirds home from work. I told them what had happened, and what I'd tried to do on their behalf. "My mother is capable of anything when she gets into one of her moods." Julian stated, as we discussed my actions around the kitchen table. "But thank you for trying all the same, Mrs Evans."

"Mam." Megan said, offering her opinion. "Julian and I think we should wait for the storm to blow itself out, before we confront her again. After all it's going to take more than a day or two for Julian's mother to calm down." And in the end that's exactly what we all decided to do.

We spent the rest of the evening watching Sky TV. We saw early episodes of 'Last Of The Summerwine' on UK Gold, and 'The Benny Hill Show' on Granada Plus. (Am I missing something here? What's the point of us installing a brand new digital satellite system to watch old television programmes from the '70s?)

August 14: Tuesday

I collected my family allowance from the Post Office, and asked Mr Baker if he would write the word 'Sold' in red ink across the description of three piece suite for sale, on our card in his window.

Outside of the Post Office, a sudden panic attack took control of my body, as I watched Mr Baker scribble the word through the advertisement of our three piece suite with his permanent marker pen. *'HOW THE HELL ARE WE ALL GOING TO*

TRAVEL TO CORNWALL???' My initial, second, and third thoughts screamed at me inside my head. *'WE HAVEN'T GOT ANY TRANSPORT?'*

Trevor has got a brain the size of a gnat... We haven't a three-piece suite in the house because Trevor never thought the circumstances of selling our old furniture through. Likewise our holiday is now in danger of following our lack of living-room furniture down the same plug-hole. Because forward planning and basic logic have never been two of Trevor's strongest suits.... Why hadn't I thought of this earlier?

Trevor said nothing but stared into open space, as the realisation of what I was saying suddenly dawned on him.

Me: Well Trevor, how are we all going to get there then?Trevor's response was negligible. Staring at him, I hoped the wooden cogs inside his head would begin to rotate.

Me: This is so typical of you Trevor. You never see anything through to the end. What's Mam going to say about this?... You haven't even got a driving licence.

Trevor: But I can drive.

Me: So what! We haven't got a car... Or any money left to hire one.

I am now depressed... No furniture... No option but to allow Julian to move in... Everything was going so well. I've never been on a proper family holiday before... I'll leave it go a couple of days to see if anything turns up before disappointing the kids.

August 15: Wednesday

Things are going from bad to worse. Our new furniture was supposed to be delivered today, but it didn't show up. Trevor still hasn't finalised our travel arrangements... When was he going to tell me?... Was he going to wait until I'd packed?

Apart from me everyone's happy. Trevor's sure something will turn up. (I can't see lightening striking on the same betting slip twice, no matter how much money Trevor invests with his bookie.) Mam phoned to say, she'd bought new clothes for her hol's. The boys have no worries, and Julian and Megan are in each other's arms... I think I'll give it until the weekend before breaking their hearts.

August 16: Thursday

No three piece suite...

I spoke to the warehouse on Mam's phone.

Me:	Hello, my name is Mrs Rhian Evans. I was promised delivery of a three piece suite yesterday.
Woman:	Sorry. What did you say your name was again?
Me:	Mrs R Evans.
Woman:	Sorry I've got no record of it here... R Evans?... I've got a Mr T Evans, and a...
Me:	That's the one. Mr T Evans. Trevor Evans.
Woman:	The brown draylon 'Picasso'?
Me:	Yes.
Woman:	I'm sorry Mrs Evans but there's been a hold-up at the factory. (Chuckle.) Silly me. When I say hold-up, I don't mean like in the cowboy films... I think the delivery drivers are on strike or something. Or maybe it's because they've run out of brown

> Picasso Draylon?... If that's the case, would you like your furniture to be covered in another fabric Mrs Evans?

At times like this I feel like giving up the will to live. She went on to say, that she couldn't give me a precise date for delivery, only a reassurance that on my furniture's arrival at the warehouse, I'd be the first to know it was there.

On to some good news. Trevor received a letter from the DSS this morning. They accept that he is unable to go to work, because he has to stay at home all day to look after me. For the first time in his life, Trevor has got an officially designated job title. 'Carer.' Good old Dr Reece whatever he wrote on those forms did the trick. The letter also went on to say, that there was a weekly payment book waiting for him to collect at our local Post Office, and an identity slip for him to hand to the Post Master when he goes to collect it; there was no mention of any rebate that maybe due to us. Trevor said that will probably be sent to us by Giro in a separate letter.

At the Post Office Mr Baker checked through the payment books he keeps in a tray behind the counter. "Sorry Mrs Evans." He said handing me back Trevor's identity slip. "Your husband's benefit book hasn't come in yet. Try again tomorrow."

August 17: Friday

No furniture, no payment book, no news of rebate, but I did receive a solicitor's letter.

Davis,Davis & Jones.
24,The High Street,
Cardiff,
15-7-2001

Dear Mrs Evans.
On behalf of our client Mrs M Jackson I must warn you to desist in your personal vendetta against the Jackson family, or further action will be taken against you. Mrs Jackson has instructed me to make this point abundantly clear to you, using the clearest language possible.

Mrs Jackson has written a statement, (Filed at this office.) that on Monday the 13th of August 2001 you trespassed the outer boundary of her property and proceeded to knock violently upon her door, (Front & Back) in such a manner that her new born baby (Sotheby Jackson) began to cry. Mrs Jackson has also secured signed statements from her neighbours stating that they not only witnessed your act of trespass, but they heard you screaming obscenities through the Jackson letterbox.
Mrs Jackson admits that there is a history of bad feeling between the two of you. She has also stated that you threatened her life during a lesson at the evening class you both attend. (Mrs Jackson can also produce witnesses to this matter, if the need be.)

On this occasion Mrs Jackson has instructed me, to inform you, that not only is she a Christian lady, but because of her deep faith in the Lord, and her strong belief in turning the other cheek, she has decided not to seek a legal recompense from you at this time. Mrs Jackson also instructs me to inform you; being a student of human nature, she has been desperately trying to understand what you have been going through over the years. Putting herself in your shoes, Mrs Jackson has been desperately trying to understand what life has been like for you having to live with a husband who's never searched for, or intended to do any kind of employed work in his life; plus the added personal burden you yourself have been under, IE suffering depression, and other forms of mental illness. Mrs Jackson concedes that these must be very difficult, and trying times for you indeed.

Mrs Jackson hopes this letter will bring an end to any unpleasantness that may be simmering between the two families, but she assures you, she will not hesitate in securing a restriction order against every member of the Evans family if matters persist.

Yours sincerely,
Mr J J Jones.

I feel very hurt.

Trevor: Ignore the silly bitch.
Mam: Rhian, you've taken away her pride and joy. You've

taken away her little boy... Of course she's going to retaliate.

Me: No I never... Megan did... I was forced to let him move in... What choice did I have?

Mam: None of that matters, Rhian love.

Gary: Bin it! Bin the letter Mam.

Julian: Take no notice Mrs Evans. My mother is always sending them to people. Last week she sent one to the new family who just moved in across the road. Their little boy kept kicking his ball into our garden.

Anthony: She's the one who is the mental case Mam, not you.

Megan: Why can't she be happy for us Mam? Why can't she just leave us alone?

August 18: Saturday

I had a terrible dream last night. I dreamt the men in white coats were coming to take me away. It's not what Mary's solicitor wrote that I care about. I couldn't give a flying fig what she personaly thinks about me. It's the other people that's got me worried.

Thanks to my Trevor, the DSS think I'm mad, and they've got written evidence from my family doctor to prove it. Mary no doubt will waste no time in spreading this rumour around the estate. The people attending my evening class were giving me funny looks the last time I attended. Am I mad? I read somewhere that if you are, you are the last one to find out.

I'm not feeling very well at all today... I wanted to curl up on my sofa and watch the afternoon film,(James Garner in 'Support Your Local Gunfighter') but when I entered my living-room I suddenly remembered my sofa wasn't there. (Damn Trevor and his bright ideas.) Torture is being alone with one's thoughts... Where are you sofa, now that I need you the most?

August 19: Sunday

Sunday dinner had been cooked, and eaten. Megan helped Julian to wash the dishes. Mam had brought a chair with her, and was quietly falling to sleep in it... After they had finished washing up Julian made everyone a cup of tea, (Mugs for Trevor and the boys.) and we all sat in front of the television.

"I've got some bad news about our holiday." I stated. My face partially hidden by my cup.

"What!" Mam shrieked, suddenly wide-awake. "I knew something would go wrong the moment you told me who we were renting the caravan off. West, Best, or whatever it is, his name is. If he's the person I'm thinking about, his family were well known as black market swindlers during the war years."

"No, it's nothing like that."

"Mam, we are still going aren't we." Megan's big brown eyes stared pleading up at me.

"We have a little problem with transport, that's all." I said. "We haven't got any."

Out came my pencil and notepad, and each mode of transport was discussed thoroughly:

Car	=	We haven't got one.
Train	=	We can't afford each individual return fare for all the family to go.
Coach	=	Same reason for not going by train.
Plane	=	Stop being silly Trevor.
Taxi	=	Stop being silly Trevor. This is all your fault.

"I'll rent a car for us all this weekend Mrs Evans, if you like?"

"Can you drive Julian?"

"Yes!"

"Can you really?" Megan asked, amazed along with the rest of us at Julian's unforeseen capabilities.

"Not only can I drive but I know a friend who works in a car rental showroom."

"I can drive, you know." Trevor said, addressing everyone. "But I've never taken my test."

"Well thank God somebody has." Mam responded. "Julian love, you're a credit to this family."

"Mrs Evans, Megan and I have been talking it over and I think I should be giving you something for my keep while I'm staying with you."

Trevor smiled and thirty pound a week was instantly agreed upon. Julian's car rental idea was also unanimously accepted. Julian wouldn't take no for an answer, and insisted the vehicle rental charges be looked upon as his contribution to the holiday... Trevor sounded off an enthusiastic, *'hear, hear.'* Until I kicked his leg underneath the table.

I feel a lot happier now that this has all been sorted out. I hope Julian doesn't think we are taking advantage of him. Is charging him thirty pound a week too much? After all, he washes and irons his own clothes, cooks his own food, (Sometimes for all the family, the washing and ironing too.) and he sleeps in a sleeping bag on the floor... Perhaps we should be paying him to live here?

August 20: Monday

No payment book. I phoned up the DSS, and they assured me it was in the post. No news of a rebate, no three piece suite.

Gary signed-on for the first time on his own this morning. Trevor said, today truly felt like a real day off.

While everyone was out I agreed with Trevor that Julian was a real dark horse. "To look at him you wouldn't think he had it in him, because he looks like such a little weed." Trevor remarked over some buttered toast. "Driving at seventeen... Rhian, he's probably got a bank account and all sorts... He's probably saving for a car too."

Julian has now become an official member of the family. Trevor reckons the more time Julian spends around our family the better. "Rhian, we'll soon have him losing his mincing ways."

August 21: Tuesday

No payment book, no rebate news, no three piece suite, but I am P.M.T. active.

After collecting my family allowance, Mr Baker assured me Trevor's benefit book had not arrived amongst the morning post. He also reminded me that my time had elapsed and he would be removing my card from his window... Would you credit it Diary. The only thing we sold was my beloved sofa, the very thing we needed to keep.

A letter was waiting for Julian on his return from work. Trevor looked out of the window when he heard the letterbox rattle. He said he saw Idris Jackson scurrying out of our gate. "He must have tiptoed up our garden path like a little mouse." Trevor observed, before slumping back down onto the carpet.

Dear Julian.
No doubt you will have seen the solicitor's letter I was forced to send to Mrs Evans. Mrs Evans is a very unstable, and violent lady. Her attack on our house/your former home was totally unwarranted, and uncalled for in the extreme.
Poor Mrs Mills from next door nearly had a heart attack, after being a witness to Mrs Evans marching around to, and heavily pounding on our back door.
Julian, I say enough is enough. You have made your point, and I agree to you having a bedroom of your own. (I also agree to your loft conversion idea.)
Darling, Megan Evans is not the right girl for you. I do understand the power of first love, but what you are experiencing is not love but infatuation. Last Friday I spoke to a lady from the Citizen's Advice about your situation. Mrs Gates, nice lady, very understanding. She informs me that you are of age, and within your rights to leave home. She also said, after considering the situation, your feelings are natural for a person of your age, and inexperience. (I'm sorry my darling, but I had to tell her you've never had a girlfriend before.) If I am correct, and it is truly an infatuation, your feelings for the Evans girl will soon fade away, then everything can return to normal. There's not a moment in the day I'm not praying you will return to your senses, and return home soon.
My dear son, please feel free to call on us anytime of the

day or night. Please don't let Mrs or Miss Evans poison your mind against your loving family. (I am willing to accept any reverse telephone calls you care to make.)

Please stay in touch. Love and kisses from:
Mama, Dada and your loving brothers and sister.
(Dominique says: Love you, miss you.)

"And that woman's got the nerve to call you mad:" Trevor scoffed, Gary and Anthony shook their heads in disbelief. "Poison your mind?... You don't think I poison your mind, do you Jay? (Julian, is now Jay in Megan's eyes.)

"I'm sorry about all this... My mother, I mean Mrs Evans. She just refuses to cut the apron strings,you see."

August 22: Wednesday

Gary's Giro came along with an accompanying letter from the DSS. I hate it when these unexpected brown DSS envelopes pop through the door. They never bring any good news, and this one proved to be no exception. The DSS want to interview Gary on August the 29th. For one horrible moment I thought Mary Jackson had grassed us up. But no, (Thank God.) it takes a cool head to deal with matters from the DSS at times like this, and as Trevor rightly assumed: "As far as the DSS are concerned, Gary is unemployed. He's been out of work for over six months, so the DSS probably want a little chat with him, and perhaps to offer him another place on a Government funded training scheme." (Please God, let it be so.)

11.30pm: I went to bed early tonight. Even so I couldn't sleep. On my way from the toilet, I popped my head over the banister and listened to part of Gary and Trevor's conversation.

Gary: I wish I had a benefit book of my own Dad.
Trevor: All in good time son. All you need to do is get married, and make out your wife is mad... It's cheaper for them to pay you, than it is to pay for around the clock care in a secure hospital.

I'll be having words with Trevor about this in the morning.

August 23: Thursday

No payment book, no rebate news, no three piece suite, one blazing row.

Ready... Boy was I ready. I was so ready, I deliberately forgot to take my Prozac, for fear of it calming me down... Anthony was sent to my mother's... Let the games begin:

Me: You're a fucking bastard Trevor, making fun of me in front of our son... Who do you think you are telling our son his mother is mad. Well I'm fucking not... You know I'm fucking not. I only agreed to go along with it to please you... Or maybe you are right, and I am mad after all. I married you, didn't I. I've had to put up with you all these years... Don't fucking lie to me good boy. I fucking heard you last night, laughing about me behind my back with Gary. I heard what you said to him. I heard what you think of me. I heard every fucking word.
Trevor: I was only joke... We were only having a laugh...
Me: Liar... Bullshitter! You run me down at every chance you get. Julian... Fucking Julian! You take more

notice of what he's got to say, than you ever did of me. (Impersonating Trevor.) I'll get the mince out of him, ha, ha, ha... Fucking Hell Trevor, if you ask me, you're the one in danger of developing a mince of your own.

Trevor: Calm yourself down. I didn't mean anything by it... We're going on holiday tomorrow.

Me: No thanks to you. If it wasn't for Julian, we wouldn't have a fucking holiday to go to... Where is my fucking sofa?

Our relationship was best described as tense for the rest of the day. Trevor tried to jolly me along after he'd been up the attic and handed me our suitcases to pack... Here's a funny story concerning my suitcases. I have three in total. (Grey nylon... Quite strong really.) One large, one medium, and a baby one. I had them free when I placed my first order with my fourth catalogue. Although they look brand new, my suitcases are in fact nearly fifteen years old. I remember this because I wanted to buy a Moses basket for Anthony just after he was born, and because I had reached my spending limit on my three other catalogues, I had to open another account with a fourth home shopping company.

Anyway, fifteen years ago they were delivered. Trevor and I had a quick look at them, and they've been living in the attic ever since.

6.00pm: I was in the kitchen making the tea. Trevor spoke to the family who had congregated around the television set...

I was eavesdropping behind the kitchen door.

Trevor: Listen... I know you always hear me making fun of your mother. Calling her a mad woman and all that... Well she's not really mad you know. She just suffers with her nerves that's all... Sometimes she feels a little bit down... But mostly she is as normal as you and me.

Trevor hasn't got a fucking clue. 'As normal as you and me!' I ask you!

August 24: Friday

At last everything is falling into place. Trevor's payment book finally arrived at the Post Office. (I've finished my period.) I am now on something called 'Incapacity Benefit' (Short time higher rate.) What this all means in English: Our claim has increased by an extra twenty quid a week... Because of the coming bank holiday there is a double payout, so along with the money I'd already put by; having enough money to spend over the weekend, shouldn't be a problem.

THE PLAN:

1. While everyone is at work, I will pack everything ready to load into the car.
2. Mam, will pack her case, turn off power and water, secure her home and wait here for the hire car to arrive.
3. Julian will pick up the hire car on the way home. Trevor will keep out of my way... Communication has resumed-between us.
4. I must remember to pack toilet rolls,bedding and my medication.
5. Hopefully we should be on our way by 7.00pm.

6.05pm: Julian draws-up in a Volvo estate, and parks it on the road in front of our gate.

"Bloody hell, you've done well. This must have set you back a bob or two?" Trevor surmised, testing the front passenger seat for size.

"Not really." Julian replied adjusting the rear view mirror. Like I said, I know someone in the showroom who owed me a favour, and he let me have it at the Fiesta rate."

An hour later and we were out on the open read. Soon we were crossing the Severn Bridge, turning right we passed Bristol, then straight on to Newquay in Cornwall.

August 25: Saturday

We arrived at the 'Poldark' Holiday Park just after midnight. Trevor proved to everyone that he couldn't read a map to save his life. We got lost a total of four times. Once on the Devon/Cornish border, once at a place called Indian Queens, (We kept driving around, and around, in circles. Anthony shouted: "We are the wagon train; where are the Indians?") and twice in the town of Newquay itself.

Our caravan is very nice. It's detached, and it stands in a row of seven, with views of the Cornish coast. On site there's a pub, (The Demelza Inn) a corner shop, (Ross's Stockade) selling newspapers,sweets, basic groceries, gifts. There is also a fish and chip shop, come pizza palace simply called 'The Pasty'. There's also a public telephone, laundry room, paddling and Olympic size swimming pool... "What a delight it is to paddle in the sea." Mam said, "the last time we did this as a family,was at Tenby in 1973." (I was twelve – No Trevor, No kids) I'm loving it. I'm reveling in every moment. The sky is of the deepest blue, the sea is its mirrored reflection. Waves of foam distinguish the water from the cloudless sky. That wonderful noise, that beautiful sound of the sea, and the calling of the gulls... A perfect harmony... Glorious weather... When I close my eyes I want to cry. The sun on my face, the sound of the sea in my ears, the sand slipping between my toes, my foot steps washed away by the incoming tide. Take me Lord, take me now. Carry me to a deserted desert island like Robinson Crusoe. For there I will truly be the happiest woman on earth.

While the family enjoyed the cabaret at The Demelza Inn, I sat outside the caravan and watched the setting sun blush orange with delight, as it paddled in the sea. Today had been a wonderful experience... It all began with Julian driving me to the nearest supermarket so I could stock up on provisions. (I found the prices being charged at the stockade a little on the steep side.) We stuffed our faces with fish and chips, Cornish pasties and Cornish ice cream on the beach. Everyone was smiling and relaxed. Trevor had gone for a swim in the sea, but ran out when the water came up to his thighs. Yes everything is perfect, and we've still got two days in paradise to go.

August 26: Sunday

Julian kept everyone awake last night with his moaning, groaning, and vomiting into a bucket Anthony had luckily discovered under the sink. I blame Trevor for this... Getting a young boy pissed, when he should know better. I also found it very annoying; every time Julian vomited, Trevor would respond: "That's it my son... Get it up... Heave ho... Get it off your chest."

"You should be ashamed of yourself Trevor." Mam said, placing a cold flannel across Julian's forehead. "This boy is much too delicate to take a part in your drinking games… Any fool can see he's not used to alcohol… If his mother could see him now, she'd have a fit… I only hope he's not suffering from alcoholic poisoning, that's all."

12.00pm: Julian was still feeling the worse for wear, yet he somehow managed to drive us all in the Volvo to Newquay Zoo. Now here is a funny thing. After walking around the zoo, I found myself sitting next to my mother on a wooden bench under a tree. Mam had fallen asleep, and Trevor had gone to buy us both an ice cream. The others were scattered somewhere in the zoo's grounds. While I waited for Trevor's return I people watched. (I found this very relaxing in itself.) I played an imaginary game, of placing funny phrases onto people's faces; one man was carrying his son in his arms. The little boy was sucking on an ice lolly. Suddenly he let the lolly drop to the ground. As quick as a flash my mind came up with the man's response: *'Did you have to drop that by* there? Couldn't you have waited until I walked past a litter bin?' A little old lady was being pushed in a wheelchair by a woman I presumed to be her daughter: *'But Jenny, I* don't want to see the lion again." Mam dozing next to me on the bench: *'Rhian, I never knew they built a zoo in Tenby?'*

Looking up through the canopy, I could see a patchwork of blue sky penetrating through the green leaves, shapes and shadows of the tree. (I wish I knew what this tree was called… Maybe oak, maybe not.) That and a trick of the sun, caused a kaleidoscope effect of shape and colour to fill my gaze… "What are you looking at?" Trevor spoke, then licked the dripping ice-cream from between his fingers. "A chimp hasn't escaped up there, has it?"

I can distinctly remember facing Trevor in an excited gush. I desperately wanted him to share with me the myriad of colour, the natural shades of fauna that was occurring under the tree's canopy. But like in the game I'd been playing; a little voice spoke, and I agreed: *'Don't bother trying to explain anything to him Rhian, he won't understand.'* So I smiled, took my ice cream, nudged my mother gently awake, who in turn grunted: "Trevor, you fool. You know I always have a ninety-nine." And kept my little glimpse of Heaven to myself.

Karaoke night at the Demelza Inn: 9.00pm: Trevor got up and sang 'What's New Pussycat'. He got up and sang it again at ten. In between, Julian sang 'Y.M.C.A', followed by 'I Will Survive' which he dedicated to his mother. Megan sang 'Like A Virgin'. Gary upset Julian by saying, he found that very hard to believe. Mam clipped Gary across the ear, and told Julian not to listen to him, adding,her Granddaughter was a very good girl really. Julian cheered up and bought everyone a drink. (I was on orange juice.)

11.00pm: Trevor was singing his 'Elvis' tribute. (He'd finished 'Fever', now he was singing the German part of 'Wooden Heart'.) Mam said the lighting in the Damelsa Inn made Trevor look a lot like 'Elvis'. (She was on her eighth gin.) I don't know if it's me but after he'd finished singing I sensed everyone in the room found it strange that Julian had a girlfriend. (Luckily, he and Megan didn't seem to notice.)

"Do all adults act like little children when they are drunk?" Anthony asked, as we both watched Trevor drop down on one knee, during the final verse of 'Glory, Glory, Hallelujah'.

"Yes." I stated, proud I had discovered enough will power to protect myself against the demon drink.

August 27: Bank Holiday Monday

Anthony and I were the only ones up to having a fried breakfast this morning. "Take that greasy pan out of my face, or I'm going to throw up." Trevor warned, and later did, after observing Anthony dip one of his battalion of crustless soldiers into a runny yoke.

I planned to do nothing today but sit on the beach and soak in the sun. If the others wanted to visit elsewhere then that was fine by me, but I was determined to stay on the beach. By midday the others were in a mood for adventure, and had gone for a little ride around the coast. Mam had kindly volunteered to stay with me, but I could tell she wanted to go for a ride, so I gradually talked her into leaving me on my own.

CORNWALL
by
Rhian Evans

The skies are blue,
The sea is too,
Hoochi, coochi, coochi,coo,
Has anybody seen my girl...

Stop messing about Rhian, pull yourself together. It's a lovely day. The sun is shining. The sound of the sea. The gulls... On my blanket I have Harmon's book of poems... Dear Diary, you must have realised I hadn't written a single verse of poetry since my evening class ended? THIS WILL NOT DO! How can I hope to be a serious poet if I don't write poetry?... I've just eaten a Cornish pasty, (Just to keep my strength up you understand.) I've poured myself a glass of cherryade... Right, concentrate Rhian, let's get down to some work.

CORNWALL
by
Rhian Evans

The skies are blue,
The sea's are too,
Hoochi, coochi, coochi,coo,
Has anybody...

It's no bloody good. I just can't get that old song from out of my head.

8.00pm: My family had returned, got changed, and were sitting in the Demelza Inn. I on the other hand prefer the sunset and my dreams. One thing I've learnt this weekend. If anything terrible happens to my family in the near future, (God forbid.) I'll be happy living here on my own.

11.15pm: "Did you all have a good time?"

"Wonderful, Rhian." Mam laughed, kissing me on the cheek. "You really should have come. You would have enjoyed yourself."

"Where's Megan and Julian got to?"

“Oh they won’t be long love. They’ve gone for a little walk along the beach.”

August 28: Tuesday

Outwardly I put on a brave face, but inwardly my heart was breaking. We were packed. The Volvo was stacked. Mam was calling me to hurry. Overhead storm clouds where forming. Rain was approaching from the sea. “Come on Rhian. I can’t wait to get home, and make myself a decent pot of tea.” One last look round. I closed the car door, I held a small shell in the palm of my hand... The sea was calling to me to stay, but I had to go away.

“Of course you do know we were ripped off.” Trevor informed us on the way home. “What with the ‘Foot and Mouth’ scare, and one thing and another. Prices on the site have gone down, plummeted, so some of the campers were telling me. Last night I was speaking to this bloke who told me he’d only paid a ton for a week’s stay in his caravan.”... In my heart, I knew the weekend was priceless.

On the Welsh side of the Severn Bridge, (Why are the tolling booths only on the English side?) It wasn’t long before we were home. I left all our luggage in the kitchen and went to lay on my bed.

4.30pm: I got up. Was the holiday a dream? In the kitchen our luggage lay where I’d left it. In the mail that had been delivered there was no news of our rebate, or three piece suite... Julian didn’t take very long returning the hire car to the showroom, strangely he had insisted that Megan didn’t accompany him when he took it back.

"Hello, this is 'Mac's Discount Furniture Warehouse'. Jill speaking. How may I help you?"

"Can I speak to somebody in authority please."

"If you tell me what it's about, maybe I can help you, madam?"

"It's about my long overdue fucking three-piece suite. I want to know when you bastards are going to deliver it?"

"Hold the line please, I'll put you through to the manager's office immediately."... Our three piece suite is being delivered tomorrow.

August 29: Wednesday

Gary phoned in sick this morning. He has an interview with the DSS at 11.00am.

9.00am: Our furniture arrived. (At last) I hurriedly hovered the living-room before I let the deliverymen put the new sofa down on the carpet... Luxury pure luxury. The room looks so much more comfortable now... I wonder how long it will be before we will be able to afford a new carpet?

"Hello, DSS, which benefit please?" (Why not strike while the iron's hot? My telephone technique worked at the furniture warehouse.)

"Incapacity."

Confidence sky high, I chanced my arm with the DSS.

"Incapacity. How may I help you?"

"Yes, it's about my claim. I was told that I may be entitled to a rebate on some back money, that may be entitled to me. But I haven't heard anything about it yet."

"Claimant's National Insurance Number?"

I told her.

"No decision has been made yet, Mrs Evans. When it has we'll let you know."... Good. At least they haven't forgot about us.

Gary came home and said the DSS want him to attend a training assessment centre in Merthyr for six months. But here's the rub. The assessment centre is situated next door to his works.

"Well boy." Trevor grinned, at his downcast son. "Talk about a mind bender. It seems to me that you are between the Devil and the deep blue sea. You can either quit your job and go to the training centre, or you can sign-off the dole and remain in your dead-end job."

Home from work Julian and Megan presented me with a wonderful bouquet of flowers: "This is just a little something to say thank you... For letting me come on holiday with you." Julian said kissing me on my cheek. "I just want to say thank you for letting Julian stay with us." Megan said, also kissing me on the cheek.

NEW PLAN:

1. Become poet.
2. Make a lot of money.
3. Buy little cottage somewhere on the Cornish coast.

August 30: Thursday

11.45pm: Dear Diary I can't believe it. The world is crashing down upon my head. All for the sake of a bunch of flowers... Flowers, I must admit I didn't ask for, or didn't need... Flowers, fucking flowers... The stupid, stupid, pair of... Now what are they going to do? What will Mary say when she hears about this?... Please let me sleep in peace tonight Lord. Good, kind, sweet, God above. Carry my spirit off to Cornwall and abandon me forever on a secluded beach.

August 31: Friday

Julian and Megan have been sacked for stealing/shoplifting flowers.

All the flowers, Julian and Megan had presented to me and my mother. All the flowers Julian had given to his mother, were all in fact shoplifted blooms.

After this bomb shell, came the inquisition. Five hours of questions and answers. Five hours it took before Trevor and I had finally got to the bottom of it.

Mr Hurst had fitted a spy camera in his shop while Julian and Megan were away in Cornwall. First thing yesterday morning, Mr Hurst confronted them with the incriminating evidence he'd caught on video tape; which he played back to them on a portable television set he'd set-up in his office. Caught red-handed, Mr Hurst sacked them both on the spot.

"Honest Mam, I didn't know I was doing any wrong." Megan wailed. "Julian told me I could take home as many as I wanted... Honest, didn't you Jay?"

"Yes."

"Mam, Julian admitted it all to Mr Hurst that it was all of his doing, but Mr Hurst wouldn't listen to you, would he Jay? Mr Hurst said if anyone was to blame, it was me for leading

Julian astray. But it wasn't my fault Mam, honest it wasn't. Mr Hurst said Julian was the perfect employee until I came along and corrupted him."

"Mr Hurst is an old friend of my mother you see, Mrs Evans. He took Megan on at his shop before my mother had a chance to spit her poison out against her. Up until then Mr Hurst had been more than willing to give Megan the benefit of the doubt."

Suddenly the beautiful bouquet I'd arranged in a vase on the windowsill resembled a pot of weeds.

REVIEW OF THE MONTH:

Brilliance followed by disaster. Yin and Yang. Good and Evil. A glimpse of Heaven, before a lifetime of Hell?Is this the beginning of the end? The start of our little world caving in upon us, and spiralling us ever forward in a downward circle?

September 1: Saturday

Dear Diary, as you can imagine I don't get a wink of sleep last night. I'm another month older but I'm certainly none the wiser.

I don't know Diary, there's something not quite right going on here. I can't put my finger on it exactly, but there was something about Julian's persona last night, his behaviour?... His attitude?... I don't know maybe it's just me, or perhaps all my feminine intuition has finally gone up the spout.

Alone on my new sofa, I tried to piece Julian's thoughts together... Why did he do it?... What was going on inside his mind?... Dear Diary, does this sound reasonable to you? Could any of this have anything to do with his mother?... Was this his cry for help?

Mam called this afternoon. Her timing was impeccable as usual. (Fifteen minutes into the BBC2 Saturday matinee 'Strangers on a Train'.) Mam knows nothing about the sackings, but it's only a matter of time before she finds out.

11.15pm: I'm in bed. The plan was for me to be asleep before Trevor came home... My plan is not working, then again Trevor hasn't come home yet... I have too many things on my mind to be bothered with Trevor's disgusting habits tonight... I'm an hypocrite. Am I the pot calling the kettle black? What right have I to judge? Trevor and I blame Julian for shoplifting and for getting Megan the sack, yet we are no better ourselves. We are a family of benefit cheats. Furthermore, Trevor has been to court in the past, while I am an ex-alcoholic who needs drugs to help me through the day.

"Hello, I'm home." Trevor's back... God, please let me fall asleep before he comes to bed.

September 2: Sunday

3.10pm: There was a knock on our door. "Hello... Ummm, can I come in?" Idris Jackson entered our living-room, and sat on the left-hand side of the sofa. He greeted his son, acknowledged Megan said hello to Mam and Trevor, and nodded his head at Gary and Anthony.

"Over the weekend," he began, "my wife had a very distressing telephone conversation with Mr Hurst an old friend of the family." Megan looked tense, Julian grinned. "Mr Hurst told Mary all about the video camera. He told her his shop had been losing a lot of stock over the past few weeks. He said taking home a few wilting daffodils was one thing, but orchids, lilies and roses was an entirely different matter altogether..."

"Hang-on a minute by here boy." Trevor said, halting Idris's flow. "Before you go any further. We know all that happened at the florists, and Julian has already admitted our Megan is the innocent party in all this."

"Rhian, what's going on?" Mam asked, giving me a searching look.

"I don't doubt it for a moment." Idris agreed.

"Will somebody please tell me what's been going on." Mam insisted.

"So you admit your son is in the wrong?"

"Yes." Idris nodded.

"Rhian, will you please..."

"Julian and Megan's been sacked by Mr Hurst Mam."

"That's why I've come here this afternoon. To try and explain to you, why my son did it."

"I don't believe a word of it... Sacked you say?... Sacked?... No, never.... There must be some..."

"Be quiet Mam. Idris is going to tell us what's been going on."

Mam, fell silent and started to twiddle her thumbs. (A bad sign.) With everyone's undivided attention focused upon him, Idris began: "It's Mary you see. She puts too much pressure on the boy. Oh, it's happened before all right. When the pressure becomes too much, he snaps and does something stupid." We all stared at Julian, who grinned. "One thing I will say," Idris continued. "He doesn't shit on his own doorstep. When he blows, he usually blows it away from the estate."

"Blows what? Rhian, will you please tell me what's been going on?"

"Shushh, be quite Mam."

"Car crime mostly." Idris said, answering my mother. "He hasn't passed is test mind... Don't ask me where he learnt to drive because I haven't got a clue, but in any case when the wife works him up, off he goes and does something stupid, like joyriding around in very posh and expensive cars."

"Rhian, I've been to Cornwall with a joy rider!" Mam gasped.

"What was that?"

"We recently spent the bank holiday weekend in Cornwall. Julian said, he'd rent a car to transport us all down there."

This was all getting too much for Megan. Bursting into tears, she ran to her room.

"Well I don't know what to say, I'm sure." Mam said, slumping back in her chair. And for once I believed her.

The long and the short of it was: Julian returned home with his father. Idris was right, Julian couldn't remain in our house, after we knew about this. Upstairs, Megan refused to come down to say goodbye. Outside Julian cut a pathetic figure walking two steps behind his father carrying his bin bags. Looking out of the bedroom window, Megan was in tears as her Romeo disappeared over the brow of an hill. Trevor also looked a little emotional, waving goodbye to thirty quid's worth of rent money a week. Returning to the living-room Mam reminded us: "I've always said they were a bad lot in that family, haven't I!"

September 3: Monday

Somebody said if a month starts badly, bad luck stays with you until a new month begins. Be that as it may, the first Monday in September heralded change for this family. Gary accompanied Megan to the dole. This was Gary's final visit before he had to make his decision. Anthony returned to school. He announced, a return to normal society was what he needed, and would come as a welcome relief,after spending a summer with us.

Megan came home, and said Mr Hurst's shop was closed for stocktaking. She'd also secured an interview on Thursday at 'Easy Fashions' as a trainee machinist.

"Mam, I phoned Julian while I was in town."

"Oh yes, what did he say."

"He seemed a bit funny with me. When I told him, we needed to have a trial separation from each other... You know, to sort our minds and everything out. He said OK!"

I said nothing to Megan, but I don't think their relationship as got much further to run. Not now Mary's got her claws back into her son.

September 4: Tuesday

Yesterday I forgot to tell you; Trevor's benefit book allows me to collect his benefit money every Monday, instead of cashing his giro every Wednesday fortnight. As you know I collect my family allowance every Tuesday, so to make life easier I've decided to collect both benefits on the same day.

While I was at the Post Office I paid Mr Baker another forty pence to display a card in his window for two extra weeks. (Anthony designed this card on the computer. The wording and prices remained the same as before, minus the furniture. On a yellow background Anthony had designed his card with a border of Disney characters from 'Winnie the Pooh' along the edge.)

September 5: Wednesday

Julian is not answering Megan's calls. She claims his mobile phone has been switched off for two days, (Trevor thinks it's been confiscated by his mother.) she's left messages and texts, but he's failed to respond to any of them.

"Perhaps he hasn't got any money for a card." I wondered sympathetically.

"Than why when I call his home, does he refuse to come to the phone?"

"These things take time love. I think you should give him some breathing space. I'm sure things will work out for the best in the end." (If there is a God up there, please let Julian run off with another girl/woman/man.)

Mam called around and admitted she'd been totally taken in by Julian. "Rhian, I've been played for a sucker." She announced, during her second cup of tea of the morning. "Rhian, I didn't think he had it in him. He's a man of mystery all right, that's what he is. He fooled me like he fooled us all. It's just a shame he was so polite and used such nice manners while he was doing it. I don't think I'll ever feel the same again when I hear the phrase, please and thank you." During her fourth cup of tea. Mam suddenly asked: "How's Megan taking it. I bet he's broken her little heart?"

September 6: Thursday

Megan's interview. She got the job. (Between you and me I don't think she would have been all that bothered, if they had turned her down.) Megan starts on Monday. It's another six month Government Scheme, but unlike most of the others there's a good chance of them keeping her on; but only if she buckles down and does well. Easy Fashions is a shop, with a little factory outlet in the rear of the building. First thing Monday morning, (8.30am) Megan begins learning how to machine zips into the back of dresses.

I've tried telling Megan this could be the new start in life she's been looking for, but Megan's not ready to appreciate advice like this at the moment. (Men! If they don't hurt you one-way, they'll hurt you another.) What Megan needs is some love and understanding from me. (Or a new boyfriend to take her mind off Julian.)

"Mam, why doesn't Julian phone me anymore?"

"If I have to hear that bastard's name in this house one more time, I think I'll go insane."

September 7: Friday

Megan is not handling her and Julian's trial separation at all well. While I was out doing the food shopping, (I'm back to counting pennies.) she went to the Jackson's house and knocked on the door. Turned away, she returned home and wailed for over an hour on top of her bed. "He wasn't there Mam. Jay was out with his mother." (I'm expecting a solicitor's letter any day now.)

Dear Diary, as you can imagine talk of Julian Jackson is dominating this house at the moment. None of us suspected or can quite believe what's been going on under our very noses.

Trevor: That boy played it as cool as a cucumber. Did you suspect anything Rhian, because I certainly didn't.

Mam: Am I an accomplice to a car crime?... Could I be done for aiding and abetting?

Trevor: He robbed that car, and drove it all the way to Cornwall and back without a care in the world.

Mam: They won't show my picture on 'Crimewatch' will they Rhian?

Gary: Well, at least we had a good holiday.

Mam: I'm sorry Rhian, but if my name is mentioned on the telly, I'll have to give myself up. At my age, I'm not prepared to go through life looking over my shoulder.

Anthony: No need to worry Gran. We're all innocent. We have nothing to worry about. We've done nothing wrong.

Trevor: You may know how to operate a computer son, but you know nothing about the law. Our innocence doesn't prove a thing.

I don't hate Julian, Diary. In fact I feel sorry for him, more than anything else. Yes, I'm happy he and Megan are no longer seeing each other. (Megan hasn't accepted this yet.) But that is for my own selfish reasons more than anything else. (I don't want Mary Jackson in our family.) But saying that Julian by hook or by crook did take us to Cornwall didn't he. And for that I'll be eternally grateful.

September 8: Saturday

I've never mentioned him before, but our next-door neighbour Mr Watson (Ken) is moving out today. I've never mentioned him because the Watson's, (When his wife was alive) were a couple of miserable buggers, and a bane of my life for the best part of sixteen years. While the kids were growing up they were a nightmare to live next door to. *'I'll call the police, I'll call the police.'* Became the Watson catchphrase that they'd yell every time a ball landed in their garden. The banging on the wall used to drive me crazy. THUMP, THUMP, THUMP... *'Turn it down in there, are you all deaf or what?'*... THUMP, THUMP, THUMP... *'Turn it down or I'll call the police.'* Okay, they had to put up with our music, (Sometimes... With my nerves in the state they were in, I couldn't stand to listen to a lot of noise myself.) but I had no option but to hear Ken coughing his guts up for five minutes every morning, not to mention the sound of him flushing his toilet like clockwork at eight o'clock, and riddling his poker in the grate.

All who have entered this house, have heard the Watson cough at one time or another. I'm sure listening to Ken in the morning, is one reason my children don't smoke. When she was alive, Mrs Watson (Phyllis) was no different, and just as petty. 7.00am: every morning she'd race out of her back door with a basket of washing, just so she would be the first person to hang a full line of washing on her line. "It's a wonder she can find anything to wash." Trevor used to remark. "There's only two of them living in that house for God's sake, they must change their clothing at least three times a day."

I'll never forget the day Trevor got up extra early to challenge for Phyllis's washing line crown. The night before I'd done our washing. At sunrise, Trevor silently slipped out the back door to the line. Unnoticed by the Watson's, items of clothing were pegged out; slipping silently back into the house we crept upstairs and waited for the fireworks to begin.

An hour later the Watson back door creaked opened. We heard Phyllis's flip-flopping slippers make their way down the garden path. (From her door our line is hidden by their overgrown hedge.) Peeping out of our window, Trevor and I squeaked with laughter at the sight of Phyllis dropping her basket in horror, at the sight of our washing hanging on the line.

Ducking below our window sill, we narrowly escaped her upward glance at our bedroom window. Bingo, the crown was ours for a day... We watched Phyllis hastily pickup her washing basket and march back into her house.

Shortly after that we were reported to the council for hoarding rubbish around our back, (They claimed it was an health hazard, and would encourage rats.) and for not cutting our grass. The council wouldn't tell us who reported us, but it was them all right. So you see, I won't be losing any sleep when the last surviving Watson moves out.

Listen to this Diary. You'll never believe what I've got to tell you: Phyllis Watson died last year. (Heart attack) Our telephone was connected at the time. Do you know old man Watson would, and did walk to a public phone box, (Two streets away, by the shops.) rather then ask us if he could use our telephone to save the life of his dying wife... Why didn't the authorities prosecute Ken for doing that?... My Mother phoned-up, and reported him to the police.

The van took his furniture away. Ken Watson slammed his front door, and leant against it to make sure it was firmly shut. He took a few steps along his path and looked back. He saw me staring at him from my window. He glared back. No acknowledgement came from either side. He closed his gate. The taxi drove him away. He was glad to go, I was happy he had gone... I only wish they had carried him out in a pine box too.

Later on, I walked down the Watson path, and stared through the living-room window... Gone,gone at last, thank the Lord he's gone.

September 9: Sunday

Peace and quiet at last. With no one living next door, it feels like we are living in a detached house.

"Mam, what would you do if you were me? Should I stay where I am, or should I go on the scheme." Tomorrow, the people at the unemployment centre expect Gary to attend a six month course at their assessment centre. Gary doesn't know what to do for the best, and quite frankly nether do I.

The easiest option would be for him to stay where he is and sign off the dole, but is it his best alternative?... Okay, he's got a full time job... It's very dead-end, but the question must be asked; is any work better than no work at all... I think not. Both pay, and working conditions at Lewis & Hudson are appalling, and who's to say the firm won't go belly-up during the next six months?

At the assessment centre Gary will be given a taste of the

trades they have on offer. You never know, given time he might come to like one of them. Okay, the money is crap, and the course ends in six months; but if he does well they might keep him on for further training, and you never know, at the end of it all he might come out with an offer of an apprenticeship, and some qualifications to help him secure a decent job in the future. In my opinion Lewis & Hudson is a dead-end job leading nowhere, but in the end the decision is up to him.

Today is turning out to be a day for preparation. In one bedroom Gary is lying on his bed wondering what to do, while staring at the ceiling. In her room solitude is the name of the game. Megan has everything ready for the first day at 'Easy Fashions'. Her overall is on a hanger, her clothes are folded neatly, with her choice of footwear waiting patiently under and between the legs of a chair. 'I Will Always Love You' by 'Whitney Houston' is being consistently played over and over again on the CD player. Megan saunters from bed to window and back again. (I can hear her footsteps walking overhead.) Her constant companion, and best friend in all the world is her mobile phone, but it doesn't ring... Gary had Megan's bedroom door slammed in his face, when he said: *'The reason your mobile doesn't ring, is because nobody wants to speak to you!'*

"Mam, why is Julian treating me like this? Why doesn't he call me?... Mam, Mam, what can I do to get him back?... Mam, Mam, Ma..."

"For Christ's sake snap out of it girl. Julian is a liar and a thief... You are better off without him... And turn that music off. It's getting on my bloody nerves!"

September 10: Monday

If yesterday was a day for preparation, then today was a day when a lot of loose ends were finally cleared up. Megan now knows why Julian hasn't bothered to answer any of her calls. He's got a new girlfriend. Not only that, but he's got his old job back with Mr Hurst. (By the way, have I mentioned Mr Hurst's shop is called 'The Blooming Daisy'?) "Mam, I had the shook of my life when I walked into the florists." Breaking the news better than I thought she would, Megan explained she intended to apologise to Mr Hurst in person for all the upset caused, even though she was the innocent party. (Megan assured me, beginning work on the opposite side of the street from Mr Hurst's shop was a total coincidence and had nothing to do with her decision.) "You should have seen him Mam. He was all 'coochi coo' with her. They were laughing, Julian was giving her the same old bullshit, he used to give me. He nearly shit himself when I strolled through the door. Mam, he run from behind the counter, (Here Megan imitated Julian's actions.) *'I don't want any trouble, I don't want any trouble.'* I've never noticed it before but hasn't Julian got a mincing way of walking... I nearly laughed in his face when I saw him coming towards me. And that slut he was with. I could tell she knew who I was all right, because as soon as I walked into the shop her face went as red as a beetroot and stood in the corner like a timid mouse.

Julian is terrible under pressure Mam, (I nearly said: all men are love. But I thought better of it and let her carry on.) he was nearly in tears... I took the blame for you... I admitted it was all my fault... Mr Hurst is a very old and dear friend of my mother, and he's decided to give me another chance... Please Megan don't start any trouble... I want to start a new life.

What a shit!... Mam, to think I was going out with a thing like him... Take the blame for me... FOR ME!... Happy to take the blame for me when it was all is fault in the first place."... I began to playfully tease Megan. I started to sing 'I Will Always Love You'. "Please Mam don't, please don't remind me about it."

Gary came home from work, and announced he'd decided to attend the Assessment Centre. "I didn't know what to do for the best, so I stood in the middle with each unit on either side and tossed a ten pence piece. Heads won, and I am being assessed. Today I was being assessed while I used a paint brush." Gary give me a wink. "On the way home (A day's work at the assessment centre is a hour less than a day's work at Lewis & Hudson. Plus Gary is entitled to holiday, sick pay and travel expenses.) I made sure no one was watching, so I popped in next door and handed in my notice."

Dear Diary, you do realise what all this means don't you?... I'm the only benefit cheat in the family. Trevor, Megan and now Gary are all legit, which leaves only me to con the country.

September 11: Tuesday
(THE DAY THE WORLD STOOD STILL.)

During the break in this afternoon's edition of 'Crossroads' there was a news flash. I suddenly found myself watching a Jumbo jet of some sort crashing into one of the 'Twin Towers' in New York... The other tower was already on fire... The newsman said another plane had already crashed into it... Moments later both towers crashed down to the ground... I saw people walking out of the dust, like zombies in an old American B-movie... Thousands must have perished... I saw people jumping out of the skyscraper windows... During one replay of the plane crashing into the building... I don't want to write about this anymore...

MY WORLD:

Personally today was one of those lazy, hazy, late summer days that are often being described in my books. Nothing happened apart from the war... I love living in a detached house. I hope next door turns out to be one of those houses the council leaves abandoned for years.

Gary made me laugh when he came home from work: "Have you got a twin brother?" One of his assessors asked him, while he was painting a coat of gloss on a wooden cabinet. "Because there's a bloke who's the spitting image of you working in the Lewis & Hudson unit next door."

"The two of them were sitting on our bench Mam. Julian and that thing, sitting together on our bench!... Eating bread rolls they were. He was telling her jokes, and she was laughing at every word he said." Megan marched through the front door, and threw her bag on the chair. "I don't know what I ever saw in him. Julian was never that funny... They couldn't see me, but I could see them. You should have seen what he did, when I stepped out into the open, and walked past where they were sitting. He shut-up, she stopped laughing and they both held onto each other for dear life." I hope Megan doesn't turn into one of those bunny boilers I've read about in the newspapers.

BACK TO THE NEWS:

Terrorists have definitely attacked America. Apart from the Twin Towers, another plane crashed into the 'Pentagon', while another crashed into a field in Pittsburgh Pennsylvania... All planes were completely destroyed. Crew, passengers, murdered. All terrorists aboard were also killed.

September 12: Wednesday

APOCALYPSE-ARMAGEDDON-KAMIKAZE-PEARL HARBOUR-THE WORLD WILL NEVER BE THE SAME AGAIN... Television and the newspapers are full of it.

WHAT THE FAMILY THINK:

Trevor: I can't believe it. It's like watching a film.

Mam: Stock-up with tinned food. If they cut the electric, tinned will last longer than fresh... Have you got any candles in the house Rhian?... Don't forget if they start bombing the safest place to stay is under the stairs.

Trevor: Who's going to bomb this estate?... What do you mean we haven't got any candles in the house!... What about the Father Christmas and snowman candles you put out at Christmas time?

Megan: (Too upset over Julian to care.)

Gary: We've all been assessing the situation down at the assessment centre.

Anthony: I know a boy in school who was talking to one of the terrorists on the internet.

MEANWHILE IN WALES:

I feel so guilty. It's my evening class tonight, and I've written bugger all, all summer.

"Welcome back one and all." Mr Davis greeted us... perched on the edge of his desk he spent fifteen minutes of my precious class spouting his opinion of the forthcoming war. (I don't understand why Mr Davis doesn't like America, or why he feels they had it coming... I also don't understand why Jew's are so hated?) "Tonight really is a case of off with the old and on with the new. First I'd like to bid a fond farewell to Mrs Jackson, and Mr Simpson from our little group.

There was no need, but both parties were polite enough to resign in writing." Removing both letters from his jacket pocket Mr Davis read: "Blab, blab, blab... Here we are... During the summer break,myself and another member of the class," Mr Davis looked up at me. "Have reached a crisis point in our relationship, from which there can be no reconciliation." Replacing the letter in the envelope, he moved his attention to the other. "La-de-da-da-daa... Here we are... There is a power struggle going on between two dominant females in the class, which I can no longer be a witness too."

Both letters were replaced in his pocket. "Rhian, you will promise to behave yourself this term wont you love?" Making a joke of it, Mr Davis introduced the class to Mr. Walker.

"What do you think of him then?" Anne asked during the break. "If my Dave wasn't here, I'd be screwing him in the girls' toilets." She sniggered.

Doug Walker is six foot of everything a woman could ever dream of, which posed the question: 'What the hell was he doing here?'

Nearer Anne's age then mine, I saw Dave's jaw drop as Doug entered the room.

"So you're the trouble maker?" Doug said handing me a cup of coffee.

"It's a long story."

"I've got plenty of time, if you'd like to tell me about it?"

Help, Trevor, Gary, Mammy. I don't feel safe with this man on my own anymore.

September 13: Thursday

They say over an hundred Brit's were killed during the attack on the Twin Towers... Countless firemen and rescue workers were also killed when the two skyscrapers collapsed... On the news I saw the people of New York lining the road cheering and holding-up banners of encouragement as the fire engines drove past... Saudi terrorist Osama Bin Laden is the chief suspect... He's head of something called the Al-Qaeda terror group... At the moment Bin Ladin is living in a cave with the Taliban in Afghanistan.

Sexual fantasies are plaguing my mind. I couldn't stop dreaming about Doug last night, and they've continued throughout the day. If these dreams turnout to be true, I shan't have a hole in my body that wont feel sore.

This is all Anne's fault. Talking about bonking in the girls' toilet. Dave's the one I feel sorry for,Dave and my Trevor... What happens if the next time we are doing it, I imagine Trevor is Doug... Does that count as cheating?... I wonder if Trevor imagines I am someone else when we've been doing it?... He's always fancied 'Viv Windsor' from 'Emmerdale Farm', (Don't ask me why?) and sometimes he likes the bedroom light off, and then on other nights he likes it on? (What's all that about?) It took Mam to bring me back to reality. She rushed around this afternoon with some more survival tips on what to do if there's a war, (An Anderson shelter was mentioned.) plus news of a very disturbing telephone call she'd received from Julian: "He was very upset Rhian. He was crying and everything over the telephone. He claims Megan is stalking him. He claims

Megan took a job on the opposite side of the street from 'The Blooming Daisy' on purpose, so she could spy on him and his new girlfriend who's just started working there. Julian claims Nancy is so scared of Megan that she's considering ending their relationship. She's also threatened to quit her job twice. Julian claims Mr Hurst is fed up of receiving silent telephone calls during business hours... Julian claims the girls working in 'Easy Fashions' are giving the shop some funny looks as they pass by. He's asked me to have a word with our Megan. He wants her to know he didn't two time her with Nancy, and he did mean everything he said at the time. But he doesn't mean it now." (Typical man!)

"Megan, Julian's been on the phone, crying to your Gran... He claims you are stalking him... For Goodness sake girl, don't you realise you are better off without the little weed. Now leave him alone, you can do much better than him... Do you hear me?... Can you hear me up there?" Megan's bedroom door slammed shut... "I mean it Megan, I don't want to hear anymore about it, OKAY?... Turn that bloody music down... Megan, Megan, TURN IT DOWN!... TREVOR GO TO YOUR DAUGHTER'S BEDROOM AND CONFISCATE HER CD PLAYER THIS INSTANT!"

September 14: Friday Trevor's Birthday - Day Of Remembrance - 3 minute silence

Before I write about Trevor, let me state here and now; on her way out of the door this morning Megan refused to give any assurances about any change in attitude towards Julian. (I'm sure I heard her mutter the word bastard under her breath.)

Trevor is forty-one years old today. I wrote him a card, and I give it to him with the three Polo shirts I intended giving him at Christmas. Trevor was really pleased with the shirts, and wore the green one for the rest of the day.

Finding ourselves all alone in the house, we celebrated the occasion in our customary manner. After... While we were lying on the bed, I asked: "Trevor, while we were making love do you ever fantasise that I am someone else?"

"You what?"

"Well do you?... Pretend I'm someone else, I mean?"

"What's brought all this on?"

"It's a simple question Trevor. Do you pretend I'm someone else or what?"

"Like Lady Di, you mean?"

"Well, yes... Like her or someone else."

"And you wouldn't mind, would you... If I did, I mean?"

"No, no of course I wouldn't... It's only pretend isn't it?... I mean, if Lady Di was alive today, what are the chances in real life of her having it off with you?"

Without me knowing it: over the years Trevor's warped and twisted mind has turned me into Rita Fairclough, Mavis Wilton and Alma Sedgewick from 'Coronation Street'. Kathy Glover, Viv Windsor, (His all time favourite.) and Betty Eggleton (He claims: '*Just to see the look on her face.*' This rule also applies to the Queen and Margaret Thatcher.) from 'Emmerdale Farm'. Jackie Corkhill from 'Brookside'. The lady in 'Juliet Bravo', Joan Collins and Kate O'Mara when they were both in 'Dynasty'. Sue Ellen in 'Dallas', and Princess Anne when we do it doggy style, or when we play the cow and the bull game on the farm... With his cast of thousands, it's a wonder Trevor hasn't been bonking me every night of the year.

September 15: Saturday

I'm getting fed-up of the media telling me that the world has changed... Mine hasn't!... Why will history never be the same again?... History is always changing... I thought that was the point!History always changes, and now I'm going to change the subject... In myself I've forgiven Trevor his lurid fantasies. After all if we could all control what goes on inside our minds, there would be no need for me to be on Prozac, would there?

Trevor's birthday tea went off brilliantly. He received his full quota of cards from the family. Each card (Mam, Gary, Megan) contained a five pound note. Anthony's was once again made on the computer, and contained this sentiment: 'WITH A DAD LIKE YOU, WHAT CAN I DO, BUT BE PROUD OF YOU.' With a tear stained eye Trevor said this sentiment was worth five pounds of any Dad's money, any day of the week.

Yes Diary, you're right. I should have written all this in yesterday's chapter, but Trevor knocked me off my stroke. He's been giving me some very funny looks all afternoon. He's even started calling me Viv!

September 15: Saturday Part 2

Trevor got my name right at last: "Rhian, Rhian, you'll never guess who's moving in next door?"

"Who? Who?"

"One of the rag's kids... The oldest boy, and his wife I think.

"Where did you hear that?"

"Up the shop. I was standing in line, and the youngest girl... You know the one. About so high only about ten, but she's got a big mouth on her. She turned to me and said: "Our Darren's moving next door to you. He went down the council to see about it yesterday."... Thank you God. That's all I need.

September 16: Sunday

Tony Blair says we are at war with terrorists... Does that include the IRA?

Trevor got up early and spent the morning repairing the fence dividing our front and back garden from our neighbours. "The barricades are in place." He announced. "Rhian, where can I lay my hands on some razor-wire?"

'All the people in the house say yeah!' The noise from the van was deafening. "They're here Mam." Anthony yelled, as the three of us peeped out at our new neighbour's arrival.

Darren Johnson, his pregnant wife, and one younger sister, got out via the front of the battered old Transit van. Resembling a scene from the D-Day landings, the rear doors swung open, releasing the Johnson masses who disembarked their carrier and charged up the beach. (Garden path.)

"This is nice." We heard Mother Johnson say to her son as he tried to open the front door.

"Yes, you'll be all right by here boy." His father agreed. "I told you the council would see you all right in the end, didn't I... The only thing you have to worry about is the neighbours. I used to enjoy a quiet drink with Ken Watson before he moved away. Ken reckoned they were a rum lot this side. (I actually saw him pointing at us.) Well you've seen what he is like for yourself haven't you, always fighting and that down the club. She on the other hand so Ken tells me, isn't all that right in the head. "

On the other side of the wall I heard squeals, laughter, footsteps running up and down stairs, banging, tapping, the toilet flushing, muffled voices... Then I pressed my ear up against the wall... "A lick of paint, and you'll have yourself a beautiful little place to live in... Donald, have you got any tins of paint left in your shed?

"What colour?"

"I don't know... White I suppose?"

"I'll have to have a look..."

After what seemed an age, the tramping of the stairs ceased, the front door slammed shut, the invading hoards re-boarded their van, the deafening music helping to mask the rattling engine, they pulled away from the kerb. They were gone... Dear God, what have I done to deserve this?

September 17: Monday

It seems to me that America is in full panic mode... Britain never fell apart like this, not even during the Blitz... For once I'm glad nobody in my family can afford to travel by plane.

The topic on 'Kilroy' was 'Proud To Be Fat'. A twenty stone woman said she was happy to be who she was and if anyone didn't like it, that was their problem, and they should keep their hurtful opinions to themselves.

'I've been to many places, I've seen so many faces'... The Johnson van was parked outside, but the music was coming through my wall. *'Yellow, blue and purple hills.'*

"What the fuck is going on?" Trevor screamed from the bedroom.

BANG, BANG, BANG, I hit the wall with the first thing that came to hand. The underside of a brass ornament sitting on the mantelpiece, and screamed: "Turn that bloody noise down."

Five minutes later there was a knock on my door: "Hi, my

name is Jodie Johnson... We are your new neighbours. When I say we, I mean me and my Darren of course... Darren and J J Johnson. Everyone calls me J.J on account of my initials... I'm sorry about the noise. You can hear the noise through these walls can't you?... These dividing walls aren't very thick are they? Typical Jerry built council rubbish I suppose... I know you won't believe this, but my Darren isn't even playing his music at full volume at the moment... Look I don't want to get off on the wrong foot, but we do have a lot of work to get done, what with the decorating and all..."

"It's not the work noises I object to." I said, finally getting a word in. "It's the music. I can't hear the television set in my own living-room."

"What's on?"

"Kilroy."

"Can I come in and watch it with you? Only we haven't got a telly yet. We haven't got anything at the moment, not even a bed. Darren can't take his bed from his parents' house, because his younger brothers and sisters are sleeping in it."

So I invited her in and we watched Kilroy. Mind you, watched is the right word because I couldn't hear a thing. Music in one ear, Jodie in the other: "I see what you mean... Loud isn't it?"... BANG,BANG, BANG... "DARREN, DARREN TURN IT DOWN. I CAN'T HEAR KILROY IN HERE!... There that's better." She said, the music was down to a muffle. "You got a lovely house." God this woman can talk. "I love your telly. Widescreen, and you've got satellite too. You wait until my Darren hears about this. He'll be around here all the time watching the football... I don't think I'll see him again... I'll tell you what... I'm sorry, I'm so sorry. There I go again. Listen to me. I'm in your house.

I'm drinking your tea. I've ate some toast, which was lovely by the way, but you haven't told me your name yet."

"Rhian." I answered timidly. God, I have no defence against this woman. Like a whirlwind Jodie has entered and taken over my life.

"Yes I can see my Darren and your husband getting on famously... What's his name by the way?"

"Trevor."

"That's a nice name... Trev, Trevor, Trev; yes, I can live with that. While your Trev, and my Dar are watching the football, you can come around to me. I'll need all the help I can get when the baby arrives."

Dear Diary the time is now 11.45pm. I am knackered. Jodie went on and on, and on. Kilroy started at 9.00am, and she finished at 4.00pm. She told me about her marriage: "Rhian, I know I shouldn't be telling this to strangers, but that bastard decorating next-door has cheated on me three times in the past two years." Before I could get a word in, up went her hand: "I know what you are going to ask me... Why do I stay with him? Why do I put-up with it?... Oh Rhian, I love him you see. I wouldn't know what to do without him... I shouldn't be telling you any of this but two of the women he went with have had his children... Tried to trap him they did, but he soon came running back to me when he found out... Rhian, is it all right if I use your toilet?" Patting her stomach, "you know how it is when you're pregnant."

She told me about her sex life: "Rhian, my Darren's a fantastic lover." She whispered, exaggerating her lips as she spoke. "He can go all night long... He's got this fantastically long tongue" She laughed. "I shouldn't be telling you any of this to you, but when my Darren calls round, I'll ask him to stick it out for you."

She met Trevor: "I bet he's a good shag?" She winked, after Trevor had said hello, and walked into another room.

I couldn't get rid of her. She couldn't, or wouldn't take the hint. She talked over me, when I told her I had things to do. I stood up, and put on my coat, but she just sat there and watched me button it up: "I don't have anything to do with my family. They don't like Darren, you see... Are you still speaking to your mother Rhian?... Are you? Oh that must be nice."

"Is that your husband calling you?" Trevor asked, in a desperate attempt of getting her out of the house. "I'm sure I heard him calling for you while I was out the back."

"Well, I must go before I outstay my welcome... It's been lovely meeting you both... Rhian perhaps we can arrange alternative coffee mornings together, when I've saved enough money to buy a cafetière. I hope you don't mind me asking... Maybe when you are free one morning you wouldn't mind popping next-door and explain what it feels like to give birth?"... Why me sweet Lord, why me?

September 18: Tuesday

ANOTHER DAY TO ADD TO THE REST
by
Rhian Evans

Blue morning - Towers standing - Jets of doom -
New York mourning.
Across the land planes are falling - Pentagon -
Field in Pennsylvania.
Jump for your life - Crash through the clouds -
Walk through the dust.

Thousands perish - Victims -
Knights climb aboard siren steeds.
The dead phoning home -
Voices captured by answering machines.
The World watches on TV - We grieve.

A week has passed since September 11. I'd like to mark the occasion with this little verse.

"Hello, I've just been to the Post Office to collect my unemployment giro, and I saw your card in the window. Have you still got your bits and pieces for sale?"

"Yes."

"Do you live on the estate? If you do, can I call round?... Say in half an hour?"

"Yes, fine, fine. The address is 29, Heol-Y-Haul."

"WHAT, NEVER... RHIAN YOU KNOW WHO THIS IS, DON'T YOU... RHIAN, IT'S JODIE FROM NEXT DOOR... Put the kettle on love, Darren and I will be around in a minute.

"TREVOR, TREVOR." Sprinting up the stairs, I yanked the bedclothes off my comatose, naked husband's body, while explaining what had just happened.

"She's off her fucking head." He muttered, searching the bedroom floor for his clothes.

There was a knock on the door.

"Rhian!" Staring directly into my eyes, Trevor said: "For Christ's sake, let's make this short and sweet."

"Darren, show Rhian your tongue... Isn't that the biggest one you've ever seen?... Darren, do that trick for Rhian. Touch the end of your nose with it... I told you it was long, didn't I Rhian?"

"What do you want to buy." Trevor interrupted, in a vain attempt to speed things along.

"All of it really." Jodie said, removing our card from her purse... "What, or this... I didn't have any paper or pen on me. So I took the card out of the window myself." Then in an attempt to justify her actions. "Rhian, did you design this card yourself?... She's very talented, isn't she Darren?"

To cut a long story short they bought the lot for seventy-five quid. Trevor had stored it all in his shed, and happily agreed to help Darren transport it all next door.

"We slept in Darren's old sleeping-bag last night." Jodie admitted, while the men carried the fridge out of the front door. "My back was in rags this morning. We haven't got a stick of furniture in the house, thank goodness Darren likes eating cold baked beans, that's all I've got to say." She continued without a care in the world. "I've got a three-piece suite, and some wardrobes coming from the charity shop this afternoon... I know I'm being cheeky, but you haven't got any old bedding, going spare by any chance?"

I promised to search some out for her: "You are kind Rhian. Darren and I have really landed on our feet moving in next to such kind and considerate neighbours as you and Trevor... Does your daughter still work in the Blooming Daisy?... She's found herself another job as she?... What's the story on the gay guy she used to work with? He lives somewhere on this estate too, doesn't he?" Handing me back her empty mug Jodie returned next-door to await the arrival of her charity furniture, and to arrange our old belongings around her home.

"Rhian, they've got fuck all in there." Trevor said, confirming Jodie's story. "But they couldn't give a shit. How old is she? Sixteen, seventeen, eighteen maybe? He's nineteen... I can't believe it Rhian, they're eating out of tins, they haven't got any plates, cups, knives, forks, bugger all. But they seem so happy together, living like pigs in shit."

"They are young see, Trev. I remember a time when we were like that." (I hope I don't pick up Jodie's annoying habit of calling my Trevor, Trev.)

September 19: Wednesday

Last night I heard my old headboard knocking violently against the opposite side of the wall. (And she's nearly seven months pregnant... We never had to put up with this when the Watson's were living next-door!)

I spent the morning sorting out old pieces of crockery, and cutlery I found taking up space in my cupboard and draws. (Trevor even popped up the attic.) I also found some old towels, pillowcases and blankets I no longer use. (We have been a duvet house for the past five years.) Trevor reckons he let the Johnson's have our old stuff for seventy-five pounds, because it was taking up too much room in his shed: "Anyway." Trevor said, handing me the money. "Nobody else wanted it did they? And if our old telly and video help to keep Jodie in her home instead of around at ours, it won't be that bad an investment, now will it?" (I believe my Trevor is just a big softie at heart.) "Did you hear that headboard banging last night? If they keep that up, it wont be long before they will be coming through the wall."

Mam called round this afternoon, and helped me carry my bits and pieces next door. I introduced her to Jodie, who immediately went into raptures about how comfortable my bed was for having sex: "Rhian, I'm surprised you've only got three, if you've been doing it in a bed like that... It supported me in every position... It's done wonders for my back."

Inside number 31, Darren had painted everything white. Walls, doors, ceiling, passage, landing,toilet, bedrooms, living-room, kitchen. "I love brilliant colours." Jodie said, during our grand tour. "We choose silk emulsion, because if the baby dabs the wall with a dirty hand all the cleaning up I'll have to do is rub the mark away with a damp cloth."

In the master bedroom Jodie introduced Darren, who was in the midst of painting an old wardrobe white to fit in with the colour scheme. Winking and patting my old bed on the way out of the room Jodie said: "Doesn't the smell of gloss paint turn you on?"

You are living next door to a sex manic." Mam said, delivering her immediate, first impression opinion on my new neighbours, as the vibrating sound of my old headboard tapped out the lovers' message against my wall. "Rhian, I know we live in a modern world and everything is supposed to be different these days, but I'm here to tell you I refused to let your father come anywhere near me, after I'd found out I was carrying you." Mam also added tapping her finger against the bridge of her nose: "Rhian, I wouldn't allow Trevor to go next door on some pretext on his own while that husband of hers is out, if I were you."

Thank God, for the sanctuary of my evening class. (A Jodie free zone.) "Fancy a cup of coffee?" Doug asked, pouring out a measure from his flask. "After tasting last week's example, I thought I'd better bring my own." He smirked handing me a plastic cup.

Politely refusing; I'm very nervous when it comes to eating and drinking strange foods, or should that be beverages offered to me via strangers. (I've never taken any sweets from strange men.) The newspapers are always full of women being date raped after drinking drugged drinks. I watched Anne accept a cup from Doug without batting an eyelid... The young have no fear.

What have I done?... I feel so ashamed... I've lied to my class: *'I mailed a selection of my work a few weeks ago, but I haven't heard anything yet.'* I told my innocent classmates... What a barefaced liar I am. I haven't written anything for ages. I haven't so much as put pen to paper... In fact I can't remember where my notepad is kept? My classmates have overtaken me in leaps and bounds. Everyone except me is receiving rejection slips in the post. Last week, Anne received two standard refusals alone.

"Isn't it exciting." She gushed, as I read one of her replies. "I look forward to seeing the postman every morning now... I've still got two letters outstanding and you never know, there my be a cheque on the way to me, as we speak."

September 20: Thursday

Life is becoming much to much for me again... I'm P.M.T active. (Which doesn't help.) I can feel matters coming to a head.

11.15pm: I heard next-door's headboard banging against my wall.

11.25pm: I was grinding my teeth, but thankfully the banging had stopped.

11.35pm: I was drifting off, but the banging rudely brought me back to the present.

Megan: (From her room) What are they doing in there?
Gary: (From his room) Mam, tell them to shut-up.
Trevor: (Lying next to me) I don't know where he gets his strength from?
Anthony: (From his room) Will you all be quite, I'm trying to get some sleep.

11.45pm: I heard an excited scream, then the house fell silent.

Trevor: (Lying next to me) That was a quick one!

8.00am: "He must be keen next-door." Anthony remarked at the breakfast table. "Darren from next-door is making an early start again this morning." I cocked my head and heard a faint tapping emanating from the opposite side of my bedroom wall. "He was hard at it till late last night... It was nearly midnight before Darren finished hammering what he was hammering together?... I think Jodie must have had an accident and sat on a nail or splinter, because I heard her screaming out in pain."

Thank God Anthony is still an innocent, and Gary and Megan weren't sitting next to him to put him right. Leaving my youngest son believe our new neighbours were experts at D.I.Y, I waited until Anthony had left for school before paying a visit to my new neighbours' home.

Her body covered by a man's white towelling bathrobe,

Jodie answered the door: "Excuse me." She yawned. "I didn't get much sleep last night."

"I know." I replied in a sarcastic tone. "My family heard you moving around in your bed all night."

The penny dropped... Her face reddened: "You heard us, did you?... Come in, come in, come in, I didn't realise we were playing to an audience." Moving to one side, a gust of wind blew underneath Jodie's robe, exposing her naked body from the waist down to the elements. Giggling Jodie hurriedly covered up her bare bump, closed the door and showed me into the sitting-room. "So you heard us then?... You should have shouted or banged on the wall or something... I'll tell you what Rhian, let that be our secret code for the future. If either of us are making too much noise in the bedroom, let the other bang on the wall... It's because I'm pregnant you know. I never used to be like this. I used to be happy to have it once a week like everyone else. It's my Darren I feel sorry for. I think I'm wearing him out... He's lost a lot of weight... Was you like this when you were having your three, Rhian?... I can't get enough... Darren couldn't cope one night." Jodie drew near to me. She looked around the room, she listened for the sound of Darren working upstairs: "I know I shouldn't be telling you any of this. Darren doesn't like me telling strangers any of our personal business. But you're not a stranger anymore are you Rhian? You are my friend. And anyway, I've got no one else to talk too." Another quick glance round told her the coast was clear. "Well the other night, I was really turned on. I mean Darren did what he could, but it wasn't enough to satisfy me if you know what I mean." Now it was my turn for my face to redden... I agreed entirely with her Darren, I shouldn't be listening to any of this, but it was too late. Once again I found myself caught between the devil and the deep blue sea. I know it was wrong. I know I should have said: *'Your personal life has got nothing to do with me Jodie,'* but I was hooked... Too much information or not, I wanted to hear the rest of the story. "Poor Darren was dog tired. He'd been working on his projects all day, and he'd been doing it to me all night, but I still made him get out of bed at half past two in the morning and bring me up a carrot so I could finish myself off... Rhian, do you think I'm a selfish person?"

What could I say after that? I've never met anyone like Jodie/J.J in my life. The woman/girl is a one off, an open book. She opens up her life to anyone who asks, or doesn't as the case may be... A stranger on a bus, train, or standing in a Post Office queue would know her life story inside out, after greeting her with a friendly hello.

FACTS I KNOW ABOUT JODIE WITHOUT ASKING:

1. Jodie and Darren are not married.
2. Darren used to slap Jodie around, but he doesn't now.
3. On the occasions when Darren's left Jodie for another woman. Jodie tried to commit suicide. (She showed me the marks on her wrist.)
4. Jodie used to be anorexic and bulimic.
5. Jodie lost her virginity at fourteen during a one night stand at the youth club.
6. Jodie's had two abortions.
7. Jodie gave up smoking and drinking, for the baby. (But not at weekends.)
8. Baby names: Holly = Girl Owen = Boy
9. Both are unemployed.
10. Jodie and Darren's parents live on the eastern side of the estate.

11. Jodie's on Prozac: "They make me feel so happy Rhian. I don't suppose a strong minded woman like you would have any idea what my life would be like without them?"

Jodie has agreed to move her headboard a little bit away from the wall, when her and Darren have sex with each other in the future.

September 21: Friday

"Hello." I could just make out the top of Darren's head popping over our garden fence." I don't want to interrupt you from hanging out your washing. But I was wondering if you were using your back garden for anything important?"

"You what?"

"Your back garden. Are you using it, or do you have any plans to do anything interesting in it?"

Dear Diary, to tell you the truth my feelings towards Darren have somewhat cooled since I've heard what Jodie had to say about him. Call me old fashioned if you like, but I believe there aren't any excuses; no man should hit a woman, no matter what she'd said or done... Take my Trevor for instance. He's never laid a finger on me, even when I deserved it.

"If you're not using the garden, I wonder if you'd mind if I stored some of my scrap metal in it?"

Bewildered, I made my excuses, and told him he'd have to talk to Trevor about it... You see, it's things like this that make my blood boil. You give an inch and they take a mile. I've bent over backwards to make our new neighbours feel welcome, but it still isn't enough. Not content with my cast off china and linen, they expect me to turn my garden into some sort of glorified scrap metal yard as well.

"My Darren's ever so clever with his hands." Jodie informed me later in the afternoon. "He loves D.I.Y, and anything to do with electric and machines."

"I'm sorry Jodie. You know I'd like to help you in any way I can. But I'm not allowing your Darren to turn my back garden into a glorified junk yard for old cars."

"Don't be silly." Jodie laughed. "My Darren can't even drive... Well he can, but he hasn't passed his test if you know what I mean... No, it's for his sculptures, silly. It's my Darren's hobby. He makes these life size garden sculptures from scrap metal he finds lying about at the scrap-yard and the local council tip. He welds them into shapes. Some of them are over six feet tall. When he's made about ten or so, he sells them at a car boot sale. He sold three the other week at fifty quid apiece."

A sculptor, a poet, a singer (Karaoke - Trevor) all living on the same estate. My God, we Welsh are a talented people.

By the way, I said I'd have to see the sculptures, before I'd agree to Darren storing them in my garden.

September 22: Saturday

Oh no, I've got writer's block. Try as I will, I can't compose a single rhyme to save my life. Alone; I thought this the perfect opportunity to practice my literary talents... But alas it was not to be, not a single line, idea, or verse.

I've tried, and I've tried, and I've tried again, but to no avail. I tried, before, during and after the BBC2 Saturday matinee. ('Escape From Fort Bravo' starring William Holden, and John somebody or other who played Blake Carrington in 'Dynasty'.) This is awful. I don't like this feeling at all. My mind is in a whirl, what with one thing and another. Next-door, Megan and Julian, my evening class. Oh my God, I'm having a panic attack... Breathe deeply, breathe deeply, come on Rhian you've suffered plenty of these in the past... Where did I put that paper bag?

9.00pm: I don't feel very well at all. I still can't make anything rhyme. I'm going to bed.

September 23: Sunday

Trevor came home early last night. He said, listening to all that action going on next-door had got him in the mood. I replied: "If you come anywhere near me tonight Trevor, I'll kill you!" (Trevor still shook hands with himself, after I'd begged him to turn off the bedside light.)

Trevor came down the stairs this morning holding his hands up in the air: "I come in peace." He said, before flopping down on the chair. Handing him a tray, containing a bowl of cereal, (I hope he's washed his hands this morning.) and a mug of tea, I apologised for what I'd said: "I didn't mean it love... It's my period talking... I'd been feeling rough all day."

Megan can finally see the wood from the trees. At last, she can see the light at the end of the tunnel. "It suddenly came to me last night Mam. What am I doing?... Why am I doing it?... Where is all this going to get me?" Megan shrugged her shoulders, and paused after each question. "Sometimes I think I'm going off my head Mam. What is wrong with me? Why do I still want to have anything to do with Julian when he clearly wants nothing to do with me?"

"It's all part of growing up, love."

"Fffff... To hell with the little bender, Mam."

September 24: Monday

Department of Social Security.
Cardiff.

Dear Mrs Evans,
It has come to our attention that you are currently receiving a weekly amount of 'Child Benefit' you are no longer entitled too. Our records show that on 10-9-2001 your daughter Megan Louise Evans, began a six month Government work related initiative, funded by the Welsh Development Agency.

Please hand your benefit book in at your local Post Office with the enclosed declaration slip, or alternately mail your benefit book back to us using the enclosed prepaid envelope.

A new benefit book with the amended amount will be posted out to you promptly. Failure to do so,is liable to result in criminal proceedings being leveled against you. In the event of our investigations proving you have been in receipt of benefit you were no longer entitled to. Any unentitled payments will be deducted from your future benefit.

If you feel you have been treated unfairly in anyway. You have the right of appeal. Please read the enclosed information provided.

Yours sincerely,
D.D.Field (Child Benefit Manager)

THE BASTARDS!

September 25: Tuesday

I feel a lot better after a good night's sleep. Looking back on it, I suppose it was only a matter of time before the DSS found me out. (At least they never found out about Megan working at 'The Blooming Daisy'.) One good thing to come out of all this is, I'm no longer a benefit cheat. For the first time in I don't know how many months my household is on the straight and narrow, which will be good for my nerves, but alas bad for my pocket.

On to other matters: Darren's older brother Mark, helped him to transport his sculptures to his new address in the Jackson family's battered transit van. Trevor also gave an hand to unload, then when he came in to get something, he mentioned: "That Mark Johnson is a hell of a boy Rhian. He hasn't got a care in the world. (A common trait with that family.) "He's driving around in that old Bedford van without any road tax, insurance, or M.O.T. You've got to laugh Rhian. He said the police will never catch him for speeding. The van won't go that fast... I'm sure he's not all there, because he said the police can't ban him for drink driving either, because he's already been banned... But like he pointed out. He doesn't drive very far. Only around the estate, to the odd car boot sale he attends, and to Tesco's each week to help his mother with the shopping."

6.00pm: Darren knocked at the door, and invited Trevor and I to a private exhibition of his work:

"And you get all the metal from the scrap yard and council tip, do you?" Trevor enquired, walking around a six foot structure I can only describe as baring a strong resemblance to the tin man from 'The Wizard of Oz.'

"I call this one 'Acid Rain'. Darren stated proudly. "Gardening folk all around the world will be dressed like this when the ozone layer finally packs in."

"I don't understand them myself. Do I Darr?" Jodie gushed proudly hanging from her partner's arm. "But as long as one of us does that's the important thing, and other people must like them loads, because you've sold a few, haven't you Darr?"

"What's this one called?" Perched behind the tin man, a ball of metal hovered above, a tripod of metal railings.

"Well spotted." (As if I could miss it!) "Rhian, I can see you've got taste. I completed this, three days before we moved into our new house, and I've dedicated it to our coming child." Darren tenderly patted Jodie on her stomach. (Did this man really used to slap Jodie around???) "I call it: 'An Embryo In A Womb Of Thorns'. I've made it to symbolise the struggle our child will face growing up in this ugly and oppressive world."

Other examples of Darren's work were entitled 'The Female Orgasm ', (Jodie squealed: "We worked together on that one. Didn't we Darr?") 'Flotsam & Jetsam', (As described by Darren: "A matching pair, with a subtle difference.") 'Faeces', (I don't want to go into this, but it had something to do with living on this estate.) and a couple of others that were following along the same lines.

"What did you make of that lot?" Trevor asked, after we'd bid the Johnson's a good night. "I can take it or leave it." I replied. "But I'll tell you this for nothing Trevor. Darren Johnson is not displaying his 'Faeces' in my back garden!"

September 26: Wednesday

There is panic on the streets... The newspapers are full of it... People are going gas mask, and identity card crazy... Mam says she'd wished she'd kept her parents' old gas masks from the war... Why on earth would anyone want to gas this estate?

Back in our world:

"Still haven't heard anything?... Never mind, I'm sure something will soon arrive in the post." At evening class, rejection slip mania as been elevated to the forefront of human achievement. In my case this has been superseded by the believable lie. I hate to say it. And it's not because I'm envious in anyway of my fellow classmates, but most of my evening has been taken up reading the many examples of their wretched correspondence, that is circulating around the classroom.

I haven't been able to get any work done for weeks now... I've lost it... Whatever little talent I had,or thought I had, has deserted me and gone away.

"Your new neighbour sounds like a laugh." Anne said, during the break. "Nearly seven months pregnant, and moving into a house with nothing but the clothes on her back, and a heap of old junk in the back garden. When I go home, I'll have to root out some of my old baby clothes for her."

"Dave looks happy Anne?"

"It's because Doug hasn't turned up." Pulling me to one side, Anne whispered in my ear. "Dave doesn't like him... He thinks I fancy Doug... I don't really, but Dave doesn't know that... It's good to keep your husband on his toes Rhian."

RELATIONSHIP
by
Rhian Evans

Relationship of a serious kind.
Worship your body, worship your mind.
I fret, when you aren't there.
Discard all matters, without a care.
Until you return to my side.
Terrors untold, abide.
Conscious of jealousy,
Suspicious friend.
Life together, or at an end.
Relationship!
Will you work?
Broken heart.
Hurt!

I'm back baby, I'm back.

September 27: Thursday

It's pay day for Gary and Megan. News of the forced rent increase (The DSS took from me, now I must take from them to make-up the short fall.) didn't go down at all well by both parties.

"If I pay you anymore, it won't be worth me going to be assessed." Gary complained, after I'd confronted him with the facts.

"Now you know how I use to feel before I got my benefit book." Trevor said, before I could tell him to shut-up.

"But Mam, mun. I can't afford it." Megan wailed. "I can't

afford to give you any more. I have bus fares to pay, mobile phone cards to buy, and I still have to save some money for new clothes."

Why wont anyone understand that I'm the big loser in all this. I can't allow the family to be any worse off, than we already are. No matter how guilty they make me feel. I'm sorry Gary and Megan, but you'll have to make-up the deductions in my benefit money, until times change for the better, or you both find somewhere else to live.

September 28: Friday

I ended my period today. (Not a moment too soon.) Trevor needed no encouragement when he heard the news, and was soon back on the nest. At some point during our love making, Jodie banged on our bedroom wall, and with an hysterical tone in her voice, screamed: "I see what you mean Rhian... Rhian, you know it's already eleven o'clock in the morning don't you?... What time did you say you are going shopping today?... Can I come with you too?" (I'll have to make Trevor pull our head-board away from the wall, from now on.) If that wasn't embarrassing enough. My next thought made me feel sick to the pit of my stomach: *'Have our former neighbours the Watson's* been *listening to Trevor and I going at it all these years too?'* The thought of old man Watson and his wife ... Listening... With his... In his hand... And her... With her fingers in her... The dirty pair of... Why are these thoughts entering my head? I feel as if I've just been sexually violated in some way.

September 29: Saturday

I have agreed to allow Darren to store his 'Embryo In A Womb Of Thorns' and 'The Female Orgasm' in my back garden, along with some sheets of cold steel. (Why do the words 'cold steel' make me think of 'Lance-Corporal Jones' from 'Dad's Army?')

Actually I find the sound of Darren working quite relaxing in a funny sort of way. The noise of his angle-grinder, the sight of a shower of sparks, arching over our garden fence, the pounding of hammer upon metal... A cottage industry around my back... I wonder if this will encourage Trevor to take up an hobby and maybe construct something of his own?

CONSTRUCTION
by
Rhian Evans

You see a sheet of metal.
I see a figure tall.
You see some rust and flaking paint.
I see a colour tone.
You reject,
I save,
For salvage sake.
I create.

September 30: Sunday

Dear Diary, nothing remotely interesting happened today. Nothing-Nil-Zilch-O. With nothing to write about I think it's about time I told you some of my views concerning 'Satellite Television'.

We have a black mesh dish secured to an outside wall of the house, angled towards the sky. Through this Trevor and I can once again enjoy a lot of programmes we used to enjoy in the seventies. Trevor's got his sport channel, I've got my home shopping channel, (I haven't bought anything yet. But it's nice to know it's there.) The kids' hog the music channel, Mam likes the DIY, cooking, and gardening channels, we all love the film channels, and Jodie hopes we'll allow her new born baby to watch the cartoons on the children's channel when its born.

To tell you the truth, the threat of losing satellite TV became a handy bargaining tool during my recent rent negotiations with Gary and Megan. The thought of returning to four channels, and a fuzzy pictured C5 was too much for them to bear.

Trevor was correct in his prediction. A increase in our benefit does cover the subscription charge. So all in all, satellite TV has worked out well for our family... Trevor: "If we increase their lodge by another £10 a month between them Rhian, (Extra £1.25 weekly increase for Gary & Megan) we could subscribe to either Television X or The Adult Channel!"

QUESTIONS ABOUT ME & SAT TV:

1. How am I expected to get on with the cooking and cleaning, when there's an array of good programmes being screened at all hours throughout the day and night.
2. 2.00pm: 'On The Buses, started. This was followed half an hour later by 'Terry & June. What should I do? Should I sit and watch, or should I make the dinner?
3. Am I a television addict?
4. Is watching sixteen hours a day too much?
5. Is it wrong of me to try and get my housework done during the commercial breaks?

REVIEW OF THE MONTH:

I have a seven month pregnant nymphomaniac, for a neighbour. I have a daughter nursing a broken heart. I've lied to my evening class. I've suffered writer's block. I've fantasised about performing sexual acts on other men. I have a mother who thinks she's going to be on 'Crimewatch', and an 'Embryo In A Womb Of Thorns' in my back garden.

On the other hand; Jodie makes me laugh. Megan is getting over Julian… Over the years Trevor has insisted: *'It's all right to look, but not to touch.'* Gary is being assessed at a training centre. Darren's sculpture is growing on me. We all love satellite TV… All in all, a very interesting month.

P.S: THE CIVILISED WORLD IS AT WAR WITH TERROR… That means us and America.

October 1: Monday

The first of the month... A time for positive thinking... A Monday, the best day of the week to start something new... Off with the old, and on with the rest of my life.

Determined to move forward I wrote to every magazine I could think of, enclosing a selection of my work, along with a.s.a.e.

Mrs R.Evans.
29,Heol-Y-Haul,
Lloyd George Estate,
Aberheol,
Wales.

Dear Editor,
As an avid reader of your magazine, I find it very informative on stories concerning the stresses and strains of everyday human emotions. In common with the ladies depicted on your true life story page, I too find the pace of modern life frightening. I am a housewife and a mother who lives in constant fear of my teenage children coming to harm, or falling in with a bad crowd.

I have a husband who through no fault of his own, is unemployed. Money, as you can imagine is in short supply and I worry that I/we can't afford to give our children the best of starts in life.

Over the past six months or so, I've felt a great need to express my emotions through the medium of poetry. (Please find inclosed a selection of my work.) If you find any of these verses could be beneficial in anyway to your readers. Please don't hesitate to publish them in your magazine. (If they are not what you are looking for I enclose a.s.a.e for their return.)

Yours sincerely,
R.Evans.

I posted eight letters into the pillar-box. Until I did my research, it never occurred to me before. A lot of female magazines share the same address??? (The building must be a skyscraper.)

I see the minimum wage has risen 40p to £4.10 per hour... Thanks for that Mr Politician. How much did you say your salary is again?... Plus expenses?

October 2: Tuesday

After collecting our benefits from the Post Office, I went to feel terrible. I have a headache, and I feel like I've got a ten pound weight attached to each eyelid... I feel rundown... I've developed a chesty cough... I want to be alone... I can't stand for anyone to come anywhere near me.(Let alone touch me.) Sunlight is hurting my eyes... I think I've got the flu... I've gone to bed.

October 3: Wednesday

9.00am: I'm in bed with flu... Trevor phoned for reinforcements.

9.15am: Mam arrived with a basket full of remedies; home-made and shop bought. (Sell by date unknown.)

9.30am: My head is covered by a bath towel. My head is bent over a large bowl of steaming hot vapour fumes. I am being ordered to inhale deep breaths though my nose (If I can?) and mouth.

10.00am: Bony alien fingers are jabbing/rubbing an unknown concoction of 'Vic's Vapour Rub'/Goose Grease into my chest. (I'm expecting vinegar & brown paper at any moment.) The smell is foul, but I'm assured it will kill off 99% of all known germs. (I'm not in the least bit surprised.)

11.00am: The enemy, (My mother) is fully encamped at the foot of the bed.

11.15am: I have already been informed: catching the flu was my fault, because I didn't leave the house appropriately dressed during this recent spell of bad weather.

11.20am: It will also be my fault if anyone else in the family catches the flu from me.

11.25am: Mam claims: "Rhian, I haven't caught a cold or the flu for the best part of twenty years, touch wood."

11.27am: Mam added: "I can't remember the last time I caught anything?"

11.28am: After a minutes reflection: "The last time I caught the flu... I don't know... Let me see... It must have been sometime during the late seventies, or early eighties, I think."

11.30am: That was my fault too!

11.45am: Time for a hot lemon drink... Homemade... Don't know, or want to know what the ingredients are.

12.00pm: I want to go to sleep. Mother won't let me.

12.15pm: Made mental note: 'Must remember to ask Mam to look after Trevor, if he falls ill.'

?????pm: Must have nodded off?

1.00pm: Mam woke me up to sip some soup... I drank another hot lemon drink.

1.30pm: Another hot bowl of vapour fumes.

2.00pm: Mam's told me not to worry about anything. She's staying until I feel better.

2.30pm: I began to hallucinate: Dressed all in black, with a tall pointed hat, Mam cackled while she bent double over her cauldron.

2.33pm: I can see a black cat sitting at the foot of my bed.

2.35pm: A broom carrying two buckets of water has entered my bedroom, and poured the water into the cauldron.

2.40pm: I can hear the sound of a man walking up the street singing, Zip-A-Dee-Doo-Dah.

2.45pm: Mam says I am in her power, and she's trying to rip a pair of ruby red slippers off my feet...

4.00pm: Mam asked me if I enjoyed my little nap. She said I must have been dreaming, because at one point I shouted out: *'Don't you dare go near that Tar Baby Brer Rabbit!'* Mam also said: "There's no place like home, when anyone is ill."

5.00pm: Mam made the family tea – Me: another bowl of soup, and a hot lemon drink.

6.00pm: I received my third bowl of steam vapour of the day.

6.30pm: While Mam was in the toilet; I begged Trevor to send her home. (I had tears in my eyes.)

7.00pm: Mam's gone home. Trevor sent her packing with

the lie: "Mair, if you don't go home and rest. What good will you be to Rhian in the morning?... I can take over from here."

7.05pm: Made Trevor set the alarm for seven-thirty in the morning. Whatever happens, he's to phone my mother first thing, and tell her I'm feeling a lot better today, and there's no need for her to call.

October 4: Thursday

Mam beat the alarm clock by half an hour. She called early to make sure Gary and Megan were up and ready for work, and Anthony had everything he needed for school. Thankfully she didn't trouble me until after nine, but I soon became the victim of her goose grease rubs, and steam bowls again.

I do not have the strength to fight back. My mother is slowly killing me. Okay, she's killing me with kindness, but she's still killing me all the same. Trevor on the other hand is living the life of Riley downstairs. I can imagine him now; sprawled out on the sofa watching TV... Make the most of it Trevor, because the sofa belongs to me, the moment I feel strong enough to leave this room.

Anne called round this afternoon, to see if anything was wrong. (I missed evening class last night.) Anne said the class felt flat without me. She also said, (Whispered when Mam had left the room.) Doug had asked after me???

Mam is getting on my nerves... I can't help it... I know she means well... No, Mam... No, I don't want another hot lemon drink... No, I don't want another steam bowl. (I must be getting better... I'm finding the strength to argue back.) I caught sight of myself in the mirror this afternoon... I look like death warmed up. My face resembles a wrinkled prune. (Must be all that steam.)

October 5: Friday

I was determined to get out of bed today, but I used up all my energy fighting my mother, who was equally determined that I stay put until after the weekend.

"What do you want to get out of bed for?" Mam argued "I'm here to see to everything, aren't I. The sight of hard work is no stranger to me, you know Rhian. I may be seventy-three next birthday,but you won't find me flinching in a family crisis."

Trevor did the family shop on his own today. I dictated a shopping list to Mam, who in turn handed it to Trevor, accompanied with a warning about selecting dented tins, before sending him on his way: "Really speaking, I should be the one who does the family shop." Mam said, plumping up my pillows. "A pound to a penny, Trevor comes home with all the wrong things. But I haven't got the strength in my arms I used to have, you see Rhian." (You could have fooled me!) I can only manage my own shopping... The little bit I buy... I haven't the appetite I used to have... But your shopping would be far too much for me to carry on my own... If only Trevor would come with me!" (I can never see that happening.)

I have a simple plan... I fall asleep for as long as it takes. I wake up, and my flu has gone... Why won't my mother allow me to find out if this method works?... No matter how provocative my mother becomes, I'm determined not to fight with her anymore. I must learn to conserve my strength at all costs. I don't care what she makes me take or do. I am her rag doll... My mother can play house if she likes... Tomorrow I'm determined to reclaim the sofa.

October 6: Saturday

"What are you doing down here, you silly girl?... Can't I turn my back for a moment, without you undoing all my good work?... Rhian, you really are a stupid girl you know. Everybody in the house will catch it from you now. You see if they don't." Removing her coat, and tying the strings of her piny around her waist, Mam hovered over me with her hands on her hips. "Trevor should have stopped you coming down the stairs. You wait until I see him. If you can't think for yourself, Rhian, you must think of other people."

"Mam, I am thinking of you." I lied. "If I'm down here, then you won't have to keep running up and down the stairs after me all day."

"You are making work for me you mean." Mam said shaking her head. "It was important I kept you in quarantine. You know how fast these germs spread. Take 'Foot & Mouth' for instance. That spreads like wildfire, just like the flu. If you stay down here, then all the family are going to catch it,and Rhian, I'm to old to look after all of you."

But in the end all the protests and hand waving came to nothing. I listened to Mam's protestations. I even found myself agreeing with a lot of what she had to say. Yes, my mother is right and if it had been anyone other than myself who was ill, then that person would indeed be in their bed. But the fact of the matter is: it was me, and I am ensconced on the sofa, and that is all there is to it.

Megan stayed at home today. She didn't say much, and spent most of her time in her bedroom. I hope she won't be the next to come down with something.

October 7: Sunday

Mam was in the kitchen cooking our Sunday dinner. Jodie called into see how I was feeling. She remarked: "Bloody hell Rhian, you look rough... You look like a ghost Rhian. Your skin looks all dry. Your face is a mass of lines and wrinkles, you look a washout... How old have you got to be before the flu becomes life threatening?"

I thanked Jodie for her kind concern, and assured her there wasn't a germ in the world who would dare threaten my life. Not while I had my mother standing at my side.

Then she recommended: "You know what you need, don't you Rhian. To put your face right I mean... Sperm!"

"You what?"

"Sperm!... You know spunk... Semen... The jizz you milk from Trevor's willy... For your face... Really works wonders it does... It'll sort out all of those lines and wrinkles for you in no time, no danger... It's the male hormone in it you see... It works wonders on the female skin... Better than all these expensive creams and soaps in the shops... Why use the bull, bear, or musk ox stuff they sell in expensive jars, when you can exploit the real thing for free?... Look at my face. You can't find a line or a wrinkle on it anywhere, can you?"

"But you're only seventeen." I protested. "Your skin is in peak condition. It's the best it's going to look in your life."

"Yes, because of Darren's spunk." Jodie bust out laughing.

"What's going on in there?" Mam shouted from the kitchen. "Jodie, you must try and keep Rhian from getting excited."

Frantically motioning at Jodie to keep it down, Jodie composed herself and went into detail: "Every two weeks or so I get Darren to pump some of his stuff into a little plastic container. Rhian I'll tell you the best ones to get, if like me you haven't got any Tupperware. Have you seen those little self-seal cartons they put coleslaw into, in Tesco's?" Embarrassingly, I nodded. "Well wash and save some of them, so after Trevor's done it for you..." Jodie giggled. "I like to milk my Darren myself..." She grabbed hold of my hand. "I know I shouldn't be telling you any of this, but we are friends, aren't we Rhian?" I nodded. All through this conversation I wore a permanent smile, set by my disbelief. "I use a cotton wool ball to dab it on my face. I do it before I go to sleep, then I wash it off in the morning... Rhian, I think it's all right to store the plastic container in the fridge for a couple of days... Would you like to try some before you ask Trevor to help you out?... I think I've got a little bit of Darren's left, if you'd like me to pop next-door and get it for you?"

Back in the real world. Megan said she didn't want any dinner. Mam looked at me and said: "She'll be the next one to go down with it, you mark my words." Then added disparagingly: "Rhian, you really should have stayed in your bed you know!"

On the war front: The U.S.A, and the U.K launched their first missile strikes against the Taliban... BBC's Antiques Roadshow was cancelled for the news bulletin.

October 8: Monday

THE ATTACK OF AFGHANISTAN DAY 2: America bombed for a second night, and the Taliban released captured British newspaper journalist Yvonne Ridley... Mam said: "What that woman was doing there in the first place is beyond me."

I'm feeling a lot better within myself today, thank God. But Mam wouldn't hear of staying away: "You should know me by now Rhian. When I start a job, I like to see it through to the bitter end." She said, shooing my protest aside. "Rhian, you could have a relapse... You could develop an infection... You could have anything. Rhian, there's many a slip between cup and lip, I don't want to be sitting comfortably in my armchair at home, only to hear news of your decline during another emergency telephone conversation with your Trevor... After all, your Trevor was the one who insisted on my assistance in the first place. (Thank you for reminding me Mam. I haven't thanked Trevor for that kindness, YET!)

Yesterday, and again tonight. I noticed Gary has got on very friendly terms with the Johnson's. After he came home from being assessed he spent all evening helping Darren work on his sculptures in the back garden. (Darren's rigged-up some lighting so he can work in the dark.)

"Darren learnt to weld at the assessment centre." Gary explained excitedly. "He said he started off like me on painting and decorating, then they moved him on to bricklaying, from there he went on to plumbing, electric's, welding, mechanics, even a bit of gardening. Darren said he didn't find, or was offered a job at the end of the course, but thanks to the knowledge he gained at the assessment centre, he hasn't got to pay anyone, or wait for the council to do all the niggling little jobs that needed doing about his house, because he can do them himself."

"If Darren loves welding so much, why doesn't he try to find himself a welding job?" I asked, hoping to shed some light on the future job prospects of next-door.

"Darren's not all that bothered at the moment Mam." Gary replied. He says at the moment he's doing very well on the dole. And what with the baby, and all. He said he's going to wait until everything settles down, before finally deciding what to do with his life."

There was something in the way Gary spoke that worried me. That devil may care attitude was there. Trevor had it... Trevor's still got it. Darren has it, and now Gary. It's a trap... How can I explain this??? When you've got nothing, the dole gives you something. Darren and Jodie have nothing, but the dole gave them a rent and rate free house to live in. The dole gives them money to spend each week. The dole has helped them more than any minimum wage would have done.

I used to agree with my mother. Trevor was out of work because he is a lazy bugger, but I was/am/ still in love with him, so what could I do?... But I and my mother were wrong. I can see, and understand it now. There is hope for people on the dole. For those who can recognise it, take advantage of it, embrace it with open arms. There is more hope for anyone on the dole, than there is for someone slaving away day after day for the minimum wage.

Darren's got dreams... Darren sculpts. The dole has given him time and opportunity to do both. You could say, the dole is subsidising a penniless artist until he gets discovered.

Trevor used to dream. Trevor had many ideas. Trevor tried to build his own business, (Admittedly on a shoe string. More about this at a later date.) but he's too old now, and anyway he's got his benefit book to support him for the rest of his life... Trevor's more or less taken early retirement."

And then there's our Gary. It's still not to late for him to find a job. With a bit of luck something will turn-up for him after he's completed his course. (God, I pray it will.) But if it doesn't, then I also pray Gary's got plenty of money making ideas, or at least like Darren develops enough skills to become a Jack of all trades (A cowboy builder) to work hobbles for the people who can't afford not to take advantage of the black market economy, or the wealthy who refuse to pay the going rate for skilled labour... God, I'm feeling weak after writing this. I think I'll go back to bed.

October 9: Tuesday

Trevor went to collect our benefits from the Post Office. Because I'm the one who usually collects our money, Mr Baker the Post Master was funny with Trevor, and asked him to show him some form of personal ID to prove who he was. (I said nothing to Trevor, but I know for a fact Mr Baker disapproves of husbands collecting their families benefit money. Mr Baker does everything in his power to try and prevent the man of the house from taking the money and pissing it against the wall.) Trevor was not a happy bunny, when he returned home. Muttering a stream of obscenities under his breath, Trevor searched a draw for a letter from the DSS with his name on it. "I wouldn't say so much... He's trying to take the piss, that's what all this is all about... Didn't know who I was my arse... We wasn't in the same class as each other, but I used to go to school with the bastard!"... We still haven't heard anything from the DSS about our rebate... I'll chase them up when I'm feeling better.

Megan's not looking at all well. She's off her food, but she's still going to work: "I'll buy myself a sandwich in town Mam." Insisting. "Please will everyone leave me alone, I want to be on my own."

"Rhian, you must make her listen to me." Mam said, marching into the living-room. "How is she going to feel any better if she refuses to drink the hot lemon drink, or bend her head over this bowl of vapour fumes I've prepared for her?"

"Mam, will you tell Gran that I'm not rubbing any of that disgusting gunk over my chest!"

October 10: Wednesday

'FLU'
by
Rhian Evans

A weight on every eyelash.
A mind that's fuddled and taut.
Too bright, is the sunlight.
Too frightening, is the dark.
I sleep and dream,
Relive shadows of my past.
Faces in the wallpaper.
My father's, captured within a rose bud's stem.
What strange feeling this?
Make me well.
Make me well mother dear.
Hold my hand until the end.

Tonight I missed another evening class, so I thought I'd better keep my hand in. I'm determined to attend next week's class if it kills me. In fact I'm determined to be fully recovered by the weekend.

Nothing much happened today. I watched 'Richard & Judy',

this morning. Of course when I say I watched 'Richard & Judy', I realise they are no longer part of the show, (They've gone to C4.) but old habits die hard, and no matter who the presenters are, the show will always be called 'Richard & Judy' to me. I suppose it's a bit like calling my vacuum cleaner a 'Hoover', when it's a 'Goblin'. (By the way, I think the shows gone downhill, since they left.)

October 11: Thursday

Anne called in to see how I was feeling. She said that Doug sends his kind regards. (Does this man fancy me or what?... I hope not... I don't think my nerves could stand it... Furthermore I'd like to say it's one thing for me to fantasise about men, and quite another for men to fantasise about me... Quite disturbing if you want to know the truth.)

Anne liked my poem. She said I hadn't lost my magic touch. I told Anne about Jodie's home-made recipe for face cream; to my surprise Anne didn't laugh and took the matter most seriously: "Do you know Rhian, I've often wondered about that." Anne pondered for a moment then smiled: "You know... After Dave and I have finished the business... Well, I suppose some little droplets of you know what... His stuff lands on me, and in the morning I wake to find little patches of very soft skin all over my body... Of course this could all be in my imagination, but it can't hurt to experiment can it?... And anyway, who's to say what they put into the cosmetics in the shops?... I'm rapidly coming to the conclusion that all members of the younger generation are stark raving mad. Somehow, I can't see Trevor being very happy if I asked him to fill a little plastic beaker for me... My mother would be horrified!

I think Megan's face looks more sad than ill. I don't believe

Megan is coming down with the flu at all. A broken heart would be nearer the truth. Megan claims she is over Julian, but I say her demeanour speaks louder than words... The poor dab.

October 12: Friday

'Best' were the first of the women's magazines to reject my work. My heart lifted a little, then sank as I saw the postman's hand push my stamped addressed envelope through my letterbox.

Dear Mrs Evans. Thank you for... Blah-blah-blah-blah-blah... Don't call us, we'll call you... Blah- blah-blah-blah-blah... Love the Editor.

One down, seven to go. On the bright side, at least I've got something to show my classmates at evening class.

Trevor did another family shop. Last weeks wasn't too bad as it happens. This morning I went over the list with him in minute detail. As he walked out the door, I shouted: "If in doubt, choose the cheapest brand."

Mam sniffed at this advise, and said: "Rhian, no wonder all your family look ill."

I received some good news from my mother this afternoon: "Rhian, after Sunday, I think you'll be fit enough to be left on your own... I don't mind staying until then, but I'm way behind on my house work as it is. And I've heard they're all missing me down at the old age club. Of course you can phone for me if you need me to do anything, but you'll be all right on your own won't you? Of course you will."

Megan looks very pale and withdrawn. She won't eat... You just wait until I get her on my own.

October 13: Saturday

For the first time in two weeks I am fully dressed. I've had a bath, but Mam has prohibited me from washing my hair: "You're not well enough, to get your head wet... Rhian, do you want to catch pneumonia, and then your death?"

I read rejection letters, two and three (Woman & Woman's Own) at the breakfast table, and a letter from the council informing us they are coming to fit our house from top to bottom with double glazing, early in the new year: "Typical bloody council." Trevor remarked, after reading the letter. "Always doing everything arse backwards. Double glazing is a summer, not a winter job. Come next January, we'll be all sitting in this house freezing our tits off while they put it in."

Jodie called round this afternoon. She showed my mother and me a scanned photograph of her unborn baby. Mam couldn't make head or tail of the photo. She said: "They didn't have things like this, when I was having Rhian. You just gave birth, and that was that."

While I was cooing over the photo, Mam inquired: "What does your Mother think about you having a baby?"

Before I could abort this line of questioning; Jodie shrugged her shoulders and replied: "I don't know. We're not speaking to each other. In fact, I'm not speaking to any of my family at the moment."

"Why's that then?" Mam probed, ever deeper. "Surely, this is a time when a girl of your age and in your condition, needs her mother the most."

"Mam, this is none of our business." I panicked. "Perhaps Jodie doesn't want to talk about it?" I said, offering my neighbour a way out.

"Oh I don't mind telling you my tale." Jodie announced,

displaying all aspects of her life as usual upon her sleeve. “You can’t keep secrets on this estate... Rhian, I’m surprised your mother hasn’t heard anything about it before, because the tom-tom drums have done the rounds on more than one occasion... Besides it’s common knowledge on the eastern side.”

“Rhian, before Jodie begins, why don’t you make us all a nice pot of tea.” In the kitchen I banged the cups and saucers down in frustration on a tray. “Rhian, don’t forget to bring in the biscuits with you.” Jodie yelled... I think it’s going to be a long day.

“Well it all started during my and Darren’s third separation.” Jodie began stirring, then placing her teaspoon in the saucer.” I’ve already told Rhian, my Darren’s left me for three different women over the years I’ve been with him, but what I didn’t tell her was: on the three times he left me, I had no option but to return to my mother’s house because I had nowhere else to live.”

“If only the young would listen to their mother’s.” Mam mused during a pause in which Jodie took a sip of tea. “If you ask me love, I’d say you would have been better off staying with your mother in the first place, then maybe none of this would have happened... Rhian, what a pig! To desert this beautiful girl three times.... In how many years love?”

“My mother, and Darren’s parents are neighbours. So you see, there was nothing that was going on between me and Darren, that they both didn’t know about.” As Jodie spoke, I could hear Darren angle grinding something in his back garden. “My eldest sister, and her husband live with my mother.” Jodie continued. “Look, I know it was wrong... I can see that now... But I wanted to get back at him you see... Julie was getting on my nerves. Forever saying Darren was the scum of the earth, and her Chris would never dare to treat her like that: *'Fancy going back to him, after he's dumped you three times.'* She'd say, in that stuck-up tone of hers. "Jodie paused, I looked at Mam who was also looking at me. "Her voice Rhian." The palm of Jodie's hand angrily slapped down upon the arm of the chair. "You should have heard her. Full of airs and graces, on what? I don't know who she thinks she is - The Queen's mother?... Julie's got nothing, she lives with my mother, her husband is on the dole... Her children, right!... Don't make me laugh... Call herself a mother!... She's only living with my mother, because she's got a built-in baby sitter for free... Gerr, Julie makes me sooo angry, I could punch her face in when I think about her."

"Yes I can see how maybe you wouldn't get along." Mam's conjecture, interrupted Jodie's gnashing teeth.

"Well, I could only put up with her praising her gormless husband for so long, couldn't I?" Jodie smiled, "so I shagged him... Mind you I only shagged him to prove to Julie all men are the same: her Chris, my Darren and I'm sorry to point this out to you Rhian, but your Trevor too!... If I popped around for a cup of sugar while you were out, and I don't know peeled down my panties and gave your Trevor a seductive glimpse of my thatch. I don't care how solid Trevor's relationship is with you. I can guarantee he will forget all about that, for the thirty seconds or so it takes him to come in my box." (I caught my mother sympathetically nodding her head during this statement.)

"There's a lot of truth in that!" I stared at Mam. Mam's cup and saucer were rattling in her hand. Composing herself, Mam enquired: "And your sister found out about your affair, did she love?"

"No, of course she didn't." Jodie laughed. "She didn't find out about it, because she didn't have time to find out about it... Less than an hour after the deed was done I told her to her face, when she returned home from taking her little ones to the park... Chris denied anything took place of course. Julie called me an evil little slut, who wanted her marriage to break up. Mam believed Julie. Chris said he never thought I'd sink so low. Then, when no one was looking, laughed in my face... Julie wouldn't allow me to talk to her kids... Mam said she was sorry, but she thought it best if I go... But never mind about all that. I've got you now, haven't I Rhian?"

My heart sank, as Mam agreed: "Yes you have love, haven't you."

October 14: Sunday

True to her word, Mam came, cooked the dinner, dusted, ran the Goblin over the carpet and passed me fit and able to carry on without her help: "I'm going to treat myself tomorrow." Mam said before she left. "I'm going to have a long lay-in, and sit around doing nothing all day."

On a more serious note, Megan has gone from bad to worse. She refuses to eat any food, and apart from going to work, she's very reluctant to leave her bedroom. She's beginning to lose weight at an alarming rate. Her face looks long, drawn, and lined with worry. The poor girl looks as if she's carrying the weight of the world on her shoulders. She refuses to talk to either Trevor or me... What can I do, if she wont talk to me?... Jodie's right... Bloody men!

October 15: Monday

I felt strong enough to tackle the DSS about Trevor's rebate this morning... The bastards aren't giving us anything. Of course they said we could appeal if we didn't agree with their decision, but after a lot of thought we've decided to let the matter drop... Trevor said: "Rhian, I don't want the SS investigating our case anymore than they have too. You never know what they might come up with... They might uncover something to our disadvantage, and take my book off me."

6.30am: I heard Megan moving around in her bedroom. I heard her go to the bathroom, and then I heard her go downstairs.

6.45am: I sneaked halfway down the stairs, dipped my head over the banister, and saw Megan sneaking some food from the fridge. 'Good.' I thought. 'At least she is having something to eat.'

7.00am: I heard Megan being sick in the toilet.

7.01am: I'm worried.

7.30am: I'm very worried. I heard Megan leaving for work.

8.00am: I don't want to get out of bed... I don't want to face this... I want to go to sleep... When I wake-up, I want everything to be all right... Julian Jackson, you bastard. If you've done this to my girl... If he's made her ill... I'll, I'll... Fucking Jackson's!

12.00pm: I haven't stirred from this sofa for hours. The telly's been on non-stop, but I haven't been able to concentrate on a thing. (Not even Robin's Nest & Man About The House.) Why aren't my Prozac working?

6.00pm: Megan came home from work. I took one look at her little face and burst into tears.

6.15pm: Megan's in her bedroom crying. Trevor wants to know if the world's gone mad.

7.00pm: Megan won't speak to me. She's in her room, and I'm in mine... Trevor doesn't know what to do or say for the best?

10.00pm: Trevor said he can't be expected to help, if he doesn't know what's wrong. I said it was about time he opened his eyes, and saw what was happening inside his own home.

11.00pm: Trevor and I are no longer speaking... A perfect end to another perfect day.

October 16: Tuesday

I couldn't sleep last night. Early this morning I heard Megan repeat the same routine, as the previous morning... This does not bode well for the future.

I am desperate. I'm out of my head with worry. I spoke to Jodie about eating disorders: "When my Darr left me for the first time, my heart was in bits. I couldn't eat, I couldn't drink, if I stood up, I'd only fall down. I lost three stone the first time. Two and a half stone the second time, and what with my sister and everything, nearly four stone the third time."

"But what if Darren hadn't come back to you?" I asked, already knowing and dreading her reply.

"Oh, I'd be dead of course." Jodie replied in that cheery way of hers. "The first time, I frightened my mother half to death. I heard her speaking with the doctor, and they were talking about filling me with tubes and everything. On the second time Mam had got used to it, and told me to pull myself together. Her and my bitch of a sister kept asking me was it worth it. Was it worth killing myself for a man who didn't give a toss.

On the third time I heard my mother say: *'If the silly little bitch wants to kill herself, then that's her look out. She's old enough to look after herself, she keeps telling me to stay out of her life. This has got nothing to do with me.'*

I told Jodie, I'd seen Megan take food from the fridge, then moments later hear her being sick in the bathroom.

"They call that binge eating." Jodie explained. "That's when somebody eats as much food as they can possibly cram inside their mouth, feel instant guilt, then make themselves violently sick in the bathroom."

"And why would anyone want to do that?" I asked, again knowing and dreading my neighbour's response."

"Boyfriend/husband, blowing them out. Because they think they're fat. Feeling guilty because they've broken their diet. Low self-esteem. Because they can't find a boyfriend, because they can't keep a boyfriend, because it's trendy, because they've read about it in a magazine, because a friends told them it's a good way to lose weight, because they want to... Who knows?"... I asked Jodie to pop in to have a word with Megan while I'm at my evening class tomorrow evening.

October 17: Wednesday

"You look well... How have you been keeping this past couple of weeks?... I hear you've not been feeling too good?"

Doug slimed his way over to my desk. His polar neck and chunky signet ring, reminded me of 'Department S' and 'Jason King'.

"Look, I've got you a coffee from the machine, I remembered you refused to take a drink from my flask the last time we met."

The first time Doug entered the classroom I thought to

myself; here's something interesting. At one point I even let my imagination run away with itself, and fantasised about us both making love in some way out exotic places. I felt this way because I am a bored housewife, and if there's anything worse than being a bored housewife, it's when a man identifies you as such and looks upon you as easy meat.

"I heard some things about you while you were away." Doug bent forward and whispered in my ear.

"All good, I hope." I flirted back.

"I hope so?" Doug winked. "Why don't you came out with me for a drink one evening, then you can tell me if the things people are saying about you, are true or not?"

"Doug." I said, beckoning him to bend his head ever closer, so I could seductively whisper my reply into his ear. "Proposition me again you bastard, and I'll cut your fucking balls off and ram them down your fucking throat."

To tell you the truth, Doug had picked the wrong time and place to launch his charm offensive on me. What with one thing and another... Megan... Trevor's blindness around the home... I was in one of the zones where I could see, and read men for what they really are... Full scale bastards of the first order, who would jeopardise their own, and anyone else's relationship for a quick shag.

"You are off your fucking head, you silly cow?" Doug screamed, lurching away from my desk. "Why would a guy like me, ever want to go out with an old slag like you?"

"You fucking tosser." Dave Huws yelled, coming to my defence. "Who the fucking hell do you think you are, speaking to Rhian like that... You make me fucking sick... Coming here driving a flash car... Looking for a bit of rough are you

Doug?... Looking to shag a bored housewife are you,you fucking wanker."

During this verbal onslaught, Dave had manoeuvred Doug to the corner of the room. "Look, there's been a simple misunderstanding, that's all." Doug proclaimed, little beads of sweat running down his forehead. "The lady misunderstood what I meant, that's all. It's an easy mistake anyone could have made."

Jabbing his finger into Doug's chest, Dave made his point as clear as daylight: "The only mistake made here tonight, was made by you Doug." Dave growled. "Now I expect you to pickup your things and leave, and I don't expect you to come back."

Doug made his excuses to Mr Davis, who had just entered the classroom, and left. Mr Davis said: "I don't know what happened here tonight, and if it's all the same to everyone here, I don't want to know either." Then Mr Davis focused his attention on me. "I can cut the atmosphere in here with a knife... Ha Rhian, nice to have you back with us again."

"I hope you didn't think I called you a bored housewife, and a bit of rough." Dave apologised during the break. "Blokes like Doug get right up my nose... While you were away... You did know he was after my Anne, didn't you?

"Isn't my Dave brave?" Anne giggled. "He's a big softy really. But when he gets going, he's a real tour de force, aren't you munchkin."

"I saw the way he was talking to you... I saw you took offence at what he was saying... If he had laid just one finger on you, I would have taken him out."

After that, the evening fell pretty flat. I presented my three rejection slips, and so did others in the class.

When I got home, Jodie was still speaking to Megan in

her room. At ten thirty, Jodie came down the stairs, and silently mouthed at me: "It's all right, I'll tell you about it in the morning."

11.30pm: Trevor came to bed. We're still not talking. While he got undressed I pretended to be asleep. I think I'll make it up with him in the morning.

October 18: Thursday

What a waste of time that was. Looking back I suppose I only have myself to blame, sending a young girl on a woman's mission: "Rhian, there's absolutely nothing to worry about." Jodie reassured me. "I had a little talk with Megan last night, and she said she's feeling a little bit run down, that's all. She said, that business with Julian hit her harder than she expected and although Megan tries to put on a brave face, sometimes it all gets too much for her... What a pig Rhian. Fancy driving your family all the way to Cornwall and back again in a stolen car... Then he gets your Megan the sack, for shoplifting..."

"What about the throwing-up?" I said, halting Jodie's assessment of the situation. "You did ask her about her being sick in the morning didn't you?"

"It's got something to do with the girls from work. Megan was in the toilets, when she overheard a couple of the girls disguising her weight... I wouldn't worry about it Rhian. And like Megan said, she doesn't feel like eating anything at the moment anyway... The taste of food in her mouth, just makes her want to heave."

I'm totally disappointed with the outcome of Jodie's investigation. I've never heard such a big load of old codswallop in all my life. Talk about a cock and bull story... No wonder Darren took advantage of Jodie, if she believes this tale… I don't know, young girls of today!… So naive… And the Government find it surprising, that there are so many teenage pregnancies… FUCKING HELL!

October 19: Friday

I've been awake all night… Please God let my intuition be wrong.

I heard Megan throwing-up again early this morning. I'd feel a lot happier if I heard her being sick in the afternoon… Bloody woman's intuition. I can't be right, can I?… I need stronger Prozac to help me cope with this… Trevor's going to go off his head, when he finds out… Mam, oh what am I going to tell my mother?… Oh fucking hell, fuck, fuck, fucking hell, this will all be my fault for letting Julian stay here… It is Julian's isn't it?

I'm at the end of my tether. My thoughts have changed since this morning. My mind has now informed/tortured me; to help her get over Julian, Megan has been sleeping around on the rebound… I defiantly need a stronger Prozac. These ones are not working. If they were, my mind should not be thinking such dark thoughts as these.

Megan came home from work. She looks very thin, withdrawn and really rundown. I can't see any sign of a bump. I could be wrong, but why don't I think I'm not?

October 20: Saturday

Megan spent the day at home today. I found it very difficult to sit still, what with us being the only people remaining inside the house, and this being the perfect moment for a private chat. My whole body was full-up of pent-up energy. Like a coiled spring, I /my intuition wanted to burst through her bedroom door, and confront her with its theory. *'Rhian, you must give the girl time to come to you with it herself.'* I kept reminding myself over and over in my head. *'Rhian if you go charging in there like a bull in a china shop, she's only going to go into denial and then where will you be?'*

Remaining seated in my chair, while imagining what terrible thoughts a lonely and desperate Megan had plaguing her mind, is one of the hardest things I've ever had to do in my life... I must give Megan more time to bring her problem to me... I must... I must... I must.

October 21: Sunday

Megan is eight week's pregnant.

October 22: Monday Mam's Birthday

We were all sitting around the table eating Sunday dinner yesterday afternoon. Mam was reminding Megan she must eat her greens, or she'll make herself ill. Gary said if she didn't want her meat, he'd have it. I told Gary to leave Megan's meat alone: "I'm going to have a baby." Just like that, no warning, nothing: "I'm going to have a baby." She repeated, to the silent table: "I'm going to have a baby." She screamed, running to her bedroom: "Well Rhian, what do you think about that then?" Mam asked, as the bedroom door slammed shut. "Of course I could see this happening all along. Those Jackson's are a bad lot. Joy riding indeed, I'll give the little swine joy riding when I see him. Our Megan was as good as gold, until she took up with that Jackson boy."

Trevor took the news better than I thought he would. I'm not sure if he was trying to be funny sarcastic, or both; when he remarked: *'She's got to be like everyone else on this estate, hasn't she. She sees all her schoolmates with children of their own, and know she wants to have a baby too... At least our Megan's wont be black!'*

I on the other hand, kept my mouth shut. I didn't let anyone know of my suspicions. I certainly didn't let anyone in on my notion, of the baby not being Julian's child.

The Post-Mortem. (Or why it was all my fault.)

Mam:	"Rhian, what did you expect... You allowed Julian to stay under the same roof."
Trevor:	"Rhian you made me change my mind. You know I never wanted her to have anything to do with that Jackson boy."
Mam:	"Rhian, you never put your foot down. You never set ground rules. You never told them what they could or couldn't do, under your roof.
Trevor:	"I told you I didn't want her going out with him didn't I?"
Mam:	"Well, it's too late now... The stable door is open and the horse has bolted... Rhian, what are you going to do about it, that's what I'd like to know?"
Trevor:	"Nobody bloody listens to me... Rhian are you happy now?"

That happened yesterday, and that's why I've drawn a line underneath it. I woke up this morning worried to death. I wanted to say so much to Megan before she left for work, but in the end I opted out of an exchange of words I knew would end in a heated argument. In order to keep the peace for as long as possible, I remained in bed listening to the sound of my daughter prowling around her room, before making her way down stairs, and exiting through the front door.

"Happy Birthday Mam." I uttered these wishes, because it was expected of me. Mam accepted them,and a peck on her cheek, but deep down neither one of us were in any mood for celebrating: "I'm seventy-three, Rhian. I wasn't made for and shouldn't be living in this world of free sex, and single girls having children by different fathers... It's not right Rhian. It's not right, and it doesn't look good for the family, does it?"

I agreed by nodding my head.

"I mean to say, it's bad enough when the neighbours are doing it. But our Megan! What happens if Julian doesn't marry her?... No decent man will want a young girl with a child... And what about the future. How many children, will she have?... How many fathers, will she have them by?... I hope I'm not alive to see it, Rhian, that's all I have to say."

On the sideboard lay Mam's unopened birthday cards and present. (I bought her a pink cardigan from the charity shop.) "I'll take these home with me, and keep them to open at a happier time." She said, putting them in her bag. "Rhian, about my birthday tea... Let's give it a miss this year shall we. I'm not in the mood."

October 23: Tuesday

Dear Diary, little did I know; while I was dreaming of being reborn on my Cornish beach, new life was indeed being conceived behind the second sand dune to the left of our caravan.

"Of course it's Fucking Julian's!" Megan screamed. "What type of girl do you take me for?" Tearing my suspicions to threads, Megan became verbally ferocious in her attack. "You think I did it on purpose, don't you?... Oh my God, my own mother thinks I shagged Julian, in order to trap him... Just because you did it, doesn't mean to say I'm the same as you... Fuck Julian... Fuck Julian to Hell... I couldn't give two fucks for the fucking wanker... Do you think I want a cunt like him around my child while it's growing up?... Well do you Mam?... Unlike you I don't need anybody. I'm stronger than you Mam... My child and I will be fine... I don't want Julian to know, and I don't want you or Gran telling him anything about it."

Between the bouts of violent aggression, name calling, and running around the house, opening then slamming doors; this is what I could make out:

1. The child is definitely Julian's.
2. The baby was conceived on a Bank Holiday Monday in Cornwall.
3. Julian and Megan only bonked the once. (She was a virgin... Unlucky!)
4. An abortion is out of the question.
5. Megan is determined to bring the baby up on her own. (This may change in time.)
6. Julian knows nothing about it, and she wants to keep him in the dark. (If she manages to keep this a secret, Megan will be cleverer than all the other single mothers on the estate.)
7. Megan's going to put her name down for a council flat of her own.
8. She doesn't care what anyone says. She's old enough to do what she likes.

Trevor's reaction: (Minus foul language, and violent actions - A lot of gesturing, but no violent contact took place.)

1. "You're not too old, to have a clip around the earhole."
2. "In my house you do what you're told."
3. "No slip of a girl is going to dictate to me."
4. "One more word out of you and you can pack your bags and go."
5. "If you are so clever, why are you pregnant?"
6. "Look after a baby, you can't even look after yourself."
7. "Change a baby's nappy... You! One - You won't be able to afford nappies. Two - You don't even know how to wipe your own arse properly."

I could go on, but the dialogue isn't very pretty, Megan... I hate it when my children turn on me. Why did Megan throw my past in my face? I was only trying to help her, then she turned... Okay, I got married because I was pregnant, but Trevor and I were committed to each other by then, and anyway what's that got to do with this?... It's Trevor's fucking family again, isn't it. They've never forgiven him for marrying me: '*Soft bastard*', his brother Wyn cried, as they watched Trevor walk me out of the Registry Office, but that's neither here or there... Oh why oh why, do my children turn on me God?... Why can't they except my help in good faith?

Trevor visits his family at least once a week... So do the kids... I have no wish to see them, and they have no wish to see me... It's been this way all our married life... I have no desire for this arrangement to change.

October 24: Wednesday

I am P.M.T active, (Red for danger) I'm in the mood to kill. Megan took one look at my eyes, and thought it best to stay out of my way. (She's gone around to Jodie's tonight. Since Jodie's little talk,they have become good friends.) Doug must have taken Dave's hint, because he didn't attend tonight's class, and I don't expect to see him again. (Doug doesn't realise it, but in tonight's mood Dave's probably saved his life.)

"During the first part of the lesson I want everyone to write a poem off the top of their head. It doesn't have to be very long, then after the break I want everyone, to recite their verse to the class." Sitting on the edge of his desk, Mr Davis issued his instructions to his students.

THE TRUTH
by
Rhian Evans

It was hard for me.
To admit the truth.
You are young,
My dreams undone.
I'm no better,
Than you I mean.
If I could turn back time.
You know I can't.
The hurt is mine.
We share the shame.
Our minds in a spin,
Over, and over again.
In truth, I meant none of this.

You nod and agree.
I'll make the best of it.
For my child and me.

I broke down at the end of my verse. Through my tears, I could read the mind of the blurred and confused of Mr Davis, staring at me from his desk: *'I have some very sick individuals attending my class.'*

In order to defend my embarrassing actions, I ended up making matters worse, by blurting out: "My sixteen year old daughter is having a baby." Realising this was not a good move, I whimpered: "I'm sorry." Before snatching up my bag, and hurrying out of the room.

A few steps down the darkened corridor, I stopped and rested my forehead against the cool plaster wall. Inhaling deep breaths I tried to stifle my sobbing, but my tears never stopped. Resting ten yards from the classroom, I saw the glow of the light shining into the darkened corridor,and I heard the scuffling sounds of my bemused classmates shuffling nervously at their desks: "Well now." I heard Mr Davis say. "There's never a dull moment when Mrs Evans is around."

October 25: Thursday

I'm never going to attend evening class again. One - It's too stressful. Two - I always end up making a fool of myself. I wonder how long it will take before Mary finds out Megan is expecting her Grandchild?

Jodie called round to let me know, Megan had told her all about it. "It's a shame isn't it Rhian." Jodie sighed. "But what can anyone do? My mother tried to stop me, but I wouldn't listen. It's human nature you see, and hormones which when you come to think about it are all apart of the same thing."

I can't believe it God... How the world has changed... I can't believe I'm speaking to an eight month pregnant woman, a mere slip of a girl herself if the truth be told... She's very young. A year or so older than my Megan... And we're conversing together on equal terms... I never spoke to my elders like this when I was her age:

"Like I told Megan last night. There's nothing to be nervous about. I'll be having my baby first, so she will be able to have a go with it if she likes." I never used to discuss these sort of things with the neighbours... The Watson's would never have put up with it... Civilisation really has turned turned upside down on itself.

When Megan came home from work, I said: "Be careful what you say to Jodie in the future." I also added: "Keep your private business close to your chest. We don't want everyone to know everything that is going on in this family."

Mam phoned to say she felt up to opening her birthday cards and present. Then thanked me for the cardigan.

Four further rejection letters have arrived. Since the news of Megan's pregnancy, I don't feel the least bit excited receiving them anymore.

October 26: Friday

Anne called around and said if only she'd heard about our Megan sooner, she would have given Megan her unwanted baby clothes, instead of offering them all to Jodie.

"Come and have a look at this." I said to Anne, leading her

to the back door. "Darren calls it an 'Embryo In A Womb Of Thorns.'

"That's, that's, yes, that's exactly what it is." Anne replied nodding her head.

"Well, I have two of them now." I responded, to Anne's flummoxed expression. "One animated example living inside the house, and that static example standing in my back garden."

"It's the way of the world." Anne remarked, an hour or so later. "Sex, I mean. Well, it's everywhere today isn't it... Rhian, do you know what I find disturbing?" I shook my head. "Children's television,and those horrible nappy commercials on the telly... Do they have to broadcast bare baby bottoms, on our television screens every day Rhian? And I hate it when they make babies up to look like adults too!... Have you seen the age of the presenters on children's telly, these days?... Some of them look barely old enough to call on my three, and ask them if they want to go down the park for a game of football... It's all sex, fashion and make-up, aimed at children today, and it's only going to get worse."

Dear Diary, I'm too young to be a Grandmother... I don't want any babies living in this house... I don't want to bring up my daughter's children... Why should I have to go through this?... Why can't everyone think about me for a change?... Megan did it!... Megan got herself pregnant, why have I got to pick up the pieces?... I am a human being too, you know... I'm entitled to a life of my own... No, I'm not... I am a mother!... What choice do I have?

October 27: Saturday

It didn't take long... By mid afternoon, I was speaking to my mother on the telephone: "It's Julian." Mam spoke in a frantic whisper. "Rhian, he's found out about Megan's condition. Don't ask me how he knows; he phoned me to ask if it's true. He also wants to sort something out with Megan before his mother gets wind of it."

Only two days after I'd let the cat out of the bag. (God, is nothing sacred on this estate.)

"Rhian, what's Megan planning to do now?" Mam's whisper became more excited as she spoke. "Is she going to speak to him Rhian?... Is she going to tell him he's the father?... Does she have to tell him anything, Rhian?... What's she going to do when Julian's mother finds out? It was all so different in my day, life was so much simpler then... Rhian, will the social make Megan reveal who the baby's father is?... Will they make Julian pay for the baby's up keep, if he refuses to marry her?What will Mary say, Rhian?... Do you think she'll be happy when her first Grandchild arrives?

Repeating: "I don't know, Mam." After every question, I was very relieved when my mother said: "Oh well, I've got to go now, or I won't be able to pay my bill."

"How the hell did Julian find out?" Megan demanded to know. "Well, the little shit's got a long wait, if he thinks I'm going to speak to his ugly face again."

Megan's language!... Since the news of her pregnancy, her language has gone from bad to worse... Pregnancy has turned my little girl into a foul mouthed fish wife.

"I hope Gran told him to fuck off, when she realised it was him she was speaking to on the phone... He's too fucking shit to phone me on my mobile, and he'll never phone this house, just in case you or Daddy pickup the telephone receiver... The tosser!"

Later on in the evening, Megan came down from her room, and said she was calling on Jodie: "So he knows then does he... Good!... Give him something else to cry about in the dark... Remember him crying for his mother, when he was living here?... The twat, and I was the stupid bitch, who had to tell him everything was going to be all right..."

I'm going to have to stop Megan spending so much time with Jodie... If only to stop her swearing. The clocks go back an hour tonight... Just what I need, an hour extra in bed.

October 28: Sunday

After we'd all finished our dinner. Mam handed Megan a little cream matinee coat for the baby. "I couldn't help myself Rhian, what with the new baby being my first Great Grandchild and all." Mam gushed, spreading the tiny woollen garment across Megan's stomach.

"It's too early to buy anything yet Mam." I protested. "You don't want to bring bad luck down on us all... Don't you dare say there's no such thing as bad luck. You never know which God may be listening?"

"I think it's a bit late to worry about that, don't you?" Trevor laughed, forcing an old chair cushion up his T-shirt, he pretended to pat his pregnant stomach."

"I don't think it's unlucky to create life." Megan remarked, developing a wobble, as she moved herself from the table to the chair. "Inside of me could be the next Prime Minister, or the greatest rugby player ever to play for Wales."

"Can I have a rise on my benefit please?" Trevor playfully asked his developing Grandchild, the country's future Prime Minister. "Blinking typical." Trevor said, feigning rebuke, after rising his head from his daughter's stomach. "Megan your baby is definitely following your Nana's side of the family. No word of a lie, I've just heard it yell out: *'Get off your arse and get a bloody job, you lazy bugger.'*"

Dear Diary, today has been a very good day considering. We all laughed and joked with each other,for the first time in ages. For once we all behaved like a proper family. No one was blamed, no one took offence, tonight Matthew we were the 'Oxo Family' from the television advert. If this is a taste of the lifestyle the new baby will bring, then I'm all for Megan having it.

October 29: Monday

"It was terrible Mam. All the people were looking at us, on the bus stop." Megan returned home from work in one hell of a state. "Julian was shouting and screaming": *'You've done this to me on purpose you selfish bitch... Why wont you leave me alone?... Why can't you get on with your own life?'*

Clearly shaken after her ordeal, Megan stated: "I didn't deserve any of that Mam... I don't even want the little prick to have access or have anything to do with my baby." And then she got angry: "Who the fuck does he think he is, accosting me like that at the bus stop. Well, it's all out in the open now... The big mouth git... Will I keep it from his mother, my arse... The little shit... How the hell does he expect me to say nothing, when he's already let the cat out of the bag?"

Dear Diary, I will not stand for Julian hassling my daughter in public like this. Solicitor's letter, or no; if he continues with these tactics, I will personally march round to Mary's, and confront the bitch in her lair.

On a happier note, the Assessment Centre has moved Gary on to bricklaying. After only one day of mixing mortar, Gary announced: "Mam, I promise one day I'm going to build an house of my own."

Megan entered the living-room. Relaxed after a soothing soak in the tub, she continued her distressing account of the bus stop incident, in a gentler tone:

"I wouldn't give him the satisfaction... Is it mine? He demanded... No it's mine actually, I teased... Julian, is a spoilt child Mam... He couldn't handle the way I spoke to him. At one point I thought he was going to pull his hair out in sheer frustration, as he jumped up and down, stamping his feet on the pavement." Megan laughed. "He called me cruel. He called himself a fool for ever having anything to do with me. Why didn't I listen to my mother, he wailed?... He kept chanting the same unanswerable mantra over and over again... He was embarrassing Mam... He even had the cheek to call our family the scum of the earth."

"Have you confirmed that Julian's the father... Have you told him?..."

"I've already told you Mam." Megan replied, cutting me off in my tracks. "I don't want... We," she patted her stomach. "Don't want the Jackson's in our lives ever again."

October 30: Tuesday

Over the years... Well, the early part of our relationship; Trevor tried all sorts to bring a little extra money into the house. Window cleaning, (Bad luck and months of bad weather kept Trevor off his ladder.) gardening... Trevor had this old lawn-mower, the old type you had to push, with a grass collecting box on the front, and a roller at the back. Trevor would walk to the posh estates with his lawnmower, knocking on doors, he'd say: *'I'll mow your lawn like they do at Wimbledon. Front and back for three and a half quid.'*

Trevor's also tried poaching, (One for the pot, and ten for his mates down the pub.) bare knuckle fighting, (He quit after he lost his first fight. But he did get paid twenty-five quid for his two black eyes... I warned him this was a bad idea at the time.) his worst plan (Trevor went around calling himself an entrepreneur... Too much 'Only Fools & Horses'.) was badger baiting. I had to put my foot down when I heard about this scheme for the first time:

1: I don't believe in cruelty to animals... I believe people should only kill animals for food.
2: I didn't want a vicious Pit Bull frightening my mother away from the house. (Trevor thought this a bonus point.) We also had very small children toddling around at the time.

Trevor's other glorious failures included; rugby club bouncer, on disco nights... Dressed smartly in black suit and dickey bow, Trevor resigned after one night complaining: *'Rhian, it wasn't much fun fighting my mates at closing time.'*

Furniture removals... Another of Trevor's friends owned a clapped out old van. Everything was going well until the van died a death halfway to Swansea, after which Trevor returned to his window cleaning round again. But this time around Trevor's former clients accused him of being a fly by night operator who couldn't be trusted to call around once a month to clean their windows.

Dear Diary, as you see; Trevor has tried to create his own

work in the past. Admittedly, apart from the window cleaning, none of his schemes would have mounted to much, or would have paid him a living wage, but then again, they weren't supposed to. They were designed to bring in what we call top-up money. A top-up to help to pay for the little extras our benefits couldn't possibly provide. Christmas time for instance... To pay for something inside or outside of the household that needed to be repaired... Extra food... Yes, Trevor drinks and smokes. Yes, the money Trevor wastes on his hobbies would be better spent on improving the life of his family, but that's life isn't it? Are any of us perfect?... Dear Dairy, take a look out of my bedroom window... Look again, and tell me what you see? How many Saints can you spot living on this estate?

October 31: Wednesday - Halloween... I refuse to celebrate Halloween. I don't want anything to do with Halloween. I wouldn't give you tuppence for Halloween. Trevor hates answering the door to the next generation of trick or treat protection racketeers. Plus I have more than enough demons of my own – making themselves comfortable – squatting inside my head – thank you very much... Imported bloody American rubbish!

At 2.30pm, the telephone rang: "Hello Rhian, this is Mary Jackson speaking." My heart sank. "I'm sorry to disturb you, after all that's gone on between us. But I thought you'd like to know about a ridiculous rumour I've heard circulating this estate... Of course, I laughed, when I heard it." My silence on the other end of the line, caused Mary's voice to tremble... She hesitated: "Um, um, some people are saying your Megan is pregnant, and my Julian is the father of her unborn child."

"Yes, that's correct." I don't care what Megan wants. Keeping the name of the baby's father a secret is a stupid idea anyway... Besides, I wasn't about to lie to my old enemy... The truth will out in the end.

"Is it true?" Mary's voice quivered, as the truth sank in. "Oh my God, it is true isn't it?... That idiot son of mine... Look, what you've done."

The truth hurts. Listening to Mary breakdown on her end of the line, I could imagine no greater pain than that of her realising the person who'd held her dreams, could be so tragically flawed.

"I'll... We'll... She does intend having this child?... You stupid, stupid, boy."

"Of course she does." The line fell silent, and then the dialling tone buzzed in my ear.

I gave tonight's evening class a miss... I feel the class and I need some space... Anyway they'll only be talking about the war in Afghanistan... Only, it's not a real war, like the First and Second World War's is it?

When she got home, Megan was not best pleased: "Why did you tell her Mam?... Why did you tell her, when you knew I didn't want them to know?"

"Because it was the right thing to do. Because I didn't want Mary calling me a liar, after she finally found out the truth."

"What about what I want?... Or maybe you think I haven't got any rights?"

"We have to do what's best. How would you like it if the shoe were on the other foot?"

"Probably relieved!" Marching off to her room, I let Megan ponder this, and her future actions.

LIES
by
Rhian Evans

Lying never works.
The truth is a cert.
Hiding - Manipulating facts.
Acting out of sync.
Causing friends to blink.
They never thought it of me.
How wrong could they be?
Truth out in the end.
A fool to one's friends.

Trevor answers our front door and is wished a Happy Halloween by two small children wearing plastic Dracula masks: "It's all right mister. We've got change for a fiver."

REVIEW OF THE MONTH:

At least the cat's out of the bag. From today all the principal players know my daughter is pregnant,and I for one feel all the happier for it.

After Megan's revelation there's nothing else to say about this month, even this so called war on terrorism has come to nothing... God, my skin looks tired. My face is a mass of wrinkles especially around my eyes... "Trevor, would you like to take part in an interesting little experiment with me?"

November 1: Thursday

Idris called round this afternoon. (What is it with the Jackson family. Can't they do anything in the morning?) Apparently Mary found out about Megan's condition, through Mr Hurst of 'The Blooming Daisy', who in turn had overheard Julian discussing it with his new girlfriend in his shop. Idris seemed delighted with the news, but admitted that his wife needed more time to come to terms with Megan's condition.

"It's the boy, I'm worried about." Idris said shaking his head. "He's taken it all really badly. He claims your Megan wants nothing to do with him. He says, your Megan also doesn't want him to have anything to do with the baby."

"It's still early days for our Megan, you see Idris." I said, sticking up for our side. "To tell you the truth, I don't think she knows what she wants for herself at the moment."

"Don't forget, your Julian was the one who blew our Megan out, and got her the sack from a job she loved." Trevor interjected." So it can't be that much of a surprise, that she doesn't want anything to do with Julian, can it?"

On hearing this, I could see a discernible change etch across Idris's face: "I'm very concerned about my boy's state of mind. All this is too much for him you see. The baby, Mary... I've told Mary to leave him alone, but will she listen to me... I may as well talk to that wall."

"What are you trying to say?" Trevor snapped, ruffled by our guest's demeanour. "Out with it man. Are you trying to warn us about something or what?"

"What, warn... Me!... Oh no... Only it's the boy you see... Well, you know what he's like when the pressure builds-up... Look, can't you ask your Megan to speak with him... Put his mind at ease as it were... He's not a bad boy really... Only..."

"He's liable to do something silly if he doesn't get his way." Trevor interrupted, with the remainder of the sentence.

"I'm not saying he will, you understand... But he could... Wouldn't it be better, if we all sat down and tried to sort this mess out between ourselves."

"Idris, if your boy comes near my Megan, I'll sort him out all right." Trevor responded, to the down trodden soul who had already accepted his son's fate. "Look, we'll have a word with Megan." Continued a cooling Trevor. "If she's willing to speak to him then so be it... She'll be in touch."

Accepting, that this was as good as he was going to get, Idris rose from his seat: "Children, everything was so different when they were small. I'll tell Julian what you said, and I hope Megan will be in touch with him soon."

Closing the door behind Idris, I turned to Trevor: "You don't think Julian is capable of doing anything silly, do you?"

"Not if he likes living, love." Trevor snapped. "Not if he likes living love."

November 2: Friday

Anthony came home from school, and announced Ivor Smith from the newsagents, had offered him a paper-round, which he'd accepted, and starts on Monday.

Trevor:	If the silly little sod wants to get up early in this cold weather, that's his lookout.
Me:	That's the wrong attitude, Trevor. You should encourage the boy.
Trevor:	Encourage him to catch the flu more like. What does he want to deliver newspapers for anyway?
Me:	Why don't you ask him?

Anthony: (Sitting opposite his father) For Christmas... So I can buy you all a present.

Trevor: If you catch the flu, boy... I warn you... I'll be moving out, if your Nana moves in.

Anthony: Don't worry about me Dad. I'm only doing it for the Christmas... I'll be quitting, in the New Year, after I've collected my Christmas box.

Trevor: Did you hear that Rhian?... He's got his head screwed on has this one.

Megan said nothing about Idris's visit yesterday, and she's said nothing about it again today... Nobody is going to shift her opinion until she comes to it herself.

November 3: Saturday

The cheeky little sod!... Fancy calling at this house when he knew I'd be here alone... Carrying a massive bouquet of flowers... Flowers!... After all the trouble they've caused.

I opened my front door: "Hello Mrs Evans, I'd like to..."

"Fuck off Julian." Instantly regretting, what I said, I slammed the door in his face... I ask you, what else could I do? (My face went brick red.)

Behind my net curtains, I watched Julian's pathetic figure make his way down the garden path. Turning to stare at our windows, he rammed the bouquet between two metal railings of the garden gate, and trudged slowly away.

"I saw it all." Jodie squealed.

The bouquet retrieved, I handed it to her. "You wouldn't believe the trouble these things can cause... Well, what did you think of him?"

"Are you sure you don't want these?" Ecstatic with my gift,

Jodie posed with bouquet in front of her bump. "That was Julian, was it?... I thought it was. I saw him working with Megan once in that flower shop... I can't imagine him being Megan's type, let alone going out with her... He looks a bit strange to me Rhian. Hasn't he got a funny walk... I don't know, I can picture your Megan going out with a more beefier hunk... So he's the one who's knocked her up!... Looking at a weed like him, I'm surprised he could raise the spunk.... Rhian, I don't suppose you could lend me a vase for these flowers could you?"

Jodie stayed with me until my children came home from town. Megan became very agitated when she found out Julian had called: "The fucking wanker, who the fuck does he think he is?... Don't be silly Jodie. Of course I don't want his fucking flowers back!"

November 4: Sunday

"I spoke to Julian for nearly two hours last night." In the kitchen, I'd wondered why Megan had followed me out of the living- room. "I phoned him at home, and he phoned me back on my mobile phone." (Later on, Anthony worked it out; at 45p a minute, the call had cost Idris fifty-four quid.)

"Julian's really lost it Mam. He was going on about refusing to pay maintenance for a child he'd never see... He spoke about blood tests, and DNA... He threatened to file for custody, on the grounds of me being a bad mother... He told me he came to the door, and you told him to fuck off. He wants to know why you hate him?... He said, he only robbed that car because he could see how much you were looking forward to the holiday."

I must admit, after hearing this, I was ashamed of my actions.

"Julian said if he could turn back time he would. His new

girlfriend has left him over this, and quit her job. (Apparently the girl came from a good home, and her widowed father owned his own house and had a bit of money.) Julian sounded really desperate Mam. He even offered to put in a good word for me with Mr Hurst, to see if I could get my old job back.

He started crying Mam." Standing motionless at the sink, I watched the little droplets of water drip from my plate. "He sounded really pitiful Mam. He said, nobody could understand what he's been going through.

I felt sorry for him Mam. Julian said, he didn't intend to hurt me. He wants us to be a normal couple, living together in our council house... I told him no..."

Megan looked down at the floor.

"He called me a slag Mam. He called me a dirty little whore... He said all the women were mad in our family... You, Gran, me. He said no judge in his right mind would let me bring up a child in such a dangerous environment... He claims that you threatened to kill his mother, and in a fit of temper, you could injure my baby."

I saw red. If Julian had been in the room, I would have ripped him from limb to limb... Megan broke down.

"I told him you wouldn't hurt anyone Mam, but he wouldn't listen to me, and insisted you would." Sobbing, Megan looked up at me. "You wouldn't, would you Mam. You wouldn't hurt me, and my baby would you?"

I felt so emotional... I felt so angry. Tears welled-up, and dripped from the ends of my eyelashes... How dare he. How dare anyone say these things about me... Viper... Viper in my bosom... I took him in when he had nowhere else to go. I listened... I tried to help him. If he and Megan had stayed together, I would have been all for them... Judas. Scum!... Son of my natural enemy... If I live to be one hundred and fifty, I will personally see to it that the Jackson's have nothing to do with my family ever again.

November 5: Monday Guy Fawkes Night

Anthony left the house at 6.00am in the pitch dark, to start his paper-round: "Good luck to him." Trevor remarked, then turned over and went back to sleep.

Christmas - Catalogue - Code Numbers. I have a three hundred pound budget. (£100 a head) Trevor and I can't afford to buy for each other... Anyway, Christmas is a time for children... Don't get me wrong if I see a little trinket in the charity shop, or at a car boot sale, I'll buy it for Trevor/Mam, but when I say I don't buy him anything, what I really mean to say is I don't buy him anything expensive.

Code numbers jotted down, I phoned through my order to the operator, who said they'd be with me within the next twenty days... With Christmas sorted for another year, I turned my attention to tonight's fireworks party at the school.

Staring at myself in my dressing table mirror, I pondered on Julian's words to Megan, and I wondered if others saw me in the same light?... I'm not mad, I'm not, I'm not, I'm not!

I caught Doug looking at me during the firework's display. I said nothing, and kept well away. (What was he doing there?... He doesn't live in the area.) Anthony bought me a hot dog. (By the way, he said his newspaper round went well, and it wasn't all that cold once he got into it.) Anne and Dave were there with the triplets, two of which were crying, while the other was laughing at the exploding rockets, with his hands over his ears.

"Nice to see you looking after your mother, Evans." Mr Davis said to Anthony, as he walked past. Dave shrugged his shoulders and said, he hadn't noticed Doug in the crowd... Maybe it was a trick of the light, because I didn't see him again after that... Anne told me she spelt her name A double N and not A double N-E... I must remember that the next time I write anything about Ann in my diary.

November 6: Tuesday

I saw Doug's car parked outside the Post Office... He wasn't in it, so I entered the Post Office collected my money, and hurried home.

Mam had a surprise in the post this morning. A £200 cold weather payment from the Government: "Rhian, I'll be able to do my Christmas shopping early now." She said, placing the Giro in her purse.

7.00pm: I've been feeling uneasy all day. My mind is playing tricks with me again?... Am I being stalked?... I'm forty-one for Christ's sake, who in their right mind would want to stalk me?

Thank you for that thought brain. Stalkers are not in their right mind, are they?

When something happens to me... When I think something is going to happen to me... I mean... If Jodie thought something was happening to her, I'd tell her not to be so silly. I'd say there was a perfectly rational explanation for what was, or what she thought was going to happen... So why doesn't this piece of good advice work for me?

If I'm seeing things, then I really am mad. If I'm not, then what in the world is going on?... Why do I feel that this has got something to do with me?... I'm a bored housewife... Am I making all this up in my head?... Do I want to screw Doug?... I don't feel very well. I want to go to sleep... I'm not paranoid am I?

November 7: Wednesday

I had to attend evening class... I felt frightened, but I had to do it... Confronting my fears, I forced myself out of my front door... No sign of Doug, his car... Good. (Very good indeed)

Safely seated behind my desk, I became excited... I'd defeated my nemesis, bringing myself justice and peace of mind. I was afraid of seeing Doug, but not enough to stay at home. Liberated, I'd faced my fears and escaped mental retribution... I could have spent the rest of my life looking over my shoulder, worrying about a stalker... Shadows lurking in the dark, no matter how imaginary... It would have been a blight on my life... But I proved myself strong enough to win... I...

"Rhian, what kind of mood do you think 'Keats' was trying to portray, when he wrote his brilliant 'Ode on Melancholy'?"

Make not a rosary of yew-berries,
Nor let the beetle, nor the death-moth be
Your mournful Psyche, nor the downy owl
A partner in your sorrow's mysteries.

"I'm sorry, Mr Davis... I, I, I wasn't listening... I have no self-confidence... I'm quitting the class.

November 8: Thursday

The truth is; I don't go out of the house... Okay, I go shopping, and to the Post Office... But apart from attending my evening classes, where do I go to?

What have I done with my life?... Apart from mailing a couple of letters, I've achieved absolutely nothing again this year... It's the truth... I have no car to take me anywhere, (A feeble excuse) but if I did learn to drive, would it change anything?... I've got no money for the lessons.

Outside forces are making my life a misery. Megan; don't get me wrong. I love her dearly... But once out the door, I have no power over her. I have no say in who she can, and cannot talk to. The same goes for Gary and Anthony. Out of sight is out of mind. Every time they walkout the door... All I can do is sit at home and hope for the best.

Trouble is transported to my house. Trouble, brought home by my family. Trouble that has nothing at all to do with me... But nevertheless, I have no option but to sort it out.

I wish Megan wasn't pregnant... Do wishes ever come true?... Will I have to become a better parent for the baby, or the baby's mother?

November 9: Friday

Jodie waddled in this morning, and immediately plonked herself down in front of the television set. This girl is my only tonic. Looking at her I can't help but laugh. I offered her a mug of tea, and after resting it down on her bump, she said: "Rhian, I've got enough room here to balance a plate of biscuits too."

I must admit, at first I did find Jodie a handful. Sex mad she may be, but she's better than a packet of Prozac any day of the week.

"Rhian, I'm worn out." Jodie complained, then uttered a silent curse, as the soggy end of a rich tea finger, sank to the bottom of her mug. "It's all this moving the bed from against the wall at night that's tiring me out. Rhian, I'm going to ask my Darr, to take the headboard off it, all together. That should stop it from keeping you awake at night."

Bending my knees, we interlocked hands, and after a great deal of tugging, I successfully helped to pull her out of her seat. "Rhian, I can't keep any excess liquid in my body. One sip, and I have to rush to the loo. Was it like that for you?... My Darr is terrified of my water's breaking, he said I needed a life jacket, a couple of distress flares, and one of those self-inflating life-rafts, instead of an overnight bag to take to the hospital... I know I shouldn't be telling you any of this Rhian, and my Darr would go off his head if he ever found out. But he's frightened to have sex with me. He's too scared to put it into me, just in case I go bang and chunks of me go flying across the bedroom... Rhian, isn't that the cutest excuse for not having sex, you've ever heard in your life!"

Dear Diary how can anyone not like Jodie. She's such an innocent, it's frightening. She's like a little girl who's playing house in real life... I'm terrified for her... I'm glad she moved in next door... I promise to keep an eye on her.

November 10: Saturday

We had an unexpected visitor in our back garden this morning. Cocking his leg-up against 'The Female Orgasm', Piccalilli's little dog had tunnelled its way out of its compound.

"Billy, Billy, here boy." Dogs really are the dumbest animals on the planet. Instead of keeping his yap shut, and make his escape complete, the stupid dog excitedly turned towards the wooden fence and barked.

"Bad boy, Billy... You're a bad boy to your Mum... Come

home Billy, come home to Mummy immediately." Demanded the voice from the other side of the fence.

Billy barked, and ran the length of the fence, left to right. Occasionally he'd stand on his hind legs, using his front paws to steady himself against the wooden slats, when he heard his mistress's voice.

Like the good Samaritan, I stepped outside to help Billy find his way home. "I'd like you to hand me my dog back, if you don't mind." Scouring at me from the top of the garden fence, (She must have been standing on a stepladder.) Piccalilli gestured for the return of her pet.

On please, no thank you, no I'm sorry Billy got into your garden, no hello, no goodbye, no good morning, have a nice day, how do you do. I handed her the dog, smiled. She took the dog, and sneered. "What's Mummy's little angel been doing in that nasty woman's garden then?" She said,climbing down, leaving me to feel a right idiot staring at my side of the fence... The frosty faced bitch... I wonder if she's a friend of Mary's?

10.00pm: The day had rambled along its well worn path, until Trevor came home... Helped home covered in blood.

"Your Trevor put up a good show." Darren remarked, as he helped me carry my husband to bed. "If he hadn't been so drunk, I think he would have beaten the five of them up, with one hand tied behind his back."

Sitting Trevor at the foot of the bed, I began by dabbing cotton-wool doused in antiseptic over his cuts. (I hope this antiseptic hasn't gone off... It's an old bottle I've kept from when the children were young... For grazed knees, and the like... I hope Trevor won't get blood poisoning!)

“He’s too old for this.” I complained. “And they’ve ruined this best shirt.”

“It had to be done, Rhian.” Darren insisted, propping Trevor up, while I continued to administer to his cuts and bruises. “I won’t let any fucker, call my daughter a slag and get away with it either.”

“Julian!” An unbelievable thought flashed through my mind. “Julian, did this to Trevor?”

“No, no, no.” Darren laughed. “That little weed... Beat-up Trev... Don’t make me laugh... Trev would squash him under his pinkie toe no problem... No these fucker’s, were some relations... Brothers, cousins, or something... Anyway Trev steamed in, took out two of them, before one of their side chaired him across the back, then they all piled in with the boot.”

Deciding it would be best to let him sleep it off, I ushered Darren down the stairs: “One more thing before I go.” Darren said stepping out of the door. “When he wakes up, tell Trevor the steward has barred him from drinking at the club.”

November 11: Remembrance Sunday

Trevor gingerly descended the stairs clutching his side... On the television Prince Charles was laying a wreath at the ‘Cenotaph’... After September 11th, and with our soldiers on the verge of entering Afghanistan, this year’s ceremony carried more meaning than most... I bet Mam had a cry while she watched it on her own television.

Luckily for Trevor, he had only superficial injuries to contend with after his war, which included a heavy amount of bruising, to his rib cage, and thighs. Lifting his shirt, Trevor revealed a psychedelic patchwork of yellow, purple and blue, covering the left-side of his torso.

"How old are you?" I demanded to know. "I don't care what was said. You had no right to get yourself into this state."

"Man trap, that's what they called our Megan." Wincing his way onto his seat, Trevor took a deep breath: "Man fucking trap, that's what those Jackson's called her... They said she'd deliberately allowed herself to get knocked up on purpose, so that she could escape your evil clutches." Trevor took another breath, while I pondered on being thought evil by a group of strangers.

"There was no mistaking it, the five of them where there to cause trouble Rhian... None of them were club members. Typical fucking Jackson's. The club's not good enough for them as a rule. They drink in that new pub in the village." Trevor eased himself against the back supports of the chair... I can't understand why anyone would want to call me evil?

"He's a fucking foul mouthed git, is that Derek Peterson. There he was, shouting the odds in the middle of the club... Four wankers, for brothers behind him... Calling you mad, and our Megan a slag... Accusing us of contaminating their family blood line... And here's the best laugh... Our Megan... Ruining their Julian's reputation."

I don't understand why people think I'm evil and mad?

"Of course, at this point in the proceedings I had to let them know that not only was their Julian an accomplished liar, but he was a shoplifter and a joy rider too boot." Trevor tenderly soothed a painful section of his bruise. "Then it kicked off... Those Jackson's have never liked listening to the truth."

In minute detail, Trevor described every kick, headbutt, and punch. Pride welled up in his eyes. He was fighting for the honour of his family. "Five to one, Rhian... The fucking bastards... Five of the scum against me, and they still couldn't get me down... Derek was the first to hit the ground like a sack of shit... Barry was next... Butt, butt, two heads, and I think I broke his nose... I could see the other three shitting themselves, but fair play to them, they still came ahead." Ducking and diving, weaving right, then left, Trevor danced his way through a personal pain barrier that left him grimacing in his chair.

"At this point Derek must have slipped around my blind side, because before I could do anything about it, he'd broken one of Harry's heavy bar stools across my back, and before I could regain my balance, the five of them made freely with the boot."

"Didn't Darren, or any of your mates help you?" I asked, wishing I'd been there in order to hear what really had been said.

"Why should they?" Trevor scoffed. "It was a fair fight, until Derek used that stool... Five, six, ten... The men of that family are nothing Rhian. When they all piled in with the boot, the boys joined in and threw them out... But like they said: They couldn't interfere straight away like. They had to give me a sporting chance to get back on my feet."

I do believe Trevor got a big kick out of retelling his tale throughout the day: "Not including a few tussles on and off the rugby field, this was my first real scrap I've been involved with since the early eighties." He proudly told his sons: "I learnt my trade touring with Cardiff City, in and outside of the football grounds of the old third division.... I can remember this time, when a coach load of Cardiff City supporters, went to Bristol, and...

...Fighting is like riding a bike. When you learn how to do it... I haven't lost my touch."

November 12: Monday

The terrorists have crashed another passenger airliner in New York... This time an airbus came down in the Queens district of the city... All the passengers and crew are dead, and streets of a residential neighbourhood are on fire... What is happening in this world?

I had a terrible night's sleep, last night. I've more or less accepted the world believes I'm mad. But now I've got to put up with it believing, I'm evil as well... Thank God I'm not thin skinned, or all this fighting and name calling would be disturbing my piece of mind.

On the other hand, Gary and Anthony think their father is Superman, and Mam agrees. She said: "Rhian, it's about time your Trevor stood up for the honour of his family."

Megan also thought him very brave, while Superman himself basked in his underdog triumph... Apparently losing doesn't matter when it's five against one."

Gary came home and after spending twenty-five minutes describing the reactions of his workmates at the Assessment Centre, said: "Lewis & Hudson are closing down at the end of the year."

"They thought I was good, did they?" Trevor asked, flexing his biceps.

"Poor Dave and Ann." I said on hearing the news.

"Some of your friends were at the rugby club last Saturday night, were they boy?"

"I bet Ann will be heartbroken when she hears the news... Just after Christmas and all."

"Dad, this guy I know said it was bloody brilliant when you head butted that bloke."

"Dave will be out of work in the New Year... Not a very happy start for them, is it?"

"Hang-on a minute son... What's your mother twittering on about?"

"I was just saying... Lewis & Hudson... Bad news for Dave and Ann."

"What have they got to do with us Rhian?... I've told you before about wasting your time worrying about other people haven't I... It's not good for you love... Megan is the only person you should be worrying about at the moment... Be thankful, love... Be thankful, our Gary got out of Lewis & Hudson when he did."

Don't worry about me Trevor, I'll be all right... You carry on enjoying yourself, reliving your triumph of taking a beating, on your ego trip.

November 13: Tuesday

Terrorists didn't attack New York after all. It was all just a terrible accident... But you can't blame the media for jumping to the wrong conclusions, can you!

Megan took a day off work, and used the time to speak with the people down at the council housing offices: "Mam, I filled out some forms while I was down there, and they've officially put my name down on the housing register."

Why my daughter wants to leave home, and bring up her baby in squalor is beyond me. But she's determined to do it, so I've decided to let her get on with it... Megan needs a short sharp shock. Living on her own will either make or break her. Jodie can fill her head with all the nonsense she likes. Sharing a lonely flat twenty-four hours a day with a screaming baby and no money, is not my idea of fun... But there again, Megan knows best.

"No, you move out of this house Megan, and you're on your own." Resiliently I held my ground staying true to my principles and beliefs: "If you no longer wish to remain a part of the family, then your family no longer wish to remain connected to you... Who do you think you are, asking me to look after your baby, while you go to work... No I will not baby sit for you to go out on the piss... Living on your own, means exactly that... If you need help, you can always turn to your family: but you don't want to be part of our family, do you Megan?... You only want us to be there for you when it suits you... You want your cake and eat it. But that's not what's going to happen my girl... You can either live with us, and receive all the help in the world, or you can tough it out on your own... Yes, we will see wont we!"

"I want a place of my own, and you can't stop me getting one." My daughter is as stubborn as a bloody mule.

November 14: Wednesday

I forced myself to go to class tonight. I'd been 'hum-ing and ha-ing' about it all day, but in the end I decided I didn't want to give up on my dream just yet.

Ann portrayed a very worried expression on her face: "I suppose you've heard." She said, before the class started. "Dave loses his job in the New Year."

"My Trevor reckons, your Dave won't lose much by being

out of work. In fact you may be better off financially." I replied optimistically.

Ann looked doubtful: "It's not the money, it's Dave's mental well being that I worry about... He gets so depressed you see Rhian. My Dave's like a tiger in a small cage, spending his day traipsing back and fore across the room. He gets so bored staying at home... No offence to your Trevor, but Dave doesn't know how he can do it day after day... Staying at home doing nothing I mean?"

I was going to say, different generation, very easily as it happens Ann. My Trevor was a boy of the sixties, and early seventies. Born at a time when work was never top of anyone's agenda. Trevor reached adulthood at a time of mass unemployment... All my Trevor did, (Apart from a few speculative business failures.) was find his niche and lie in it... But I said nothing.

"My Dave couldn't say at home all day twiddling his thumbs... No offence." I gestured, that no offence was taken. "I know what will happen, you mark my words. When he's made redundant, Dave will pretend the first two weeks of his unemployment are an holiday... He'll be as happy as Larry for those fourteen days. All the little jobs that need doing around the house will be seen to, and then the depression will sink in." Ann looked down at the floor. "Rhian, I don't know what to do. I don't want to go through it all again... Dave's been doing ever so well at work. He's happy to get up in the morning. He's all smiles when he comes home at night. His nerves have improved no end."

"Nerves?"

"Look, keep it to yourself... Rhian, I know I can trust you. You've been a good friend to me and Dave in the past." Ann looked around to check no one was listening. "Like you Dave is on Prozac for his nerves."

As bad as it sounds, I was overjoyed to hear this.

"I know we've never said anything about it to you in the past. But Dave doesn't like talking about it you see... He's a very private person, is my Dave. He doesn't want people thinking he's schizophrenic or something."

I felt overjoyed, because I don't feel alone... I'm not the only one who's mad.

"My Dave is also a big worrier. He worries about everything. Money, the house, the kids...

"My Trevor isn't." I interrupted. "He's completely the opposite of your Dave. If anything goes wrong he believes in doing nothing, and leaving it to fate."

"Do you remember the morning I had to drag Dave in from the street?"

I nodded. I did indeed remember my mother's handiwork.

"He was like a wild thing possessed, after he'd read that letter from the child welfare... Rhian, I don't want to go through something similar again."

Back home I thought to myself: it really is true. None of us truly know what goes on behind closed curtains.

November 15: Thursday

"That bastard wants to pay for me to have an abortion, Mam." Julian had accosted Megan at the bus stop again. "Fancy promising me, he'd pay for me to go private... In front of all those people in the bus queue, Mam!"

"I'll have a word with him, the next time I see him." Gary said, without turning his face away from the television screen.

"It's about time someone had a word with the little shit." Megan replied, agreeing with her brother's point of view.

"Because, he won't listen to me. Julian refuses to listen to a word I say."

"No one is going to say, or do anything. Do you understand me?" I said, making sure Gary understood. "If Julian persists in making a nuisance of himself, then we'll take a leaf out of his mother's book... Mary's not the only one who can send out solicitor's letters you know."

November 16: Friday

Megan has been attacked on her way home from work... She's in hospital... The doctor said they want to keep her in because they want to monitor her and her baby over night... Megan has been hit over the head with a blunt instrument, and kicked in her stomach. The person who did this left her for dead and run away.

A policeman knocked at the door. I saw him, and instantly thought something terrible had happened to my mother... He said Megan had been found in a dark alley/walkway, people use as a short-cut between streets.

Trevor took the thoughts out of my mind and asked, if she'd been raped?

The policeman replied: he wasn't sure of the circumstances, but what he'd seen, made him think that whoever had attacked Megan, had given her a good hiding... The policeman gave Trevor and I a lift to the hospital.

Megan was sitting up in bed, when we arrived. Her head is bandaged, and she's linked up to a machine monitoring the baby's heartbeat in her stomach.

She said she didn't see who attacked her, because the coward crept up on her from behind... We all cried.

November 17: Saturday Anthony's Birthday

Anthony is fourteen today. 9.00am Mam called round with a card and a present for Anthony. She became distraught when I told her about Megan lying in hospital, then insulted because I'd forgotten to let her know about it when it happened.

"Has she been raped?" Mam asked.

Putting her mind at ease: "Megan has only been attacked, Mam."... Only!!! "The doctor said, if she wasn't pregnant, they'd have allowed her to come home today. But because of the baby, they are going to keep her in until Monday for checks."

In the hospital, Megan told us the police had taken a statement. She said: "I don't know what good it will do, because I didn't see or hear a thing."

"Are you sure you wasn't interfered with love." Mam asked, as we all squirmed uneasily in our seats.

"Of course I wasn't." Megan answered, as if the notion had never entered her head. "I was mugged that's all. I have a cut and a lump at the back of my head. Whoever did it was probably after my pay."

Looking at the faces around the bed, I could see no one there believed this explanation for a second.

"Do you think Julian had anything to do with it?" Mam's steam rolling interrogation took no notice of my facial expressions. Her jackboot like stance, wouldn't and couldn't tolerate my pleading for tolerance in this situation. I wanted to give my daughter time to come to it herself. While Mam wanted to lance the boil there and then, and to hell with the consequences.

"Your mother's told me all about the trouble you've been having with Julian. (On the way to the hospital. I thought it wise to bring my mother up to speed.) Don't you find it strange that this has happened to you, at this moment in time?"

"No!... Well, I don't know?... I think not!... Mam, you don't think Julian would seriously hurt me, do you?"

I could see the confusion building in my daughter's eyes. "I didn't see who did it. So I suppose he could have... And the mugger didn't runaway with my money... Mam, you don't think he tried to murder me do you?... He did ask me to kill my baby..." Watching my daughter sobbing hysterically Trevor, Anthony and I turned to face my mother.

"It's no good hiding from the truth Rhian. These matters have to be faced, and the sooner the better if you ask me."

"Not much of a birthday for you, is it Ant." I said as we walked along the corridor. Outside, in the open air I realised Trevor had said nothing for the whole time we were there... Mam spoke, but I don't think anyone of us heard a word she's said, and then I remembered Gary. Gary hadn't returned home last night. Apart from me I don't think anyone else had noticed... On the bus home we all sat in silence... I for one am not looking forward to finding out what fate has in store for my family.

November 18: Sunday

I was in bed, when Gary come home. My alarm clock told me it was 12.30am, when I heard him turn on the bathroom taps. Through the open door I watched, as Gary let the running water flow over the knuckles of his hands.

"What have you been up to?" I asked, as his red face turned towards me.

"Nothing... Ah, on my way home I tripped, and my knuckles scraped against a wall."

"Where was this?"

"Outside... Nowhere you know... We were just messing

about... You know, me and the boys, when I over balanced and grazed my knuckles against the wall... That's all."

Back in bed, I could only sense events gradually getting worse.

We all spent the afternoon visiting Megan. She understood, we couldn't come again during the evening, what with the buses being on Sunday service and all. But like she said, she was feeling a lot better, and she'd be home sometime tomorrow in any case.

On his way back from the toilets, Anthony said he had seen the Jackson family entering another ward. Peeping through the glass window in the door, he said he could see Julian in bed, with his family weeping around him.

I looked at Gary.

Gary looked at the floor.

I stared at Gary's hands.

Gary put his hands in his pocket.

Mam said: "What goes around comes around."

Megan, didn't know what to think.

Trevor went with Anthony to make sure he hadn't been seeing things.

"Julian's in one hell of a state in there." Trevor informed us on his return from his spying mission. "Julian's face is a grotesque mask of pink flesh."

"Perhaps the mugger who attacked me, attacked him?" Megan uttered hopefully.

Doubting this instantly, my suspicions were confirmed as Gary questioned his sister more carefully: "I thought Julian was the one who pasted you over?"

"I think Julian's on some sort of life support machine,

because he has tubes and all sorts sprouting out of him... We could hear the machine go beep as we stood outside the door, couldn't we Ant?"

Confirming the type of noise the machine made, Anthony added: "I think someone caught Julian trying to steal their car, and give him a good hiding."

"Megan, it must have been Julian who attacked you." Gary insisted.

"Well if he didn't, he's only got himself to blame." Mam nodded.

"If it wasn't Julian... It must have been Julian... Who would have done such a thing to you it if it wasn't Julian?" Gary searched his sister's face for the answer. "You must have heard something Megan... A voice... Footsteps behind you... Something to let you know who it was."

"Why are you questioning me, like this?" Megan, snapped. "I've already told the police everything I know... Mam, tell Gary to stop pestering me... I don't know! Hearing all this about Julian has suddenly made me feel sick... Mam, I want you to help me to the toilet, and then I want to go to sleep.

November 19: Monday

THE MIDDLE OF THE NIGHT: Jodie's agonising screams from next-door woke the house up. "My God Rhian, if I was married to that woman, she'd wear my heart out." Trevor said, turning over in the bed. "I mean there's no need for it, is there?... Making all that noise at this hour of the night... Why doesn't Darren stick a pair of socks in her mouth?"

Another ear piercing scream, had Trevor out, and thumping the wall: "Keep it down in there... There's people trying to sleep in here." (I've decided to cut down on the bad language used during this statement... Flipping through the pages I feel ashamed, as I'm constantly reminded about the amount of swear words I and my family use in everyday life.)

Somebody was banging heavily on our front door.

Trevor: If that's kids at this time of night, I'll bloody kill them.

Me: (Praying for mercy) Please God, please don't let it be the police coming for our Gary.

"TREVOR IT'S ME, PLEASE OPEN THE DOOR, IT'S AN EMERGENCY" Darren pleaded through the letterbox. "IT'S JODIE, SHE'S STARTED... THE BABY IS COMING... JODIE'S WATERS HAVE BROKE ALL OVER THE BED... I DON'T KNOW WHAT TO DO... SHE'S CALLING FOR RHIAN... CAN I USE YOUR TELEPHONE TO CALL FOR AN AMBULANCE?"

2.45am: I was holding Jodie's hand in the ambulance.

3.45am: I helped Jodie breathe in some gas and air.

4.15am: I overheard a very tired looking doctor utter the phrase: 'Caesarean Section'.

4.30am: I held, Jodie's hand as she pushed. (The Caesarean Section wasn't needed.)

4.35am: Jodie is mother to a beautiful nine pound baby girl.

5.00am: Jodie fell asleep, and I went to Megan's ward and sat with my daughter.

I stayed with Megan, until the doctor passed her fit to come home. We visited Jodie, who was in the middle of breast feeding her baby.

Jodie: I've promised Darren I'd give it a go, until this little one begins teething.

Megan looked frightened to death, when Jodie asked her if she would like to hold the baby... She nearly fainted, when Jodie removed the baby from her breast, and told her: "You'll be doing this in a couple of months' time."

Promising Jodie that I'd come and visit her tomorrow. I helped a frail looking Megan to the bus stop... At last: I believe the reality of Megan's situation, is finally beginning to sink in.

Megan: (On the bus, on the way home.) Mam, I've been thinking. Before my baby and I move into a place of my own, I think it's best, if we stay with you and Dad until I'm strong enough to stand on my own two feet. (Surprise, surprise.)

November 20: Tuesday

Mary and I passed each other in the hospital. (I know in my heart my Gary beat her Julian to a pulp.) We ignored each other in passing. (I know it's only a matter of time before the police come to question him.) Further down the corridor, I saw Idris loitering outside Jodie's ward.

"May I have a word in your ear, Rhian?"

"Look Idris, I know absolutely nothing about what happened to your Julian." I lied.

"Listen, I'm sorry about Mary's family... You know...

Fighting with your Trevor." I'd forgotten all about that. "And I can assure you, Julian had nothing to do with the attack on your Megan."

"How can you be so sure Idris." I enquired. "Where you with him at the time? Well, were you?"

"As a matter of fact I was." Idris interrupted. "Mary and I had taken the family to Cardiff for the day... We've told it all to the police... We've given then our shopping receipts... We've been helping them with their inquires, you might say."

Idris took hold of my arm and drew me to one side. "I know your Gary did it." My heart sunk. "Julian told me, when his mother had left the room." I kept my eye's down, and stared at the floor.

"Don't worry Rhian, he's not going to do anything about it." I looked up. "He knows he deserved a beating for the way he's treated your Megan... But it's the wife you see." There's always a but, I thought. "She wants vengeance... She thinks it was one of your lot who attacked her son, and she's told the police as much."

Idris let go of my arm. "I want to have contact with my grandchild, Rhian. Keeping this silly feud going isn't doing anyone any good... I'm helping your son to stay out of trouble, and I expect you to help mine to have access to his child."

"What about Mary?"

"I'm sure her heart will thaw when she holds her first Grandchild in her arms." Idris tapped the side of his nose with his index finger. "Rhian, this is between you and me." He said walking away. "Between you and me you understand. No one else needs to know a thing."

I spent the next three hours visiting Jodie... She's like a little girl playing with a new doll.

November 21: Wednesday

Jodie came home from the hospital with her new baby today... First thing this morning I ventured next-door with my dust pan and brush: "Rhian, you're a real treasure." Darren said, as I pushed past him. "If it were left to me, I wouldn't know where to start... I'm an outdoor man you see, Rhian. Indoors, is a mystery to me."

While Darren got himself ready to collect his wife and child. I gave the place a quick flick over with my feather duster, (To be honest with you, the Johnson's haven't got much in the way of ornaments or such like, so it didn't take me long.) washed-up his dirty dishes, collected the dirty washing, setting it to go in my machine, vacuumed around the rooms... Two hours later, the house sparkled like a new pin.

"You think they'd have brought the baby home by taxi, wouldn't you, Rhian." Mam pointed out, as we watched the proud parents walking down the street. "The poor mite, not a very good start to life is it. Coming home on the bus."

"It could have been worse." Trevor laughed. "Darren could have asked his brother to pick them up in his old van."

I give evening class a miss tonight... Well, Jodie asked me to call round (I think she needed me there for support.) and Mam tagged along too, and between the three of us we had a really good gossip. (Darren went next-door to watch the football on Sky with Trevor.)

November 22: Thursday

8.00am: A worried Jodie invited me into her house, and asked: "Does my baby look all right too you?"

Looking at the little mite sleeping in her crib, I felt her forehead, I listened to her breathing, I felt inside her mouth for any sign of a blockage... To me the baby seemed perfectly healthy, if not a little cold. I advised Jodie to cover her with extra blankets on cold nights.

"Rhian I've been shitting myself all night." Jodie admitted. "I couldn't get a wink of sleep... I'm terrified she'll stop breathing... Rhian, do you know anything about cot death... Did you use to worry like me, when you had your three?"

To be perfectly honest, in my day women gave birth and got on with it... Well I did anyway. Now I come to think about it, I had my mother with me. Mam was my rock to lean on. Jodie's got no one. At times I must have been worried, but then Mam would always be there to set my mind at ease... I am Jodie's surrogate mother... I don't mind being a sounding board for her.

"I blame the hospital for all my insecurities." Jodie said, after I'd finished giving her baby a medical. "I thought I'd be in hospital for at least a week. But no. As soon as they took this little one out of me, they expected me to vacate the premises. It's like being on a conveyor belt in that maternity ward Rhian. One at a time we were all wheeled in, then wheeled out again, cradling a nine plus pound bundle of joy."

Times had indeed changed, I agreed.

"How do they expect me to know what to do?" Jodie stared at me for an answer. Thankfully she spoke before I could think of a suitable response. "Right, I thought to myself, I'll be in hospital for a week, the nurses will show me how to feed and help me change the dirty nappies of my little girl. In the middle of the night, they will came and tell me what signs to lookout for if something goes wrong. If I have any questions, they will be at hand to answer them for me... But it wasn't like that Rhian. They told, and showed me nothing. They didn't have time to, because I wasn't in there long enough for them to tell or show me anything. Rhian, the R.S.P.C.A wouldn't allow anyone to keep a dog if they didn't know how to look after it properly... I think the hospital should have shown me what to do. At least they should have told me something about the basics of bringing up my baby... No Rhian,that's not an excuse. They shouldn't rely on you or my mother telling me what to do. What if I had been a orphan?"

6.00pm: Jodie, Darren, and baby entered my living-room: "Rhian, Darren and I have decided to name our daughter Leah, and if we decide to get her Christened, we'd like you and Trevor to be baby Leah's Godparents."

November 23: Friday

The White Arrow man delivered Christmas... Thankfully everyone was out of the house at the time. Standing on a chair, I bundled the delivery into the attic. (Alternative hiding places have become scarce over the years.)

Dear Diary, what Idris said has been playing on my mind... Jodie's baby has helped to blank my feelings over the past few days, but nevertheless I have to face-up to it. Sooner or later, I'll have to engage in another battle with the Jackson's. (God help me!)

Gary's been very quiet since last weekend. I think he realises he's made a big mistake and got the wrong man, but he's said nothing to me about it... I don't want to say anything to him, until I persuade Megan to allow the Jackson's access to their Grandchild.

Megan's taking some time off work to help her get over the attack. She's also been very quiet since the weekend. The assault, and the reality of Jodie's baby has really taken the wind out of her sails... Indestructible? At Megan's age, I think we all believe we are. Only this episode has made her feel very vulnerable. I hear Megan crying when she thinks no one is listening... Sobbing some nights. It can't be easy replaying the attack over and over inside her head. If only she knew who was behind it... That would be something... It would help to put her mind at ease.

Trevor seeks vengeance, Mam thinks it's a shame, I want our lives to return to the way they were. Money!... Money's no good at a time like this. Money, job, my dreams, poetry, I'd settle for nothing,just so long as piece of mind returns to the lives of my family.

November 24: Saturday

Mr E Dunstable.
Islington,
London.

Dear Mrs Evans.
Please allow me to take this opportunity to introduce myself. My name is Eric Dunstable. For the past twenty-six years I have been a literary professor at the London Collage Of Further Education.

My Dear Mrs Evans: poetry is my one true indulgence. Like you I employ verse to express my feelings - elaborate on every day situations - understand my experiences, and to fathom out the mysterious enigma of life confronted by my good self throughout the working day.

Mrs Evans: unbeknown to you, we owe a great deal of thanks to one Ms Stella Davis, assistant to the assistant editor of 'Bella' magazine. Stella, (A former student and great personal friend.) knows all about my little project. At the moment it's at the gathering stage, and at the gathering stage Mrs Evans, is where you come in.

Titled 'Tunes of the Mind', I plan to publish a book of poetry, from yet unknown and unpublished writers like your good self.

My dear Mrs Evans, all poems selected for my book have one thing in common. 'The Mind'. That complex mass of untapped, human, electricity, imprisoned inside our cranium castles of bone.

Mrs Evans I think you'll agree this is a rare opportunity for you to see your name in print. Alas I can offer no monetary gain to you at this time, but if any of your work is selected for the book, of course I will be delighted to negotiate the question of royalties with you, at a future date; which I can assure you will take place well before the completed manuscript goes into print.

Yours sincerely,
E Dunstable.

PS: A new web site will be up and running shortly. (New Year-ish) Address and detail information will be sent on completion of said site. All rejected poems from the manuscript, will be presented on said site, with author's permission of course.

I have been in tears all day. I can't believe it, I can't believe this as happened to me. On top of everything that's happened, it's wonderful. It's too much... Just too much.

November 25: Sunday

What goes up must come down... My heart sank like a lead balloon this morning, when the police came and knocked on our door to question Trevor and Gary about Julian's assault.

Nine o'clock they knocked at the door. For twenty minutes Trevor and Gary denied everything, apart from knowing Julian had been admitted to hospital. On the whole the police have been very understanding, what with Megan and all. They questioned Trevor about his fight with the Jackson clan... I just wish they believed Gary's story a little more, and not take it with a pinch of salt, which I'm sure they did. (I noticed both officer's eyebrows rise, as they listened to Gary telling them his tale.)

"They'll be back." Trevor said, as he closed the door behind them. "It's obvious isn't it. We grassed their Julian for attacking Megan, and now in a tit for tat retaliation campaign the Jackson's have grassed me and Gary up for assaulting their son."

I haven't had a chance to tell anyone yet about what Idris had to say... Well I have, but I don't know how best to approach the subject. I also haven't said anything about my letter. Now is not the right time... Maybe during Christmas dinner?... Maybe when the book comes out?

"Well, Julian's attacker must have struck in the same manner as Megan's." Trevor remarked,settling down in his chair. "Or the police would have arrested him." I watched Gary hanging on his father's every word. "It stands to reason doesn't it. The police say Julian is lying wide awake in his hospital bed... They've questioned him... Don't you see?... Like Megan, Julian doesn't know who attacked him either." A smile grew broadly across Gary's face... It sickened me... I'm the only one who knew, Julian was keeping his side of the bargain.

I'm P.M.T Active once again... This doesn't help, either!

November 26: Monday

Megan had decided to take another week off, on the sick. Physically she had made a good recovery. The wound on the back of her head had healed nicely, (Stitches out on Wednesday) while the bruising to the upper and middle side of her body, had faded to an unpleasant memory. With Trevor and Megan both in their beds, I reread Eric's letter and pondered on how much it would cost for the Evans family to go on the internet?

November 27: Tuesday

On my way to collect my benefit money, I noticed Doug's car parked outside the Post Office again. Just as before there was no sign of life sitting behind the wheel, and just as before the vehicle's owner wasn't to be seen anywhere on either side of the street. Walking past the car the hairs on the back of my neck suddenly sprang into life. It had been a cold, windless morning, but until that moment my goose-pimples had remained dormant under my skin.

I don't know how, or why I sensed it, but there was some sinister meaning going on with this car... Eerie, creepy, I didn't feel right. Call it woman's intuition if you like. I hurried myself into the Post Office, then I hurried myself home.

My mind is nagging at me. I'm beginning to imagine all sorts. I know Julian didn't attack Megan, so maybe Doug did???... Why should he???... To get back at me???... Am I being stalked???... Just because I saw his empty car, why am I thinking this way???... Who would believe me if I said anything about it???... I wouldn't if I was listening to someone else describing exactly what I was thinking.... Have I got extra sensory perception???... Am I really mad???... Why can't I get this silly idea out of my head???

Changing the subject: AOL are sending me a start-up CD, so Anthony can gain free access to the internet for a month.

I can't walk into a police station... I'd be a laughingstock if I walked in and said: "Officer, I've just this minute walked past a parked car, and sensed the car owner to be the person who recently attacked my daughter." Who would believe me???... I wouldn't... What can I do???

November 28: Wednesday

Waiting in the doctor's surgery, I asked Megan: "Did you notice a red sports car parked, anywhere near to where you were attacked?"

She answered with a resounding: "No!"

"Megan's stitches came out beautifully." The nurse remarked: "With your lovely head of hair my love, no one will ever see anything is there." (She was talking about the little scar at the back of Megan's head.)

Outside the surgery I guided Megan towards a bench, pausing to sit for a moment I blurted out: "Gary beat Julian up."

"How do you know?" Megan's eyes were filled with excitement. "Has he told you?"

"No. Idris told me at the hospital... When Julian came round, he told his father what Gary had done."

"Bullshit!" I could see the contempt etched across Megan's face. "Why hasn't he told it to the police then?" Megan shook her head. "They're pulling your leg Mam, that's all. They're only guessing. His mother would love to put our Gary in it if she could. She hates you..."

"They want you to allow then access to your baby." I watched Megan's face crumble. "If you won't let them have access to their Grandchild. Then they will report Gary to the police."

"NO!" She screamed. "NO! NO! NO! NEVER!" She stamped her feet heavily onto the pavement in utter frustration. "Why does everyone want to hurt me, Mam?" She wailed, braking down and sobbing on my shoulder.

"Now, now," I said, handing Megan a paper tissue. "We have a long time to go before your baby is born. We might have lost this battle, but we have a long way to go before this war is over."

"What do you mean?" Megan sniffed.

"I mean, you allow them access, or at least say you will... Their Julian makes a speedy recovery... Our Gary keeps his freedom... The baby isn't born yet love... The Jackson's are blackmailing us."

"Yes, so?"

"We don't have to keep our word with blackmailers."

"But won't they report our Gary to the police if we don't?"

"Not if we turn the tables on them, and blackmail them back...

We can tell the police they are only making these untrue accusations because you won't give them access to their Grandchild... We can threaten the Jackson's with, withholding information... That's a criminal offence in itself, you know... We can do all sorts of things, when the time is right... But just now we have to agree to the Jackson's terms."

"And Daddy, and Gary don't know anything about this?" I could see the gleam returning to my daughter's eyes.

"That's right darling, and why should they? You know what men are like in a time of crisis... Like bulls in a china shop, each and everyone of them. They go steaming in, just like our Gary did for you. Only this time he got the wrong man."

Megan cheered up after our little talk. She understood my plan beautifully. She was also both proud and surprised, that her seemingly uncaring brother had stuck-up for her in the way that he did. With a renewed confidence in her step, she said: "Mam, I think I'll return to work on Monday after all."

November 29: Thursday

Megan and I spent the morning around at Mam's. Although Megan is feeling, and looks a lot better than she was. She still doesn't feel safe staying at home on her own. (Gary's at work, Anthony's at school and Trevor's nipped out for an hour... Don't ask me where?)

Today is the day of my mother's traditional Christmas dinner, held every year at the old age centre. In the past this highlight of the pensioners' year, took place on the final Thursday before Christmas Day, but like everything else in the world times change and what with one thing and another, a lack of volunteers, council organisation, commitment and resources.

The day of the dinner has been gradually forced back to its present date.

I for one think it's an absolute disgrace that my mother, and the other old age pensioners on this estate have to chip in so much of their pension each week, in order for the dinner to take place at all.

Dear Diary, excuse me while I have my little rant: The Labour council around here are so tight when it comes to the old. They were one of the first councils in the country to do away with the meals-on-wheels service, when the Government gave them the green light to do so. They refuse to repair any damage caused by vandals to the old age centre, but think nothing of spending thousands of pounds of taxpayers' money on their little fact finding holidays... Sorry, I mean jaunts around the more exotic parts of Europe and the world. (Checking out how pollution is controlled on the Great Barrier Reef, then failing to apply what they've supposed to have learned when the time comes to clean-up the local canal.)

It comes to something; when in this country and in this day and age, old men and women of eighty plus can be seen daily, and in all types of weathers, using ordinary soap and water to scrub all indiscriminate graffiti from the side of their beloved building. (My Trevor, God bless his heart,sometimes helps to remove the higher echelons of graffiti art work with the aid of his ladder.)

Mam is the treasurer of the pensioners' fighting fund. All sub's collected from the members, (50p a week) are held in a building society account, whereby no less than three members of the elected committee (The building society keeps a record of their ever changing names... Due to death.) have to be present at all times when club funds are withdrawn.

The fighting fund pays for everything apart from electric heating, and light. (The council still subsidises that.) All cleaning, and toilet sanitation products, tea and coffee, the ladies make sandwiches and cakes, the men - allotment holders, supply the produce for the Harvest Festival dinner and dance, (The local vicar is invited to this gathering to say a few words. He also attends the Christmas dinner... Ah, to say some additional words... If the date of the Christmas dinner is put back any further. Harvest Festival and Christmas dinner will merge together!... Is there such a thing as a Christmas Harvest?)

"Don't tell me about our council." Mam said, while I used up half a can of hairspray, in setting her home perm. "They've been dying to get their dirty little fingers on our club for years. They want to knock it down, and turn it into flats for single mothers... No offence Megan."

"You don't know that for sure, Mam." I said removing a final curler from the back of her head.

"Of course I do Rhian. Mr Bryant used to serve teas, during council meetings and he said they've been trying to think of away of getting their hands on our club at nearly every meeting." A steely determination etched its way across Mam's cheeks. "They'll never get their hands on our club, not if I have anything to do with it. Hitler tried to bomb it in the forties, (That would have been the old club. The new club was built along with a new prefabricated school in the early sixties.) and the council, this council are no better than terrorists, that's what they are... They'll never get our centre. Look what they did to the Boys' Club Trevor and you used to attend in your youth. (It's an off licence now.) No wonder there's so many children causing trouble, and running wild at all hours of the day and night on the streets. Nowhere for them to play you see love.

Just like us old ones who'll have nowhere to go if they get their way and close our club... They are trying to kill us all off one by one Rhian, that's what they're trying to do. They are trying to kill all us old one's off to save the NHS, and to keep the private pension companies from going bankrupt... We're no use to them anymore... We no longer contribute taxes... We are a burden on the state."

Call me old fashioned if you like, but Father Christmas, a Carol Service and a turkey dinner with all the trimmings, seems a tad out of place at the end of November.

Ex-Beatle George Harrison died today... I liked him.

November 30: Friday

First bit of luck for a good while; my period ended this morning. I am no longer P.M.T active. (It's very lucky to begin a new month without a period... Here's a thought: wouldn't it be great to remain festive free!)

After he came home from work, Gary held the stepladder steady, while I entered the attic to hunt out our Christmas decorations. (I've hidden all the presents up there, so I couldn't let Trevor, or the children climb into the attic and find them, could I?) Trevor loves to be kept totally in the dark when it comes to knowing what Christmas presents I've bought for everyone. This gives me a free hand, plus all the blame if I get it wrong. Trevor's like a big kid at Christmas time. He enjoys the excitement of his children discovering what Santa's (Me) brought for them... Well, I suppose it's not a lot to ask, is it. After all, poor Trevor doesn't get many Christmas presents of his own.

I handed Gary down four boxes, (Ex- K.P. crisp boxes.) plus an oblong box containing our Christmas tree. Gary is another big softie when it comes to Christmas. Like his father, he's a better giver than a receiver. (Apart from the dole of course... Receiving usually makes him flush red with embarrassment.) On the sofa with Megan at my side, the three of us spent a pleasant evening working our way though each box, dusting, Sellotaping torn trimmings, with the room's grotto design in our minds... Why can't family life always be like this?

A MONTH BEFORE CHRISTMAS
by
Rhian Evans

1.
Familiar boxes, one, two, three.
Holding treasures created by me.
Santa up a chimney - On card - Crayoned red.
Cotton wool beard, with brown felt-tipped sack.
A star coloured lantern,
In the box now collapsed.
A fairy for the Christmas tree.
Hair and wings out of place.
Uncle Fred's Christmas card,
In such terrible bad taste.
A Yule log from the garden,
Fully seventeen years old.
Some holly, some mistletoe,
Last years - Out of date.
My toilet tube snowman - Poo, what a state.

2\.

November the 30th,
The eve of the 1st.
The first day of Christmas - December the first.
I prepare like a child, for the twenty-fifth day.
In my boxes are friends, who all feel the same way.
Made at school, when I was five, nine and six.
Innocence kept, for the prayer that I pray.
Let all believers, believe in this way.

I feel strangely weepy after writing this poem... This month has really been too much for me... Trevor, Gary and Megan all involved with violence... Come on now, you silly old thing, pull yourself together... I'd better had, hadn't I... Blackmail, who are the Jackson's to try and blackmail us?

For two new pins, I'd... Thank God we've all made it through the month okay.

REVIEW OF THE MONTH:

Please read previous statement.

December 1: Saturday

I am distraught... I am utterly undone... Will those Jackson's never keep their word?

The morning started perfectly. Carried away by the ambience of the night before, Megan and Gary forgo their usual outing to the city, in favour of helping me hang-up our Christmas decorations.

Busying ourselves throughout the morning, (Which meant working around Trevor, who was reading his newspaper in the chair.) apart from the Christmas tree, (Traditionally kept for last.) our living-room, passage and kitchen sparkled in gold and silver tinsel, with individual strands of red,and green tinsel twirling, twisting, snaking up and around every rail of the banister on the stairs.

By midday only the tree was still waiting in its box. Settling down with a mug of coffee each, the three of us gazed in a wondrous silence around the room. Overhead, an intricate network of gold spiral chains, fringed at each link, spread from the centre to the corner of our ceiling. Sectioned like a giant box of 'Dairylea' cheese slices, each wedge (Eight in total) alternatively housed a multicoloured paper ball, bell, Chinese lantern within the centre of its network.

Father Christmas, a snowman, each with fold around paper tissue stomachs, hang upon the walls. Pride of place went to the wall above our grate. Knick-Knacks, mementoes, assorted handmade cardboard cutouts, traced by pencil and crayoned by my children when they were small, were blue tacked ceremoniously to the wall.

"I can't believe you've kept this old thing." Megan squealed, finding her name on the back of a Santa, desperately holding onto the final remnant of his cotton wool fringing, balding along the bottom of his coat. "I was in Mrs Graham's class when I made this."

"And so was I." Gary laughed, holding up a older yet identical modal, retaining a little more of its original cotton wool.

"Three, two, one, I have great pleasure in declaring this house ready for Christmas." Gary announced turning on the Christmas tree lights... The police came and arrested Gary for the attack on Julian Jackson shortly after... Anthony ran to the rugby club to tell his father... Megan's locked herself in her room... Anthony is also in his room. (His door is open.)... Trevor hurried home and the two of us have been sitting in silence ever since. Trevor's upset... I told him about Idris's offer... We put on a brave face when Jodie and Darren brought baby Mia (Jodie had a rethink... Deciding against Leah, in favour of Mia.) around to see our Christmas lights.

December 2: Sunday

The police made Gary spend the night in the cells. (My poor lamb, I bet he's petrified.) Officially, the police say they're keeping Gary in for questioning, and to help them with their inquiries... Over the telephone I begged the desk sergeant to let him go. I pleaded: "My son wouldn't intentionally hurt a fly." But the sergeant only sneered: "But he has Mrs Evans, hasn't he!"

Trevor couldn't sleep, I couldn't sleep. I couldn't get up either, I was somehow trapped within a limbo world inside the confines of our bed.

12.00pm: I phoned the station and spoke to the arresting officer. He told me Gary had confessed to the assault, and would be up before the magistrate first thing tomorrow morning. I told him to tell my son, his father and I wouldn't rest until we had found him the best solicitor legal aid could buy.

Gary has to spend at least another night in the cells. Hopefully and with all fingers crossed the magistrate will grant him bail in the morning. (The arresting officer told me, Gary's already been offered the services of a defending council... Please God let him/her be a good one.)

3.00pm: Trevor answered the door, and dragged Idris in by the scruff of his neck. "IT WASN'T MY FAULT, IT WASN'T MY FAULT, THE BOY CRACKED." Idris screamed, cowering at the foot of our stairs. "I'VE COME TO TALK, WE CAN STILL WORK THIS MESS OUT." He pleaded, as Trevor arched menacingly over him with his clenched fist. "PLEASE LISTEN TO ME TREVOR... YOU KNOW I'M NOT A FIGHTING MAN... BUT I COULD BE YOUR BOY'S ONLY HOPE." Pulling Trevor off our terrified guest, with a few choice words that made him see sense. I helped Idris up off his knees, and led him into the living-room.

"Julian came home last Friday night." He began. "Well, you know what Mary's like." He spoke in a more relaxed tone. "Mary's so tenacious at times, she's like a dog with a bone." Trevor drummed his fingers impatiently across the top of his thigh, and snarled at our visitor. "I tried to tell her to leave our son alone... The boy needs rest, I said. The doctor told you that at the hospital." Idris bowed his head. "Mary acted like a woman possessed. Not for a moment did she believe Julian didn't know who attacked him, and was determined to find out who had beaten up her son... Julian had been protected in hospital you see. If his mother got to much for him, he would summon a nurse who would shoo his mother away. But at home, on her own patch she was relentless." Idris furtively glanced into my and Trevor's eyes. "I did my best... I stuck up for my son... I tried everything I could think of to stop my wife from finding out." Trevor stood up. Idris tried to make himself disappear,and held his hand over his face.

"Well you didn't try fucking hard enough, did you boy?" Trevor retorted, before returning to his seat.

"I tried to make her see sense." Idris whimpered. "I said, the boy doesn't know who assaulted him... If he did, don't you think he would have given his attacker's name to the police."

"Then how did she find out?" Trevor snapped.

"Yesterday morning, while I was out doing the shopping... Julian's very weak, you see... You know what he's like under pressure... He cracked... It's the strain his mother puts him under you see. He broke down and told her your Gary did it." Idris remained silent for a few moments. "He begged her not to tell the police... He tried to tell her about the baby, her Grandchild." Idris bowed his head again. "Well, you know the rest."

"Why are you here, Idris?" Trevor growled.

"Because I want to see my grandchild. Julian wants..."

"Fuck you, and your cunt of a wife." Trevor retched, and made a grab for Idris's throat.

"STOP IT, STOP IT." I screamed, as I once again found myself standing between both of the baby's future Grandfathers.

"We won't be pressing charges if it goes to court!" Backing

away Trevor and I returned to our seats. Flushed in the face, Idris made comfortable adjustments to his clothing. "Julian won't be pressing charges if it goes to court." He repeated his sentence, in a whisper.

"So our deal is still on." I interjected. "Gary's freedom, in return for access to your Grandchild."

"Exactly." Idris smiled, then gestured.

"Don't you fucking grin at me, you fucking twat." Trevor made a lunge, but fell a long way short of striking our house guest. "Before you come here making deals. There's the simple matter of your whore of a wife, and trying to get her to keep her big gob shut."

"M-M-Mary's n-n-not th-thinking about our Grandchild at the moment." Idris stuttered. "When she does, she'll see sense." Slowly rising out of his seat, Idris edged his body towards the front door. "Don't worry about anything." He said, trying to put our minds at ease. "Trust me... It won't go much further... I'll talk Mary round... I'll get her to play ball, for all our sakes... Trust me." The front door closed. Peering out of the window, I watched Idris hurriedly walk down our garden path, and home.

On the eve of my son's first appearance in court, Trevor and I had sex with one another. By no stretch of the imagination could anyone call what we did to each other, making love... We were like two wild animals caged in the bedroom... Lion, and lioness... Trevor said he was a warrior... I said I was an huntress... I bit, he slapped, I raked my nails down his back... Trevor played my senses like a fine toothed comb.

December 3: Monday

I woke up this morning racked with guilt. I can't believe Trevor and I did what we did last night with our eldest boy languishing in a police cell.

8.00am: Mam opened her door in her night-gown, and listened in stark silence, as I begged her to lend me my father's old suit. (My thinking: When the magistrate notices Gary wearing his Grandfather's old suit... The suit will help him win the sympathy vote.)

9.00am: Arrive at court, hand Dad's suit to the court usher, who in turn takes the suit to Gary who is already waiting in the cells. I insisted on going to the court alone. (1. I can handle disappointment a lot better than Trevor. 2. If Gary goes down, and Trevor heard the Jackson's laughing... Matters could only get worse.)

10.30am: Gary's case is finally heard. Gary stood in the dock and pleaded guilty to the charge. (Who would have thought my eldest son would have come to this?... He isn't wearing his Granddad's suit.) Gary's solicitor makes a plea for bail. He mentions Megan's troubles, and Gary's previous good character, and hopes of future job prospects after being assessed at the Assessment Centre.

Magistrate: (In summing up.) Yes, yes, yes... Unblemished record, of previous good character... Nevertheless, I hope you agree with me that a serious assault of this kind can not go unpunished Mr Jenkinson. We as a society can not have ordinary members of the public walking the street harbouring this unhealthy, revengeful, vigilante attitude of judge, jury, and in this case executioner. Also, on this occasion, I am happy to say it has been proved beyond reasonable doubt, that the innocent party on the receiving end of Mr Evans's rough justice, had indeed nothing in the world to do with the aforementioned assault on his sister. Therefore Mr Evans, (The magistrate, addressed Gary.) the seriousness of your crime, by that I mean your vicious and unprovoked attack on one Mr Julian Jackson, leaves me with no option but to remand you in custody until your case comes to trial at a later date... Bail refused, take him down.

11.00am: Gary looked a frail and shattered figure standing in the dock. On his way down to the cells he looked up at me, and whispered a faint goodbye. I was in tears. Turning to my right I saw Mary nodding her head in triumph.

11.30am: The usher handed me back Dad's old suit. Gary's solicitor told me it was pointless to appeal. "Look on the bright side, Mrs Evans." Mr Jenkenson said, as he glanced down at his gold hunter timepiece. "However long your boy serves on remand, that time will be deducted from the time he has to serve when his sentence is passed." (When Gary's case does go to court I think I'll find him another lawyer.)

12.30pm: The police allowed me to spend ten minutes with Gary. "Don't give up hope." I cried. "Julian won't be pressing charges against you."

2.00pm: On the bus home, I found myself sitting two seats

behind Mary... How I'd love to force the tip of my umbrella through the middle of her forehead.

2.45pm: Mam, Trevor, and Megan were anguishing over Gary's fate, as they waited for me in our living-room.

(Anthony was at school.) I didn't say a word as I entered the room. I didn't have to... My tears told the story for me.

5.30pm: Mam took Dad's suit home. She wasn't very happy about being kept in the dark. (Again) I wish I could take all our Christmas decorations down. I wish I could get out of this life for good... What makes it worse, is knowing that Gary loved and looked forward to Christmas so much every year... What kind of festivities can he look forward to now?... I went to bed.

PS: Mam collected her £10 Christmas bonus, along with her usual pension money from the Post Office today.

December 4: Tuesday

What a night I've had of it. I couldn't get the face of my poor boy from out of my head... What on earth must it be like for him?... It doesn't bear thinking about... Gary's never been one for sleeping in a strange bed. I tried to imagine what it would be like to hear the sound of the heavy steel door slamming shut behind me, and finding myself all alone in my cell... But what if Gary isn't alone?... On remand Gary could come into contact with quite an array of strange, and undesirable characters.

As usual Anthony was the first to rise from his bed. Listening to him scurrying around his room, I tried to imagine what Gary's first day inside would be like... Was he awake I wondered?... At this moment for instance, was Gary lying wide-awake staring at the stars through his cell's barred window?

6.45am: Quietly as he could, Anthony closed the front door behind him. Thankfully it hadn't been raining during the night, but outside it was still very dark and uninviting. Raising a corner of my curtain I could see nothing outside apart from the bleakness, and cold rivulets of condensation trickling down the glass pane.

"Stop fidgeting." Trevor mumbled, as I let the curtain drop back into place. "The boy will be all right. He's got a good head on his shoulders has our Tony. If all the street lights go out, he'll probably navigate his newspapers around the estate by the stars."

"Go back to sleep Trevor." I mumbled, slumping down on my half of the bed.

My poor boy. My poor, poor, boy... Right, that's enough of this feeling sorry for myself. Until further notice I am the captain of our ship. If I go down, we all go down... But our ship is going down, and there's nothing I can do about it... Pull yourself together woman, it's Christmas... My poor, poor, boy... How can I cope?... I must, I must, I must... But I can't. I haven't got the strength to continue, I'm weak of body and spirit... Christmas, what good is that to me now?... But I believe... I've always believed in... The three wise men, Santa... Why am I so negative?... Why do I always look on the dark side of life?... Baby Jesus, meek and mild. Come and help your fallen child... Me,me, meeee!... If Mrs Thomas from across the road can stand it, then so can I... That's it! You can do it girl... Mrs Thomas's eldest two have been in and out of jail for years, and I always see her coming out of her house with a happy smile on her face.

I can do this... For my family, I can do this.

December 5: Wednesday

My evening class went wild, after I'd shown them Eric's letter. (God, I needed that confidence booster.) Once more I was Queen for the day. Mr Davis said: "It just goes to show what a little time and effort can archive." Addressing the class he continued. "Out there is a market place just waiting for you all to discover. It's only a matter of time and patience before every one of you find a publisher."

"I'm so happy for you." Ann whimpered, with tears in her eyes. "You and I have had such bad luck lately, what with one thing and another."

"Well done Rhian." Dave said, putting a comforting arm around his wife's waist. "Take no notice of Ann... You know, she's been feeling very emotional lately, what with me losing my job and all. I'm also very happy for you... I've tried telling Ann not to worry, but she won't listen to me... I'll have a lot more time to spend with her and our kids. This break from work, will give me the time I need to finish the house..."

"Isn't he brave?" Ann sobbed into the chest of her husband's fluffy black pullover.

"There, there, you silly thing."

Watching Dave playing with Ann's spiky hair, while speaking to her using such gentle tones... Ann's panda eyes smudging her cheeks, tears glistening, reflecting like dark pools of glistening water... Are all Goth's this loving?

“If I was your Gary, I’d have done the same thing.” Pressing Ann’s head ever tighter into his puffed out chest, Dave issued his threat. “God help anyone who interferes with my family.”

“If I could have your attention please.” Mr Davis said, bringing the room to order. “This year our Christmas party will be held in this very classroom on Wednesday the nineteenth of December. Please feel free to bring along a bottle, can, or indeed any festive tipple of your choice. We will have a poetry reading of the festive variety, with us all wearing silly paper hats upon our heads. If anyone would like to bring a Christmas cake, mince pies, or anything of an edible nature all the better.

‘Twas the night before Christmas,
when all through the house
Not a creature was stirring, not even a mouse.

“Class starter for ten, what is the correct title of this poem? And for a bonus point: name the poet, and tell me the year the poem was composed?”

(Answer: ‘A Visit From St Nicholas’ by Clement Clarke Moore 1823)

December 6: Thursday

BREAKING NEWS ON SKY: The fall of Kandahar. Looks like the war in Afghanistan is nearly over with the fall of the last Taliban controlled city. Mind you I’m bored to death with this story, and so are the newspapers, judging by the coverage... Other News: Sophie the Countess of Wessex was airlifted to hospital with an ectopic pregnancy. Jodie said shame, while Megan asked me what an ectopic pregnancy is?

Prison visiting cards popped through our letter box this morning, accompanied by a Christmas card for Trevor from Littlewoods Football Pools.

What have I got that is suitable to wear for a prison visit?... Jeans I suppose. Jeans, black boots, sweater and a coat if it's cold or raining.

5.00pm: I'm shitting myself. I've never visited a prison before... The thought is too terrible to contemplate... God, what must it be like for our Gary?

7.00pm: Mam called around. (Seven o'clock was very late for her, what with it being dark outside, and in the middle of winter.) "Who would have thought it?" She said to no one in particular. "A daughter of mine going to visit her son in prison."

"Here we go." Trevor muttered under his breath.

"Trevor was always very quick with his hands, and I hold him solely responsible for filling the boy's head with fighting at football matches... Rhian, I'm worn-out, I can't eat or sleep... My Grandson's rotting in prison, and my daughter going to visit him... Rhian, it's breaking my heart." Mam pulled out her hanky, and began to weep. "They've all heard about it down at the old age club... They're all saying like father, like son." Trevor sighed heavily, at hearing this. "You do right to sigh, my lad." Mam said, rounding on her son-in-law. "If you'd been bothered enough to show Gary how to talk... How to express himself with words, instead of his fists. Then maybe this family wouldn't be in the mess it finds itself in today."

"I wondered how long it would be, before you'd blame me." Trevor snapped.

"Not in that tone please Trevor." Mam countered. "We all know about your temper thank you very much. I said to Rhian at the time, you were going to get into trouble if you didn't look out... Beware the sins of the father Trevor. They will always catch you out."

"What the bloody hell does that mean?"

"It means, because of your past. Your son, my Grandson and their brother, (Mam pointed at Anthony and Megan.) is rotting in prison and I am breaking my heart."

Mam's outburst reduced everyone in the room, apart from Trevor into floods of tears. "Well, it's late and I've said my piece, and now I have to go." Mam, said buttoning up her coat. "Rhian, when you come home tomorrow, give me a call and let me know how you've got on."

Richard and Judy have a new show on C4... It's been on for a couple of weeks... It feels strange watching them at teatime... I think they were better in the morning.

December 7: Friday

Even a double dose of Prozac couldn't calm my nerves this morning. I began shaking as soon as I got out of bed, and if truth be told I'm still shaking now.

In the middle of winter: Cardiff Youth Detention Centre is a grim place. An uninviting,inhospitable, fortress of a building holding some of Wales and the rest of the UK's most dangerous and hardened young offenders, plus my Gary. Handing our visiting cards to a warder, I was searched first by a metal detector, then a drug trained sniffer dog sniffed me up and down before we were led into a large hall like room lined with tables and chairs.

To tell you the truth I didn't know what to expect, and in

a way that made it all the more frightening. Don't get me wrong, I've seen all the police shows on the television, but I still wasn't one hundred percent certain if they were made-up or not. Expecting to speak to my son by way of a two-way telephone while staring at each other through a bullet-proof glass shield, I was pleasantly surprised to find myself in what I can only describe as a very friendly school dining hall complete with waiter service offering free coffee and tea.

Selecting a table near a window with a view of the prison yard, Trevor and I sat in silence until a door at the rear of the hall was opened, and the inmates filed in.

Around us family reunions were taking place, private little groupings, select, confidential little gatherings in full view of the authorities, were happening.

"Hello Mam!"

Gary stood before us in prison regulation collar and tie. Trevor was the first to react... Standing up he hugged his boy with tears in his eyes, until a warden walked over and told Trevor to break it up, informing Trevor no contact was allowed and to sit down.

It was all too much for me. Seeing my son like this. Wearing a red square patch of cloth, I'd last seen worn by a girls' netball team draped over his front and back.

"How are you Mam?" This time it was Gary's turn to break-down.

"What are we like." Trevor said, dabbing his face. "Underneath we are all as soft as shit."

Before we could get any sense out of each other, our time was over. Our parting once again reduced us all to tears... My poor, poor, boy.

After our prison visit, Trevor and I went to Tesco's to do our weekly shopping. Trevor reckons our next visit will be much easier, and a lot better than this one was, now that we know what to expect. "It was the initial shock, you see love... We didn't know what was happening... We were overwhelmed... We didn't know how much time we'd get... It will be much easier, next time... Now that we know I mean... He'll be all right love, you'll see. Gary will be all right in the end."

December 8: Saturday

Thank God for Saturday, the one day of the week I can usually rely on, to be on my own. The one day of the week I can meditate... Analyse my life... Think things through... Try to figure out where it all went wrong? Or where my life is going to, and after the week I've had, boy do I need it... But instead of solitude I got this: Last night's phone call wasn't enough for Mam. First thing this morning she needed a face to face, a one to one conversation/confrontation with me.

"What was it like?... Was it really depressing?... You said our Gary cried when he saw you. Has he been beaten up?... Are the other convicts beating him up?... What are the guards like?... Did they speak to you?... What did they say?... I bet they are a rough lot in there... Did you see any killers?... Is Gary sharing a cell with people who have killed?... Do you think Gary will be all right mixing with those sorts of people?... Do you think Gary will pick up any bad habits when he comes out?... Rhian, did you tell him that I love him?... Did you tell him that he's constantly in my prayers?... God give him strength to face his ordeal... Did you tell him that Julian is not pressing charges?... Does he know if he'll be home for Christmas?... What are is cell mates like?... Is he getting enough food to eat?... What about going to the toilet?... He's not blocked-up or anything is he?... I'll buy him some luxury quilted toilet paper on Monday. You'll have to take it into him, the next time you go... Gary does understand why I can't visit him, doesn't he Rhian... My heart wouldn't stand the strain of being frisked by a prison warden.

Four hours I had of that. Four hours of nonstop questions and answers. How I got through it all I'll never know, but at the end Mam seemed happy with my answers, and left the house believing Cardiff Youth Detention Centre was really a BBC Television set for the sitcom 'Porridge', and the show's stars 'Fletcher', and 'Lennie Godber' had taken Gary under their wing.

Good old Trevor, I can always depend on him at a time of crisis, undaunted by recent family history, he continued to pursue his Saturday pastimes down at the rugby club. (His ban for fighting only lasted 24 hours... The bar takings must have plummeted!)

For whatever their reasons, Megan and Anthony have decided to stay at home with me this weekend... To tell you the truth Megan had been determined to return to work last Monday, and seemed ready to put all of her misfortunes behind her... But she didn't go. All this with Gary has set her back, and it's a shame because last Saturday when we were putting up the Christmas decorations together, (God, that feels like a lifetime ago.) she was so full of herself. A little of her old confidence had returned, but all to no avail. What's happened to Gary has knocked her for six... Never mind she's determined to start again on Monday:

"I have to make a stand Mam... I have to build a life for me and my baby... What good will I be to anyone if I'm afraid of my own shadow?"

Secretly, I feel Megan wishes Monday never comes.

Anthony; good old Ant makes me laugh. You should hear some of the things he's been coming out with lately. Take Friday for instance. (The day of our prison visit.) Before he left for school,Anthony asked Trevor to remind Gary to keep his back to the wall, especially when taking a shower. He added: "If our Gary accidentally drops his bar of soap on the floor, tell him to leave it there."

Daily, Anthony has been coming home with tales from the school-yard. Rumour, after rumour has reached my ears. Stories, ridiculous fabrications of Gary being a cross between Jack the Ripper, and some sort of axe murderer have reached epidemic proportions at the school. Some children are saying Gary turned bad on the day a teacher give him the dap for refusing to do gym... And more hurtful accounts of him turning outlaw on the day he discovered his mother was mad. (Where are the children getting this rubbish from?... It must be their parents!)

Dear Diary, I started this page hoping to spend the day alone... Instead, I haven't had a second to myself.

December 9: Sunday

I got up extra early. (5.30am) I made myself a pot of tea, and half a dozen slices of toast. I carried my breakfast into the living-room on a tray, and set it down on the coffee-table. It was pitch dark outside, (Of course) so I sat with only the Christmas tree lights on, green, red, yellow and blue. Isn't it funny what comes into your head at a time like this. At 5.30am in he morning I found myself thinking: *'I'm glad our fairy lights don't flash on and off, and aren't musical like the ones I've seen for sale on QVC!'*

Dear Diary, have you ever sat in the dark, and stared at a Christmas tree, with your eye's scrunched-up, squinting at the colours? (What am I talking about? Of course you haven't.) It's great watching all the coloured light-bulbs join-up, and blend into one another. Alone inside my Christmas grotto of tranquillity... It's beautiful... It's silent... Not a sound could be heard, not even a mouse... I feel as if I'm, I've been transported back to the '40s, '50s, '60s, '70s. I feel I'm in a winter wonderland, a picture on an old time Christmas card, or etched upon a lid of a box of chocolates. Nothing feels real to me anymore. The surreal world of Christmas time... My beautiful fairy lights... My beautiful, beautiful boy.

When I awoke my toast resembled cardboard, and the pot of tea had turned stone cold on the tray.

8.45am: I'm still the only one not in bed. (Anthony doesn't deliver newspapers on a Sunday.)

After dinner, Jodie called in, and immediately told me there was nothing to be ashamed of. Bouncing baby Mia up and down on her knee, she stated: "Rhian, no one could have been a better mother than you. You're a natural darling. You didn't know me from Adam a few months ago, yet you've taken me and my little one to your heart. My Darren was only saying last night, you don't deserve this. Bad luck, that's what he said... Young Gary, he's not a violent boy... Just sticking-up for his sister, that's all he did... It's just so unfair of that judge locking Gary up the way he did. For his first offence and all... Take that Labour politician during the last election. Nobody said a dickey bird when he punched that farmer, and they caught it all on television... So Rhian, are you still looking forward to

Christmas this year, or do you think Gary being in prison has put a downer on the whole proceedings?"

For once I wished Jodie would go. I'm fed-up with people offering me unwanted sympathy this weekend... Gary has to buck his ideas up too, if he is to survive, and so must I... Positive thinking from now on!

December 10: Monday

4.00pm: The telephone rang. "Hello Mam, Gary speaking."

Just like that, out of the blue. "What, Gary?" My mind went into a panic. "What, have they let you out son?... Have you escaped?... Do you need money for a taxi home?... Just jump-in, I can pay the taxi driver I mean, at this end."

"Don't be silly, Mam." God, it was good to hear him laughing again. "I'm still inside... I don't get issued with my own telephone card until I've worked my week in hand. So I've swapped those sweets you brought me for ten minutes of talk time, which I've been trying to use all weekend."

"HOW ARE YOU, ARE YOU ALL RIGHT?" I don't know why, but I yelled my words into the receiver like one lunatic speaking to another lunatic, phoning from a deaf planet.

"I'm fine. Mam, you don't have to shout. You can speak normally. No one is listening to what you are saying."

"Have you got a television in your cell?" I have no idea why I asked him that.

"There's one in the common room. There's also a pool-table, table-tennis table and board games like chess and draughts."

"I hope you're not playing for money?" I wish I could stop talking like my mother for the rest of this phone call.

"I started work in the kitchen, this morning." Gary said taking control of the conversation. “I had to grill the sausages, about two thousand of them and see to the bacon.”

“I hope you didn’t burn any.” I laughed.

“No, they like um like ‘The Royal Family’ in here. Dead, dead, crispy. I’m on eggs tomorrow Mam, sunny side up whatever that means. For dinner we had a pork chop and chips, followed by Spotted Dick and custard for afters. In a minute I’ve got to go and get the teas ready, but I’m not sure what we’re having yet.”

“You sound a lot happier today, I must say.”

“Mam, you wouldn’t believe how many people who went to school with me are in here. It’s like a class reunion... You’ll never guess who I spoke to this morning... David Thomas from across the road...”

“Hello Mrs Evans.” A strange voice spoke to me.

“David Thomas speaking. I had the shock of my life when I saw your Gary this morning... Now don’t worry about a thing, me and the boys will look after him for you. Can you give my love to my Mam, the next time you see her Mrs Evans.”

I thanked David, (I think I was doing the right thing?) and just had time to say goodbye to Gary before his phone card expired.

The family were delighted to hear Gary had phoned:

Mam: That was a turn-up for the books.

Trevor: I always said that David Thomas was a good boy at heart.

Megan: Good for our Gary... It’s nice to have friends.

Anthony: Can I visit the prison during my school holidays?

Jodie: See Rhian. I told you everything would turnout for the best, when he'd settled down.

More good news: Megan did return to work today. She said her boss and the other girls were very understanding... "Mam, I feel so proud of myself today. I only cried twice."

What a great day. Things are slowly returning to normal. In my mind's eye, Gary has gone to work at the Dorchester Hotel in London to train to be a TV chef... Knowing that he's with friends, and hearing him sound so happy, has made all the difference to me... Yes, I finally believe we're going to enjoy a good Christmas this year after all.

December 11: Tuesday

Good Christmas did I say; Bah! Humbug! The morning started with a lie, and it steadily got worse from there.

"Who's 'D'?" Trevor asked, handing me a Christmas card addressed to Rhian and family, and signed with a red felt-tip pen.

"Oh, it must be from a woman in my evening class." I don't know why I lied about the sex of the sender. "You think she would have saved the expense of the stamp and handed it to me herself." I really couldn't tell you why I was making this story up? "But you know what some people are like. More money than sense I suppose."

"Stupid bitch." Trevor said, standing the card on the shelf.

Doug's car was once again parked unattended outside the Post Office. The hair on the back of my neck, and my goose pimples, jumped at the sight of it.

I hurried home... I had a think... I've decided to return to the

Post Office tomorrow morning to see if the car would still be there... I'd go to the police if I didn't think they'd laugh at me... Doug's Christmas card unsettled me for the rest of the day.

December 12: Wednesday

In my head I prayed for Doug's car to be still parked in the same spot. Turning the corner of my street I could see it wasn't... On returning home, I ripped up the card and threw it in the bin.

	Questions:	Answers:
1.	Am I being stalked?	Don't Know?
2.	Did Doug send the card?	Yes. 99%
3.	Is he playing mind games?	Yes. 75%
4.	Did he attack Megan?	Don't Know 50%
5.	Why?	Because of what happened between us in class.
6.	What can I do?	Don't Know?
7.	Who will believe me?	No One 100%
8.	What can I do?	Hope Doug grows up.
9.	Am I making all this up?	I Don't Know?
10.	Coincidence?	Maybe?
11.	Will women's intuition stand up in a court of law?	No 100%

No terrorising tactic, imaginary or otherwise is going to stop me enjoying my life. Men!... Why can't little boys grow-up? (I placed the torn card in a envelope for future evidence... You never know. I may not be mad after all.)

Speaking of psycho's, child killer Roy Whiting was jailed for life for the murder of Sarah Payne... After the sentence was passed, the court heard that Whiting had only served two years for abusing another little girl... I've got a great idea. Instead of society worrying if Whiting and his kind will offend again, why not execute them all... Let the punishment fit the crime... I think 'Paedophile' is such an ugly word.

Flat, would be the word to describe tonight's evening class... Well, flat and boring actually, but hey-ho there's always the class Christmas party to look forward to next week!

December 13: Thursday

A person form Gary's Assessment Centre phoned, and said: "Carol from the Centre here. I'm just phoning to remind Mr Evans to send us a doctor's paper, if he intends spending anymore time on the sick. Thank you."

"Excuse me love, but our Gary is currently on remand." It made me squirm, to say this to a total stranger... I could read her mind as I spoke: *'Not another one!'*

"Ummm, so he won't be coming in then?... I, I'll tell you what Mrs Evans, leave it with me, all right... Goodbye."

Trevor: Never mind, Gary can always reapply to be assessed when he comes out.

Mam: Life goes on you see Rhian. There are other people in the world who need to be assessed too.

Jodie: My Darren said it was a shit-hole of a centre anyway.

I don't know. Being employed gave our Gary that air of respectability. Now he's like all the other young lads on this estate, in prison. Only our Gary isn't like that... Why does society tar everyone with the same brush?

December 14: Friday

Trevor was right. It doesn't happen often, but this time he was spot-on. The cool winter sun shone down on Cardiff Youth Detention Centre. A clear blue sky, reflecting, shimmering upon numerous windows, dazzling our eyes. Inside a hall I will for now and ever refer to as a school canteen, Gary approached us with a spring in his step, and a beaming grin broadly spread across his face.

"Mam, Dad, I've seen the light. I want to be a locksmith when I get out of here." He announced before we could get our *'How are you?'* Out of our mouths. "Dad, did you know a locksmith earns over twenty pound an hour, plus a call out charge in Cardiff. More if I worked in and around the London area."

"Steady on now boy." Trevor said trying to cool his son's ardour. "What's brought all this on then? I'm glad to hear you are making plans for the future, but a locksmith you say... Where did that idea spring from?"

From there Gary went into some five minute story about all the best locksmiths coming from the criminal classes. Our assessment centre news didn't phase him in the slightest.

"They couldn't assess a bag of peanuts in that place." Gary scoffed. "I firmly believe everything is done for a reason Mam. (I've been telling him that for years.) Coming here has helped me understand that... I've assessed myself, that's what I've done... Mam, Dad, I'm going self-employed when I get out of here."

On a more serious note, I asked Gary if he wanted me and his father to find him a better legal team to fight his case for him. But he wouldn't hear a word of it: "No, don't bother." He quipped. "Mr Jenkinson has got me this far, he may as well go the distance."

In all my years of living with Gary, I'd never seen him this optimistic before: "I'll need to buy myself a small van... Tools of the trade, Dad did you know I can make and adapt some of those myself?... Mam can you find out for me how much it costs to place an add in the Yellow Pages... If that's too expensive I could always advertise in the local newspaper or have some posters printed up." Gary was more or less bouncing up and down in his chair with excitement as he spoke.

"Where's all the money coming from to finance all this?" Trevor asked, trying to bring his son down to earth. "You'll have to go to locksmith school or something, because at the moment you can just about manage to open your own front door with a key."

"Listen now Dad." Gary said, taking a uppity stance. "People are always locking themselves out of their homes, cars and things. And there's a lot of people earning excellent money when they do."

Sensing an argument brewing I tried to change the subject, but I couldn't stop Gary's new found entrepreneurial mind from dominating the proceedings: "I'm moving-on up when I leave here. I'm going to learn the trade, and then I'm going to build an empire of my own."

"Boy, when you locksmith your way out of this prison, then I'll believe you. Until that happens, as far as I am concerned you are just talking out of your arse."

Thank God, the warden came and told us our time was up... At least we parted company on amicable terms. (In other words we were still speaking to one another... Oh yes, Gary said he'll give me a call sometime over the weekend.)

Do you think Gary was on something?" Trevor enquired, as we walked down the baked bean aisle in Tesco's. "Only, he seemed very up to me."

“He was very excited, that’s all... He didn’t want us to feel upset... Perhaps he thought if he showed us he had hope for the future, then everything would be all right.” I turned my back on Trevor midway through my explanation. Of course my son was on drugs, the silly fool. I’ve never seen our Gary that excited about anything in his life. (Not even when the cartoon series ‘Transformers’ was on the telly.) “He’s got big plans Trevor, that’s all.” God, why have you added yet another worry to my already over burdened heart?

December 15: Saturday

The Saturday Matinee: Santa Claus spoke to a little girl in Dutch, during BBC2’s re-screening of the evergreen black and white Christmas classic ‘A Miracle on 34th Street’, starring Edmund Gwenn... Forget 34th Street, what I needed was a miracle on the Lloyd George Council Estate to save me from going insane.

My mind is reeling. I haven’t slept very well at all. Gary, my idiot son is on drugs. What kind, I don’t know... But he’s definitely on them.

His behaviour yesterday morning was astounding... He was so up, so full of life... Thinking on it he was also very fidgety.... He couldn’t keep still... His eyes and his head, were constantly on the move... He couldn’t look Trevor or I in the face... Why is he doing this to us and himself?... Boredom?... It can’t be much fun being locked-up for hours on end... To be one of the boys?... He did try smoking pot when he was a member of a rock group... I hope he’s strong enough to realise what he’s doing now, is the wrong thing to do again.

What if Gary comes out of jail with an habit? I haven’t got to start hiding my purse, have I?... What about our new widescreen television and video. I'm not letting him sell them for drug money. Mam will have to be told. I can't have him going round to her house on some innocent pretext,before ransacking the place while Mam pop's into the kitchen to brew her favourite Grandson a friendly pot of tea... My mind is racing. All I can see is doom and gloom... Please Gary, please snap out of it boy... What are those prison guards doing about it, that's what I'd like to know. Probably selling the drugs to Gary on the sly, no doubt?... This world makes me sick... Those bastards are supposed to be helping Gary, not making matters worse!

Here's a thought. If I can prove my son was drug free before he went into prison, and he comes out with a drug habit; can I sue the prison authorities for failure of their duties?

Trevor, Megan and Anthony have gone out. Mam... Mam doesn't want to see or speak to anyone, all this with Gary has finally caught up with her... I don't blame her for wanting to be on her own. I wish I could be on my own too.

At the end of 'A Miracle on 34th Street', everything turns out fine, and they all live happy ever after... I so hope we do too!

December 16: Sunday

Trevor woke me up in the middle of the night, and tried to encourage me to allow him to have his wicked way... Do I need to say anymore? Do I need to write; we are no longer speaking to one another?... How could he... Pissed or no, Trevor only thinks about himself.

Okay, let's get down to it. He accused me of shagging him a day after the police came and took Gary away... I responded: "Well that's not now, is it!" Stripping the bed of it's duvet, I stormed out of the room, and went to sleep on the sofa.

Trevor growled his way through the morning, and when Gary

phoned at two, he yelled from the background: “TELL HIM, IF HE SPEAKS TO ME AGAIN LIKE HE DID LAST FRIDAY, HE’LL FEEL THE BACK OF MY HAND MAKING CONTACT WITH HIS FACE.”

Gary sounded very down over the phone. He said he’d helped to prepare a Yorkshire roast for the inmates dinner. He also said he’d made a real custard using fifteen egg yokes. Johnny Price, (Gary’s cellmate) showed Gary how to pick a padlock, using a hair-clip. Where the hair-clip and padlock came from, I don’t know, because at that moment we were cut off. Still, it was good to hear from him again while the phone call lasted.

December 17: Monday

Idris knocked the door, entered, then plonked himself down before I had chance to invite him in.

“Well, he’s done it now.” Idris said throwing his hands up at a startled Trevor.

“Your Julian?”

“No, your Gary. Why couldn’t he keep his big mouth shut. He’s admitted everything to the police.”

I knew Gary would be no good under pressure.

“We’ve held-up our part of the bargain. Julian’s dropped all the charges. But it’s no good because your son has already owned up to the assault, and the case is still going to court.”

“So what you’re saying is.” Trevor spoke slowly. I could hear the cog wheels ticking over inside his head. “If our Gary had kept his trap shut and denied everything, he would be coming home tonight.”

“Yes, more than likely.” Idris nodded “You should have heard Julian arguing with the desk sergeant: *‘I am a born again Christian... I believe in turning the other cheek... Let him who is without sin, cast the first stone.*' Julian really gave it to him. '*I believe in forgiving those who trespass against me.*' But the sergeant wouldn't listen to him so we had to come home."

"So that's that then." I said. "Whatever happens our Gary is going to court, and there's nothing any of us can do to stop it."

Idris looked down, then he said: "I had a quiet word with the desk sergeant when Julian left the station. According to him, if Julian refuses to press charges Gary will still be found guilty, but because of the time he's already spent inside the judge will probably let him out on probation... You know, bound over to keep the peace."

Trevor showed Idris out, and thanked him for trying. It's news like this that bind a family together. Idris has admitted, he and Julian have gone behind Mary's back... When she finds out, look out!

"Gary will be pissed-off when he hears about this." Trevor said, flopping his head onto one side. "That Julian's got some neck on him, I can tell you... Born again Christian... The cheeky sod... Why couldn't our boy keep his yap shut, Rhian? So much for telling the truth... It's true what people say: when you're in the shit, keep your big mouth shut." As you can see Trevor and I are back on speaking terms... Yes indeed, Trevor. Yes indeed?

On a much lighter note. Anthony made some posh Christmas cards for us on his computer. Anthony had superimposed our facial images onto the heads of a family of snowmen. (Mam's face replaced the head of a robin.) Inside the card our address was placed neatly in the bottom right-hand corner under the verse:

Snowmen point the way,
For Santa and his sleigh.
Seasons Greetings to you all,
From Rhian, Trevor & Family at
Number 29, Heol-Y-Haul, Aberheol.

December 18: Tuesday

Double benefit payout at the Post Office today. (The Post Office is closed next Tuesday, for Christmas day.) Doug's car was parked outside again. Fuck Him!... I'm not letting a twisted little shit like Doug spoil my Christmas holiday... I kicked his wheel as I squeezed between his and another parked car. Mam loved Anthony's cards: "Rhian, how did our Anthony know the robin is my favourite bird?" Mam cooed, then cooled. "I don't believe the Jackson's said anything of the sort to the police in our Gary's defence... They hate us Rhian... I can see fun and games happening when Megan's baby comes along... Rhian, I'd take it all with a pinch of salt if I were you. Gary's on his own, and the Jackson's only want the baby. It's up to us to make sure Gary spends the shortest time possible inside, and to make sure the Jackson's aren't allowed to bribe the affections of Megan's unborn child with toys."

My mother can be a wise woman at times. We can't relay on anybody but ourselves. We must take the initiative, because there's no one to take it for us... If only my poems could earn us some money. I'd abandon everything, (Including our new television & video combo.) and move us all to Cornwall to begin the good life.

December 19: Wednesday

I bought two bottles of wine, and two boxes of Mr Kipling's Cherry Bakewell Slices from Ivor Smith's newsagent, come off licence, come corner shop. (Both these items were buy one, get one free offers... The cakes were only one day past their sell by date.)

After she'd come home from work, Megan helped me with my hair. I decided to wear my hair up with a trailing fringe, and curly strands teased with glitter. Megan loaned me her black blouse, that went well with my jeans, and matching high heel shoes.

Trevor said I looked great, then discreetly announced: Christmas had come early this year, and if I remained a good little girl, he would let me unwrap one of my presents later."

Outside my gate I waited for Dave and Ann to approach. The night air was cold. My breath became visible, and wafted up past my nose. Frost had settled on cars, and grass sparkled by the light of the moon: "Looking forward to it?" Dave asked, swinging his carrier-bag in his hand. "Ann's spent all day getting ready in the bog."

"Nerves." Ann grimaced. "I know I'm being silly, but I'm always the same before attending a local function, or social event."

Inside the classroom, Ann and I both squealed: "Special Offer." After we'd simultaneously produced identical twin boxes of Mr Kipling's Cherry Bakewell Slices from our plastic carrier bags. "At least we bought different colour wine." I giggled, matching my two bottles of white, alongside her two bottles of red.

"If you'd like to place your food and drink on the tables to my left." Mr Davis had lined four desks against the left wall of the classroom. “I’ve managed to scrounge some paper plates, and some plastic cups from the school canteen... So if you’d like to place what you’ve got there, then I can quickly say a few words, and the quicker I can say them, the quicker we can begin.” In an orderly line, the class filed pass the tables placing either their bottles of wine or four packs of beer next to a stack of plastic cups, then edging along the desks they stockpiled their boxes of food adjacent to the stack of paper plates.

“Mmm, yummy.” Mr Davis sighed eyeing the main ingredients of our Christmas fare. “I see ‘Mr Kipling’, and ‘Carlsberg’ are our main sponsors again this year.” He quipped, before munching a cake. “Mmmm, Cherry Bakewell, my favourite.”

“I think we should bomb them, and all the other countries that harbour terrorists.” Mr Reed demanded. “That’s where we went wrong during ‘Desert Storm’... With Saddam Hussein, I mean. We had him cornered in his lair, and for no apparent reason we let him off the hook... We can’t allow the same thing to happen this time around.”

Through the open classroom door, my eyes followed the corridor until the darkness spreading from the other classrooms dimmed my view.

“After all said and done.” Dave said, taking a slightly opposing view. “If they had crash dived those jumbo jets into the middle of London instead of New York, this so called war on terrorism would not be taking place at all.”

“Rubbish.” Reed, scoffed into his can.

“Terrorists have bombed us before.” Dave stressed. “But this country just picked itself up, and got on with it... What about the Falklands? Did the Americans want to know about that?... Did they fuck. It was more important for them to remain friends with Argentina.”

Along the corridor the children had decorated the walls with paintings and drawings depicting world peace.

"That was different." Reed countered. That was country verses country. This is a band of outlaws attacking everybody."

"Killing is killing whatever the reason." Dave reasoned. "Look at that Welsh soldier who was burned, (Simon Weston) and the others who perished when their ship was hit by that exocet missile... It seemed important at the time, but who gives a fuck about the Falkland Islands now?"

A child had painted a circle of people dancing around a giant Christmas tree, with a silver star shining at the top. Brown, black, yellow, white, pink, happy smiling faces...

"You can't compare this to the Falkland Islands." Reed continued.

I wanted to scream: 'CHANGE THE FUCKING RECORD, THIS IS SUPPOSED TO BE A FUCKING CHRISTMAS PARTY. A HAPPY TIME... YOU'RE FREAKING ME OUT!'

"Why?"

"Because this is different. Times are different. The world is different... They've got chemical weapons, and they'll use them on us if they could..."

'I'd like to teach the world to sing in perfect harmony...' The words from the old 'New Seekers' song filled my mind, as I studied the children's simple pictures decorating the walls of the corridor.

"Well all I know is this." Dave said, patting Reed on his shoulder. "If the war on terrorism is won or lost. I'll be on the dole come the New Year." Emitting a gormless laugh, Dave raised his can to the light-shade dangling from the ceiling and said: "Gentlemen, charge your glasses please... The Dole, and all who claim from her."

"You don't think we'll be gassed do you." Ann timidly asked. "Happy New Year, on the dole and gassed Rhian. It's one hell of a life, isn't it!"

All this war talk spoiled the Christmas party for me. War, Gary in prison, Megan's baby... I hoped the party would take me away from all that. I hoped to escape my life for a few hours. I wanted to discuss, and hear poetry, light-hearted banter while nibbling on a Bakewell tart. I wanted to laugh but instead I ended up standing in silence sipping a drink, I didn't want to drink. Listening to opinions I neither wanted or cared to hear. The children's artwork I studied exhibited more sense and understanding of the environment, than all the actions I'd just witnessed in the adult world... Perhaps Blair should see what I've just seen, before his finger squeezes the trigger.

December 20: Thursday

What a disappointing let down last night was... Bloody War!... Why did we have to talk about that when there are so many nicer topics we could have debated?... Poetry, the arts, or the children's naive water-colours on the corridor wall!

Jodie called round this morning, and asked me if I thought she should get baby Mia Christened, or not: "Rhian have you had your three done?"

"No."

"I don't know what to do for the best. Should I do it now, or should I wait until Mia is old enough to choose what religion she wants to follow herself?"

I shrugged my shoulders and replied: "It's up to you."

"What if she doesn't believe in God?... I suppose the

Christening would have been a bit of a waste of time in that case wouldn't it?... What if she chooses another faith? Don't laugh Rhian, it could easily happen you know. Have you noticed how many black people there are living in Cardiff these days."

God, this girl makes me laugh and she asks the funniest questions: "Rhian, if I decide to have baby Mia done. Has the ceremony got to be performed in church, or will they perform it for me at the registry office?"

"For Christ's sake." Trevor groaned, raising his newspaper to cover his eyes. "Does she have to do that, while I'm in the middle of eating my breakfast?"

As natural as the day is long; lifting up her top, Jodie suckled her child: "I didn't realise I'd have to pay." She said ignoring Trevor's protest. "I thought it was free to join the Christian faith. I didn't think Jesus would demand a subscription charge from the poorest members of his congregation... Perhaps I could apply for a grant from the DSS?... Rhian, do you think that is the reason people are turning away from the Christian church in order to join other faiths?... Do you know if you have to pay anything to become a Muslim?"

"Religion is the opium of the masses." Trevor grunted from his chair. "Like all the other forms of mind control drugs, religion doesn't come cheaply no matter which sect you belong too."

"Rhian, hurry with a damp sponge." Trevor yelled, pointing at a damp patch of draylon. That idiot girl has squirted some of her breast milk over the arm of the chair... Rhian, you must remember to have a word with her about it." Trevor threw his exaggerated arms about, as he searched for the right expression. "Doing that in public. What if our Gary, or Anthony had been in the room. You can't tell me it would have made the slightest difference to her... It was bad enough for me, and nobody can say that I don't like looking at a fine pair of tits... But not when they are used for that sort of thing... She's got no shame, that one... Well, I'll say this, Rhian. When our Megan's baby is born, she'll be using the bottle from day one. No matter what her mad friend has to say about it."

Today was also Anthony's last day at school until Monday the seventh of January, which brings me back to last night's Christmas party. I can't remember when I've felt so let down in my life. (I can, but I don't want to go into that.) Last night was my final evening class of the year. It should have been an evening of celebration, instead of a requiem of reflection. A premature post-mortem of our modern world... Am I selfish to want to be happy at a time like this?... Or am I selfish just to want? Towers fell, thousands died, movies and the news have desensitised me from what is reality or fantasy... It's not possible for me to change the world. The best I can hope for is to alter the circumstances surrounding our own personal universe for my family.

December 21: Friday

Firstly, Anthony was upset because I wouldn't allow him to accompany Trevor and I on our journey to visit Gary at the Youth Detention Centre. (Our final visit until the New Year.) At the Centre's search area, I handed the warden Gary's Christmas presents. (I'd made up a little box of tangerines,toothpaste, shower gel, soap, flannel, disposable razors, Milk Tray, Dairy Box, dry roasted and salted peanuts, plus Trevor spent last night cracking open the hard shells of Brazil nuts, to get at the the nutty kernels of which he placed inside a plastic bag.

(These were later confiscated by the warden, and sent away to be analysed.)

Inside the hall the prisoners had decorated the ceiling with gold fringe trimmings, similar to the type hanging in our living-room. In one corner a string of Christmas light's twinkled around the edge of a cork framed notice-board advertising the dates of future visiting days, and the telephone numbers if needed, for the Criminal Help Line, Crisis and The Samaritans.

Waiting patiently by a tree shedding it's needles, Trevor sighed, then said: "It'll be a strange Christmas this year without Gary in the house."

We didn't have to wait long before Gary appeared. I told him about the parcel we'd left with the guard, and about Idris and Julian speaking to the police. "I know." Gary said, with a faint smile on his face. "Mr Jenkinson told me all about it... He told me I'd have probably been released, if I hadn't owned up." With his head in his hands, I watched my son fall into a pit of despair. "Mam, I've been charged under section 20 with GBH. In the worse case scenario I could get ten years." The tears rolled down Gary's cheeks. "I can't face that, Mam." He cried.

"Did Mr Jenkinson say anything about a court date?" Trevor asked, hoping the question would help his son to raise his moral.

"The middle of next month." The words stumbled out of Gary's mouth in sobs and whimpers.

"You've got to remain positive, boy" Trevor growled. "If Julian sticks to his born again Christian story, then you must believe the judge will show mercy and let you out."

"Mr Jenkinson reckons I've got a good chance." Lifting his

crestfallen head, the fringe of his hair matted with tears. Gary's eyes caught the reflection; crystallised into a kaleidoscope of colours drawn from the tree's twinkling fairy lights.

"That's right boy." Trevor said, noticing the changed expression on his son's face. "Don't give the bastards the satisfaction of seeing you cry. You've got friends in here, have a laugh and a joke with them, and remember to keep your head down... You'll be home soon."

When the time came it broke my heart. I hated leaving Gary feeling like this. Gary looked so timid, so fragile... I knew I wouldn't see him again until the New Year... I wished him a Happy Christmas... We hugged and kissed, and when he left the hall, I cried.

I bought one or two Christmas presents in Cardiff, and then we went food shopping at Tesco's.

THE BIG SHOP OF THE YEAR:

2 x Large Christmas Pud's, Large Jar of Mincemeat, Christmas Cake, 2 x Large Jar Pickled Onions,2 x Large Jar Red Cabbage, 1 x Large Jar Pickled Baby Beetroot, 12 LB Turkey, Leg of Pork, 2 x Large box of Paxo Sage & Onion Stuffing, Large foil, 99p Turkey Tin, Tin of Quality Street & Roses, After Eight Mints, Matchmakers, Terry's Chocolate Orange, Box of Christmas Crackers, Box of Crackers for Cheese, Cheese, (Stilton & Cheddar) Fancy Box of Biscuits, 2 x Squirty Cream, 2 x Tiptop Cream, Tin of Shortbread Fantail Biscuits, Box of Bird's Trifle Mix, Nuts, (In shell & out) Crisps, Fruit & Veg, (Fresh & Tinned) Beer, Lager, Stout, Cheap Brand of Whiskey, Vodka, Gin, Pop, Orange and Lemon Squash, Figs, and two boxes of "Eat Me" Dates... Plus my usual household cleaning products and goods.

Today was also Megan's final day at work before the holiday. The girls from her factory had tried in vain to coax her to go for a drink with them, but she remained adamant, and didn't go. (I'm absolutely delighted Megan didn't go. A young girl drinking to drown her sorrows is a sure recipe for disaster... I for one should know.)

December 22: Saturday

On my sofa I feel like a contented squirrel, hibernating with a nest full of nuts. Trevor is out, and my two remaining children are lazily doing whatever in their rooms... Earlier this morning Anthony was in one hell of a strop. Returning home after completing his paper round he said newsagent Ivor Smith is refusing to hand over his Christmas tips, until all the newspapers have been delivered on New Year's Day."

"Ivor's not as silly as he looks, is he boy?" Trevor said, patting his youngest son on the head. "He's seen it all before, and no doubt he'll see it all again... I bet you young boys think you're being clever by quitting your newspaper round after all the newspapers have been delivered on Christmas Eve. I bet you thought you'd have a good laugh at old Ivor's expense, didn't you. Tucked up in your nice warm beds at six-thirty am, Boxing Day morning. Meanwhile poor Ivor forced outside in the cold, cursing every last one of you with no option but to deliver all the newspapers on his own... No Ant, you'll have to get up pretty early in the morning to pull the wool over that old sod's eyes."

Dear Diary, I love to hear the rain lashing against my windowpane at Christmas time. It makes the house feel so warm and cosy. Mam doesn't like to see it raining on Christmas Day.

She says it spoils it for the children who've found bicycles in their stockings.

My concern for Gary has grown throughout the day. I hated leaving him yesterday... I do hope he can enjoy some sort of Christmas when the big day arrives.

December 23: Sunday

Would you believe it, I'm going to be P.M.T Active for Christmas after all!

Jodie called round, and said she'd booked the little chapel on the edge of the estate for the Christening: "My Darr knows the chapel caretaker." She chirped, letting me in on the arrangements. "We're having Mia baptised on Sunday January the sixth, after morning worship has finished."

"January 6th!"

"That's right Rhian. The first Sunday of the New Year, plus Darren and I would like both you and Trevor to be baby Mia's Godparents."

Of course I accepted, (I also accepted on Trevor's behalf.) but it didn't stop me from thinking Jodie had taken it all for granted.

"Rhian?" Coy, and sweetly sugarcoated the question left Jodie's lips, as her puppy dog eyes toyed with my heartstrings. "What are you doing for Christmas?"

I knew what was coming, but still I played along with it.

"Celebrating at home, why?"

"Oh nothing... Only, me and Darr are also celebrating at home on our own, and we were (She was) wondering if you'd mind at all... I mean, very much, if you could see your way some how to allow us all to celebrate together?"

You've got to give the girl ten out of ten for cheek... She invites me to a Christening, and herself to Christmas dinner.

"Brilliant, I was only saying to my Darr last night. Wouldn't it be great if the Godparents of our child could spend the whole day with her at Christmas time... Darren said you might have made alternative arrangements, but I said no, you'd love to have baby Mia here."

Three more to dinner... No, two - Jodie will be feeding baby Mia herself... I must remind her not to breast feed while we're all sitting around the table.

December 24: Monday Christmas Eve

Let me state from the start. I regard this day as being the best day of the year. There's not one thing about Christmas Eve, I don't like, and over the years my mother and I have perfected a well rehearsed routine, which we perform like a well oiled machine.

MAM & MY CHRISTMAS EVE ROUTINE:

8.00am: Mam arrives. She will not return home until the day after Boxing Day. (This year Mam will be sleeping in Gary's bed.)

9.00am: After a cup of tea, Mam will make a start on stuffing the turkey, and scoring the crackling on our leg of pork.
While she is doing this, I will be cleaning the house from top to bottom. (Megan & Anthony will clean their own rooms. The only day of the year I insist they do so.)

11.00am: Turkey stuffed, pork scored, stuffed and tied, Mam makes a start on the pastry. The house is clean. (I've left the bathroom, until we've all washed.) I make us all a mug of coffee. (Mam insists on a cup.)

12.00pm: The turkey is in the oven. (We don't believe in cooking it on Christmas day... Too much hassle.) Mam has rolled out and lined four individual, twelve sectioned baking trays with pastry, and I'm helping her to fill them with mincemeat, strawberry jam, and lemon curd. (The mince pies have pastry tops - Jam, and lemon curd tarts have a pastry criss-cross latticework pattern laced across the top of them.)

1.30pm: We have a light lunch. (Porkpie salad) Trevor is at the pub/rugby club. (For the day... Until midnight.)

2.30pm: The turkey is basted. We take it in turns to have a bath. The tin of sweets are opened, Mam has a sherry. We are all very relaxed, and behaving very civilised to each other.

4.30pm: The turkey comes out of the oven, and the tarts go in. The Turkey is left to rest upon a turkey plate covered with foil. (TV chef Gary Rhodes said this will help the juices seep back into the body of the bird.)

5.00pm: The tarts come out, and the pork goes in. Mam relines the baking trays with pastry for the second load; and we enjoy a little chat while I help her to fill them up. Mam said: "The more the merrier." After I'd told her Jodie and Darren were coming for dinner. Mind you, she'd had three sherry's.

7.00pm: The pork came out of the oven to be basted. We've all had a bath. One good thing I will say about satellite TV, (And Mam agrees.) they're showing all the Christmas shows we used to watch in the seventies, and eighties.

9.00pm: The leg of pork comes out, the second batch of tarts have gone in. Mam has made enough pastry for a third batch just in case we haven't made enough. Jodie's called in with baby Mia dressed like a little angel. Mam kept hold of, and rocked the baby to sleep in her arms, then passed her over to me when her tarts were ready to come out of the oven. (She'd drank five sherry's by this time.)

9.30pm: The second batch came out of the oven, and ten minutes later the third batch went in. (We'd run out of strawberry jam and Lemon curd. So I've used up the apricot, blackcurrant and raspberry jam dregs, I kept in the fridge.) The turkey, having cooled and rested, is placed inside the fridge.

10.15pm: The final batch of tarts came out of the oven. Removed from the tray, and placed on serviette covered plates; the tarts are given a light dusting of icing sugar.

11.00pm: Mam made a start on the veg. Apart from the roast potato's, and the packet of dried Leo's peas that were left over night to soak in a saucepan. The ordinary boiled spuds, Brussels sprouts, and carrots, were peeled, washed, chopped and put in pots of cold water, are left to stand overnight on the electric rings on top of my cooker.

12.00am: After its rest, our leg of pork went into the fridge on a shelf under the turkey. On the kitchen table Mam had covered the mince pies and tarts with a clean tea-towel. There was a carol service on the television. I insisted that Megan and Anthony went to bed. Mam said she would go up too.

1.30am: I completed wrapping all the presents before Trevor came home, and placed them under the tree. Gagging Trevor, as he opened the front door, I guided his drunken body to the bedroom, where he collapsed on top of the bed. (Earlier in the day I'd placed a sick bucket and towel by the side of the bed, just in case he wanted to be sick during the night.) Mission accomplished, I fell asleep.

December 25: Tuesday Christmas Day

"Trevor, I don't care how bad your head his. Come downstairs, and open your presents." Choking,coughing and spluttering his way into the living-room, the family greeted the late arrival with a merry Ho-Ho-Ho, and a glass of foaming 'Andrew's Powders'.

Anthony was over the moon with his computer games, and AOL internet start-up disc. (I'd also bought him a telephone extension cable, so he could plug into the net from his bedroom.)

"That's a dear do." Trevor ignorantly groaned, on hearing the word internet. "How much is that going to cost me; because you can't tell me anything connected to the telephone comes cheap."

"Relax Dad." Anthony reassured him, spinning the disc on his finger. "It's free for a month, then when the trial period expires, I can always find another internet server to sign-up with for free again."

"As long as it's free boy, I couldn't give a toss who you choose to service you." Trevor smiled. "Thank your mother son. Now, that's what I do call an excellent Christmas present."

Megan was happy with her new clothes, and trainers. (The correct designer label this year.) My foraging throughout the year resulted in Trevor, and Mam being happy with their little bits and pieces too.

Mam bought me another M&S cardigan for the third year on the trot. (This one was cream with a flower motif.) She bought Trevor a 'Charlie Dimmock' gardening book, in the hope of it encouraging him to take-up a new hobby in the New Year.

The kids got their usual Cadbury's Selection Boxes, and a ten pound voucher from Argos. Trevor told me to close my eyes, and to take hold of his finger... Before I did this, I made him promise he wasn't going to do anything rude... And anyway, it would be in extremely bad taste to do it in front of my mother.

Laughing, Trevor told me not to be so silly, and to trust him for once in my life... I burst into tears directly after opening the little box he'd placed in my hand.

"I know it's not a lot... You see I kept a little bit of my winnings back... Well, you said you would love to own one of those silver Diamonique rings on Q.V.C... You deserve it after all you've been through this year love."

I was gobsmacked. All I could do was cry. I'd never owned an engagement ring before. Until today, the only ring Trevor had ever bought me was my wedding band. "How come I never saw the postman delivering this?" I mumbled tearfully. My words mixing with the emotion of the occasion.

"I asked them to deliver it to my mother's address." Trevor replied, kissing me on the cheek.

THE SADDEST SIGHT IN THE WORLD:

Gary's presents looked so alone under the Christmas tree. Mam asked me to hide them in another room, because the mere sight of them was breaking her heart. Solemnly Anthony helped me carry them to my bedroom, where I placed them out of sight on top of the wardrobe.

10.30am: Jodie, Darren, baby Mia, and twelve cans of 'Carling Blacklabel' were knocking on our front door. 'This is a bit early.' I thought to myself. 'But hey-ho it's Christmas.' Thrusting baby Mia into my arms, Jodie yelled: "Merry Christmas everyone." As she entered the living-room. "Rhian just you wait until you see what my Darr's given me." She said, pointing at her matching gold-plated stud earrings, bracelet (Which she jiggled around her wrist.) and necklace, which she carefully lifted from underneath her T-shirt. "These are from the 'Buckley Designer Collection'." She boosted proudly. "Darr bought them from that shopping channel you are always watching."

"Q.V.C?"

"Yes, that's it. Darr said, during half time when Trevor switched channels, he saw them and ordered them on the spot... You can't tell these are not real gold can you? Darr said, the man who made this costume jewellery has won awards for it. Darr said, all the film stars wear this sort of jewellery because they're afraid of getting mugged. Rhian did you know Julia Roberts, Catharine Zeta Jones and the rest of them keep all their real jewellery locked away in the bank?"

"Have you seen my ring?... Trevor gave it to me?"

"A solitaire diamond ring." Jodie squealed. "Darr, come and see Rhian's ring... Trevor the DSS must be paying you a lot of Incapacity Benefit for you to be able to afford a ring like that."

I let Jodie believe my ring housed a real diamond. (Holding it up to the light, neither of us could tell the difference... By the way, I also told her the silver was really platinum.)

1.00pm: We all sat down to dinner. (Darren helped Trevor carry our battered old kitchen table into the living-room... It didn't look too bad under a tablecloth.)... Our table wasn't big enough for everyone to sit around, so Megan and Anthony had to eat their dinner off trays balanced upon their laps. Trevor proposed a toast to absent friends, and Jodie told Baby Mia she'd have to wait until after dinner to be changed, but Mam insisted Jodie change her child immediately because the mere thought of it, and the ever increasing smell of Mia's soiled nappy was putting her off her food.

The main course was a triumph. Contented murmuring continued throughout the eating of the pud... Mam's home-made mince pies drenched in squirty cream also went down a treat. Jodie and Darren agreed that this was the best Christmas dinner they'd ever had in their life. (They've already made reservations for next year's feast.)

CHRISTMAS DINNER
by
Rhian Evans

Christmas dinner is over.
No dirty pots and pans, or saucepan lids.
No messy 99p non-stick turkey tin,
With welded-on crusty bits.
No plates, no bowls, or tureens of any kind.
No knives, no forks, or spoons -
In filthy dishwater, left behind.

No cups, no mugs, or glassware of various
shape and size.
Yes my love the food looked and
tasted wonderfully nice...
Yes my darling, it was a marvellous idea of yours
to eat out on Christmas Day.
But lover of mine...
What will my husband and your wife say?

5.00pm: Mam helped me to make a large plate of turkey sandwiches. I forked some pickles and red cabbage into bowls. We placed some jam tarts and mince pies onto anther plate. I opened our Tesco Christmas Cake and Chocolate Log... Using our dinner table as a buffet bar, I placed a stack of plates, bowls and eating utensils by the side of the fare, and announced that everyone were welcome to help themselves, and to take what they wanted. (The buffet bar did not include the tins of sweets, dates, figs, bowl of fruit and nuts... These were on the coffee-table.)

"Well, it's as far away as it ever is." Mam philosophised, while breaking an excess bit of pastry off her lemon curd tartlet. "Rhian, I do hope Gary enjoyed his day too."

"I feel like a beached whale. Jodie admitted, blowing out her stomach. "I can't remember the last time I ate so much. Rhian, I'll have to come round tomorrow and help you eat up all the leftovers. I hate seeing good food go to waste... Did I mention I'm going on a diet in the New Year?"... One by one we drifted off to sleep.

9.00pm: Time for supper:

Trevor: I may as well finish off those sandwiches. Rhian, cut me a slice of cake will you?

Anthony: I don't want anything Mam. I'm going upstairs and play on my computer.

Mam: Just a cup of tea for me please, love. OK, you've twisted my arm, I'll have a slice of chocolate log too.

Jodie: Rhian, if you're opening that tin of shortbread biscuits, I'll dunk some in my tea.

Darren: I'll stick with this can, thank you very much Mrs Evans. I'll have another Quality Street if I want anything to eat.

Megan: Mam, I want to be sick.

Jodie: That's probably the start of morning sickness.

Baby Mia: Crying for her milk.

Jodie: Mia, you'll have to wait until Mammy's finished eating her biscuit.

Me: I think I could just about manage a tangerine.

11.00pm: Megan had gone to bed, Anthony was playing on his computer in his bedroom, Mam is in a coma, Trevor's eyes were barely open, Darren was asleep; his can dripping onto the carpet. Jodie tried to speak, but kept losing her thread. Baby Mia was happily wide awake... I'd had enough, and insisted they all buggered off home, so I could go to my bed.

12.00am: Everyone apart from me is fast asleep. I'd cleared up the best I could considering the circumstances. I made sure everything electrical had been turned off, and plugs pulled out... Apart from Gary not being here, its been a wonderful day.

December 26: Wednesday Boxing Day

Question: Why is today called 'Boxing Day'? I refuse to believe this has got anything to do with sport. Years ago in Victorian times so my mother says, the day after Christmas was the day the Victorian dustmen used to call round and clear-up the boxes after the rich people had opened their Christmas presents... This can't be right, surely?

A little after midday, Darren called for Trevor, at the same time depositing his partner and child in the care of me and my mother: "It's traditional love." Trevor winked, kissing me on the cheek. "A Boxing Day pint down the club, before the game starts... I'll try not to be home too late." He yelled slamming the front door shut behind him.

"Rhian, have you got anything for heartburn." Jodie asked, rubbing her chest. "I was up all last night with it. It's the turkey that does it to me... Especially if I mix it with pickles and red cabbage."

"I don't suppose you'll be wanting any dinner then?" Mam said, giving my neighbour a quizzical glance.

"Why, what are you having?"

"Cold turkey, pickles, and red cabbage." Mam grinned.

"Mmm, lovely." Jodie replied "I love turkey, but turkey doesn't love me... And it is Christmas after all."

After lunch, Megan was playing with baby Mia on the carpet, when the telephone rang: "Mam, it's Gary. I'm sorry that I didn't phone you yesterday, but all the phones in here were chock-a-block, what with it being Christmas and all."

God, it was good to hear Gary's voice again.

"Mam, I made Christmas dinner for everyone yesterday... That old joke is true. The prison turkey is a very strange bird; a thousand legs, and no breast."

Gary sounded very happy. I only pray chemicals are not helping him to feel this way. "We all ate individual Christmas puddings and everything... Some bloke said it was just like being in hospital without the broken kneecaps... We pulled crackers, I wore a paper hat and we all read aloud those stupid jokes. We had a carol service around the tree... The centre's chaplain said a few words, and we all sang 'Silent Night' before being sent back to our cells."

I could feel a lump rising in my throat.

"I'm going to a pantomime this afternoon. The prison players are doing their own version of 'Snow White', called 'Mistress Black and her Seven Gimps'..."

The line went dead. "Mam," I said turning to my mother. "That was our Gary. He said he's having a marvellous time. They're putting on a pantomime, for the prisoners this afternoon."

"Oh that will be nice for him... Rhian, I wonder if anyone famous from the TV will be in it?"

I stayed up late to make sure Trevor wouldn't burn the house down before he went to bed... My God,it's hard work enjoying yourself.

December 27: Thursday

7.00am: It was still dark outside when I got up, fifteen minutes after Anthony had left for his newspaper round. It was good to be alone in my living-room, with only the twinkling fairy lights for company. Overall this was turning out to be a very good Christmas, considering Gary wasn't here. Christmas dinner had

> been a real scream with us all wearing our paper hats... The bang produced from the crackers was really loud this year, and it frightened baby Mia who was trying to wriggle away from the noise on the floor... Mam upset herself of course... But she was happy it hadn't rained, for all those children who'd recently discovered new bicycles in their stockings.

Darren ate like a Gannet... To be perfectly honest with you, I think it's the first decent meal Darren's ate since he moved next-door. (No wonder he's so thin!) Trevor tried to tell him to pace himself, but he wouldn't listen and wolfed his dinner down before it could touch the sides. Then to everyone's amazement, (We all made eye contact, but nobody said a word.) he preceded to help himself to our tin of 'Roses' while he waited for us all to catch him up... I think Jodie felt a little embarrassed because on more than one occasion he yelped: "What?" After she'd kicked his shin under the table.

CHRISTMAS
by
Rhian Evans

White ground,
Cool, crisp, crunch, under foot.
Red berry, hidden among a thorny crown of green.
Smiles, squeals, giggling laughter.
Fresh smell of pine.
A crackling log on an open fire.
Stocking filled, gifts a plenty.

A bulging table.
Paper hats, feathered tickling whistles, balloons.
Trimmings, turkey, leg of pork.
A fairy on top of an artificial tree.
Multicolour lights, twinkle or still.
Nativity of the Virgin Birth.
Sentimental music, and television spectaculars.
Mistletoe, Uncles, Aunts, Nieces and Nephews.
Grandma in her chair, recounting her youth.
It's a time I love best.
It's Christmas - Happy Christmas.
Season's Greetings - All the best.

9.00am: Mam broke my daydream... I made us both a pot of tea.

For once it felt good to be out of the house. Good, clean, fresh air. I inhaled deeply, and took my fill. The Post Office is closed next Tuesday, (New Year's Day) so Mr Baker the Postmaster is allowing an early payout today. The walk to and from the Post Office really took it out of me. I expect the excitement from the past few days, has started to catch up with me. After Mam went home, I decided to have a early night, and went to bed... It's very cold outside. The weather has taken a nasty turn for the worse. It's blowing a gale, and it's started to snow.

December 28: Friday

Sometime during the early hours of this morning, Baby Mia died.

Lord, why do you make us suffer, so?... On the celebration

of your son's birth... Why Lord, why oh why do you mercilessly transform our feelings of happiness into those of despair?

December 29: Saturday

Jodie is under sedition in her bedroom. Her mother and sister are at her side. (Typical Welsh family. At each others' throats until trouble arrives.) Darren has been outside in his back garden all day tirelessly sculpting a metal headstone, in the freezing cold.

"He'll get pneumonia, if he carries on like that." Mam predicted, over the clanking of the hammer. "He hasn't stopped since half past seven this morning." (Mam stayed the night when she heard what had happened. She didn't feel happy staying in her house all alone.) It's nearly three in the afternoon now, and it's already getting dark. I don't think he's had anything to eat and drink all day."

6.00am, last Friday morning: The scream, when it came got everyone up, and out of bed. Rushing to the front window I saw and heard Darren banging on our front door, screaming for one of us to phone for an ambulance.

Inside Mia's bedroom, I found Jodie rocking her baby in her arms. In front of her lay the open pages of a nursery rhyme book, the lyrics of which Jodie recited to her infant in mantra fashion, over and over again.

> *'Three blind mice. Three blind mice.*
> *See how they run. See how they run...'*

"Jodie, let me take a look at Mia." I asked softly, trying to ease the baby out of her arms. "Let me see if there's anything I can do for her love." Jodie wouldn't listen, or couldn't hear me. "Please love, let me see if everything is all right." I begged her.

'...She cut off their tails with a carving knife,
have you ever seen such a thing in your life...'

I tried to take the baby from her, but she'd buried Mia's little head deeper into her chest... I was so frightened, terrified, scared... Then I saw Mia's poor little blue face... I'll never forget that for as long as I live.

"Are you hungry, darling?" I couldn't believe what I was hearing or seeing... I didn't know what to do... Jodie was trying to suckle her baby at her breast.

'Sing a song of sixpence...'

"Jodie can you hear me?" I waved my hand in front of her eyes.

'...Four and twenty blackbirds baked in a pie...'

"Mam, are you up there Mam?"

I sprinted for the bedroom door, and closed it before Megan could discover what was going on inside the room.

"It's freezing in here Mam, and the heating is turned-up full, but it isn't working."

The ambulance came and took the family to the hospital. Darren, who was in shock, but still had his wit's about him, asked Trevor if he'd tell his parents what had happened. (Trevor did.)

We heard nothing until 9.00pm that evening, when they returned home. (I'd tried phoning the hospital, but they wouldn't tell me anything because I wasn't a member of the family.) Jodie wasn't in a fit state for anything, and went/was carried to her bedroom. Darren laughed, cried... He didn't know what to do?

"The baby's dead." The news came from Darren's father. "My boy tells me you've been good to him and his family, so I suppose you have a right to know. The poor mite froze to death in her sleep... They didn't have any money to feed the gas meter... Spent it all on Christmas you see, buying new toys for the little one; and this snow doesn't help... The lass is taking it badly. My boy; I don't think it's sunk in yet... Well if it has, it's only now starting to come out of him." (On cue Darren curled up upon the sofa and burst into tears.) "Poor bastard." His father continued. "Fuck God to Hell, that's what I say. God only craps on people like us. People like us are better off praying to the Devil."

"Rhian, if you didn't know they didn't have any tokens to feed the electric meter, how could you have helped them love?" Back home, Mam was trying her best to make me see sense. "Of course you would have lent Jodie the money if you had known... But look at it this way. You gave Jodie the best Christmas of her life. What kind of Christmas would poor Mia have had, if you hadn't invited them?... You're a good woman Rhian Evans, and nobody could've done more for that family than you and Trevor... Not even their own would have given them so much."

The news on the telly is full of the Chancellor of the Exchequer's wife Sarah Brown; who give birth to a 2lb 4oz premature baby in Kirkcaldy... I can't see her baby dying from hypothermia. Megan's taken the news badly... She's forever touching her bump. (She's started to show.) "Mam, that could have happened to me." She sobbed. "What if I'd moved into a council flat on my own?"

At a time like this, life seems so clear to me. The right road to go down, and the wrong turning to avoid... Life's map, magnified to stand out a mile in my mind... If only I'd listened to this. If only I'd done that. From here I can see where I went wrong. I know what I have to do to put my life back on track... Only sometimes... I hope it's not too late.

December 30: Sunday

God. I hope you don't mind me saying this... But you can be a funny bastard at times. I am a staunch believer... Okay, I don't go to church, but then again why should I. I can converse with you here,within these four walls just as easily as I can there. (Without paying for the privilege.) I believe in good and bad, and I also believe that we are all made up of an equal measure of both. Fate, Lord... No one believes in fate more than I. Throughout my life you have shown me what will be will be. My family and I celebrate all the Christian festivals of Easter, Christmas, and even Whitsun if we only know what it meant... Pancake Day, Good Friday, (I always buy at least six packets of hot cross buns from the supermarket.) you name it Lord, if we've heard of it, we'll celebrate it... Lord, the Evans family are C of E Christians. Lord, the Evans family are traditionalists. Gary in prison, Baby Mia... Lord, how do you expect my family and I to ever think of Christmas in the same light again?

A vicar called next-door while Trevor and I were there. (Apparently the same one who Jodie had booked to perform Mia's Christening.) He spoke to Jodie: "At the moment I don't expect you to understand why; but God did have a reason for taking your little one away." After some uneasy questioning from Darren's side of the family, he said: "All will be revealed when the time comes for you to be reunited to the recently departed soul of your loved one, in the Kingdom of Heaven."

The more he spoke, the more uncomfortable he made me feel... I thought he was very young to be a vicar... He sounded more like a magician than a man of God.

"God works in mysterious ways..."

"Are you saying, God had a reason for taking our Mia?" Darren interrupted?

"There is a reason for everything. We may not be able to see or understand the reason at this moment in our existence, but in the fullness of time..."

"I can't take anymore of this bullshit." Darren said getting up, but before leaving the room he turned to face the vicar. "There is no good in any of this. I don't give a fuck about God's reasons for doing this and that... Don't come here spouting your bullshit... We are fucked, because we've got fuck all... Are you going to help me pay my gas bill,Vic?... What about your church?... What do you collect money for in that fucking church, anyway?... A new roof?... Gold candlesticks? Or maybe you just stash it into your Swiss Bank account every week, because whatever you collect money for it's not to help the poor on this estate, is it?... No fucker on this estate has ever seen a single penny of it, have they?... The fucking old age pensioners have to pay for their own fucking Christmas party for Christ's sake."

"Steady now boy." Thank God, Trevor was there to put a reassuring arm around Darren's shoulder otherwise I honestly believe he would have attacked the vicar there and then.

Not surprisingly, shortly after this conversation had ended the vicar made the sign of the cross and beat an hasty exit.

"BASTARDS!" Darren called out before his father had time to

close the front door. "FUCKING HYPOCRITES EVERY ONE!... Fucking gas, and electric light company... Tossers down the DSS... We've got nothing... MIA!..." Darren punched and kicked the wall. "MIA!... MIA!... MI..."

Trevor released Darren from his grasp, his hand tightly held my arm as I angrily raised my head and sneered at the ceiling: *'Gentle Jesus meek and mild... Enough is enough God. THAT WILL DO!'*

December 31 Monday New Year's Eve

Dear Diary, no offence against you, but I won't be sad to see this year come to an end... Jodie returned to her mother's house last night with Julie her sister. She looked terrible. I don't think she knew who or where she was going... I wouldn't be surprised if she ever returns/steps inside her house again. I don't think I could... Not in that house... Not after what's just happened.

9.00pm: Dear Diary, I've spent the day reflecting on the year. Flicking through your pages, I think I can pin point the exact moment our luck changed for the worse. August Bank Holiday Monday; the evening of which Megan lost her virginity, and became pregnant... The trigger for all the catastrophic events that followed from there.

HOPE FOR A HAPPY NEW YEAR:

1. Gary, released from prison.
2. A healthy baby for Megan.
3. Megan's attacker prosecuted. (The police have no clues yet... We haven't heard anything from them for weeks.)

4. My poems published. (I will take it as a sign you haven't forsaken us.)
5. Happiness.
6. Jodie... I hope she and her peace of mind return soon.

REVIEW OF MONTH & YEAR:

Of the month, I haven't the heart to dwell on this sorry tale. Of the year it had my moments, but on the whole... Good Riddance!

NEW YEAR'S RESOLUTION:

None!... Same as last year. (Go on a diet, be happy, fight the good fight, etc.)

FINAL THOUGHT:

Dear Diary, we've come to the end of a long and sometimes very difficult journey together. After what we've all been through, I'm amazed we're still in one piece... Dear Diary, you've helped me more than you can know. You've helped me to see myself clearly for the first time in my life. You've given me the opportunity to write down my thoughts... Express my feelings... Unburden my soul. You are/were my sanctuary at a time of chaos. My calming influence in a crisis... Time of stress. You've given me the confidence to attend evening classes... Think for myself... As I look out of my window, onto an uninviting desolate estate... Dear Diary, I've been watching the snow falling. The snowflakes are large, beautiful, fluffy... Is this a sign?... Lord, I ask for nothing more... Tomorrow I pray I wake up to a new beginning... A fresh start... A change of life... Happiness!... Maybe happiness is asking for too much. But I'd settle for a contented heart.

POST-MORTEM:

Rhian: I'm sorry if my best isn't good enough... I'm sorry if my three little dots have driven you to the verge of suicide... I'm sorry if my feral apostrophes live a life of their own, and in some cases vanish from the page altogether. But most of all I'm sorry I neither learnt my lessons at school, or from the personal mistakes I've continued to make at regular intervals throughout my adult life... Whatever!... Not your problem!... I remember one of my former teachers saying: '*It's the story that counts*', and something else about punctuation looking after itself... At least, that's what I think he said?... '*Experimental tinkering with the educational system.*' That's what Trevor calls it. '*Rhian, they didn't even give us the opportunity to sit the 11-Plus!*'... I don't know what to think any longer. It happened such a long time ago.

ISBN 141202637-7

9 781412 026376